Praise for *Nine Lives*:

"Wendy Corsi Staub's writing sparkles and the book fairly crackles with suspense. Her characterizations are spot on and you are sucked in from page one . . . If you're looking for a different type of cozy, then this one's for you!"

—*Night Owl Reviews*, Top Pick

"A good cozy by a good writer telling of a town that is its own character, just as much as the people that reside there"

—*Suspense Magazine*

"*Nine Lives* achieves just the right balance of charming and quirky, with Staub offering up a loveable cast of characters who will hopefully be haunting readers for years to come."

—*Hartford Books Examiner*

"*Nine Lives* is not just a mystery, but a story of a mother's determination to provide a life for her young son . . . I definitely recommend it to mystery and nonmystery fans alike. It's just that good a read."

—*Long and Short Reviews*

"The strength of this new series, written by award-winning suspense author Wendy Corsi Staub, is how her heroine very realistically transitions between states of vulnerability, anger, strength, and overwhelming sadness . . . Lily Dale extends a warm welcome to readers, who will find themselves charmed by its superstitious population of believers and practitioners."

—*Kings River Life Magazine*

"Wendy Corsi Staub's *Nine Lives* hooked me from page one. In fact I didn't want to put it down: with warm characters, an intriguing setting, and just a touch of the unexplainable, it's a thoroughly satisfying read.

—Rhys Bowen, *New York Times* bestselling author of the Molly Murphy and Royal Spyness mysteries

"Wendy Corsi Staub weaves a spectacular tale of suspense . . . Lily Dale would definitely be on my must visit list. It's an appropriately quirky town with an even quirkier cast of characters—and a cat, Chance, who's adept at pulling Houdini acts. Who could ask for anything more? Definitely a must read."

—T. C. LoTempio, national bestselling
author of the Nick and Nora Mysteries

Praise for *New York Times* and *USA Today* bestseller Wendy Corsi Staub:

"If you like Mary Higgins Clark, you'll love Wendy Corsi Staub."
—*New York Times* bestselling author Lisa Jackson

"Once Staub's brilliant characterizations and top-notch narrative skills grab hold, they don't let go."
—*Publishers Weekly*

"As always, Staub leaves us wanting more."
—*RT Book Reviews*

"When it comes to mysteries of the home and hearth, Wendy Corsi Staub is unrivaled. Just when you think you've figured her out . . . think again!"
—John Valeri, *Hartford Books Examiner*

Something Buried, Something Blue

Something Buried, Something Blue

A Lily Dale Mystery

Wendy Corsi Staub

CROOKED
LANE

NEW YORK

Copyright © 2016 by Wendy Corsi Staub.

Published in the United States by Crooked Lane Books, an imprint of The Quick Brown Fox & Company LLC.

Crooked Lane Books and its logo are trademarks of The Quick Brown Fox & Company LLC.

Library of Congress Catalog-in-Publication data available upon request.

ISBN (hardcover): 978-1-62953-772-6
ISBN (ePub): 978-1-62953-802-0
ISBN (Kindle): 978-1-62953-803-7
ISBN (ePDF): 978-1-62953-804-4

Cover design by Louis Malcangi.
Book design by Jennifer Canzone.

Printed in the United States.

www.crookedlanebooks.com

Crooked Lane Books
34 West 27th St., 10th Floor
New York, NY 10001

First Edition: October 2016

10 9 8 7 6 5 4 3 2 1

For the real people of the real Lily Dale

For the real Chance the Cat and Li'l Chap

For my sons, Morgan and Brody

*And for my husband, Mark, on our
twenty-fifth wedding anniversary*

Prologue

"I now pronounce you husband and wife."

Charlotte Ackerly-Toombs—now officially Charlotte Ackerly-Toombs Driscoll—smiles up at her handsome new husband.

"Happily ever after, darling," Thad murmurs, then leans in to kiss his bride.

"Happily ever after." She feels light-headed, and not necessarily in a swoony, head-over-heels way.

Yes, Thad is the man of her dreams. And yes, she's elated to be marrying him. But something isn't right.

Is it altitude sickness?

She's not used to being six thousand feet above sea level. She and Thad live in Florida. The wedding is in Colorado Springs—a destination wedding, because who wants to get married in the tropics in August? Still, she was fine yesterday after they got here. When she woke up this morning, she felt a little jittery, but wedding-day nerves are to be expected.

Maybe she shouldn't have had that omelet for breakfast. She usually just drinks a cup of black coffee, but one of the fellow guests, just some random person who happens to be staying at the inn, kept insisting that she eat something.

"You don't want to faint on your wedding day, do you? Try the applewood-smoked bacon. It's delicious."

It *was* delicious. But it doesn't seem to have agreed with her.

Why did you listen to a total stranger? Why did you . . .

Wait a minute. Did you marry *a total stranger?*

1

Confusion churns into the nausea as she stares at the man beside her.

No, of course not. He's Thad.

Isn't he?

Is he?

Come on, Charlotte. Who else would he be?

His handsome face is blurry, but she can see that he's smiling at her. She forces a return smile and shifts her gaze.

There's the minister—a woman wearing a white robe. She's standing right here in the little gazebo with Charlotte and Thad, but her face is blurry, too. The guests seem to shimmer and shape-shift, seated in folding chairs on the lawn beyond.

Even the vast panorama of the Rocky Mountains is hazy, though the temperature is a crisp sixty degrees with a cloudless blue sky and zero humidity.

The string quartet begins the recessional, sounding as if they're perched on a neighboring crest. Bows glide across strings with jarring dissonance.

"Charlotte!"

She turns toward the whisper.

"Here, take this." Her maid of honor, her friend Miranda, thrusts something into her hand.

Right. Her bouquet.

The flowers are in shades of deep purple, mossy green, and white. So are Miranda's floral print dress, the satin ribbons festooning the chairs, even the candy heaped in glass bowls on the dessert buffet table.

Sheer perfection, Charlotte thought when she first glimpsed the finished effect.

For her, as a graphic artist, the wedding's color scheme was perhaps even more important than choosing her own dress. Brides wear white, but the rest of the day was an empty canvas onto which she could splash her most vibrant palette. She chose to reflect the surrounding mountain peaks, snowcapped even in summer.

Charlotte gulps fresh air, clinging tightly to Thad's arm as they make their way along a grassy aisle strewn with purple-and-white petals. Mercifully, the discordant Bach concerto fades to a murmur

2

of voices, but they, too, sound warped. Someone hands her a slender flute of champagne garnished with plump ripe blackberries.

She sips. Swallows.

The world swims before her. Fragments of conversation float toward her as if from distant peaks:

Congratulations . . .

So happy for you . . .

Cheers!

Her mouth smiles and attempts to say all the right things.

Her brain peptalks her like a coach trying to keep an injured player in the game.

Come on, you can do this. You're just nervous, you're just jetlagged, it's just the altitude, it's just the champagne . . .

No. I can't do this.

You can. Take a break. You just need a minute.

She excuses herself to go to the restroom.

Dusk is falling.

She is falling.

She tilts into a doorjamb, banging her arm hard.

At the sink, heedless of her painstakingly applied makeup, she splashes cold water onto her face. It helps a little. There she is in the mirror, a distorted vision in white and green and purple: silk gown, flowers and ivy woven into her blonde chignon with a pouf of illusion veil, and a large ugly bruise forming on her arm.

She sways back to Thad.

"What happened here, darling?" He gently touches her arm.

"It's nothing. I just—I think . . . I'm tipsy."

"You need to eat something."

Dinner is served on the terrace. Strings of lights glitter in the trees, and votives flicker on round tables covered with more purple, green, and white: linens, flowers, petals.

A salad course with more of the same: oak leaf lettuce, radicchio, blue porterweed blossoms, goat cheese in a lavender vinaigrette.

Charlotte nibbles at it.

Sips champagne.

Clinks for toasts.

Nibble . . .

Sip . . .

Clink . . .

Crystal shatters on flagstone.

Her flute has dropped from her hand.

Her chest constricts.

Her throat constricts.

I can't breathe.

I can't breathe.

I can't . . .

"Charlotte!" Thad cries out in alarm as she falls. "Someone help! Help!"

Human shadows loom; voices warble.

"Is she choking?"

"She's turning blue!"

The last sound Charlotte Ackerly-Toombs Driscoll will ever hear is her husband's frantic plea: "No! Please, someone . . . help her!"

Above her, white lights twinkle like stars in lush green branches against a deep purple twilight sky that slowly fades to black.

Chapter One

Lily Dale, New York
Labor Day, One year later

"Destination wedding?" Isabella Jordan echoes, gaping at Odelia Lauder.

"It's when the bride and groom decide to get married in a faraway place, and their guests travel from all over to be there."

"No, I mean, I know *what* it is—I just . . . *here*? In Lily Dale?"

"Yes!" Odelia's curly carroty head bobs with enthusiasm. "Can you think of a more beautiful spot in the world? Look around, Bella!"

Bella looks.

On this balmy Monday afternoon, the view really *is* spectacular. Tucked into western New York's rolling green hills, Cassadaga Lake shimmers in late-afternoon sunshine. White seagulls swoop and dive from the deep blue sky while fat brown ducks bob alongside swimmers and small boats. Bella's five-year-old son, Max, and his pal, Jiffy Arden, are skipping stones from the weathered pier that juts from the pebbly shallows.

She and Odelia are seated in a pair of painted red Adirondack chairs, surrounded by abundant flower beds in full bloom on a wide lawn that stretches to the water's edge. A gentle breeze jangles the wind chimes dangling in nearby gingko tree branches and the porch eaves of Valley View Guesthouse behind them.

The Dale's rutted lanes are dotted with nineteenth-century cottages. Valley View, painted lavender gray with white trim, towers over them all, rising three stories. There's no shortage of Queen Anne gingerbread on its gables, porches, and "witch's hat" turret.

When Max first heard Bella describe it that way, he asked, "Are there witches here?"

"Nope. It's an architectural term," she assured him, though he appeared more curious than fearful. "No witches here."

"Only ghosts."

What was she supposed to say to *that*?

Lily Dale, New York, isn't just the most beautiful spot in the entire world. It is, according to a painted blue sign posted beside the gated entrance, *The World's Largest Center for the Religion of Spiritualism*.

For well over a century, Spiritualist psychics, mediums, and healers have populated the compact lakeside village. They announce their metaphysical specialties on painted wooden shingles that dangle from cottage signposts up and down the narrow streets, much like business signage in any other charming small town.

Only here, the locals aren't advertising their services as hair stylists or tax attorneys.

In Lily Dale, things are a bit different.

Patsy Metcalf, Spiritual Healer

Reverend Doris Henderson, Clairvoyant

Andy Brighton, Psychic Consultant

And, of course, right next door to Valley View: *Odelia Lauder, Registered Medium*.

Bella may not be convinced her new neighbors can talk to dead people, but plenty of others are. Hordes of map-toting tourists in sneakers and fanny packs roam the Dale throughout the official summer season. They seek healing, enlightenment, and counseling, and nearly all of them hope to contact lost loved ones through a medium. Many even want to learn how to do it themselves via a full daily schedule of classes, lectures, and workshops. Visitors gape in awe at local landmarks like the Fairy Trail and the Pet Cemetery.

They gather at Inspiration Stump, a mystical spot deep in the Leolyn Wood that's said to be teeming with energy vortexes. Back at the guesthouse in the evenings, they breathlessly recap their experiences, and Bella marvels at human nature and the power of suggestion.

So . . . *are* there ghosts here?

"No ghosts," Bella told Max, which was not exactly a lie.

After all, her medium friends strictly refer to the dearly departed as "Spirit."

So even if Bella were to believe—*which I don't*, she frequently assures herself, with varying degrees of conviction—she wouldn't call them ghosts.

Over the two months she's spent in Lily Dale, she's become well versed in the local vernacular, which includes such catchphrases as "There are no coincidences" and "Expect truth."

As a former science teacher, she's approached the peculiar setting with healthy skepticism, but she can't deny that a couple of strange incidents have occurred here. In the moment, they seemed convincing, but she later chalked them up to coincidence or electromagnetic energy or sensory phenomenology.

She hasn't actually *seen* Spirit hanging around the Dale, and seeing is believing, right? This may be an extraordinary place, but she's witnessed no filmy apparitions lurking in attic windows, no ladies in white drifting along midnight streets, no eerie lights or dissolving figures.

"Did I ever tell you about Johneen, my granddaughter Calla's old college roommate?" Odelia asks.

"The one from Florida who rode her bike to Alaska?"

"No, that's her friend *Jeannine*, from her writer's critique group. This is *Johneen*. She lives in Pittsburgh, originally from Philadelphia, and they call her Johnny. And I'd be surprised if she's ever even ridden a bike down the street. She's a little bit—I'm trying to think of a nice way to put it."

"Clumsy?" Bella certainly can relate to that, as can Odelia, who until last week was on crutches from a bad fall she took last spring.

"No, she's not clumsy, she's . . ."

"Lazy?"

"No, she's . . ."

"Prissy?"

"Exactly!"

"So we're talking about this prissy girl—woman?—named Johnny because . . ."

"Because she just got engaged, and she wants to get married at Valley View." Odelia waves her hand at the guesthouse behind them.

"Wait, what now?" Bella stares at Odelia, who is, as always, quite a sight to behold.

Odelia seems to take the same approach to her wardrobe as she took to planting the flowers behind her house next door. Once, when Bella remarked on the colorful beds, Odelia said, "I just went to the nursery and bought any seeds that had bright colors on the packets, dumped them all together, closed my eyes, and tossed them out into the dirt. Wherever they happened to land, they grew. I don't like fussy-looking gardens."

In Odelia's yard, delicate pink morning glories and frilly fuchsia sweet peas scale trellises and birdhouse poles as if in a desperate attempt to escape a sea of bold scarlet poppies and orange zinnias.

On Odelia's person, a violet-sprigged halter top clashes with her green-and-yellow madras skirt and with her hair, freckles, cat-eye glasses, and lipstick, all in contrasting shades of red. Bella has grown as affectionately accustomed to Odelia's quirks as she has to Lily Dale itself.

Still, she can't help but ask, "Wouldn't it be better to have the wedding at a place that . . . you know . . . puts on weddings?"

"What is a wedding, really, but a spiritual ceremony and a celebration? We do those things every day here in the Dale." Odelia has a way of making the most illogical things seem logical.

"Weddings are much more than that. You need wedding planners and caterers and—"

"What is a wedding planner or caterer, really, but someone who—"

"Someone who knows what she's doing! Come on, Odelia. This is crazy."

"Crazy like a fox, sister," Odelia says. Or perhaps she says, "*Crazy like a Fox sister.*" Not that either comment would make any more sense than hosting a wedding at the guesthouse. But the Fox sisters were largely responsible for launching the Spiritualist movement back in 1847. As far as Bella can tell, that practically makes them patron saints of the Dale. There's a commemorative plaque and memorial garden on the site where their cottage once stood.

The conversation zooms forward, as Odelia conversations tend to do. "Do you want to stay in Lily Dale?"

"Of course I do. Which is why I'm staying in Lily Dale."

"At the mercy of Grant Everard?" He, of course, is Valley View's new owner, having inherited the guesthouse in June from his late Aunt Leona.

"What does he have to do with—"

"You need this wedding to happen here as much as the bride does, Bella. Maybe more. Valley View is dead at that time of year, and—"

It's Bella's turn to interrupt with a sly, "I thought there was no such thing as dead."

Odelia rewards her with a smirk. "Listen, why would a high-powered, high-tech businessman with homes all over the world hang onto one more? He's not about to give up globe-trotting and making gazillion-dollar deals to become an innkeeper and kitten wrangler in Lily Dale."

"*I* did. Well, minus the gazillion-dollar deals and globe-trotting. But Grant is the one who hired me to stay here over the winter, remember? It's not as if I'm squatting on his property."

"You might as well be. As soon as he sorts out the estate, he's going to slap on a 'For Sale' sign, and you and Max will be out on the street."

That's exactly what their landlord did back home in the New York suburbs. Bella tells herself Grant is different. "He might decide not to sell it."

"Why wouldn't he? Right now, it has no value to him."

"It has sentimental value. Leona was his only family, and the house is still filled with her belongings."

"Do you think Grant cares about trinkets and tchotchkes and stacks of paperback novels? Trust me, all that matters to a business-man like him is the bottom line."

"Well, Valley View *is* a business."

"A tiny one that's only busy two months out of the year and that has been losing money for years."

"That's true." She sighs. "I wish I could just buy it myself."

"You couldn't even if you wanted to. Real estate purchases in the Dale are restricted to members of the Spiritualist Assembly."

"That's right. Well, at least it won't be easy for him to find a buyer."

"And if someone makes an offer tomorrow, he'd need a hell of a good reason not to take it. You and Max can only stay here if Grant hangs onto the house. Face it, Bella. You're in limbo."

"Believe me, Odelia. That is *not* news to me."

Back in June, having recently lost her husband, her teaching job, *and* the roof over their heads, she was en route with Max to Chicago, her late husband's hometown. She had planned to move in with her mother-in-law, Millicent, whom Bella privately calls Maleficent.

Though hardly warm and fuzzy, Millicent loves Max, just as she loved her son Sam. And she's the only family they have in the world.

But the woman is impossible. Living with her would have been . . .

Impossible.

Fate intervened in the form of a pregnant mackerel tabby sitting directly in their path before they even reached the state line. They detoured to Lily Dale to find Leona Gatto, who owned both the footloose feline and Valley View Guesthouse.

Unfortunately, Leona had died suddenly—or crossed over, as Odelia would say. In truth, she'd been murdered, though Bella didn't suspect that until after she'd settled in to help out with the guesthouse and Chance the Cat's eight kittens. She had never dreamed that the killer was much too close for comfort, or that in this community of clairvoyants, she herself would be the one to solve the case. Nor could she have predicted that come September, she and Max would still be here, much less that their new Lily Dale friends would feel more like family than . . . well, Maleficent.

All summer, she'd been planning to continue on to Chicago in the fall. All summer, Max had been begging to stay in Lily Dale. And all summer, even Bella had been torn.

Last week, as she was privately lamenting the impending departure to Chicago, Grant offered her a handsome salary to stay on in the guesthouse through the off-season. The money might have been a drop in the bucket for a gazillionaire, but it was far more than she had ever made as a middle school teacher.

"I still haven't had a moment to figure out what I'm going to do with Valley View, and it can't just sit empty over the winter," he said on the phone.

"But there won't be any guests, and it sounds like everyone else in town leaves after the season," she felt obligated to remind him, though her heart was already pounding with jittery anticipation.

"Aunt Leona always stayed year-round. So does Odelia, and there are plenty of others. Plus, we still have a houseful of kittens," he reminded her. We—as if he and Bella are a team.

Ah, the power of a well-placed pronoun.

Still, she hedged. "Doctor Bailey"—the local vet, whose first name is Drew—"told me the kittens will be ready for adoption soon, and everyone who meets them wants to keep one. I'm sure they'll all find homes."

"But they aren't ready yet, and what about Chance? She lives at the guesthouse. She and her babies need you, Bella. *I* need you."

Even over the phone, she wasn't immune to his charisma.

In person, it's downright dangerous. He has a way of making people—well, certainly Bella—change their minds about even the most inconsequential things. Like going out to dinner when they planned to stay home. Or being attracted to dark, good looks when they have no intention of getting romantically involved with anyone ever again. Maybe that was why she was trying so hard to find a good reason to turn down Grant's offer. Everything about it felt precarious.

Though repelled by the thought of anyone taking her place with the little feline family, she managed to say that she was sure he could hire someone to take care of the kitties and the guesthouse.

"I just did. You."

"I haven't said yes."

"You haven't said no."

"I might."

"But you won't."

She didn't.

Forget her own attachment to Lily Dale, the people, the house, the pets. How could she uproot Max again so soon? By spring, she might feel differently, but for now, they're staying.

At the mercy of Grant Everard.

Odelia steeples her hands beneath her double chin and levels a look at Bella. "If you can convince Grant that the guesthouse might be profitable year-round, there's no reason for him to get rid of it. All you need to do is pull off this wedding."

Ah, the power of an ill-placed pronoun, Bella thinks wryly. "All *I* need to do? What happened to *we*?"

"I mean *we*. But *you're* the one whose future is hanging in the balance. It's a perfect plan."

A perfect plan that hinges on the impending nuptials of a headstrong bride named Johnny?

"Why Lily Dale, Odelia? For the bride and groom, I mean."

"This is halfway between Pittsburgh, where Johnny lives, and Toronto, where her fiancé, Parker, lives."

"There must be other places around here that are available even last minute. Maybe not on that particular Saturday, and maybe not a country inn, but restaurants and banquet halls can probably—"

"Johnny has her heart set on that Saturday and on a country inn. And believe me when I tell you that once she makes up her mind, she doesn't change it."

"She sounds a little bit spoiled."

"Oh, she is. But Calla loves her anyway, and any friend of Calla's is a friend of mine. And any friend of mine is a friend of yours. So is it settled?"

"I . . . don't know."

"Why are you trying so hard to resist the obvious solution to your problem?"

"Because . . . I don't know. I guess it's what I do."

Odelia reaches out and pats her arm. "You've lost so much that you can't bear the thought of losing anything more. You're trying to make yourself immune to the pain by not taking risks. But that approach is only going to guarantee more loss. Your son is counting on you."

She's right. Bella never thought she'd find a home that would even come close to the one they'd lost. If she doesn't want Grant to sell Valley View out from under her, she's got to show him that it can earn its keep, and so can she.

"I know I'm bossy," Odelia says gently, "but I really do have your best interests in mind here, Bella."

"I know you do."

From the moment she beckoned Bella and Max onto her porch during a June thunderstorm, Odelia's been more of a mother than Bella's own mom, whom she'd lost as an infant. More, too, of a mother and grandmother than Millicent ever cared to be.

To be fair, Sam's mom did sound surprisingly disappointed when Bella finally called last night to tell her they weren't coming to Chicago after all. Funny, she'd expected her mother-in-law to be relieved. Millicent is one of those people who likes things to be just so. And Bella is one of those people who, no matter how hard she tries, can never seem to pull off perfection.

No wonder she and Odelia have hit it off so well. Warm, welcoming, and more than slightly wacky, the new next-door neighbor has filled a void in Bella and Max's lives. In one too-fleeting summer, she's become their family, just as this ramshackle house and this strange little town have become their home.

I can't lose it just yet. Or maybe ever.

She sighs. "Tell me about this wedding I'm—*we're*—hosting."

Odelia grins broadly and leans back in her chair. "They just got engaged, and they've set a date for the second Saturday in October. Johnny has always wanted to get married at a charming country inn, but of course everything in the area is long booked."

"Don't most people confirm a spot to have the wedding before they consider the date *set*?"

"Johnny likes to do things her way."

"She sounds like a piece of work."

"She's Calla's friend."

Calla is in her late twenties and came to live with Odelia as a teenager after losing her mother, Odelia's daughter. Much to her grandmother's pride, she recently published her first book and has spent the summer at a writer's retreat working on a second one. Bella has yet to meet her, but she sounds lovely.

Unlike this soon-to-be bride named Johnny.

"Will Calla be back for the wedding?" Bella asks.

"Of course. She called this morning to tell me that Johnny has agreed to have it here."

Bella clears her throat. "I thought it was Johnny's idea?"

"Oh, it was, it was."

Sure it was. "Is she hiring a wedding planner and caterer?"

"Just us."

"You and Johnny and Calla?"

"Us." She wags her index finger back and forth in the air between them. "You and me."

"I really don't think this is a good idea," she tells Odelia. "I have no idea where to even begin planning a wedding, and I'm not—"

"It's simple. *You* got married. *I* got married. We'll figure it out. We just need to take care of the food, the cake, the flowers, the ceremony, and the photographer. Calla will help us. The bride will do the rest."

"The rest, meaning . . . *rest up* for the big day?"

"So you've met Johnny after all." Odelia's smile has thinned considerably.

Bella sighs.

"I'll admit this is going to keep you busy, Bella, but things would have been a little too boring around here now that the season has ended."

Boring is dangerous. When Bella has too much time on her hands, she thinks about Sam, the life they had, and what might have been if only . . .

If only is dangerous.

Thinking is dangerous.

"Calla says Johnny will pay you very well, and believe me, she can afford to," Odelia tells her. "She comes from a wealthy Main Line family."

"Why aren't they getting married in Philadelphia, and why isn't her family handling the arrangements?"

"Oh, they're estranged."

Terrific. "What about the groom's family?"

"From what I hear, they're out of the picture, too."

"That doesn't sound good."

"It depends on how you look at it. The guest list will be nice and small. And no family means there's no meddling mother of the bride."

"Or groom." Bella nods, thinking again of Millicent. "When should we get started?"

Odelia looks at her watch. "The bride and groom will be here in about twenty minutes."

"*What*? They're coming *here*? *Today*?"

"Why don't you go freshen up while I put on a pot of tea?"

I need to hang out a shingle, Bella thinks as she scurries toward the house.

Only it would have to be a billboard.

**Bella Jordan, Mom, Innkeeper,
Roundabout Resident of the World's Largest
Spiritualist Community . . . and Wedding Planner**

Chapter Two

Lily Dale is a far cry from New York City, where Bella was born and raised, and even from Bedford, the relatively sleepy suburban town where she lived from newlywed to widowhood. She'd still be living there if her landlord hadn't sold the building and kicked out the tenants.

She's had a couple of months to adjust to living in a place where things move more slowly than her last-period chemistry class. Thus it's ironic that the painstaking pace doesn't apply to the destination wedding.

One moment, she was out in the yard gaping at Odelia; the next, she was rushing up the stairs to make herself presentable for the bridal couple.

As always, she'd started the morning freshly showered, her brown hair falling in loose waves down her back. She'd been wearing white wedge sandals, a white denim skirt that flattered her long, sun-browned legs, and a crisp sleeveless blouse in the same cobalt shade as her eyes.

Bella blue, Sam called the shade.

That was his favorite nickname for her, in fact: Bella Blue. He was always making silly little rhymes out of it: *"Where are you, Bella Blue?"* or *"I love you, Bella Blue."*

Sometimes, in quiet moments here in Lily Dale, she can almost hear his voice.

But *almost* doesn't mean she's really hearing it. He isn't here with her, no matter what Odelia and the others would have her believe.

Yes, there were times when she heard things—wind chimes, voices—that she shouldn't have heard. There was even a moment, back in July, when she found a necklace and allowed herself to believe that it was a heaven-sent gift from Sam, but . . .

She can't go around thinking for one instant that he's hanging around here. Then she'll start expecting to find him at every turn, looking back instead of forward.

That would be dangerous for a widow.

No. No way. Every minute, every day, you just have to focus on what lies ahead. You have to move on.

Bella thought it would get easier with time, that every day would be better, brighter than the one before. Some of them are. But every so often, she finds herself engulfed by a fireball of anger, sorrow, and disbelief—usually on days when she doesn't have enough to do.

Today wasn't one of them.

After her final guests checked out, she snapped a rubber band around her hair and changed into ratty old shorts, a T-shirt, and sneakers. Then she spent hours scrubbing bathrooms and bedrooms, emerging limp, sweaty, and smudged.

Another quick shower leaves her clean, if bedraggled and chilled. A promisingly steamy start led to a shivery finish, courtesy of the fickle, old hot water heater. Sometimes, it goes for weeks without acting up, but once in a while, it goes cold without warning.

Luckily, it's only happened to one guest, and he was good-natured about it. She's since posted warning placards in all the bathrooms. The icy flash usually only lasts a minute or so, if you have time to wait it out. Unfortunately, she doesn't. Wrapped in a towel, she retreats to the Rose Room.

The large bedroom at the head of the stairs previously belonged to Leona Gatto, and it's been Bella's private haven from the first night she arrived here. Filled with ornate, antique furniture and decorated with old-fashioned floral wallpaper, upholstery, bedding, and area rug, the room is decidedly feminine. Towering crown moldings and several tall windows make it seem more spacious than it is.

After catching a glimpse of her disheveled self in the bureau mirror, Bella checks the bedside clock. If the bride and groom are on time, then they're probably already downstairs with Odelia, who, in typically unruffled fashion, told Bella to take her time getting ready and promised to keep an eye on the boys.

The towel comes undone and drops to the carpet as she zips across the room to grab a sundress from the closet.

Nine pairs of eyes, all of them green, are fixated on her.

"Nothing you haven't seen a hundred times before, right everyone?" she asks Chance and her kitten octet. They're watching from their nest, a wide drawer Bella lined with a spare quilt when the litter got too large for the crate they'd been using as newborns.

Now just over two months old, seven of the kittens—whom Max named after the days of the week—are plump and sturdy, fully weaned, perpetually underfoot, and into everything.

The eighth kitten, Spidey, is a tiny black puffball who never strays far from his mama's side. He was the runt, so fragile for the first few weeks of life that Bella hand-fed him around the clock.

Drew Bailey recently assured her that little Spidey is past the danger zone and will most likely survive and thrive. "But he won't be ready to be adopted out until long after his siblings are gone."

Overhearing the vet's warning, Max spoke up. "We're keeping Spidey forever, just like Chance."

"You are?" Drew raised his dark eyebrows at Bella.

"We are *not*," she said quietly, regretfully. "We can't keep either of them."

Her mother-in-law's city condo isn't kid friendly, let alone pet friendly. If Grant really does sell this place in the near future, where else would they go? She doesn't have a nest egg, having spent every spare cent of her summer earnings trying to pay down lingering debt and medical bills from Sam's illness.

Odelia is right, she thinks as she hears a door slam out front. *This wedding has the potential to turn things around for us . . . and here comes the bride now.*

She glances out the lace-curtained window overlooking the aptly named Cottage Row. The narrow thoroughfare is better suited to the pedestrians who traipsed it all summer than to cars, especially the enormous SUV parked at the curb.

Beside it, a young couple, equally blond and beautiful, stands gazing up at the house. The man is wearing loafers without socks and madras shorts with a pink button-down shirt—untucked, sleeves rolled up. The woman has on a white linen shirtdress accessorized with gold sandals, belt, and jewelry.

Bella ducks out of sight before they see her naked and spying, though not before she catches the blatant dismay on the woman's face. How can she help eavesdropping, though? The window is open and their voices float clearly through the screen.

"When Calla said this place was quaint, I asked her if that was a euphemism for dump. She assured me that it wasn't. Apparently, she lied." The woman's aristocratic accent is pure Katherine Hepburn in *The Philadelphia Story.*

"Now, Daisy, don't be that way. I think it's full of charm, and I'm sure it's perfectly lovely inside."

Daisy, not Johnny. Maybe this isn't the bride and groom after all.

But they're coming up the walk . . .

And Bella isn't expecting any new check-ins today . . .

And the woman mentioned Calla . . .

Of course it's the bride and groom.

Bella pulls the white eyelet sundress over her wet head and shoves her feet into her white wedge sandals from this morning. There's a smudge of dirt on the canvas fabric. Oh, well. She'll cross her feet so that it doesn't show.

Story of my life.

She grabs the towel from the floor and rubs it over her hair, then glances into the mirror. Courtesy of fluster and the sun, her face is the same shade as the wallpaper's splashy cabbage roses. She hasn't worn makeup in so long that she can't even remember where she stashed her cosmetics bag. If she knew, she'd be compelled to put on some lipstick and powder, lest the bride judge Bella's facade as harshly as she did the house's.

You haven't even met her yet. Don't decide she's a snob based on a first impression.

The bride might be as lovely inside as she is out. Many people are.

* * *

Johneen Maynard is not.

Five minutes into a conversation with the bride-to-be and her fiancé, Parker Langley, Bella is not only convinced that her first impression was correct, but she's also having trouble remembering why she even thought the woman was lovely on the outside.

Yes, her features are delicate. Her skin is peaches-and-cream perfection. The highlights in her silky mane are the same shade as the softened honey butter Bella sets out for her guests with blueberry coffee cake leftover from breakfast.

But there's a pinched set to Johneen's expression from the moment she walks over the threshold, casting a distasteful look at the clunky brass andiron beside the heavy wooden front door.

"I use it as a doorstop on nice days," Bella explains quickly. "The door used to stay open, but there's something wrong with the hinges."

"Why don't you get someone here to fix them?"

"I haven't had a chance."

The heels of Johneen's gold sandals tap hollowly across the century-old hardwood floors as Bella leads the way to the breakfast room at the back of the house.

She remembers her own first impression of Valley View the night she and Max came in out of a torrential storm. For her, the dark woodwork, burnished period wallpaper, and vintage furnishings were reassuring as a warm hug from an old friend.

With towering ceilings, tall windows, and plenty of alcoves and cubbies, the place looks, and even smells, like the old house they'd left back in the New York suburbs. She barely noticed scarred wood and timeworn textiles, but Johneen scrutinizes every flaw. Her eyes are the same opaque gray as the duct tape patch on the storm door's screen, covering a hole that was big enough for a wayward kitten to squeeze through.

"When Calla said that she knew the perfect inn for our wedding, I thought it would be . . . an inn."

"It *is* an inn." Odelia's voice is perfectly pleasant but with a shade less warmth than usual.

"I was referring to the kind of inn that has . . . facilities."

"Oh, never you mind. We have plenty of restrooms here."

Johneen's impeccably sculpted eyebrows shoot up in dismay, and Bella bites back a smile, well aware that Odelia deliberately misunderstood her.

"I meant facilities like a restaurant, a cocktail lounge, perhaps a spa."

Bella replies, "We don't have any of those *facilities* here at Valley View. You might want to look into—"

"No, this is perfect," Parker interrupts. He reaches out to clasp his fiancée's hand. "Every wedding needs 'something old, something new, something borrowed, and something blue.' The house can be our 'something old.' The ring is new, and you said you wanted to borrow that bracelet from Calla, so—"

"Do you mean Calla's emerald bracelet?" Odelia cuts in.

"Yes. Green is my favorite color."

"Have you asked her if you can borrow it?"

"No, but she'll say yes. After all, it's for my wedding day."

Odelia tilts her head and raises her brows as if to say, "Don't be so sure."

Bella suspects that the emerald bracelet is more significant to her, and to her granddaughter, than a mere piece of jewelry.

"Bella," Odelia says, "why don't you tell Parker and Johneen a little about the guesthouse?"

"Um . . . sure." She clears her throat. "What, exactly, would you like to know? It was built back in the eighteen hundreds, and it's been both an inn and a private home over the years. Most of the woodwork and fixtures are original."

Poised in the archway between the parlor and dining room, she presses a concealed button to release a small bronze lever. Pulling it, she slides a polished and ornately carved cherrywood panel across the opening. "There are pocket doors like this throughout the house, and they were restored by Pandora Feeney and her husband Orville Holmes when they owned it a few years back."

Parker and Johneen's faces register not a hint of recognition, eyes glazed over like unwilling museumgoers held captive by an overzealous docent.

When Bella arrived in Lily Dale, she frequently found herself similarly blank when engaged in conversation with the locals. She didn't recognize celebrity mediums like Orville Holmes. She mistakenly assumed the Fairy Trail was simply a lakeside trail leading to a ferry, as opposed to a woodland neighborhood populated by tiny creatures.

Before she can go on speaking, Parker cuts to the chase. "All we want is an intimate spot where we can be married in October. This fits the bill, doesn't it, Daisy?"

Johneen nods and forces a smile.

"*Daisy?*" Odelia echoes.

"It's my pet name for her, because of her coloring," Parker explains, as if they might actually attribute the nickname to her sunny disposition.

"And," he adds, "because she looks like the actress who played Daisy in the *Great Gatsby* film."

"Mia Farrow?" Odelia squints, trying to envision it.

Johneen shakes her blonde head vigorously. "Of course not! He's talking about the remake from a few years ago. We weren't even born when the old one came out."

Neither was Bella, but she had watched plenty of classic movies with her father, and she owns a dog-eared copy of F. Scott Fitzgerald's novel. As far as she can tell, there's as little resemblance between Johneen and Daisy Buchanan as there is between uptight Johneen and the cheerful field flower. The Fitzgerald character's trademark is her lyrical voice; Johneen's Main Line lockjaw is the complete opposite.

"Huh," Odelia says. "I thought your nickname was Johnny."

"No, that was just a silly college thing. It doesn't suit me at all."

"No, it doesn't," Parker chimes in. "It's ridiculous. I don't know what that gaggle of girls was thinking."

"They were probably being ironic." Odelia, whose granddaughter Calla was part of the ridiculous gaggle, still sounds fairly pleasant, but Bella notes an ominous set to her jaw. "College students do appreciate irony."

"I guess that's true. And my freshman roommate's name was Francesca, so I suppose it was inevitable that we'd become Frankie and Johnny." Johneen flashes a brief smile, the first genuine one Bella has glimpsed since she arrived.

"It sounds like you know everything you need to know about the house," Bella says. "Why don't we go sit down?"

She leads the way to the white-wainscoted breakfast room and pulls out chairs at a round café table by the windows. Odelia had brewed a pot of tea while Bella was getting changed and pours it into four mismatched china cups.

Having skipped lunch, Bella slathers a moist blueberry-studded cake square with butter and tries not to devour it in one unlady-like bite. What she wouldn't give to be with Max and Jiffy, blowing bubbles on the back steps in the sunshine.

"Are there *children* here?" Johneen asks as their merry laughter floats past the screens on soapy, iridescent orbs.

Bristling at her tone, Bella fumbles her cake, scattering cinnamon crumbs. A plump berry splats onto her lap. She dabs at the indigo stain on her white dress.

Ah, there we go. There's something blue. Guess we're all set for the wedding.

"Bella's son, Max, lives here with her, and his friend Jiffy lives next door to me on the other side," Odelia explains. "They're good kids."

"We *love* children." Parker isn't entirely convincing. "Don't we, Daisy? We're going to have a bunch someday."

"In a few years, maybe. But we don't want any of them at our wedding."

Producing a pen that was tucked somewhere in the cloud of red hair above her right ear, Odelia jots *adult reception* on a paper napkin.

"Yes, definitely adults only," Parker agrees, and Odelia underlines her note.

"Absolutely no children!" Johneen is adamant, as if she were engaged in a bitter dispute even though no one is arguing.

Odelia underlines again and adds exclamation points. Then she asks, ballpoint poised, "What did you have in mind for the ceremony?"

Johneen bristles. "No childr—"

"No, I mean a church or a chapel or right here at the guesthouse?"

"Here," Parker says conclusively.

"Do you want a religious ceremony?"

"The ceremony doesn't matter much to me, although I would prefer not to have anything long and drawn out," Johneen decides, then gestures at Parker. "And he's an atheist."

"Well, I've performed plenty of weddings," says Odelia, who's an ordained minister among other things. "I'd be happy to officiate, and I'll keep it short and sweet and nonreligious."

This time, Parker doesn't bother to consult Johneen. "That would be fantastic."

Bella decides that he's the more personable of the two, with a relaxed, almost lazy lilt to his accent. Still, he isn't exactly oozing warmth even in comparison to his frosty fiancée. The two of them seem to float above Bella and Odelia in an iridescent little bubble of perfection, impervious to crumbs and stains and other messy complications.

As Fitzgerald said, *The rich are different.*

"Then that's settled. The ceremony will be here, and I'll marry you," Odelia briskly tells the couple. "Now let's talk about the *adult* reception. How many guests will you have?"

"Just a few of my friends and their dates," Johneen says firmly. "No family."

"What about your side, Parker?"

"There's no one."

"No family?"

"None who can make the trip."

"How many friends?"

"No friends."

"It's not that he doesn't have any," Johneen speaks up quickly, "but he's lived everywhere. Right now he's in Toronto, and before that, he was in Beijing for a few years. So his friends are scattered all over the world. They won't have time to be here on such short notice. We're going to have another reception later in the year so that I can meet them all."

"Why not just hold off on the wedding until then?"

Bella's question seems reasonable, but the couple does not look pleased by it.

"We're getting married in October," Parker says firmly. "Why wait?"

Why not *wait? This is clearly not a shotgun wedding.*

"So what do you do, Parker?" Bella asks as another possibility occurs to her.

"I beg your pardon?"

"Your career. You've lived all over the world . . . ?"

"Yes. I'm a freelance photojournalist."

"You're Canadian?" Maybe they're in a rush to wed so that he can obtain citizenship.

"No, I'm American. I was born down South, went to boarding school in New England and then college in California."

There goes the green card theory. But it explains his slight drawl.

"Where will you live after you're married?" Odelia asks.

"Where we live now, for the time being."

"Separately?"

"Only until his assignment is over," Johneen says.

"Why not just wait until then for the wedding?"

"Because we're in love!" she tells Odelia.

"And life is too short as it is," Parker puts in.

Bella, of all people, can hardly argue with that.

"Besides, I already have the gown. It's very elegant. Nothing frilly or puffy."

"She doesn't do frilly or puffy," Parker informs Odelia and Bella, who nod politely.

"And no veil. I'll just wear flowers in my hair, as long as they aren't scented. I don't do scents, either."

"Daisies will be perfect."

"Yes, daisies. And maybe some baby's breath. Something delicate."

Odelia allows the bridal couple to smile contentedly at each other before she resumes questioning them about the wedding. "Were you thinking of a sit-down dinner or a buffet?"

"A *buffet?*" Johneen recoils as though she'd suggested that they serve live crickets.

"Or a cocktail reception?" Bella says quickly. "It could be elegant, and we could do it outside as the sun sets over the lake. The weather can be beautiful at that time of year."

Oops. Seeing the look on Odelia's face, she remembers that October snow is hardly unheard of around here. Located about an hour southwest of Buffalo, in the heart of western New York blizzard country, Lily Dale sees its share of unseasonable storms.

"Cocktails by the lake." Parker nods. "I like it."

His bride tilts her pretty head. "I suppose we could do it with a shabby chic flair."

Bella doesn't have to be psychic to know they're thinking the same thing: *Heavy on the shabby.*

"What would you do for shabby chic food?" Johneen asks.

Good question.

"There are plenty of vintage platters and serving pieces around the house," Bella says.

"Yes, and we can do finger foods."

The bride flinches violently at Odelia's suggestion. "Finger foods? Do you mean like mozzarella sticks and those horrible little hot dogs?"

"Of course not. We'd do . . . we'd do . . ."

"We'd do scallops," Bella says before Odelia, whose culinary skills are as creative as her wardrobe, can make a suggestion. "And grilled shrimp."

Johneen and Parker nod. Yes, this is more like it. Seafood is always chic.

Odelia gives her an *attagirl* nod, so Bella goes on improvising. "Steak would be nice sliced and served on toasted baguettes. And cheese and crackers, and crudités, and grapes in wicker baskets . . . and maybe we can serve the drinks in mason jars," she adds, remembering that the basement shelves are full of them . . . along with plenty of spiders.

Parker warms to the idea. "We can have buckets of wildflowers on the tables, and you'll have them in your hair and bouquet. We'll make sure there are plenty of daisies for my Daisy." He pats her porcelain hand, which is French manicured and sporting an oversized diamond.

Wistfully remembering her own wedding and Sam, Bella decides that Johneen and Parker aren't so bad after all.

"Do daisies even bloom in October?" Johneen asks.

"They do in my garden," Odelia assures them. "And the meadow over by the main gate is full of wildflowers right up through the frost."

"What about a wedding photographer?" Bella asks.

"I *am* a photographer," Parker says.

"But you won't be in any of the photos if you take them."

"I'm sure the guests will be perfectly capable of pointing and shooting," he tells Bella.

Johneen nods her agreement. "We've talked about it, and we'd prefer not to have a wedding photographer posing us for endless portraits. That would distract from what the day is really about."

Well, that's refreshing. Bella would have pegged her for someone who can't get enough of the spotlight. All things considered, this has gone better than she expected.

"And the religious thing won't matter off-season, right?" Johneen asks Odelia as they stand to embark on a tour of the upstairs guest rooms.

"What do you mean?"

"All this Spiritualism stuff . . . it doesn't happen in October, does it?"

"Lily Dale is a Spiritualist community," Odelia replies somewhat stiffly. "If that's a problem for you—"

"No, it isn't," Parker says hastily. "We love it."

"We just don't believe in it," Johneen says. "Is that a problem for *you*, Odelia?"

"No. To each his own."

"But I have to wonder why you want to get married here, of all places."

Parker answers Bella's question for both of them. "Because it seems as if it's a million miles away from the rest of the world."

"And you want to get away from the rest of the world because it's romantic?"

Johneen hesitates long enough before her "yes" for Bella to suspect there's more to their story than they're letting on.

She takes them upstairs to peek into the guest rooms, glad that they're tidy and vacant. The tour seems to leave them underwhelmed.

Back downstairs at the door, Johneen gives one last look at the makeshift doorstop, then clears her throat and turns back. "One more thing, Bella . . ."

"Yes?"

Here we go. They're going to back out. So much for Odelia's perfect plan and my and Max's happily ever after in Lily Dale.

"This is a bit awkward. I hope you won't take this the wrong way, but . . ."

"Yes?"

"I'd appreciate if you'd refrain from wearing white on my wedding day."

Bella glances down at her blueberry-stained dress. "Don't worry. I wouldn't dream of upstaging you."

Johneen raises an eyebrow and looks at Parker, who chuckles as though that's the most ridiculous thing he's ever heard.

Bella and Odelia stand on the front porch, watching the couple drive away down the dusky dappled lane in their oversized luxury vehicle.

The engine fades, leaving only the sounds of Max and Jiffy calling to each other in the backyard, a distant lawn mower, and wind chimes tinkling from the eaves of this and every other house along Cottage Way.

At last, Odelia speaks. "You know, I've only met her a few times, when I visited Calla at college. Johnny was always spoiled, but I don't remember her being quite this high maintenance. I'm sorry."

"No, it's fine. I've got this."

"You do. You sounded like a pro in there."

"I did?"

"You had Bridezilla eating out of your hand when you were talking about all that fancy food."

She smiles. "I did, didn't I?" She'd been remembering the outdoor parties she and Sam attended back in New York. They'd had a nice social life for a short window of time before the economy tanked and Max came along. "You know what? I can do this. Maybe it'll even be fun."

"Really?"

"Who am I kidding?" Bella sinks onto the porch swing and swings her feet up onto the opposite railing. "But we can laugh about it later, right?"

"Let's hope so." Odelia sits beside her. "She really is self-absorbed."

"Most brides are. Weddings are stressful."

"Was yours?"

Bella thinks back. "Not really. It was the happiest day of my life. I was head over heels in love with Sam. All I wanted was to be his wife, and I couldn't wait to start living happily ever after. I meant every word of my vows."

They were tested so soon afterward.

She and Sam had been rich and poor. They'd had sickness and health, though not in that order.

As for the rest . . .

Till death do us part.

The words are bittersweet now.

How can she fault Johneen and Parker for rushing into a wedding because they're in love? Life really is too short.

Of course, here in Lily Dale, plenty of people—Odelia included—don't necessarily consider death a relationship obstacle.

Sometimes, Bella welcomes that philosophy. It's nice to imagine that her late husband really is still with her, even though she usually can't feel him, and she certainly can't see or hear him.

"How about you?" she asks Odelia. "Was your wedding stressful?"

"Not at all. But my marriage made up for it," she adds wryly.

Odelia doesn't often talk about her ex-husband, who left when their only daughter was young. Bella knows he didn't support her Spiritualist beliefs, which are, as she once mentioned, a more important part of her life than her ex-husband ever was.

"Is that why he left you?" Bella had asked. She'd learned never to expect a simple answer from Odelia, but that time, she got one.

"Yes."

"Did he tell you that?"

"In so many words."

"I'm sorry."

"Don't be. There are worse reasons for a man to leave a woman."

On that day, as on this one, they sat a while longer in cozy silence, swaying the porch swing so that it made a gentle squeaking sound. Bella has spent many a contented hour in this very spot, rocking and reading, watching butterflies or fireflies, listening to the crunching footsteps and murmuring voices of passersby as they leave the Spiritualist message services.

I'm going to miss summertime, she thinks, wondering if she'll regret the decision to stay for the winter. Will Lily Dale be so welcoming when the lake-effect snows blow in from the west, burying the village in eight-foot drifts?

Sam would have been happy here. "'*I love snow and all the forms of the radiant frost*,'" he'd quote Percy Bysshe Shelley to Bella whenever she bemoaned winter weather.

Sam loved poetry as much as he loved snow.

"Easy for you to say. You can ski and ice skate. I just slip-slide around and fall down a lot."

"Well, you might as well make a snow angel while you're down there, Bella Angel."

That was his other nickname for her because her maiden name was Angelo. On her birthday last year, he gave her the stained-glass angel wind chimes that now sway gently from the porch rafters.

"Angel bells for my Bella Angel," he said, smiling a sad smile. He was already ill. "When you hear them, think of me."

They didn't ring much back in Bedford, where the weather was far more tranquil. But here in the Dale—

"I probably shouldn't share this." Odelia's voice intrudes upon the tinkling chimes and Bella's memories.

"Share what?"

"Spirit is warning me about something."

Spirit, Bella knows, refers to the energy Odelia channels from the Other Side or the Great Beyond or whatever one chooses to call the place souls reside before they come to earth and after they leave. Bella has always called it heaven, ever since she was a little girl trying to cope with the fact that her mom was there instead of with Bella where she belonged. Now Sam is there too, along with Bella's father.

Whenever Odelia starts to deliver one of her cryptic messages, Bella gets her hopes up. But they're never from Bella's loved ones.

"My obligation is to tell you what Spirit wants you to know," Odelia always reminds her. "Not what you want to hear."

"What is Spirit warning you about?" Bella asks her now.

"Something to do with Johnny's wedding gown . . ."

"What about it? Is it puffy? She doesn't do puffy."

Ordinarily, Odelia would crack a smile. Not this time.

"Nothing like that. Spirit just keeps showing me the bottom of a long white dress, and it's dripping wet. Maybe . . . It sounds strange, I know, but I feel as though something bad is going to happen because of it."

"Because of what? The hem of her dress?"

"Yes. Maybe she's going to trip over it, or maybe she'll slip in a puddle of water and get hurt."

She falls silent.

Bella waits.

Odelia's eyes are closed. She isn't in a trance, but she's wearing an intent expression, as if she's seeing something Bella can't see and hearing something Bella can't hear.

Which is—if you buy Spiritualism—exactly the case.

Does Bella buy it?

Normally, no.

Occasionally, like right now . . .

Maybe.

"And there's a spider."

Bella hates spiders, and so does Max these days. A fan of *Charlotte's Web* and Spider-Man who'd even named his favorite kitten Spidey, he'd never minded them much. But there are some hairy, horrible ones in the basement of this old house, and he was imprisoned down there on a harrowing day back in July. The experience could have resulted in something far worse than sudden-onset arachnophobia, Bella knows.

"Mom!" he shrieked last night in the kitchen, "A giant spider!"

In the old days, he'd have called, "Dad!"

Now it's Bella's job to nudge the horrible creatures out into the night with a broom whose handle isn't nearly long enough. She tells Odelia about the latest eight-legged interloper. "Is that what you were seeing in your vision?"

Odelia doesn't answer, deep in concentration.

After a long time, she murmurs, "There's something else."

"What is it?"

"A closed door. I see the key in the keyhole. That's important."

"What does it mean?"

"I have no idea." Odelia opens her eyes abruptly. "It's Spirit shorthand. I have to figure it out."

"Refresh my memory. What is Spirit shorthand?"

"We all have unique methods of communicating with Spirit, interpreting the messages through symbols. For example, when Spirit shows me a pink helium balloon, it signifies a little girl. A blue helium balloon is a little boy. Or when I see a shiny black car, I know someone is going to cross over."

"What does a closed door mean?"

"When I see a door *closing*, it means that someone is about to make some kind of transition. But in this case, I'm seeing it already closed and locked."

"Are you sure it has something to do with Johneen?"

"Absolutely."

"Do you think it means she shouldn't be getting married to Parker?"

"I wouldn't go that far, but . . ." Odelia frowns. "Something isn't right about this."

"Are you going to warn her?"

"I don't want to alarm anyone. I'm not sure what it means. I'll wait and see what else Spirit shows me."

Chapter Three

October
One month later

Wearing comfortable old jeans the same shade as the sky and clutching her car keys, Bella steps out the front door of Valley View into a sunlit mosaic of red and gold, maroon and orange. Leaves float lazily from the branches, and a vibrant carpet blankets the Dale, infusing the air with a heady, earthy perfume.

The perfect weather won't last much longer. According to the forecast she just spotted online—and contrary to this morning's report—the balmy sunshine won't stick around over the weekend after all. This time tomorrow will usher in a cold front with strong thunderstorms and a killing frost, just in time for the Maynard-Langley wedding.

So much for the meticulously planned outdoor ceremony and reception, she thinks as she hurries toward her car.

During the season, the small parking area across the lane would be crowded with cars. Today there are only a few. Bella recognizes all of them, including a familiar white Lexus that belongs to one of Odelia's regular clients. Alana Rotini keeps a standing two o'clock Friday appointment with the medium the way some women do with their hairdressers.

Bella checks her watch and makes a mental note to call Odelia after three to discuss a rainy day backup plan.

So much to do, so little time.

She hadn't intended to add an emergency spay surgery to the week's agenda, but intense feline wanderlust seemed to blow in on the warm Indian summer wind. Yesterday, Bella opened the interior doors to enjoy the crossbreeze, and Chance beat a hasty exit through the faulty-hinged screen door when she wasn't looking.

It wasn't the first time the cat had pulled a vanishing act. When they first moved in, Bella and Max were baffled by the way she'd disappear from a room on one floor and reappear behind closed doors on another. Max assumed she was magical, and Bella was inclined to agree. Then they discovered a network of secret passageways that had been used by bootleggers back in the Roaring Twenties.

Last summer, Chance wasn't the only one coming and going through the secret tunnels, but she is now, thank goodness.

Who can blame her for wanting to nap undisturbed on the cushioned bench in the parlor's bay window or on the blue braided rug in the breakfast room, away from her litter's adorable but exhausting antics?

She always dutifully returns to the nest after a brief respite. Last night, however, she was gone at least a few hours before Bella figured out that she was outside, a lapse she blames on both wedding tasks and her mother-in-law.

Millicent has been calling a lot lately, having gotten over her disappointment—and yes, irritation—that Bella and Max decided to stay in Lily Dale for the school year. She'll ask Bella countless questions, then want to talk to Max. She asks him the same questions, almost as if she's expecting different answers.

When yesterday's hour-long call finally ended, Bella found a couple of kittens performing death-defying stunts on the stairway and realized she hadn't seen their mama in any of her usual haunts. Nor had Chance escaped to the basement through one of the secret passageways upstairs. If she were there, she'd have come running when Bella shook the treat bag at the top of the stairs.

"She must have gotten out of the house," Bella told a worried Max. "But I'm sure she'll be back."

"What if a wild animal eats her?"

"There are no wild animals in the Dale."

"What if she gets run over?"

"There aren't many cars in the Dale either, now that the season's over."

Bella wasn't nearly as worried about traffic as she was about tomcats. The last thing anyone needs right now is a fresh batch of kittens.

Chance ultimately turned up on the doorstep, indignantly meowing to be let in, as if she'd been pushed out of the house in the first place. But as soon as she'd visited her kittens and eaten a can of food, she tried to escape again and caterwauled when she couldn't.

Bella called Drew Bailey.

"Do you think she's sick? Or rejecting her kittens?"

"Nope. She's in heat."

"Uh-oh. She was out there for a while. I hope she didn't get . . . romantic."

"Believe me, when the cat's away, the cat will play," he said dryly. "If you're going to let her out, then you need to—"

"I'm not going to *let* her out. She *got* out. The door is broken."

"Well, then, I guess I'd better fix them both."

"Both?"

"The cat and the door."

"Oh, you don't have to fix the door. Just Chance," she said above howls from Chance as well as from a couple of amorous tomcats parked beneath her open window.

"Let's see . . . I have an opening next Tuesday afternoon."

"*Tuesday*?" How was she supposed to pull off the Maynard-Langley wedding amid a cacophony of unsated feline lust? "Is there any way you could do it sooner? Like . . . first thing tomorrow? Please?"

He hesitated, then agreed to squeeze her in.

"Really? Thank you so much. You're my hero!" she blurted.

As she hung up, flustered, she could have sworn she caught something about Drew coming to fix the door on Saturday morning. But she couldn't be sure, and she didn't know how to bring it up when she dropped off Chance after a sleepless night spent unsuccessfully trying to drown out the incessant wails with headphones and a pillow over her head.

She was unexpectedly emotional as she gave the restless cat a last loving pat and told Drew to take good care of her.

"I always do, don't I?"

Yes. He always does. Still, worry dogged Bella as she went about yet another day crammed with wedding errands. She was relieved when Drew called to report that Chance was safely in recovery. Now the cat, like Max, just needs to be settled at home before the bride and groom arrive.

Bella drives down the lane to the gatehouse at the entrance to the Dale. A two-lane road winds past, tracing the shoreline of Cassadaga Lake. It's lined with scattered houses, trees, and the occasional clearing with a boat dock jutting into the water.

She exchanges a friendly wave with a mailman leaning from his truck to deposit mail into a roadside box just outside the gate.

"You drove to the bus stop today," he calls to her. "Everything okay?"

"Everything's fine. Have a good weekend, Smitty!"

He drives on, and she parks her car alongside the now-familiar blue sign with its inscription *The World's Largest Center for the Religion of Spiritualism.*

Whenever she sees it, she's grateful for her tunnel vision on the stormy June night she first drove into the Dale. She was so focused on her mission to return Chance the Cat to her rightful owner that she hadn't noticed the sign. If she had, she never would have considered the Dale a haven.

Flanked by redbrick pillars, the low-roofed windowed hut was unmanned then, as it is now. During the season, it's occupied by an attendant who collects a modest visitor's fee. Most days, it was Roxi, a pretty teenage girl who babysits for Max once in a blue moon when Bella has a social life. That has consisted solely of seeing a movie with Odelia, attending a housewares party down the street, and—if you count it—getting an emergency filling at the dentist.

Odelia is always telling her she needs to get out more and even dared to encourage her to date. *Yeah, sure. The Dale isn't exactly crawling with eligible bachelors.*

Although . . .

Speak of the devil.

Blue Slayton, wearing khakis and a navy cardigan sweater, appears at the foot of a nearby driveway leading to a house that is, unlike the ones inside the gate, no simple cottage. Perched on a knoll above the lake, the grand, turreted gingerbread structure stood empty all summer. Odelia had mentioned that its owner, the renowned celebrity medium David Slayton, now resides mainly in Los Angeles, where he tapes his cable television reality series, *Dead Isn't Dead.*

Even Bella had heard of the show prior to her arrival in Lily Dale. She caught an episode over the summer and found David Slayton's on-air persona to be the antithesis of the mediums she'd met here. His aggressive and arrogant method of relaying Spirit messages is hallmarked by dismissive impatience with his guests if they don't readily recognize the lost loved one trying to communicate.

Blue Slayton materialized one mid-September day as Bella was waiting here for Max's bus. If she believed in ghosts—and around here, it's hard not to, though she continues to wear her skepticism like a shield—she might have pegged him for one.

He popped up out of nowhere in a spot she'd had all to herself on weekday afternoons. While a handful of Lily Dale kids attend the elementary school a few miles down the road, Bella is the only one who ever meets the bus here daily.

Fortunately, the guy wasn't a ghost. He was just a guy. A good-looking one, albeit a little too buttoned up, neatly combed, and unrumpled for her taste. She'd assumed he was around her age, but Odelia mentioned that he's a few years younger, not quite thirty. He dated Odelia's granddaughter Calla when they were young and both living in the Dale. From what Bella gathers, that relationship didn't end well. Blue has never mentioned it. They see each other daily as she waits for the bus and he retrieves his mail, but their conversations are casual.

Today, flipping through a stack of catalogs and envelopes, he glances idly at her car and then does a double take. Recognizing her in the driver's seat, he comes over to her open window.

"You drove today," he observes, and she marvels at the clockwork precision of Lily Dale life in the off-season. Now that the crowds are gone and life has settled into a predictable rhythm, you can't make a misstep without someone noticing. Most days, it's nice to know people keep an eye out for each other, though she supposes the scrutiny might be intrusive under certain circumstances.

"I have to scoop up Max and take him out to the animal hospital to get our cat," she tells Blue. "She had spay surgery this morning."

"Yeah? That's good. I mean, I'm guessing it's good?"

"It's definitely good, since eight kittens are all we can handle, although the timing could have been better. I've got a houseful of guests on the way."

"That's right, this is the wedding weekend, isn't it?"

She doesn't remember telling him that. He must have heard about it from someone else. Not Odelia, though. She has no use for Blue Slayton and mentioned just yesterday that she's glad she hasn't run into him yet. "I don't know why he's still hanging around here at this time of year."

"He said he's doing some work on the house."

At Bella's comment, Odelia rolled her eyes. "That's not true."

"Does Spirit tell you that?"

"Common sense tells me that."

"Victorian houses need constant repair," Bella pointed out mildly.

"The Slayton house is no Victorian. It was built about fifteen, maybe twenty years ago after David went Hollywood. And even if it does need work, that man is rich enough to hire the world's best contractor. His son doesn't need to play handyman and can't be any handier around the house than I am."

"Spirit or common sense?"

"You saw him. Does he look like someone who'd be wearing a tool belt?"

"Not exactly," Bella admitted, thinking for some reason of the veterinarian, Drew Bailey. Now *that* man, even in surgical scrubs, looks like he'd be just as comfortable holding a hammer as a scalpel.

She wouldn't mind finding out if that's the case and wonders if he'll mention fixing the door when she sees him. If he does, she can say that tomorrow morning is a bad time, but maybe another day. If he doesn't, well, she can always hire someone, or . . .

Or park yourself outside Drew's office howling like Chance?

As the yellow bus rolls around the bend flashing its red lights, she reminds herself that her relationship with Drew Bailey is strictly professional and platonic.

"Good luck with the wedding," Blue tells her as he heads up the driveway with his mail. "Too bad it's going to snow. But that's Lily Dale for you."

Max bounds off the bus with a handful of other kids who live in the Dale. He and Jiffy Arden are each clutching rolled-up, rubber-banded poster boards that Bella recognizes as last week's art projects. Now the boys are holding them to their eyes like telescopes, peering at the sky.

"Not yet," Bella hears Jiffy tell Max, "but we gotta keep looking."

Her son is dismayed when Bella waves him over to the car.

"I want to walk home with my friends! We're looking for snow clouds!"

"We have to go pick up Chance from Doctor Bailey. You can look on the way."

Her mention of the veterinarian magically erases his scowl. Suddenly agreeable, he climbs into the car, shouting to Jiffy that he'll see him later.

"Okay," Jiffy shouts back. "Don't forget about the snowboards!"

"Snowboards?" Bella asks as she pulls out onto the road.

"Yep. Me and Jiffy are going snowboarding this weekend, so we need to go buy snowboards."

With an inner sigh, she decides not to waste her breath defusing the latest kid conspiracy. There will be plenty of time for that later.

Max chatters on about the snow and school and *Candy Corn*, the animated Halloween movie being released today. Naturally, he wants Bella to take him to see it tomorrow. Apparently, all the kids from school are going to the Saturday matinee. Yep, every single kid, he insists. But he's sounding drowsier by the second, and by the time Bella reaches the dirt road turnoff, he's fast asleep.

The first time she ever traveled this particular shortcut from Lily Dale to Lakeview Animal Hospital, she was a stranger in a strange land and had just begun to suspect that Leona Gatto had been murdered.

Leona's nephew Grant was at the wheel that hot summer night. Max, Chance, and her hours-old litter were in the back seat, with

Spidey in urgent need of emergency veterinary care. Bella doubted the fragile runt would survive the journey.

She wasn't sure any of them would, as Grant, a stranger she'd just met, sped deep into a foreboding green tunnel of dense night forest.

What a difference a season makes.

Thinking of her mile-long to-do list, Bella presses the gas pedal.

Weather aside, this wedding is going to be perfect, just as she promised the skeptically intrigued Grant Everard.

"I never thought of Valley View as a destination wedding spot," he said when she first mentioned it over the phone last month. "Especially considering what just happened there."

He was referring, of course, to Leona's death and the subsequent murder investigation, during which a few other lives, including Bella's, were in jeopardy. The case did make the local papers after the culprit had been apprehended, but the national media was fortuitously distracted by an exploding political scandal. Dubbed "Pantygate," the salacious situation in Washington far eclipsed the obscure not-so-accidental drowning that had happened weeks earlier in a remote corner of western New York.

"Most people don't know about that, and they don't have to. Think about it, Grant. People fly to islands in the Caribbean and South Pacific so that they can get married off the beaten path. After the summer, Lily Dale feels just as remote, but it's a whole lot easier to reach."

"I hate to break it to you, but Valley View is no Bora Bora Four Seasons."

Trying not to resent the note of amusement, she reminded him, "Most people can't afford the Four Seasons. We can position Valley View as a budget-friendly, picturesque wedding venue in the middle of nowhere, even though it's not."

"That's debatable," he said, before telling her she might be onto something. "But the place needs a lot of work to bring it into the twenty-first century, and you can't sink that kind of money into a maybe."

"I can help with the makeover," Bella tells him. "I can plant some flowers, paint the walls, make some new curtains . . ."

He laughed. "What needs to be done at Valley View will take heavier equipment than a trowel, a paintbrush, and a sewing machine. We're talking about ripping out all the old plumbing, replacing the furnace, a complete electrical overhaul, professional landscaping. Not only that, but we'd need a decent website, an online reservations system, major advertising and promotion . . ."

"Not all at once. We can start small. And I'll take care of the most pressing cosmetic stuff before this wedding, if that's all right with you."

"Have at it and send me the bills," he said amiably. "We'll see how it goes."

It was hard not to find his lackadaisical attitude maddening. To him, Valley View is nothing more than a nuisance and perhaps a mildly interesting experiment. To her . . .

It's home. I have to make this work.

She brakes, spotting the familiar sign that reads, *Lakeview Animal Hospital and Rescue.*

Bordered by woods on one side and acres of grapevines on the other, it's little more than a clapboard hut. But within four cozy walls, Drew Bailey works miracles on sick or injured pets and strays.

Today, Bella and Max find him in his usual scrubs and razor stubble, finishing a splint on a little brown duckling's broken leg.

"Guys, meet Bob," he says.

"*Bob?*" they echo.

"Bob."

Max giggles. "That's a crazy name for a duck."

"Well, what else would you like me to call him? It's exactly what he does on the pond out back."

Puzzled, Max looks from Drew's solemn face to Bella's.

"He bobs," she explains.

Drew confirms, "When he's not laid up with a broken leg, anyway."

"He lives out back?" Max asks.

"He did, but it's dangerous. There's a fox den out there." Drew gently places the duckling on a blanket in a small cage and closes the door. Max peers in at him.

"Are you going to keep him, Doctor Drew?"

"No, but I'm sure someone will adopt him."

Predictably, Max turns to Bella. "Mom, can we—"

"Sorry, no room at the inn, kiddo."

"But—"

"Max, we can't."

"Hey, Max," Drew says over his protest, "you want to go visit Swash?"

"Yes!" He dashes off in search of Swashbuckler, the chatty parrot who lives in a cage in the back room.

Drew meets Bella's grateful smile with an angled dark brow. "Come on, you really don't want a warm, fuzzy duckling?"

"Thanks, but no thanks. No offense, Bob," she adds, and Drew grins the grin that sometimes makes her forget that he's her vet and not her friend.

Max *always* forgets.

She was relieved when school started and her son no longer accompanied her to weekday appointments at the animal hospital. Every time they come here, he bonds as much with Drew as with his furry and feathered patients.

On the way home, Max would ask her things like "But why *can't* we adopt a baby goat?" and "Why *can't* we invite Doctor Drew over for dinner?"

Back in July, those questions seemed equally preposterous, but Doctor Bailey—*Drew*—has since made house calls to Valley View. And once or twice, after tending to the kittens, he's stuck around to help them polish off leftovers or pizza.

But it isn't as if she's ever actually cooked dinner for him.

It isn't as if he's a friend.

And it certainly isn't as if he's anything *more* than a friend, she reminds herself yet again.

Steering the conversation back to the business at hand, she asks how Chance is doing.

"Let's just say she's feeling no pain."

"That's good."

"It is, but you might have your hands full for a while. She's still loopy from the medication."

Uh-oh. "How loopy is she, exactly? Because I'm hosting a wedding at the guesthouse, and my hands are pretty full already."

"I didn't know you did weddings."

"Neither did I, until I . . . um, found myself doing a wedding."

"How did this come about?"

She hesitates, wondering if she should explain about Grant Everard and needing to make the guesthouse profitable in the off-season. But that's a long and complicated story, so instead she simply says "Odelia."

He chuckles. "Now *there's* a one-word answer that explains absolutely nothing, yet absolutely everything. Come on, let's go see Chance."

He leads her past a bulletin board covered with fliers picturing lost dogs and cats as well as strays who need homes. His dream, Bella once overheard him telling Max, is to buy a large piece of property and turn it into a sanctuary for all the homeless animals.

"Why don't you just do it?" Max asked.

"Because I can't afford to."

"Why don't you charge your customers more money?" he persisted with kid logic.

"Because they can't afford to pay more."

Some, Bella knows, can't afford to pay anything at all. Yet she's never seen the man treat a living creature with anything but the utmost tenderness and respect, regardless of whether it's attached to an owner who can foot the bill afterward.

Chance is in the small recovery room, lounging on a cushion in a wire kennel. Bella reaches in to pet her, and her green eyes pop open, pupils hugely dilated.

"Hey, there, sweetie. Are you ready to come home?"

Chance meows, rolls onto her back, and stretches, revealing a shaved belly with a small scar and stitches. Then she stands up, falls over, stands again, and walks into the wall of the kennel. She emits an offended meow, promptly crashes into the opposite wall, and meows again.

Alarmed, Bella turns to Doctor Bailey. "Is she okay?"

"Like I said, she's loopy. It'll wear off. Just keep her contained and keep an eye on her. I'm going to go get some medication for you to give her. I'll be back in two seconds."

As he steps out of the room, the phone rings, and he calls over his shoulder, "Make it three seconds. I have to get that. Lorinda leaves early on Fridays."

Lorinda is his young vet tech assistant, who does everything from answer the phone to foster homeless animals in her tiny apartment.

Hearing Drew's brusque "Lakeview Animal Hospital," Bella remembers why she found him gruffly intimidating when they met.

He does come across that way at first, or when he's in the midst of a pressing medical issue. But he has a soft spot for animals and children, and the moment Bella saw him in action with Chance and Max, she liked him.

Of course, she changed her mind in the next moment, when his guard was back up. By then, so was hers.

On that traumatic day, she and Max had already driven away from Bedford for the last time. Heartbroken, destitute, and homeless, she had no idea what was going to happen next. For her son's sake, she'd pretended the road trip was a great adventure. But never in her life had she felt more terrified, or more alone.

Then, out of the blue, there was Chance, sitting in the middle of the road. They had to pull over.

Every time Bella recounts the tale in Odelia's presence, that's Odelia's cue to remind Bella that cats are mystical creatures.

"If she hadn't popped up where she did, you and Max would be in Chicago right now with Millicent. You never would have found your way here."

But they did, after first finding their way to the animal hospital, where unflappable Drew took them all in stride: one ownerless, pregnant cat, one fatherless boy, and one shell-shocked widow with all her worldly belongings packed into a car that wouldn't have made it to Chicago anyway.

Troy Valeri, the mechanic who eventually fixed it, couldn't believe they'd made it that far. "There was a bad storm that night. You're lucky this car didn't break down and strand you on a highway in the middle of nowhere."

Luck?

Destiny?

Chance? *Chance?*

Thanks to you, we found our way to Lily Dale, Bella thinks as the aptly named feline head-butts her hand, nuzzling and purring loudly.

Amid snatches of animated conversation between Max and Swash, Drew is all business on the phone discussing a client's ailing pet.

Parrots are chatty and ducklings are warm and fuzzy. Doctor Drew Bailey is none of the above. Yet he patiently answers the concerned pet owner's questions and follows up with many of his own. He's obviously concerned; the call is going to keep him a lot longer than three seconds.

Bella checks her watch. Odelia has probably finished her reading by now and will be getting ready to head over to the guesthouse. She pulls out her cell phone, enters the password to unlock it, and presses the number she's had on autodial since her first night in the Dale.

"If you need anything at all, you just call me," Odelia said. "I don't care if it's the middle of the night. I'll answer."

Not, however, in the middle of the afternoon, when she sees most of her clients. Bella has learned that when Odelia tunes into the Spirit world, she tunes out the physical world.

Like the other Lily Dale mediums, she has a small room in her house reserved for readings. There are no crystal balls or Ouija boards. Just a candle or two, a table and a couple of chairs, paper and pens, and boxes of tissues. Presumably, hearing from one's dead relatives can make one weepy.

Bella wouldn't know firsthand. She hasn't had a reading, despite repeated offers from Odelia and others.

The only offer Bella might consider has come from Pandora Feeney, of all people. Insufferable in many ways and eccentric in even more, she's the last neighbor with whom Bella would have expected to establish a bond—here, or anywhere else on the planet. But Pandora visits often, having owned Valley View Guesthouse before her ex-husband sold it to Leona Gatto after a bitter divorce. For all her faults, there's something almost endearing about her.

And once in a while, she'll utter a cryptic comment that makes Bella wonder whether she's channeling Sam.

Maybe it's just that Pandora wants to channel Sam, or wants Bella to believe that she is.

Why would Bella's level-headed, down-to-earth husband communicate with her through a feigned-accented, occasionally petty woman like Pandora? Surely Sam would have chosen Odelia instead, or maybe Andy Brighton, an affable male medium who lives across the way.

Unless he has no choice. Maybe Pandora is in tune with his energy and the others aren't. Maybe it has something to do with the house. Maybe . . .

So many maybes when it comes to Spiritualism.

Odelia answers the phone with a breezy "Wedding Bellas are ringing."

"Wow, you must be psychic," Bella teases. "That, or you have caller ID. You sound cheerful. I take it your reading went well this time?"

"It did."

That isn't always the case. According to Odelia, Alana Rotini is a demanding client. She's been trying desperately to make contact with her late twin brother, who has yet to show up, and she isn't always gracious to the Spirits who do come through.

"Did you finally put Alana in touch with Alfie?"

"No, but Miriam made her laugh." Miriam is the resident Spirit whose husband had built Odelia's house back in 1883. "Oh, and then we had a rollicking chat with Lennon."

"The Soviet leader? Vladimir Lenin?"

"The Beatle, John Lennon. He pops in now and then with messages for Yoko."

"You know Yoko?"

"Does anyone really know Yoko?" Odelia says mysteriously, then changes the subject. "How is Chance doing?"

"She's . . ." Bella watches the cat bat an invisible object around on the table. "She's great. The anesthesia just left her a little . . ."

"Stoned?"

"That sounds about right."

Odelia laughs. "Cheech and Chong and Chance."

Bella grins at that, but it fades when she remembers why she's calling. "Listen, I'm still at the vet, but I'll be heading home soon. Can you just keep an eye out for guests next door until I can get there? Oh, and by the way, the forecast for tomorrow seems to have changed all of a sudden."

"Welcome to western New York. What are they calling for?"

"Forty-five and sleet."

During the moment of silence as Odelia digests that news, Bella marvels that for all her psychic premonitions and predictions, Odelia is perpetually caught off guard by the weather. Then again, positioned as it is on the eastern end of the volatile Great Lakes . . .

Blue Slayton's earlier words echo in her head. *That's Lily Dale for you.*

"This isn't good." The cheeriness has evaporated from Odelia's voice. Clearly she, too, is aware that if a warm and dry Johneen can be unpleasant on an ordinary day, a sopping, shivering, wedding-day Johneen will be downright beastly.

"We'll have to move the wedding indoors," Bella tells her. "We'll get the furniture out of the dining room and set up the round tables there, and the ceremony can be in the front hall with the guests looking on from folding chairs in the parlor. The bride can come down the stairs instead of down the aisle, and—"

"No!"

"What?"

"We can't do that. We'll just . . . rent a tent."

"It's going to be freezing out."

"We'll rent a heated tent. No stairs, Bella."

"Why not?"

"Because Spirit has been warning me that the bride is in terrible danger," Odelia says ominously. "I'll explain when I see you."

As she hangs up, Bella shivers, thoroughly chilled though the bright sun is still shining outdoors . . . for now.

Chapter Four

An hour later, Bella hears a thumping sound at the front door of the guesthouse. *It can't be Odelia. She always walks right in. The bridal couple must have arrived—with a battering ram?*

But it *is* Odelia, and she wasn't knocking. She was kicking the door with a foot clad in a bright yellow rubber rain boot. She's also wearing an orange sari and a tweed newsboy cap. In her arms are a stack of envelopes and catalogues and a large basket filled with cellophane-wrapped, ribbon-tied . . . *something.*

"What do you have there?"

"I grabbed your mail from the box for you." Odelia hands it to her. "And these are wedding favors," she adds, holding up a jar of . . .

Something.

"I asked myself what I could make that would best represent the wedding."

"And that would be . . . ?"

"Lemon-habanero marmalade," Odelia says, as if she should have guessed.

Still stumped, Bella nods politely.

"It's marmalade to fit the country shabby chic theme, it's yellow to match the color scheme, and it's spicy because . . . well, the wedding night." She winks and sets the basket on an antique piecrust table. "Then again, with those two . . . they're not exactly the most unbridled bridal couple I've ever met."

"I just hope they like their accommodations." Bella has been working for days to transform the Teacup Room into the honeymoon suite for their wedding night.

Officially, she's supposed to get Grant's approval before making any home repairs or significant expenses. Deciding a cosmetic makeover didn't fall into that category, she managed the makeover for a minimal cost, though it took maximum effort and a hefty toll on her back.

She painted and redecorated in crisp shades of white, cream, and gold. Leona Gatto's collection of delicate china teacups and charming tea party wall prints went into a box on the basement shelf, replaced by a couple of vintage wedding portraits she found there and displayed in gilt-sprayed dime-store frames.

"Fit for a queen," Odelia proclaimed when it was finished. "Or a bride. Even Johneen. Although, did you get her permission to dress the room in white? We wouldn't want those lace curtains to upstage her."

Now she looks up the flight of stairs, shaking her head.

"Uh-oh. What happened to 'fit for a queen'?" Bella asks. "You don't think she's going to like the suite?"

"No, no, it's wonderful. It's the stairs that worry me."

"Odelia—"

"We can't take any chances."

"Well, I can't exactly move their accommodations to the first floor."

"No, but I'm not worried about what happens *after* the wedding. We can't have Johnny descend that stairway in a long, white dress to be married."

"Because you had a vision of her tripping and falling down the stairs?"

"I didn't see her tripping and *falling* down the stairs. Spirit just keeps showing me the bottom of a long white wedding gown and the bride's feet in heeled satin pumps."

"And they were dripping wet," Bella reminds her.

"Yes."

"Maybe it was just a warning that it was going to rain on her wedding day and that she'd better stay indoors."

Odelia shakes her head. "That doesn't feel right. The spider . . ."

"What kind of spider was it? A daddy longlegs? One of those creepy-crawly furry ones?"

"It wasn't creepy at all. It was . . . just sitting there nicely in a web."

"Do you think it has something to do with Spidey?"

"You mean Max's kitten? I doubt it. If Spirit wanted to show me the kitten, then Spirit would show me the kitten."

"And there was the door . . ."

"Right. A closed door with a key sticking out of the lock."

"The door comes after the hem. Before the spider."

"Is that relevant?"

"It might be."

Odelia has mentioned this recurring vision before. Bella isn't sure why she's so convinced it means Johneen is in some kind of danger, and Odelia herself admits that there's nothing conclusive about what she's seeing. The images are open for interpretation. For some reason, hers is dire.

And with everything at stake here, dire is potentially catastrophic.

She takes a deep breath. "Look, we can't drench a bride and groom at an outdoor ceremony. Especially *this* bride and groom. You know what I mean?"

"Of course I do."

Of course she does. They both know a lot of things now that they're wedding planners.

For example, they know that there are countless shades of yellow and white, and that if a bride e-mails photographs of her preferred shades, you can plug them into an online image search engine to find sources for matching ribbon, invitations, and even the wedding cake's embellished icing.

They know that the nearest liquor store doesn't keep cases of Dom Pérignon in stock, so it has to be ordered, and paid for, well in advance.

Bella already knew that oyster season is any month that ends in an *R*, but she didn't know, though should have guessed, that Johneen's favorite shellfish aren't readily available four hundred miles from the ocean.

She explained to the bride in one of their countless e-mail exchanges that the nearest fresh seafood market is an hour away, not an easy jaunt to make on the wedding day. Plus, someone would have to shuck them all.

Parker offered to have oysters flown in from New York City and even hire a professional shucker who would, Bella figured, also have to be flown in from New York. *"If my Daisy wants oysters, then oysters she shall have,"* Parker wrote, at which point his Daisy decided to drop the raw bar idea in favor of a carving station. *"Tres* chic, and all the rage in Paris," she claimed.

"So is the Eiffel Tower," Odelia muttered to Bella, "and the next thing you know, she'll order us to build one out of baguettes."

The carving station demanded a cutlery purchase, as Bella could barely find pairs of matching steak knives in the guesthouse drawers, let alone eleven that were similar. She did, however, locate twelve gilt-rimmed white Limoges dinner plates in the china cabinet. They were perfect.

Were.

Moving them in pairs from the dining room to the kitchen, she dropped and broke two. That left her one short, until Odelia managed to find a reasonable knockoff at a tag sale.

Overly passionate felines and psychic visions aside, it's been smooth sailing ever since.

Right into a perfect storm.

"Well, at least someone is ready for the rain." Bella glances at Odelia's rubber boots.

"These? No, there's a hole in one of the soles and it leaks," she says with Odelia logic. "I never wear them in the rain."

"Then why do you keep them?"

"Because they're the most comfortable shoes I own, and we're going to be on our feet until late tonight. Plus, they match the wedding theme."

"Rain?"

"No! They're shabby, yet chic, and they're yellow." Odelia pats her arm. "Don't worry about the rain. We aren't going to drench the bride and groom. I'm borrowing a chuppah."

"A . . . what, now?"

"A *chuppah*. It's a canopy used for Jewish wedding ceremonies."

"This isn't a—"

"No, but you were right about it being too late to rent a tent. A chuppah will do the trick. They're really quite lovely."

"Where did you find one?"

"I have a rabbi friend at a synagogue in Buffalo who's happy to loan it as long as we go pick it up either late tonight or tomorrow morning. Luther has offered to do that for us."

Luther Ragland is a longtime friend of Odelia's. But Bella can't imagine the virile, retired police officer turned part-time private detective voluntarily choosing chuppah detail in the midst of an active Friday-night social life and a sacred Saturday-morning tennis game.

She quirks a brow at Odelia. "He *offered*?"

"Well, I asked him."

"And he said yes?"

"I can be very persuasive."

Yeah, no kidding.

"Luckily, I caught him before he left the country," Odelia adds. "He had just picked up his date."

"He was leaving the country with his date?"

"Just Ontario. He was taking her to Niagara-on-the-Lake for dinner and a show."

Bella exchanges the exotic globe-trotting scenario her mind had conjured for a more pedestrian outing. The picturesque Canadian town is a mere ninety-minute drive from the Dale. Luther treated her and Max to Sunday brunch there last month, en route to Niagara Falls.

Max had already glimpsed the massive waterfall from the American side, but Luther insisted on crossing the border for the full effect.

Bella's protests that he didn't have to go so far out of his way fell on deaf ears. He seemed to really enjoy playing tour guide that day, and he and Max developed a sweet, if unlikely, kinship over the summer.

A brief youthful marriage gave Luther no children of his own. Content with his bachelor lifestyle, he's quite the ladies' man. Sometimes, Bella thinks Odelia might like to change that, but as far as she knows, that hasn't happened.

Bella found him intimidating when they first met, and he isn't the most easygoing guy in the world even now that they're friends. But Max brings out the best in him, and Luther is in some ways like the grandfather Max never had.

Sam would be pleased that there's a male role model in their son's life. Two, if you count Drew Bailey.

Bella doesn't. Or at least, shouldn't.

She flips quickly through the stack of mail, making sure it's nothing that can't be stashed in a drawer for a couple of days while she's otherwise occupied.

A postcard from a candidate running in the upcoming county elections, a couple of Christmas catalogues—*already?*—a credit card bill, yet another debt consolidation offer forwarded from her old address, and . . .

What's this?

Frowning, she stares at a rectangular white envelope with a printed label bearing her name, care of Valley View Guesthouse. There's no return address, and it bears a Lily Dale postmark.

She's about to open the envelope when a voice calls through the screen door. "Gammy?"

Bella turns to see a young couple standing on the porch.

The man, lanky and handsome, has a light brown complexion and jet black hair. He's holding a quilted floral duffel bag and is standing at the top of the steps, a few feet behind the strikingly pretty young woman. Tall and lithe, she's wearing a houndstooth blazer and snug jeans tucked into boots. Her hair is long and brown with gilded streaks, and her wide-set eyes are the same amber-green shade as Chance's.

Odelia throws open the door and envelops them both in a fierce hug. Recognizing Odelia's granddaughter Calla Delaney and her boyfriend, Jacy, Bella tosses aside the unopened envelope with the other mail.

"I've heard so much about you," Calla tells her after Odelia makes introductions.

"Same here. Both of you."

"Uh-oh. Are you talking trash about me again?" Jacy asks Odelia, and she gives him another affectionate squeeze.

"More the opposite," Bella says with a grin.

Whenever Odelia mentions her granddaughter's significant other, it's in glowing terms. She calls him Jay, and he calls her Dee Dee.

Bella knows that Native American Jacy was born and raised on a reservation until his abusive parents lost custody. He was later adopted by his foster parents, Lily Dale mediums Walter and Peter.

He and Calla dated in high school and on and off in college. After breaking up for a few years, they found their way back to each other and have been together ever since. Their future is bright, with her recent publication of her first book and Jacy about to finish med school.

"You look beautiful, Gammy. I love this." Calla touches the orange silk fabric of Odelia's sari.

"Thank you. A friend brought it back for me from Mumbai years ago, when Mumbai was still Bombay and I was still thinking I might remarry someday. It's a wedding sari, so naturally, I never used it for that purpose. But I thought it was fitting."

"The hat goes really well with it," Jacy comments with a wink, and Odelia pats the newsboy cap.

"Bad hair week. I need to have it cut and colored, and I just haven't had the time. How did you two know where to find me, anyway?"

"A little boy on a scooter told us," Calla says.

"Along with a lot of other things we didn't even ask about."

Grinning at Jacy's addendum, Odelia tells them it must have been Jiffy Arden.

"Is he the boy whose mother is renting Evangeline's house?" Calla asks.

"That's him."

Jiffy had knocked on the door at Valley View after school to see if Max wanted to come outside to play, but Bella had told him no.

"But Mom! Why not?"

"Because I'm too busy to come out and keep an eye on you."

"Jiffy's mom isn't keeping an eye on him."

No surprise there. Misty Starr, a young medium whose husband is overseas with the military, takes a laid-back approach to parenting.

The neighbors tend to watch over her little boy, who has a way of emerging unscathed from harrowing scrapes and escapades. But Bella isn't any more comfortable letting Max roam unsupervised on the Dale's deserted off-season streets than she was with the summer's transient crowds.

Bella invited Jiffy to come in and help Max keep an eye on Chance and the kittens, offering him the same dollar an hour she's paying Max. To her son's disappointment, Jiffy opted to ride away on his scooter instead.

"My mom told me to go blow the stink off," he informed them, then added hastily, "That doesn't mean I stink, by the way. It's just a saying that means get outside and play in the fresh air. My mom says it all the time."

"By the way, my mom never tells me to blow the stink off," Max complained, incorporating Jiffy's signature line. He's been saying it all summer: *by the way* this and *by the way* that.

Shaking her head at Jiffy's latest escapade, Bella asks Calla, "I hope he was wearing a helmet? He wasn't earlier, and I told him to go home and find one."

"He must have. He was wearing one."

"Now if only I could get him to stop talking to strangers."

"Good thing it was only us," Calla says. "We might be strange, but we're not strangers."

After flashing a brief smile, Jacy clears his throat and tells her, "I guess I'd better . . . right?"

Calla nods. "I guess you should."

"He should what?" Odelia asks sharply.

"It was great seeing you again, Dee Dee, and nice to meeting you, Bella, but . . . unfortunately, I have to head back up to Buffalo."

"What? Why?"

Calla answers her grandmother's dismayed question before Jacy can. "He has too much to do this weekend. He's on duty at the flu shot clinic tomorrow morning at the reservation."

"Jacy does volunteer work with the Seneca Nation," Odelia informs Bella proudly, then turns back to the couple. "But what about the wedding?"

They hesitate just long enough for Bella to pick up on a prickle of tension between them.

"I hate to miss it, but I don't think I can get away."

"That's a shame. Are you sure you can't—"

"Gammy, he can't," Calla says sharply. "Believe me, I already asked."

On that note, Jacy asks her if she wants him to carry her bag up the stairs.

"No, I've got it. Thanks. Have a safe trip back."

"Let me know if you want me to pick you up on Sunday."

"I told you, I'll catch a ride with Frankie."

Jacy nods, says his goodbyes, and heads out the door.

Odelia stares after him. "I can't believe he's going to miss the wedding."

"It's fine, Gammy. He barely knows Johneen, and even I haven't ever met Parker."

"But he should be here with us."

"You mean, with me?" Calla shakes her head. "He's busy. I can count on one hand the waking hours we've spent together lately."

"Well, you were away writing all summer. Now that you're back . . ."

"Right. I'm back, and he's never around."

"Be patient with him, Calla. He's working his way through med school, and he's one of the most gifted healers I've ever known."

"I *am* patient, Gammy. But even when he's around, he's a million miles away. I swear he doesn't even hear half the things I say to him."

"I've heard him say that about you when you're lost in a writing project, too. Anyway, it'll change when he finishes his residency."

"I hope so. Right now, I'm lonely."

"Writers need to be alone."

"Not every minute. Not in a relationship."

"Why don't you get a kitten to keep you company? Bella has eight of them upstairs."

Calla's face lights up. "That's right! I forgot. How are Chance and her babies?"

"They're great. Chance is recuperating from spay surgery, and the kittens are adorable."

"Aw, I raised their great-grandmother, Gert. She was a tiny baby when I first got to Lily Dale. I'll never forget the day Gammy brought her home for me."

"Pets are wonderful therapy for grieving children, especially when they're uprooted after a loss," Odelia says. "Bella's son Max has been through the same thing."

"Yes, he has," Bella says. "Although he's much younger than you were, Calla."

"It's hard at any age. I'm so sorry. But it sounds like he's adapting and making friends."

"Just like you did," Odelia reminds her. "Remember? Jacy, Evangeline . . ."

Calla nods. "And Willow, and Blue."

At the last word, Odelia's lip curls.

"Blue is a good guy," Bella can't help saying.

"You know Blue?" Calla asks in surprise.

"I've met him a few times. He seems very nice."

Odelia rolls her eyes and makes a *ffff* sound.

Ignoring her, Calla asks Bella, "Where did you meet him?"

"Around the Dale. I see him at the bus stop every afternoon, and he jogs past the house every night around dusk."

"Speaking of jogging," Odelia steers the conversation back, "Jacy was such a talented track star in high school that he was recruited by every top college."

"Not *every* top college, Gammy. But he did wind up getting a full undergrad scholarship." She turns abruptly back to Bella, obviously wanting to change the subject. "I take it Bridezilla's not here yet?"

"Calla!"

"Don't worry, Gammy. I won't tell *her* that's what you call her."

"I only said it once!" Odelia protests, turning to Calla. "She was being impossible."

"Was it the piano day?" Bella asks, remembering when Johneen requested that they rent a grand piano so that she could walk down the aisle to a live rendition of "Fields of Gold," their chosen wedding song. As it turned out, even if someone had been willing to transport it over the uneven, narrow space between the houses, no rental company was willing to place the instrument outdoors on the grass beside a lake.

"No, it was the day she insisted on a fireworks display even though we can't get a permit approved in this dry weather."

"So much for that." Calla shakes her head.

"The fireworks?"

"The dry weather. I just heard it's supposed to snow tomorrow."

"*Snow?*" Bella and Odelia echo in unison.

"Well, they said rain for the wedding day, but it's changing over to wet snow before dawn on Sunday. Johneen isn't going to be happy."

"Don't worry. I have it all under control." Odelia tells her about the chuppah.

"Why don't you just move the wedding indoors?"

Odelia sighs heavily and shakes her red head.

Calla looks at Bella, who explains. "She had a vision of Johneen falling in her wedding gown."

"*Not* falling!" Odelia protests, then quickly describes what she's been seeing. "I'm not sure how to interpret it."

"Are you going to tell Johneen?"

"I might if I had something more concrete to pass along, but I don't want to frighten her."

Can't you request more specific information from Spirit? Bella wants to ask, but she knows better. She's learned that Spirit conversation involves less asking than receiving, and it doesn't exactly come with a customer service line for maximum efficiency.

Every medium has her own method of communicating with the Other Side, and no one's process is foolproof. There are frequent communication gaps, resulting in attempts to interpret cryptic messages. It sometimes seems like an elaborate guessing game. A frustrating one, as there are no definitive answers.

"I'm sure everything will be fine," Calla says, "and Grant will decide to keep the guesthouse, and everyone will live happily ever after."

"Including you and Jay," Odelia puts in.

Calla clears her throat. "Can I see the kittens?"

"Sure. They're upstairs with Max. Are you still planning to stay here?"

"There's no need for her to do that now," Odelia pipes up. "She can sleep next door in her old room. A twin bed works fine since it's just her. And I have a big pot of menudo on the stove."

"The boy band?" Calla asks with a grin.

"The Mexican soup. You knew that."

"I did. But I love to tease you, Gammy. Bella, have you ever tasted menudo?"

"I haven't."

"I make it whenever there's a party," Odelia explains. "It's a tried and true Mexican hangover cure, and it sounds like we'll need it with that signature cocktail you're whipping up for tonight."

Calla clears her throat. "Gammy, I think I'm going to stay here at the guesthouse with all my friends. We haven't spent time together in so long."

Odelia's expression says *neither have you and I.* But she keeps her mouth shut.

Maybe she realizes Calla is distancing herself from a weekend of unsolicited advice from Team Jay. More likely, she's thinking she can work her Odelia magic and get her to move next door later.

Calla sniffs air fragrant with the pumpkin-scented jar candle flickering on the desk and the homemade strudel Bella baked earlier. "It smells so nice in here. And it looks beautiful, too."

She takes it all in with an appreciative eye: the mantel with its arrangement of pumpkins and gourds in harvest shades that complement the vintage honey-toned brocade wallpaper, the grand staircase with its intricately carved balustrades and frosted gaslight globe on the newel post. Her focus turns to the antique registration desk. A cut-glass bowl of M&Ms sits near the candle, along with a leather-bound register lying open to today's date.

"Leona," she murmurs, wearing a fond smile as if she's seeing not a piece of furniture but an old friend.

Bella raises a questioning eyebrow at Odelia, who says in a low voice Calla doesn't even seem to hear, "She's feeling Leona's energy."

"Leona's here?"

"Where else would she be?" Odelia asks with Odelia logic.

Bella follows Calla's gaze, searching for a hint of otherworldly activity. She sees nothing out of the ordinary, other than a thin layer of dust that's settled since she polished the furniture this morning.

When she first arrived in Lily Dale, Odelia told her that anyone can learn to tune into Spirit. Bella isn't sure that's the case, though Odelia did say that some people are more gifted than others and that psychic ability runs in families. She likened it to the way some people are born with natural athletic prowess, while others have to work extra hard at developing it.

Calla stares at the spot near the desk for another moment, then seems to snap out of it and looks again at Bella.

"Um . . . if you're ready to go up, I have you in the Jungle Room on the third floor. Max is hanging out with our little animal kingdom in the Rose Room."

"Shouldn't the cats be in the Jungle Room?"

"I wish I'd thought of that before they got settled in my room. They enjoy pouncing on me in the night and sleeping on my head. But I can't uproot them now. They're creatures of habit."

"Aren't we all."

Bella notes the wistful expression on Calla's face, as does Odelia, who puts a firm hand on her arm. "Calla, go on up and introduce yourself to Max. You'll love him, and you'll love the kittens. Pick one out."

"You make it sound so easy, Gammy."

"Most things are easier than they seem."

"That makes no sense."

Odelia looks at Bella. "*You* know what I mean, don't you?"

She hesitates. "Maybe I wouldn't say *most* things. But some things certainly are."

"And many are much harder." Calla sighs.

Trying to think of something uplifting to say, Bella settles on, "Whether or not you're going to adopt a kitten, I'm sure Chance will be happy to see you again. I have to warn you, though, that she's . . . under the influence."

"She's a drinker now?"

"Pain meds. She just had spay surgery. Last time I checked, she was attacking the plastic kibble container in the closet as though she hadn't just devoured two bowls of it. Can you please tell Max to make sure that door stays closed?" She hands over a set of keys. "The silver one is for your room and the brass one is for the dead bolts on the front and back doors. It opens both."

"So you're not using the old-fashioned skeleton keys for the guest rooms anymore?"

Bella shakes her head and explains that Grant had all the antique locks replaced with modern ones over the summer after . . . what happened.

"But we're still using the key rings Leona had made before she passed away." She indicates the heart-shaped disc imprinted with the letters *VVM*, for Valley View Manor.

"Nice touch." Calla runs her fingertips over the engraved surface, wearing a faraway smile. Then she looks abruptly up the stairs as if someone just called her name from above.

Watching her ascend the flight with her gaze fixed on the upstairs hall, Bella decides she's merely appreciating the familiar setting. Yes, of course she is, because she can't possibly be glimpsing someone who used to live here. Someone who died.

Calla seems much too . . . *normal* for that.

Not that the mediums Bella has gotten to know are *abnormal*. They're wonderful, loving friends who have welcomed her and Max into their fold. Yet by and large, the neighbors are a colorful bunch. A few are so quirky that Odelia seems conventional by contrast.

Most are considerably older than Calla, who'd look more at home sipping margaritas at girls' night out than hobnobbing around the Dale channeling Lennon or Lenin.

As soon as she's out of earshot, Odelia looks at Bella so sternly that she wonders if she read her mind. It wouldn't be the first time.

But instead of scolding her for making a sweeping, if silent, generalization about what a Spiritualist should and shouldn't be, Odelia says, "Blue Slayton is bad news."

"Bad news how? He seems like a decent guy."

"First impressions can be deceiving, Bella. You of all people should know that by now."

"I do, but—"

"I don't trust him not to break her heart. *Again*. I'm rooting for Jacy."

"No way, Odelia, *really*?"

"Was I that obvious?"

"Well, you didn't have pompons or shout 'gimme a *J*, gimme an *A*,' but yes, you were pretty obvious."

Odelia sighs. "I've always tried to bite my tongue whenever Blue comes up, but I guess I'm out of practice. She hasn't seen him in years. Why does he have to hang around here now, of all times?"

"Maybe he's changed since you last saw him."

"People don't change."

"You just told Calla that Jacy will change when he finishes his residency."

"I didn't say he would change. I meant the circumstances."

"Sometimes people change."

"Not often. You can waste a lot of time and energy wishing it would happen."

Bella thinks of her mother-in-law. She used to think Maleficent would mellow toward her once she and Sam were married. Then she thought a grandchild would do the trick. And, you would think, when her son became ill, and when he . . .

Well, shouldn't she have put aside her resentment of Bella?

She didn't seem to. And although she's occasionally glimpsed a kinder, gentler side, Bella still finds her mother-in-law thoroughly intimidating.

"I don't know why you find her so scary," Sam once said. "She's just a tiny little woman."

That's true. Bella is only five foot four, but she towers over Maleficent, who barely tops five feet in her signature leather pumps. Yet with her imposing personality and forthright conversational style, Sam's mother evokes great physical stature.

No mama's boy, Sam did occasionally acknowledge that Millicent can be controlling. Yet he'd counter that by referencing his wonderful childhood memories. His mom took him to the Shedd Aquarium and Navy Pier, and she chaperoned his field trips. She baked Christmas cutout cookies from scratch, and she let him cut all of them into the wreath shape because he liked to eat the little circle scrap of dough from the center. On nights when his father had to work late, she let him eat breakfast for dinner, both of them wearing footy pajamas.

Sam always treated his mother with affection and respect. The first time she ever saw her husband and mother-in-law together, Bella correctly assumed their relationship was an indicator that he'd treat his wife the same way. That part was good.

The Millicent-as-mother-in-law part? Not so good.

Bella finds it impossible to imagine her in jeans, let alone footy pajamas. She's the kind of woman who wears makeup and pantyhose wherever she goes, never reads best sellers or watches television series, and probably never eats potato chips. But her lifestyle, however joyless from Bella's perception, has never been the issue.

From the time she and Sam were newlyweds, Bella has been aware that his mother didn't consider her worthy of Sam.

"It isn't just you," he assured her time and again. "Trust me, my mother never thought any woman was good enough for me."

"But it *is* just me. I'm the one you married."

"And I love you, Bella Blue. Don't worry. She'll come around sooner or later."

Sooner came and went.

Later came and went.

Now it's just too late. Sam is gone. It no longer matters whether Millicent thought Bella deserved him; it doesn't even matter that sometimes, Bella secretly agreed with her that she didn't.

Hearing a knock on the door behind her, Bella pushes away the memory of her troubled relationship with Sam's mother. Here comes the bride, and as long as this wedding opens the door to a prosperous new future for the guesthouse, she'll never have to turn to Maleficent for anything.

But when she turns around, it isn't Johneen standing on the purple welcome mat.

It's . . .

Bella's eyes widen in disbelief. *"Mal—Millicent?"*

Chapter Five

Stunned to see her mother-in-law standing on the doorstep, Bella's first thought is that Odelia is right. Anyone is capable of working this so-called Lily Dale magic. She seems to have conjured the dreaded Maleficent just by thinking of her.

Her next thought, a familiar one, is that that's a ridiculous assumption. Millicent is here because . . . because . . .

Why is she here?

How is she here?

"It's good to see you, Isabella." Millicent pulls her into a lacquered hug as Bella wracks her brain, wondering if she'd somehow arranged this visit from her mother-in-law and then forgotten about it.

Right. Sort of like you'd forget about an appointment to have four wisdom teeth pulled without Novocain?

Maybe it would be different if Millicent reminded her at all of Sam—sweet, rumpled Sam, with his cowlick and round glasses and always just a hint of irony in his warm, brown eyes. Other than his coloring, he looked nothing at all like his mother, yet she always claimed he was her spitting image.

Nor had Sam resembled his late father. Blond and strapping, Thierry Jordan was an avid sailor and skier with ruddy Nordic features. Bella hadn't known him but couldn't imagine what he'd seen in Millicent.

Against her powdered-porcelain complexion, her red lipstick seems harsh as a splotch of blood on snow. Her black patent-leather pocketbook, which she would never call a "purse," dangles primly from her forearm on leather horseshoe straps. She's wearing pumps, of course, along with a two-piece skirt suit that reminds Bella of Margaret Lockwood in *The Lady Vanishes.*

If only this lady would vanish.

Bella closes her eyes briefly, but when she opens them, Millicent is still there, standing on the welcome mat beside a ginormous . . .

"Is that a steamer trunk?" Bella asks. She's not quite sure what a steamer trunk is, but whenever she's read about one, she pictures exactly this: a large, black rectangle with brass trim and a latch.

"It is." Millicent nods proudly. "It belonged to my grandfather. One day, Max will get it."

"It's beautiful." The compliment comes from Odelia, standing behind Bella, who finds herself at a loss for words.

"Thank you." Millicent clears her throat uncomfortably, not making eye contact.

"I'll bet you can cram a lot of stuff in there."

"Cramming destroys fabric."

"Huh." Odelia considers that. "Is that why you don't use a regular suitcase?"

"Well, I do when I'm only going on a short visit."

Alarmed, Bella looks from the trunk to Millicent, wondering how long she's planning to stay and why . . .

Why is she here? Why? *Why?*

"How on earth did you manage to get that up onto the porch?" Odelia asks, breaking another uncomfortable silence as Bella struggles to form a question. "It must weigh a ton."

"It does, but my driver met me at the baggage claim with a cart and then he carried it up here to the porch."

Odelia shoots Bella a look: *she has a driver.* Not a question—an observation. As in, *of course she has a driver.*

"Where *is* your driver?" Bella asks, looking around.

"He had to get back to the airport. It's well over an hour away, and he had another client to pick up."

"So you flew in?"

"Yes, from Chicago."

"Did you get one of those last-minute airfare sales? Last spring, I saw round trip to Chicago for less than two hundred dollars."

"Unfortunately, it was more than twice that one-way."

One-way. Bella gulps.

Thank goodness for Odelia, still holding up her end of the conversation, and Bella's, as well: "And how was your flight?"

"It was a little bumpy."

"You went right over the lakes, I'm guessing. I've been to Chicago. Not in years, but I remember the flight path. You just zip across Lake Erie from Buffalo, cut across Michigan, then Lake Michigan, and you're there. Easy breezy."

Millicent's pencil-darkened brows furrow as she digests this.

"Yep," Odelia agrees with herself. Then she seems to have run out of things to say, other than a final *"Eeeeasy* breezy."

Bella's inner voice screeches into the ensuing silence.

What the heck are you doing here?????

At last, Millicent clears her throat. "May I come in?"

"Oh—of course. I'm sorry, Millicent."

"Call me Mother," she tells Bella, same as always.

Bella can never bring herself to do that. She already has a mother, though Rosemary Angelo passed away long before Bella could imprint a memory of her. If she did want a stand-in mother in her life, however, Millicent would not be a prime candidate.

But oh look, here she is anyway.

She steps over the threshold and then looks back at her trunk. "If you can call someone to take that . . ."

Someone . . . like who? Max? A couple of kittens?

And take it . . . where?

"Do you mean a bellhop?" Odelia asks Millicent. "Because this isn't really that kind of hotel. It's more of a guesthouse."

"I see." Millicent takes in the round freckly face, orange sari, and pouf of rusty hair billowing beneath the newsboy cap. "Are you . . . ?"

She trails off as if she can't quite decide who, or what, Odelia might be.

"I'm Odelia Lauder, a friend of Bella's and Max's. And you're . . . ?"

"I'm Max's *grandmother.*" If this were a card game, Millicent would have laid down a winning hand.

"How wonderful that you've come to visit him in his new home." If this were a card game, Odelia would have trumped her.

"*Home*?" Millicent echoes. "It was my understanding that this is a hotel, although . . ."

Clearly, she uses the term loosely.

Bella straightens her spine, takes a deep breath of Millicent's perfume, and tells her, "It's home for Max and me. He's making friends, and he's already adapted to his new school."

"What kind of school is it, exactly?"

"It's an elementary school."

"A *regular* elementary school?"

As opposed to . . . what?

"Yes, it's a regular school. Not private, or . . ." *Irregular.*

"Not religious?"

"No, not religious. Just . . . regular. Millicent, if you don't mind my asking . . . I mean, I'm just . . . I'm so surprised to see you, and I can't . . ."

"I told you I'd visit sometime."

She might have. Their conversations tend to ramble. But Bella never imagined her coming here, to Lily Dale.

"Is this a bad time, Isabella?"

"This weekend is super busy. We're hosting a wedding here."

"A regular wedding?"

What does Millicent mean by that?

"Yes, a regular wedding. You know, the kind that has a bride and a groom"—*not that two brides or two grooms would be irregular,* she wants to point out, but refrains—"and vows and food and guests and music . . ."

And rain. Maybe snow. Good times.

Millicent frowns, looking oddly unconvinced.

"What other kind of wedding is there?" Odelia asks.

"There are plenty of different kinds. There are . . . well, you see those mass weddings on the news."

"Wedding masses on the news?" Bella echoes cluelessly.

"No, *mass weddings*. With thousands of brides and grooms. You know, like . . ."

"Like the Moonies?"

"Precisely!"

Bella frowns. "Um, this is just a regular wedding. One bride. One groom."

Which might just be two too many, she reminds herself, remembering the rain and Odelia's vision.

"Don't worry," Millicent says. "I won't bother anyone. I'll stay out of the way in my room."

"Your room? But—"

"I saw some photos online, and the Teacup Room looks most like my style, but if that's been booked, I suppose—"

"They're all booked!" It's a white lie. There is a vacant third-floor room. But Bella doesn't want Millicent in it, and not just because the roof leaked in a recent storm, soaking the rug and rendering it temporarily uninhabitable. It's become Max and Jiffy's temporary playroom, strewn with Lego bricks and Matchbox cars.

"How can this place be booked? It's enormous."

"Like I said, there's a wedding party checking in, so . . ."

"So you're saying you don't have a room for me?"

Bella hesitates.

Sharing a leaky roof with the woman would be challenging enough, but *this* weekend? With a storm, a stoned cat, all those kittens, and a wedding upon which her future depends?

What are you going to do? Turn her away?

"I just wish you had called first."

"I would have, but . . . I wanted to surprise you." Millicent doesn't meet her gaze.

She's lying.

That isn't Spirit's voice in her head. It's Bella's own, loud and clear.

Look at her. She's obviously up to something.

This isn't an innocent visit. This is . . .

What is it? An ambush? Is she here to talk Bella into leaving? Is she . . . what if she wants to prove Bella is an unfit mother? What if she wants custody of Max?

That's farfetched, even for Maleficent. But Bella doesn't dare trust her. Not now.

"We really don't have anything available this weekend," she lies.

Forgive me, Sam.

"Well, then, I'll just stay someplace nearby."

"There *is* no place nearby. And you don't even have a car!" Bella's voice sounds thinner and higher-pitched by the second.

"There's my house. I'm right next door. You could stay with me."

Bella turns to look at Odelia, as does Millicent.

"Oh, I couldn't," she says quickly.

"She couldn't," Bella agrees.

"Of course she can. You can. It'll be fun." Odelia sounds about as convincing as Bella promising Max, last spring when they found themselves homeless, jobless, and Sam-less, that everything was going to be okay.

But everything really is *okay.*

As long as Millicent stays away.

"No, really, I insist. I have my granddaughter's empty bedroom clean and ready for guests." Either Odelia's psychic powers have kicked in and she knows Millicent is up to something, or she grasps that Bella won't survive hosting her mother-in-law *and* a wedding.

Having her right next door isn't ideal either, but who knows? Maybe it will be fun for Odelia to have some company under her roof. And maybe a dose of Odelia will take Maleficent down a notch or two.

Besides, the bride and groom will be here any second, and Bella would rather her nemesis wasn't part of the welcoming committee.

"It's so sweet of you to offer, Odelia. And since it's our only option, we'll take you up on it." Ignoring the alarm on her mother-in-law's face, she suggests that the two women head directly next door so that Millicent can see the accommodations.

"That's a great idea." Odelia pats her unwilling houseguest's arm. "I'll take good care of you, I promise."

"But . . . but what about my trunk, Isabella?"

"I have some strapping young men checking in for the wedding." Does she? Probably. Maybe. Who knows? Who cares? "I'll have them carry it right next door when they arrive."

"But I can't just leave it sitting there on the porch! I have special gifts inside for Max. What if someone steals it?"

"This is Lily Dale," Bella tells her. "There's no crime here."

All right, there *was* a murder. But she isn't about to disclose that to Millicent, whose mouth tightens.

"Crime is everywhere, Isabella. Especially where one least expects to find it."

Something in her tone makes Bella wonder if maybe she did hear about Leona after all. But if she had, she wouldn't have kept it to herself. She doesn't keep anything negative to herself.

Odelia speaks up. "Crime is everywhere. You're right about that. But this is a summer community, so the only people here now are the locals who live here year-round. And we've been known to stop many a crime before it happens. I like to say that this is the world's most efficient neighborhood watch because we—"

"Because in a town this small, the residents can immediately spot anything and anyone out of the ordinary," Bella cuts in before Odelia can mention that the neighborhood watch is largely made up of psychics or that the residents themselves are decidedly out of the ordinary.

Bella had told her that that Lily Dale is a lakeside summer colony and nothing more.

"Yes," Odelia agrees, "and we—"

"Besides, it would be impossible for anyone to steal something that large in broad daylight," Bella interrupts again, gesturing at the trunk. "And I just have to ask—whose initials are carved on the lid?"

Predictably, Millicent's gaze goes to the trunk, allowing Bella to nudge Odelia and mouth the words "Don't say anything!"

Odelia's eyebrows shoot up and she mouths back, "About what?"

"Anything!" Bella screams the silent reply, concluding—not for the first time—that Odelia might be psychic, but sometimes she doesn't have a lick of common sense.

Meanwhile, Millicent is gaping at the trunk. "What are you talking about? There are no initials carved on the lid."

"There aren't?" Bella steps out onto the porch, holding the door open behind her. "Are you sure?"

Predictably, Millicent follows her out and peers at the trunk, trailed by Odelia. Bella closes the screen door firmly after them, as if they're wayward cats who might escape.

"Where are you looking, Isabella?"

"Right there, see?" She waves at the trunk.

Odelia, too, is peering. "I don't see any initials."

"You don't?" Bella leans in. "Oh, you're right. Trick of the light. Or maybe it's my eyes. I'm not getting any younger. Well, anyway . . . as soon as a couple of he-men show up, I'll send them right next door with it."

"What about the wedding?" Odelia asks. "We were going to figure out—"

"I think we're all set for now. Let's touch base after the bride and groom arrive. Millicent, you must be starved, and Odelia is a wonderful cook."

Before Millicent can request again that Bella call her "Mother," Odelia takes the hint.

"I have some nice soup on the stove," she says, steering Millicent down the steps. "Have you ever had menudo?"

Bella, who somehow doubts that very much, watches them disappear next door.

Saved.

For now, anyway.

She closes her eyes and inhales deeply. Exhales.

Breathe. Just breathe. It's going to be okay.

She opens her eyes.

Inhale. Exhale. Breathe.

Carpeted in fallen leaves, its scallop-shingled gables bathed in late-day autumn sunlight, the Dale is steeped in earthy mulch, wood smoke, and bruised fruit scattered beneath an apple tree across the way. *Aromatherapy*, she thinks.

Breathe. In. Out.

It's going to be okay.

Or is it?

A sudden breeze stirs the boughs, releasing a fresh scarlet confetti shower. Remembering Odelia's premonition, Bella watches the leaves litter the landscape like droplets of blood.

* * *

71

In the flurry of arrivals—the first infinitely more welcome than the unexpected second, with a third looming any moment now—Bella forgot all about the mail.

Remembering she'd tossed it into a large wicker basket beside the door, she sees that it's perfectly camouflaged for the time being. But curiosity gets the better of her and she grabs the envelope she'd been about to open earlier.

It's probably just more junk mail, and she can toss it, along with everything but the credit card bill, into the recycling bin. That will give her something to do, other than pace and fret about Millicent, while she awaits the bride and groom.

The envelope contains a single sheet of paper, folded into thirds. The short note was typed in a bold font.

Dear Ms. Jordan:

Please do everything in your power to stop this wedding.

Signed,
A Friend

"What in the world?" she murmurs, staring at the bizarre message.
Who would write such a thing?
Possibilities race through her mind.
Is it a prank, or a warning?
Did it come from a well-meaning friend of the bride or groom?
Or perhaps from one of the mediums, as it was mailed locally.
Was it Odelia herself?
The idea is counterintuitive, considering she's the one who came up with the plan in the first place. But what if this is an anonymous attempt to halt the wedding due to her premonitions?

Bella can't imagine that her friend would do such a thing, but who else would . . .
Wait a minute. What about Millicent?
She claimed to have arrived just today, and the letter was post-marked yesterday, but maybe she was lying. Maybe she's been poking around the Dale, and she knew all about the wedding before she

showed up here. Maybe she wants to sabotage it because she wants Bella and Max to come to Chicago as they were supposed to.

Would she be manipulative enough to do such a dastardly thing?

Hearing voices on the porch, Bella hurriedly folds the letter and shoves it into her back pocket. Johneen and Parker have arrived.

"There you are! Happy wedding weekend," she says, pasting on a cheerful smile as she opens the door.

"What is *that*?" Johneen wrinkles her regal nose at the steamer trunk as if it were a coffin containing a fresh kill.

"Oh, it . . . belongs to a guest."

"Not one of *my* guests."

"No," Bella admits. *And not exactly one of mine, either.*

"It can't stay there."

"Don't worry, it won't. I'm going to have it moved as soon as possible." Sizing up Parker, she concludes that he's less than the half the he-man who might accomplish that task.

Today, he's wearing khakis, tasseled navy loafers, a suit coat with an open-collared shirt, and designer sunglasses. Johneen is in ivory slacks and a creamy cable-knit sweater, with a filmy chiffon scarf tied around her blonde ponytail.

In the month since Bella last saw them, she managed to forget just how striking a couple they are—and just how frumpy they make her feel.

She's never believed in blaming others for one's own insecurity, and she's rarely insecure. She may not be drop-dead gorgeous, though Sam thought so, and that was all that mattered when he was around. But she's no hideous crone, either.

Yet Johneen Maynard's withering visual assessment implies that she is. The woman wears her displeasure in Bella's appearance as comfortably as Bella wore her tatty jeans and bleach-splotched T-shirt until this moment.

She invites them in, thinking of the note in her pocket and almost wishing that she could take the anonymous advice to stop the wedding.

But that would lead to homelessness, which in turn would lead her right back to Millicent. *No way. This wedding is going to happen.*

"What's that stench?" Johneen asks, sniffing the air as she steps over the threshold.

Bella looks around, wondering if one of the kittens wandered too far from the litter box and had an accident. "I don't smell anything."

"It's . . ." Johneen sniffs again, making a face. "It's like fruity bathroom spray or something."

"Fruity . . . um, I baked a strudel." *And if you call* that *stench, you're in the wrong house.*

She'd better make sure Johneen stays away from the kittens—and from Jiffy, who isn't always successful at blowing the stink off.

Zeroing in on the pumpkin candle flickering on the registration desk, Johneen walks over to extinguish it with a sharp exhalation and an exaggerated "*P.U.*"

"She doesn't do scents," Parker informs Bella.

"I already told her that," Johneen says, as if Bella is invisible.

Parker drops a bag at the foot of the stairs, then returns to the car to unload three more suitcases and two garment bags as Johneen stands by, yawning and complaining about being exhausted. She wonders aloud whether there's time for a nap before the rehearsal dinner.

"If you'd like to go lie down, I have the suite all set for you."

"Suite? What are you talking about? We requested the Teacup Room, didn't we, Parker?"

"Yes, we did." He deposits the last suitcase on the hardwood floor with a dent-worthy thud. "You said the Teacup Room was the biggest room here. Were you holding out on us, Isabella?"

"No, it's actually the same room. I just gave it a makeover last week, and you'll be the first ones to stay in it. Fresh paint, brand-new curtains and duvet . . ."

"I'm so relieved! I didn't want to have to look back on my wedding night in some dingy, old room filled with chipped saucers and an ugly bedspread and that awful threadbare rug."

Bella's smile vanishes, magically transferred onto Johneen's face. She, for once, is beaming.

Is now the time for Bella to mention that the awful, threadbare rug is still there? No. She rearranged the furniture to cover the worst worn spots. Johneen might not even notice.

Oh, who are you kidding? Of course she'll notice. Just like she'll notice the rain when it turns her into a drowned rat. Instead of a regular rat.

"Why don't you two sign the guest register?" She directs them to the desk and hands the suite key to Parker. "And help yourselves to some M&Ms, too. The previous owner always kept this bowl filled for her guests, so I've kept up the tradition."

"Mmm," the bride replies. Not *mmm* as in "yummy," but *mmm* as in "who cares?"

Parker turns to Bella as Johneen signs the register with a flourish. "The previous owner . . . is she the one who was murdered by that—"

"*Murdered*?" Johneen echoes, dropping the pen. It rolls off the desk and skitters across the floor. "Someone was *murdered* in this house?"

"No, not in this house. She was drowned." As opposed to *she drowned*, which is what Bella was told when she got here. If she'd had an inkling then that it wasn't an accident, she never would have spent that first night here.

"But she was *murdered*? Do you mean there's a murderer out there who might—"

"No! The person responsible is in jail, and it wasn't a random crime." Bella quickly explains what happened.

Parker nods. "I suppose everyone has her share of enemies."

Johneen, who undoubtedly does, clutches his sleeve. "How can we get married here after—"

"Now, Daisy, you need to just take a deep breath and—"

"How can I? This is awful! The wedding is ruined!" she rails on melodramatically. "I can't believe you didn't mention this earlier!"

Bella isn't sure whether Johneen's accusation is aimed toward her or Parker. Her gray gaze flits wildly from one to the other and then around the room as if she's expecting to find Leona Gatto's killer lurking behind the potted palm.

"You're a wreck," Parker says in a soothing voice. "Calm down and don't start crying. Your face will get all puffy."

Johneen, who doesn't do puffy, does appear to be on the verge of tears.

"Come on, Daisy." He picks up two large suitcases. "Let's go up to the suite and you can lie down and think this through."

"Think *what* through? We can't get married here now."

"Of course we can. You heard yourself that there's no danger. The killer is in jail."

"But it's . . . *tainted*. How can we—"

"How can we *not*? Everything is ready. Our guests are on their way. We're in love and we're getting married tomorrow. Isn't that all that matters?"

Johneen's face softens just a bit. "I never meant that it wasn't. I just suddenly feel so rushed. I've dreamed of the perfect wedding since I was a little girl."

"And that's what you shall have. I promise, and so does Isabella. Right, Isabella?"

"Absolutely." Again, she pushes the thought of the anonymous letter from her mind. "It's going to be just . . . perfect."

"See? All better now?"

"I guess so," Johneen says. "Thank you, Parker."

You're welcome, Bella thinks. Sheesh.

She's momentarily gratified when Parker turns to her, undoubtedly intending to share the credit.

"Isabella, would you mind giving me a hand with these bags, please?"

Seriously?

Johneen, already on the stairs, empty-handed, doesn't even look back.

Yes. Seriously.

Fine. The sooner Bella gets them out of here, the better. She doesn't want to say or do anything she'll regret.

Like show them the evidence that an anonymous correspondent doesn't want them to get married tomorrow. Maybe she should, and maybe she will, but not until she's had time to reexamine the letter and perhaps run it by someone.

Ordinarily, she'd turn to Odelia. But if she's behind this, she'll deny it. And if she isn't, she'll take it as a sign that she's not the only one having wedding premonitions.

Bella picks up one of the garment bags and reaches for the other.

"Careful—that's Daisy's gown," Parker says. "She's very particular about it."

Then she shouldn't expect minions to cart it around for her, should she? Bella wants to growl.

"I'll come back down for it," he tells her. "You just get that other suitcase."

Good thing I'm strong, Bella thinks as she lugs it up one step at a time, with Parker behind her, still wearing his sunglasses. *Otherwise, I might lose my grip and let this stupid thing drop on his stupid head.*

"Try not to bump it around too much," he says behind her. "She has fragile jewelry in there."

Right. Bella might just lose her grip anyway. On the suitcase and everything else.

At the top of the stairs, she can hear muffled laughter from the Rose Room: Calla and Max, playing with Chance and the litter. With any luck, they'll all stay behind closed doors for the time being. Johneen might be thrilled to see her old friend, but she assuredly won't feel the same about a kid and eight kitties.

Down the hall, the door to the honeymoon suite is ajar. Bella can see that Johneen is already lying on the bed, her shoe-clad feet plunked down on the brand new white duvet.

Bella dumps the garment bag on the upholstered bench just inside the door. She's not about to play bellhop, hanging things in the closet and fetching ice—ice! She forgot to refill the freezer trays for the cocktail party tonight.

She swivels and shoulders past Parker, heading back down the hall and down the stairs. At the bottom of the flight, she pauses, hearing the door to the Rose Room open above. Calla's and Max's voices float out into the hall.

"Careful, Calla! Saturday is trying to escape!"

"Whoa, get back in there, little girl! Got her, Max?"

"Got her. She's a bad influence on Spidey, by the way. Now he wants to escape."

"Aw, Spidey, you're too tiny for the big, bad world! You stay here with Max. He'll protect you!"

Bella smiles. Apparently, her son and the kittens have made another friend in Lily Dale.

Then she hears Parker's voice. "Calla?"

"Yes? Oh—are you Parker?"

"I am. It's a pleasure to meet you."

"Congratulations! Where's Johnny?"

"I'm right here," the bride calls, sounding almost like a regular person.

Eavesdropping below, Bella smiles, listening to a happy reunion between old friends. Then Calla introduces Johneen and Parker to Max, Chance, and the kittens.

"It's nice to meet you. All of you." Johneen is civil, but it's clear from her stiff tone that she isn't thrilled to find children and animals sharing the same roof on her wedding eve.

"Hello, there . . . everyone." Parker's attempt at an avuncular greeting ends in a strangled cough. Or maybe it was a sneeze. *Possibly fake*, Bella finds herself thinking.

"Are you all right?" Calla asks.

"I am. I'm just . . . allergic."

"To kids?" That's Max, sounding intrigued.

"To cats."

"Really? You never told me that," Johneen says.

"You never asked. I didn't think you were interested in having pets."

"I'm not. I just—"

"You had a kitten in college," Calla cuts in. "Remember? Her name was Coco."

"Like Cocoa Puffs?" Max again.

Calla laughs, and Johneen, who probably hates *puffs* as much as she hates *puffy*, promptly sets him straight. "No! After the designer."

"Huh?"

"Coco Chanel," Calla explains. "Don't worry, Max. Before I met Johnny, I never knew the difference between Coco Chanel and Cocoa Puffs either."

"We should probably let you know, Calla"—that's Parker—"that she's not going by that nickname anymore."

Bella rolls her eyes at the stiff admonishment.

It's followed by a high-pitched cry from not-Johnny. "This cat! It's . . . it's trying to eat my foot!"

"Chance!" Max scolds. "Stop that! Sorry, she's just really hungry today."

Calla's laughter fills the upstairs hall, punctuated by the sounds of Johneen hurriedly retreating to her suite and Max wrestling Chance back into the Rose Room. Two doors slam shut, and Bella sighs.

As she turns toward the kitchen, she spots something white poking out from beneath a fold in the long draperies at the window. Stooping to lift the hem, she sees that it's one of her bras.

"Terrific," she mutters. Chance is forever dragging garments out of the laundry room and stashing them around the house. She thought she did a thorough search and recover earlier today, but she was bound to miss something. Oh, well. At least it wasn't a pair of Max's dirty underwear tucked under Johneen's pillow—yet.

It's going to be a long weekend, she thinks, glancing at the steamer trunk still waiting on the front porch.

A white-clad figure stands beside it.

She gasps. For a split second, Lily Dale has rubbed off on her and she's certain it's an apparition.

Then a decidedly alive-and-well human voice drawls an apology: "*Ah'm* sorry! Did *ah* frighten you? *Ah* was just about to ring the *bay-ell*."

Bella's first ghost has turned out to be a regular old person. Probably one of the wedding guests. Maybe even a relative, judging by her appearance, though Johneen and Parker had said there would be no family here.

She's wearing a white sweater dress that clings to her curves. With her creamy complexion, delicate features, and lithe figure, this lovely blonde could pass for a more mature version of the bride herself. She appears to be in her late thirties. Maybe an older sister? Perhaps a youthful aunt?

Before Bella can find out, she hears Parker behind her, halfway down the stairs, sans jacket and the sunglasses.

"Virginia? What are you doing here?"

A smile lights the visitor's face. "Surprise!"

"What are you doing here?" he repeats, hurrying down.

He does look surprised to see her. Surprised, dismayed, and yet delighted, all at once. He gives her a heartfelt hug but repeats his question a third time.

This time, she drawls a simple explanation: how could she not be here on his wedding day?

"You didn't have to come all this way. You really shouldn't have."

Bella detects the hint of drawl she heard in his voice the first time she met him and remembers that he has southern roots. This guest must not be from the Maynard side after all.

"It wasn't all that far, Sugar."

"Sure it was."

"I'd do anything for you."

"I know you would, Ginny, but we were planning a reception later for the family."

"I'm the only kin that matters, Parker, and I couldn't miss y'all's big day," she says sweetly, all *ah'm* and *ah* and *way-ell* and *Pah-kah*.

"I should have known you'd show up." With a pleased, helpless smile, he turns to Bella. "This is my cousin, Virginia. Virginia, this is Isabella. She's the wedding planner, and she's singlehandedly running this place."

"Well, bless your heart." Virginia clasps Bella's hand warmly, telling her it's wonderful to meet her. "How on earth do you do it all? You must have housekeeping help, at least."

She glances down at the bra in her hand. "I wish."

"What is that?" Virginia asks.

Embarrassed, Bella admits, "It's . . . one of my bras. I have a cat who likes to carry laundry around the house. Particularly anything with straps she can chew."

Virginia bursts out laughing. "See now, this is why I love kitties so much. They're always up to something!"

Bella wants to hug her. Resemblance or not, she should have known right away that this sweetheart isn't related to the ice queen upstairs. Parker isn't exactly a teddy bear, but who would be, dealing with a woman like Johneen on a daily basis?

Not, Bella reminds herself, that they even live together, or plan to immediately after the wedding. But distance must work in their favor. Clearly, absence doesn't just make the heart grow fonder; it makes the brain overlook gaping character flaws.

"I can't wait to meet your future wife," Virginia tells Parker. "Where is she?"

"She's having a little lie-down. You'll meet her later."

You might want to change your outfit before you do, Bella wants to warn her. *Only the bride is allowed to be all dressed in white.*

"I'm sure she needs her rest. Poor thing has been through so much." Virginia shakes her head sympathetically, as if planning a wedding is akin to mortal combat.

Unless Bella is mistaken, Parker gives her a warning look and shakes his head slightly, as if she's said something she shouldn't have.

Yes, and Virginia's eyes flick to Bella before she adds hastily, "I'm sure it was a long drive up here."

It was only a few hours from Pittsburgh. And Parker had flown there last night from Toronto so that Johneen wouldn't have to make the trip alone.

Virginia turns to Bella. "I hope y'all have room for me here at the inn? I probably should have called ahead, but I didn't want to ruin the surprise."

Bella's thoughts whirl. There's the third-floor room with the leaky ceiling. Unlike Millicent—or, for that matter, Johneen—Virginia strikes Bella as the kind of woman who won't fuss over a dollop of dampness.

"Actually, I do have a room for you."

"Really?" Parker's cousin thanks her profusely and thanks her lucky stars; Bella, smiling, silently does the same. Now, no matter what happens next door, she really doesn't have room for her mother-in-law.

Bella quickly explains the ceiling issue but assures Virginia that it's dry now. She offers a low rate and runs through the usual check-in spiel, running through the hours for coffee and continental breakfast and adding that she'll make up the room between eleven and one tomorrow.

"Any questions?" she asks, handing over the key.

"Just one. I'm assuming the inn is nonsmoking?" At Bella's nod, Virginia says, "Then I'll just step outside and have a quick smoke before I go on up."

"And I'll come with you and bum one," Parker says.

"I thought you quit."

"I did. Daisy hates it."

"Well, then, maybe you shouldn't be sneaking cigarettes."

"Consider it my last hurrah," he says, holding the door open for her.

Her good-natured reply is lost as the door slams shut on its squeaky hinge.

Bella starts toward the stairs, needing to make sure there's no stray Lego bricks littering the empty room. Conversation drifts through the open screen on a whiff of tobacco smoke.

"I probably shouldn't have just shown up last minute," Virginia is saying. "It's ever so rude, but I couldn't help myself. I wanted to surprise you. I'm sorry, Parker."

Unlike Virginia, Maleficent hadn't bothered to apologize. And she came with an ulterior motive, besides.

It's going to be a long, hard weekend, Bella thinks. *I just hope I can survive it.*

"You did surprise me, but you can't fool me," Parker says, out on the porch. "I know why you're here, Virginia."

"Well, you can't blame me, can you? I'd never forgive myself if something were to happen on your wedding day."

Bella freezes with her foot on the bottom step, eyes wide.

"Nothing is going to happen," Parker says. "That's why we chose this spot. It's secluded and safe. No big splashy wedding to draw attention and tempt fate."

"But no place is really safe. You could have been followed here."

"Well, if we were, I'm here to protect my Daisy."

"And so am I," Virginia says. "But that will be our little secret, okay, cuz?"

He agrees, and their conversation shifts to the weekend's schedule of events.

Realizing, belatedly, that she has no business eavesdropping, Bella pulls the sheet of paper from her back pocket and rereads the message.

Please do everything in your power to stop this wedding.

Does it have something to do with what she just overheard?

Her first instinct is to tell someone—Odelia—immediately. But Odelia has a way of jumping to conclusions. She'll undoubtedly assume that her vision really does foreshadow a wedding-day disaster. She'll want to warn Johneen.

Maybe Bella misinterpreted the conversation.

She runs through the details again in her mind, trying to remember the precise wording. To her ear, it sounded like the bridal couple, specifically Johneen, might be in some kind of danger.

Hearing the front door open and close again, Bella hastily shoves the paper back into her pocket.

"I was about to run upstairs to make sure the room is all set for you," she tells Virginia. "It's made up, but I wasn't expecting anyone in it, so—"

"Oh, I'm sure it'll be just fine, thanks."

Chatting companionably, Parker and Virginia go upstairs. She leaves him to enter his suite on the second floor and continues on up to the third.

Long after the two doors have opened and closed, Bella remains standing there, trying to figure out what to do. She needs to run this by someone trustworthy. But if not Odelia, then whom?

Not her other medium friends or anyone living here in the Dale, where gossip is as plentiful as colorful foliage at this relatively idle time of year.

She considers telling Drew but quickly dismisses that idea, too. They're friends, but not the kind who share personal dilemmas or call each other for advice.

The one person in whom she might safely confide—the one person who'd know what to do in this situation—is Luther Rand. Living ten miles away in Dunkirk, he's well-removed from the Dale's daily grind but is no stranger to what goes on around here. He met Odelia years ago when she volunteered her psychic services to help him solve a case, and they've since joined forces on others.

Odelia had mentioned that he's up in Canada tonight, and his phone is probably turned off to avoid international roaming charges. He instructed Bella to do the same when they crossed the border last month.

She dials his number anyway, hoping he'll pick up.

He doesn't.

She hesitates, then opts not to leave a message. There's no immediate danger, and most likely, no danger at all.

But who, she wonders, could have followed the bride and groom here?

Is it the same person who mailed the note? And what—other than Bella getting to stay in Lily Dale—might happen if the wedding goes on as planned?

Chapter Six

Friday evening, Bella stands in a cluster of round tables beneath the gingko trees' daffodil-colored foliage, trying to put her mind at ease.

The weather is unseasonably balmy, perfect for an outdoor dinner. The temperature has risen over the past few hours, and the breeze off the lake is more temperate than on a typical August evening around here.

The shore is tranquil without the summer crowds. There are no bugs. The overhead branches have dropped enough leaves to allow a view of the dusky sky. Stars are beginning to glitter even as "Stardust" floats over the speakers she propped in a back window.

According to Odelia, Spirit has been known to manipulate electronics.

"Did you ever hear a song come on the radio at just the right moment?" she asked once. "That's Spirit."

How often, since Sam died, has Bella been driving along thinking of him when suddenly, she hears a song that reminds her of him?

Then again, every song reminds her of him, and she thinks of him all the time, so . . .

"I find it hard to believe that Spirit manipulates the radio to send messages from the Other Side," she told Odelia.

Electromagnetic energy is one thing, but paranormal deejays defy logic.

"You find many things hard to believe. But the next time you hear a song that suits the moment, it might not be so random after all. Remember that."

Bella remembers that. She remembers pretty much everything Odelia has told her about the how things work in the Spirit world and here in the Dale.

But there's nothing mystical about the fact that "Stardust" is playing just as the purple dusk of twilight falls over the Dale. The music is coming from her own iPod, courtesy of the wedding playlist of romantic Great American Songbook standards provided by Johneen and dutifully compiled by Bella herself.

She looks around, wishing the weather would hold out through tomorrow night. It's hard to imagine a violent storm roaring through the peaceful setting like a freight train, but anything can happen in twenty-four hours.

She can only hope the snow will be the right shade of white for Johneen's taste.

Dozens of candles flicker in mason jars on the tables and hang in the trees. The tables are set with ivory linen cloths, crystal goblets, and Limoges china. The centerpieces are simple but festive: vases of yellow and white roses clustered on the most colorful golden leaves Max and Jiffy could find. As dusk descended, she promised them a nickel per leaf and now owes them enough money to buy "ice cream cones for, like, twenty years!" according to Max.

"Forty years, with waffle cones and sprinkles!" Jiffy amended. Then he asked, "How much do you pay for finding kittens? That should be worth way more than a leaf. Especially since he's blue."

"A blue kitten?" Bella asked doubtfully.

"Yep, bright blue. Like your eyes, by the way," added Jiffy, ever the charmer.

"Can we keep him, Mom?"

"I think we have enough kittens for the time being," she told Max.

"But we don't have any blue ones."

Because there's no such thing as a blue kitten! Bella wanted to shout, but Max was so earnest, and this *is* Lily Dale. You just never know.

The boys insisted the kitten was hiding in Odelia's garden, camouflaged by the blue morning glories. They attempted to lure him out with preternaturally shrill *"Here, kitty-kitty-kitties."*

Bella wasn't surprised that a bright blue kitten failed to emerge. Now Max and Jiffy are on the back steps eating hot dogs and potato chips—a quickie dinner she whipped up instead of sending them next door to dine at Odelia's kitchen table as planned. She didn't want to risk any chance encounters with Maleficent just yet.

Earlier, Odelia reported that Maleficent had been upstairs lying down ever since she arrived.

"Travel took a lot out of her," she told Bella as they set up the rented folding chairs and round tables. "But she isn't so horrible. She really seems to care about Max. She said she can't wait to get her hands on him."

It might be a typical thing for a grandmother to say, but the words struck a fearful chord in Bella. If the boys hadn't been in earshot, she would have asked Odelia whether she senses anything malevolent about Maleficent's unexpected visit.

It isn't that she thinks her mother-in-law is planning to kidnap her son and take him back to Chicago. Surely if that were the case, Odelia would be receiving warnings from Spirit.

Unless she can only tune into one potential disaster at a time? She's still preoccupied with the fact that Jacy didn't stay for the wedding. She didn't even bring up Spirit's cryptic warnings about Johneen again. If she had, Bella might have felt compelled to mention the note and the overheard conversation.

Maybe she's just paranoid. Maybe the note really was Odelia's misguided attempt to sabotage the wedding. And maybe Bella read something into Parker's conversation with Johneen that wasn't there.

Yes, and she probably imagined Millicent's deceitful expression too, because she's so used to thinking of her as the enemy. And because if they were on better terms, she might be guiltily inclined to move to Chicago after all.

In this moment, listening to "Stardust," Max and Jiffy's cheerful conversation, and the gently lapping night water, she can't think of a single reason to ever leave the Dale.

She checks her watch and calls, "Time to head home, Jiffy."

"My mom said I can stay as long as I want."

Bella doesn't doubt that, and ordinarily she'd let him stick around for a while longer. But tonight, she needs Max upstairs and ready for bed before the bride and groom appear.

She sends her son inside, then walks Jiffy across Odelia's yard to his own back door, ignoring his protests that he doesn't need an escort.

"I don't like you wandering around here after dark alone."

"Because there are kidnappers."

"No, it's not that." She wishes she could see his expression, wondering if he read her mind when she was thinking about Millicent and Max or if he's had some sort of premonition. "There aren't any kidnappers around here, Jiffy."

Instead of reassuring her, he says, "I dreamed about it."

"You dreamed about what?"

"About a kidnapper."

Coming from any other kid, that would mean nothing. But from Jiffy—who last summer shared an eerily accurate, dreamlike vision of Leona Gatto's murder—it's unsettling.

Then Jiffy goes on, "But don't worry. In the dream where I get kidnapped, it's cold and snowy and it's not October."

"*You* get kidnapped?"

"Yep. But it's not that scary, 'cause I'm brave. See you tomorrow, Bella." Jiffy skips into his house.

Frowning, Bella returns to her own yard and idly flicks a fallen gingko leaf off one of the gold-rimmed Limoges plates.

Her ten settings would have been enough after Jacy backed out. But when Parker's cousin Virginia made her last-minute appearance, Bella had to include the tag-sale lookalike, which isn't as identical as Odelia had claimed. She confirms that it's nowhere near the seat reserved for Johneen, who will undoubtedly zero in on it with a critical eye.

"Wow. Everything looks beautiful," a voice says.

She jumps, then turns to see Calla behind her. Her face is made up, her hair is loose and wavy, and she's changed into a flattering red dress with a scoop neckline.

"Do you need anything from the store?" she asks Bella. "I forgot my contact lens solution."

"I'm sure there's some in the lost and found in the second-floor hallway."

Guests tend to leave behind everything from toiletries to phone chargers to underpants. The latter goes into the trash, but Bella collects the rest into a big basket marked "Forget something? Help yourself!"

"That's okay," Calla says. "I need a certain kind."

"You sure? You'll have to go all the way down the road to Cassadaga."

"I don't mind. Can I pick up anything for you?"

"No, thanks. I can't believe I'm saying this, but I think I'm all set for tonight and tomorrow." *Weather, cryptic threats, and Millicent aside.*

"That's good. And by the way, in case no one else mentions it, you did a nice job out here. It looks beautiful."

Bella smiles and thanks her, quite certain no one else—namely, the bride and groom—will offer that compliment.

Jangling her car keys, Calla turns to go, then looks back. "Bella? I know Johnny's been driving you crazy."

"Did you just read my mind?"

She smiles. "Pretty much. But listen, I wouldn't be friends with her if she were all bad, so . . ."

"I figured that. She's probably had a rough life."

"Well, I wouldn't go *that* far."

"So she's not a poor little rich girl?"

"No! She's a rich little rich girl. She comes from old money. Brattiness is the family legacy. Even her parents are spoiled rotten. And they don't get along."

"You mean her parents, with each other?"

"I mean all of them. Most families argue and then they kiss and make up. But the Maynards—they don't kiss, they don't make up, they don't even talk. It doesn't seem to bother them, though. That's just the way it is."

Is that what Virginia and Parker were talking about, then? Are they worried that some loose-cannon relative might show up and ruin the wedding?

Would that be ominous enough that Parker's cousin found it neces-sary to be here to help him protect Johneen?

"I hope Johneen can break the pattern with this marriage, but she hasn't made the best choices when it comes to relationships." Calla looks over her shoulder, making sure no one has come up behind her before adding in a lower voice, "I really don't know Parker, so maybe I'm wrong, but . . . I'm not sold."

"You don't like him?"

"I'm sure he's a decent human being, but he's probably too much like Johneen for Johneen's own good. Opposites attract for a reason."

Bella can't help but think of Sam. "Yes, but sometimes similar souls can be soul mates."

"I used to think that. Now . . . I'm not so sure." Calla looks so wistful that Bella almost asks her about Jacy.

But then the keys make the restless clanking again. "I'd better run, Bella. Tell Gammy I'll be back soon, in case I miss the begin-ning of the party."

"Don't worry, you'll have plenty of time. The market is right down the road. Just go out through the gates, make a left, and follow Dale Drive all the way into town, make another left, and—"

"Oh, I know where it is."

"Sorry, I keep forgetting you grew up here. You seem so . . ."

Calla grins. "You were going to say 'normal,' weren't you?"

She was, but . . .

"I don't suppose a polite lie would work on you?"

"Nope. But don't worry, I'm used to it. Whenever people find out where I'm from, if they've heard of the Dale, they ask if I'm 'one of them.'"

"A medium?"

"Right. And if I admit that I am, then they always say . . ."

Bella completes the sentence in unison with her: *"But you seem so normal!"*

Calla laughs. "Right. So if you're worried about Max growing up here—"

"I'm not." *Anymore,* she adds silently. But her mother-in-law cer-tainly will be when she figures out exactly what goes on in the Dale.

"By the way, Bella, I really am thinking of adopting a kitten. Max said I can choose, other than the little black one—Wilbur, I think his name is?"

"No, that's Spidey. But Max probably mentioned that he was a runt just like Wilbur, the pig in *Charlotte's Web*."

"Right, that's exactly what he said. He also mentioned that it's fine if I decide not to adopt a kitten after all, because he'd like to keep them all together."

"Oh, he did, did he? Well, feel free to adopt one. Or two. Or half a dozen."

"He also offered me a blue kitten, but I didn't see that one. Max said he was outside hiding in my grandmother's garden."

"So I've heard. Does Jacy like cats?"

Her smile dims. "He does. But not just because he . . . likes cats. He was raised to believe that they're mystical creatures. He said that they turn up in our lives when they seem to need us most, when they're sick or young or vulnerable . . ."

"Or lost and pregnant," Bella says, thinking of Chance.

"Exactly. But usually, it turns out to be the other way around. They show up and make us care for them in times when *we* need *them*. They possess powerful healing energy."

It isn't the first time Bella has heard that—and not just in this place where people converse with the dead, believe they've lived a dozen lifetimes, and navigate the world aided by ancient Spirit guides.

Last winter, Max's very respectable and intellectual child psychiatrist suggested that a pet might help him work through his grief. He cited scientific studies that suggested cuddling a cat would boost brain chemicals that help ward off depression.

That, of course, is medicine, not magic. Last year when Sam was dying, Bella didn't believe in either of those things. But here in the Dale, the two seem to collide fairly often in a way that almost—*almost*—makes sense.

Watching Calla leave, Bella wonders whether Odelia's granddaughter, too, might need emotional healing. Her longtime relationship with Jacy seems to have hit a rough patch, or perhaps run its course. Is she trying to hang on, or trying to let go?

I was doing both when I got to Lily Dale. I couldn't imagine a new life anywhere, let alone here, without Sam.

Yet the days kept coming, and she always managed to move through them, past them.

"When Sunny Gets Blue" plays softly over the speakers, with its lyrics about the rain beginning to fall.

Pitter-patter, pitter-patter . . .

Bella takes one last look at the tranquil lake and starlit sky, and in this calm before the storm, she heads toward the house to try reaching Luther again.

*   *   *

An hour later, Luther still isn't answering, the bride is late for her celebratory dinner, and Calla has yet to return from the store.

The other guests are gathered on the lawn beneath moon- and candlelit trees.

Maid of honor Liz is, like the bride herself, a willowy, attractive blonde. She doesn't say much, and Bella isn't sure whether she's shy or standoffish. Her square-jawed fiancé, Ryan, is neither. He's already cornered Bella in two lengthy conversations and managed to drop his Ivy League degree into both with the subtlety of an air horn in a library.

Francesca and Tanya are Johneen and Calla's former college suitemates. Tall, stocky, brunette Frankie, as she prefers to be called, coaches women's hockey at a college in Buffalo. Tanya is a married dental hygienist who is already wistfully missing her husband and six-month-old daughter.

"I haven't been away from Emily for more than a couple of hours since she was born, and Jack and I haven't spent a night apart since we were married," she confided in Bella, who did her best to muster an appropriate amount of sympathy.

Rounding out the newcomers are Johneen's Pittsburgh coworkers. Hellerman, a robust, redheaded guy with a beer belly and an infectious laugh, reportedly has a first name, but no one ever uses it, according to Andrea. A raven-haired spitfire, she's accompanied by her boyfriend, Charlie, whom Bella had initially pegged as an insipid plus-one. Guys like him often seem to pop up at events like this with a vivacious woman on his arm, and you have to wonder what she sees in him.

Charlie, however, has long since come out of his shell . . . and then some. He's peppering the conversation with curse words and lowbrow humor of which the bride would undoubtedly disapprove, though Virginia is certainly getting a kick out of it.

Holding court in a dark corner of the yard, she's changed out of her white dress. Did Parker warn her about upstaging his future wife?

She looks ravishing in slinky black satin and is as comfortable socializing with the women as she is knocking back drinks with the guys. She prefers bourbon, neat—"like any good Southern gal," she said in a throaty drawl, chain-smoking cigarettes.

Yet another burst of raucous laughter erupts, courtesy of yet another off-color joke from Hellerman. Good Time Charlie is pouring himself a second (or is it his third?) drink. Even Ryan has lost his necktie and rolled up his custom-shirt sleeves.

"Good thing we got those he-men to move the steamer trunk over to my house before we started serving them your signature cocktails," Odelia tells Bella. "I don't know what's in them, but they pack a wallop."

Bella found the recipe while browsing a vintage cookbook in the guesthouse library. Not only does the tawny liquid, served in martini glasses, compliment the color scheme, but it's aptly named the "Brandy Daisy." Even Parker is having such a boisterous time that he barely seems aware the other Daisy is conspicuously missing— feeling a little under the weather, he explained when he showed up solo.

"She'll join us as soon as she's up to it," he promised.

Bella hopes the fun will continue after Johneen shows up, though she wouldn't bet on it.

Her hostess duties keep her much too busy to dwell on her lingering concerns about the anonymous note and the overheard conversation. She scurries into the house with used glasses, out with more ice; in for a lighter, out to ignite the Sterno pots beneath the chafing dishes; in for crackers, out with crackers, only to return again for the forgotten cheese.

Odelia is helping in her own haphazard way. She can't move around as efficiently, and whenever she sets out on an errand, she seems to get waylaid, caught up in conversation with various guests—some unseen.

She tells Bella that Miriam—also known as the shy but friendly ghost next door—is hanging around the yard.

Odelia often talks about Miriam as fondly as if she were a dear friend, and a mischievous scamp.

"Miriam hid my reading glasses again," she'll say, or "Miriam is making herself scarce this week. I wonder where she's gone off to?"

Now she explains that Miriam is "feeling social" and accompanied by a couple of otherworldly cronies who were household names back when they were alive.

"Yes, soirees are much simpler when you don't have to make the gin in the bathtub, Al," Odelia murmurs as Bella adds more clusters of concord grapes to a nearby platter. "Not that *I* would know . . . Of course not! How old do you think I *am*?"

Ordinarily, Bella is as bemused by those one-sided conversations as she is amused. Tonight, she's just relieved that the only apparent party crashers aren't bothering anyone but Odelia.

Going over to the bar to check the ice supply, she finds that it's running low again. She grabs the bucket and crouches to refill it from the dwindling chest beneath the table.

"Hey, can I bum one of those?" she hears Hellerman ask Virginia and looks up to see him refilling their glasses as Virginia puts a fresh cigarette between her lips.

She removes it to say, "They're unfiltered."

"Good. So am I."

"In that case . . ." She pulls her pack from her little bag—a vintage one with black sequined straps—and holds it out to him. "What do you think of my cousin's fiancée?"

"You really want to know?"

"I really asked, didn't I?" She takes out a lighter and lights his cigarette, then hers.

"I'm here, aren't I?"

"What does that mean?"

"It means I made the cut, so we must be friends."

Through the smoke screen, Bella sees Virginia narrow her eyes at Hellerman's comment. "Were you ever anything more?"

He laughs. "Why would you ask that?"

"Just a vibe."

"I'm giving off a vibe that tells you I had a fling with Johneen Maynard?"

"Maybe just that you wanted to."

"What are you, one of those crazy Lily Dale psychics?"

"Hell, no. I'm just a very, very smart woman."

"Well, I'm not a stupid man."

"Meaning?"

"I never kiss and tell. Not at a wedding. Not to the bride's cousin-to-be."

"Fair enough," Virginia says, and they make their way back to the group.

Intriguing, Bella thinks as she heads into the house for another tray of hot canapés. Hellerman doesn't seem like Johneen's type. It's easier to imagine him making a move on her and being rejected than to picture the two as a couple for even one night.

Would that cause him to write a threatening anonymous letter and drive up to Lily Dale earlier in the week to mail it?

That's even harder to picture, but she supposes anything is possible.

Back outside, Bella finds Odelia scolding Rudy—as in Valentino, one of her so-called regulars—for mischievously pinching the shy Miriam on her posterior.

"Now you've gone and scared her away! Why would you—oh, now look what you've done! You're incorrigible!"

Bella pauses to watch Odelia pick up a votive candle. A wisp of smoke trails from the wick as if it's been abruptly extinguished . . . on a windless night.

"Rudy," she explains to Bella as she relights it. "He's saying he's sorry he got a little too rambunctious and that he won't do it again."

Mildly star struck despite herself, Bella says, "Tell him that I . . . um . . . accept his apology and would appreciate it if he didn't blow out the candles."

"There, you hear that? Now go behave yourself," Odelia tells thin air, then turns back to help Bella arrange the canapés on a serving platter. "Spirit does love a party, and we're long overdue for one around here."

She explains that crowds are teeming with energy, and energy attracts Spirit. Thus whenever a large group gathers for a festive occasion, ghostly visitors are bound to join the action.

"Sometimes," Odelia adds, plopping down the last miniquiche and setting aside the serving tongs, "Spirit can even draw enough energy to manifest."

Any other night, that might spook Bella. Tonight, she's warier of human intruders.

She glances over at the house next door. A light is on in the upstairs bedroom where Millicent is staying, and Bella can see a female figure silhouetted in the window, looking down on the festivities.

Either Spirit is spying on the festivities, or her mother-in-law is.

"Where the heck is Calla?" Odelia mutters, shaking her head and looking at her watch. "She should have been back by now."

She's right. It's been more than forty-five minutes since Calla left to make the ten-minute round-trip drive to Cassadaga.

You'd think a medium might be spared restless moments over loved ones' well-being. But according to Odelia, an emotional connection to someone can block psychic energy.

"That's why Calla was so frustrated and skeptical when she first arrived in the Dale," she said. "It was right after we lost her mom, and she expected to connect with her here."

"She couldn't bring her through?"

"No, and neither could I. Not for a long time. Our grief was too raw," she added with a meaningful look at Bella, who got the message loud and clear: her own grief is still too raw for her to have connected with Sam.

Yes, Pandora Feeney claimed to have heard from him, and the woman did know things about him that she shouldn't have known.

And then there's the tourmaline necklace she's wearing tonight. It matches her eyes and her dress . . .

Bella Blue.

When she found it back in July, she was convinced it was from Sam on the Other Side. In that moment, it seemed possible, and it was what she needed to believe. But then . . .

Then time passed, and Sam seemed farther away than ever, and I came to my senses.

Regardless of how it came to be hers, the necklace reminds her of Sam.

What doesn't?

Even the Rodgers and Hart song wafting from the speakers makes her think of her husband.

"Blue Moon . . . You saw me standing alone . . ."

Sam: *"I love you, Bella Blue."*

Then she hears Odelia say, "Oh, thank goodness!"

Bella turns to see that Calla is back.

She isn't alone.

Blue Slayton is wearing a dark suit with an open-collared starched white dress shirt and a big grin. Clean-shaven, with his sandy hair parted on the side and combed across his forehead above classically handsome features, he'd be right at home on Wall Street or in a boardroom.

"Look who I just ran into!" Calla announces. "Francesca and Tanya, you two remember Blue from when we were in college, right?"

They do, and seem lukewarm about seeing him again.

As Calla introduces him to the others, Odelia jerks the plastic wrap off a platter and mutters to Bella, "I should have known he'd show up."

"I don't think he just showed up. It seems like she invited him."

"Maybe, but it isn't her party."

"No, but she did have a plus-one who couldn't make it."

"Not a plus-one. *Jacy.* You don't just replace a wedding date with any old guy. Her parents taught her better manners than that, and so did I."

He isn't just any old guy, Bella guesses, watching Calla and Blue. Even she can sense the renewed chemistry between them as they stand in a group conversation with their shoulders nearly touching.

She wants to remind Odelia that they were mere kids back when he broke Calla's heart. Things change. People grow up. Judging by the way Blue is looking at Calla, he's thrilled to see her now. And judging by the way Calla is looking at Blue, Jacy's absence isn't nearly as disturbing to her as it is to her grandmother.

"We don't have room for one more," Odelia tells Bella. "Where are we supposed to put him?"

"We'll add a chair. Now at least we have an even number of guests."

"And an odd number of place settings."

"We'll figure out something."

"Tell that to the bride. She's not going to be happy."

"Is she ever? Anyway, this is just a dinner party, Odelia. He's not coming to the wedding."

"Wanna bet?"

Bella follows Odelia's dark gaze to Calla and Blue, their heads bent together as they laugh over some private joke.

"That's up to the bride and groom," she reminds Odelia. "Speaking of which . . . where the heck is the bride? My chicken cordon bleu is going to get cold."

"I don't—speak of the devil!"

Following her gaze, Bella sees Johneen framed in the back door. Statuesque in heels and wearing an ivory-colored pantsuit, she's surveying the scene like a lioness atop Pride Rock.

"Daisy!" Spotting her, Parker hurries over. "I was beginning to worry."

Was he? Bella wonders. *Or was he having too much fun without her to worry about where she was or whether she'd show up?*

She's beginning to think there might be something to Odelia's premonitions. Not because the bride is doomed but because the marriage is. These two might share affection, mutual admiration, and an affinity for the finer things in life, but that doesn't mean they're destined to live happily ever after. Maybe Spirit is trying to warn them, via Odelia, not to go through with it.

Parker takes Johneen's arm and leads her away from the crowd, close enough to the food table that Bella can hear every word they're saying.

"How are you feeling, Daisy?"

"Have you seen the weather? It's going to *snow*, Parker. Snow, in October!"

"That can't be right. You must have looked at the wrong forecast."

"I'm not an idiot. I looked at Lily Dale and it said snow."

"Well, there's nothing we can do about that, is there? Let me get you a cocktail. It's named after you."

"Just water, Parker. Please."

As he goes to fetch it, Johneen, who does indeed look wan, pastes on a smile and turns to greet her guests.

Watching her, Bella is struck by a fragility she never noticed before.

For a moment, she almost feels sorry for Johneen Maynard. No bride should come down with something on the eve of her wedding, even if her marriage isn't exactly meant to be. Or perhaps *especially* if her marriage isn't meant to be.

Then Bella remembers how she treated Max upstairs earlier.

The woman deserves whatever misfortune comes her way. Karma can be a real—

"I'm sorry, I don't think we've met."

Bella sees that Johneen has zeroed in on Parker's cousin, cornering her beneath the apple tree as Virginia stubs out a cigarette in a makeshift, plastic-cup ashtray.

"Why, I'm Virginia, your future kin. And you're as pretty as a picture, just like Parker said."

She flashes a tight-lipped smile and makes a feeble attempt at small talk.

Watching her, Odelia shakes her head. "Spirit doesn't like this. Not one bit."

"What are you seeing? What is Spirit saying?"

"I'm trying to figure it out, but it doesn't make any sense. Or maybe it should, but I just can't . . ." She trails off, looking over at her granddaughter.

Calla is still with Blue, cozily clinking cocktail glasses in a toast for two.

Scowling, Odelia turns toward her house. "I'll go rustle up another plate. But I guarantee that it won't be pure white, and it might be chipped," she adds darkly.

Watching her shuffle away, Bella is grateful that she herself lacks the so-called gift of clairvoyance. It's hard enough to face things that have already gone wrong and worry about the ones that might. Odelia, convinced that disaster looms as inevitably as tomorrow itself, must feel that awful, frantic helplessness that permeates a nightmare in which you're absolutely certain a psycho killer is about to get you . . .

But then you wake up.

Maybe Odelia's "vision" will turn out to be sheer imagination, and Johneen and Parker will safely leave the Dale to live happily ever after. Even so, Odelia and her fellow mediums, many of whom Bella has grown to know and love, never get to just . . . wake up and live their daily lives in ignorant bliss.

When Parker returns with her ice water, Johneen drags him off to the side of the yard, beyond the mood lighting's perimeter.

Standing nearby, Bella finds herself inadvertently eavesdropping for the second time today.

"You don't just spring an uninvited guest on the bride at the last minute," Johneen hisses.

"Your friend Calla did."

"That's different. I knew Blue Slayton back in college."

"Isn't he the one you didn't like?"

"That's beside the point, and I had a good reason."

"What was it?"

"We had a little bit of an entanglement that ended rather messily."

"Oh? Does Calla know?"

"It wasn't behind her back. They were on again, off again."

"So while she was *off*, you were *on*? Nice, Daisy. Really nice."

"At least he isn't a total stranger showing up at my wedding."

"Virginia isn't a stranger either. She's family."

"Then why didn't you invite her in the first place?"

"Because I didn't think she'd come."

"Well, she did. And . . . and she smokes cigarettes!" she flings at him.

"What does that have to do with anything? And it isn't *your* wedding. It's *our* wedding, and she came all this way. Come on, Daisy, don't be jealous."

"Why on earth would I be jealous of your *cousin?*"

"Because you, my dear, are accustomed to having me all to yourself. And I love you for it, but—"

"That's not true. I rarely have you all to myself. I enjoy my space, and you enjoy yours. I'm not one of those needy women who smothers a man."

"No, but you like to be in control, and you don't like surprises."

"I adore surprises. Just not *surprise visitors.*"

Yes, well, who does? Bella wonders, thinking of Millicent's ambush. She glances up at the bedroom window next door, where her mother-in-law's silhouette hovers like a raptor.

"I don't like her," Johneen informs Parker. "And she doesn't like me, either."

"She doesn't even know you!"

Unlike Johneen, whose upper-crust inflection is strained but holds steady within its usual octave, the perpetually collected Parker seems to be rapidly losing his cool.

"I saw the way she looked at me the moment I stepped outside, Parker. Pure contempt."

"That's ridiculous!"

"Shhh!"

There's a pause, as if they're listening to make sure they haven't been overheard.

"I'm sorry, Daisy. I know your nerves are on edge and I know what you're thinking. But you don't have to worry. Just because Virginia showed up doesn't mean anyone else will."

There's a pause. "What if *he* does?"

"He won't. He's a million miles away."

"You don't know that for sure."

Johneen sighs a slightly muffled sigh, and Bella imagines that she's leaning her head on his shoulder. She thinks of the letter, tucked in the drawer of her nightstand upstairs, and wonders if she should show it to them. It was postmarked in Lily Dale, so if it was written by *him*—whoever *he* is—then he isn't a million miles away at all.

"It's going to be all right," Parker tells her. "I promise."

"You shouldn't make promises you can't keep."

"I never do, Daisy. Now let's go celebrate. All right?"

A long pause.

"All right."

When they emerge from the shadows hand in hand, Johneen appears to be her regal, self-important self again. They slip into conversation with the others, but Johneen keeps her distance from Virginia, and Virginia keeps a wary eye on Johneen.

Maybe she's the one I should tell, Bella thinks, but quickly dismisses that idea. She's not supposed to know anything might be amiss.

She quickly makes her way back to the house and slips into the small study off the parlor. When Leona lived here, she used the room to do psychic readings for her clients. It was off-limits to visitors; its French doors were locked and its window blinds drawn.

Bella transformed the space into a sunny, public nook where guests can use a desktop computer and print boarding passes. There's even a landline phone, since certain carriers' cell service can be spotty around Lily Dale.

The walls are painted a buttery shade, complimented by blue and white window-seat cushions. During the day, with the blinds raised, the room is bright and cheerful.

But at night . . .

As she turns on the desk lamp and closes the door behind her, she wonders uneasily if someone is out there, watching her through the unobstructed glass.

Oh, come on. Why would anyone do that? You're not the one with a stalker. Johneen is.

Or is she?

It certainly sounded that way . . . didn't it?

Clearly, the couple was concerned about a potential wedding crasher. Yet as she replays the conversation in her head, Bella realizes that it could very well be something—*someone*—utterly innocuous. The unwelcome guest might just be one of those pesky relatives who lurks in every family tree if you shake hard enough. Maybe Johneen has an uncle prone to political pontification or a wayward brother who tends to overindulge. Why had Bella assumed it was a stalker of some sort?

For one thing, the conversation wasn't just laced with ordinary concern. It was more dramatic than that.

But then, she's Johneen, Bella reminds herself. *To her, every potential hindrance is fraught with disaster.*

What about the note? And Parker and Virginia's conversation?

And, as much as Bella hates to include it as potential evidence— what about Odelia's foreboding vision?

In her mind, it all adds up to the very real possibility that some one sinister is lurking.

She jerks down the blinds to cover the window just in case and dials Luther's cell phone.

Again, it bounces directly to voice mail. This time, she leaves a message. "Luther, it's Bella. Give me a call, please, if you don't get back too late. If you do . . . I guess I'll just see you tomorrow when you drop off the chuppah. It's nothing urgent," she adds. "No big deal."

Are you trying to reassure Luther or yourself?

Hanging up, she looks at the computer. She shouldn't, but she can't help herself. She opens a search engine and types "Johneen Maynard."

As the results pop up, the back door opens and someone urgently calls her name.

Bella closes out the screen and hurries to the kitchen, where she finds Tanya.

A small, mousy woman, she's wearing no makeup and has on an unflatteringly blousy teal dress with sensible, brown shoes she probably wears to work at the dental office.

Seeing her distressed expression, Bella braces herself. "What's wrong?"

"Are you going to be serving dinner soon?"

"Dinner?"

"Yes. It's so late. I really need to eat."

"Sorry, it's ready right now." As Bella opens the oven to remove the foil-wrapped entrées, Tanya goes on to tell her that she's not used to having cocktails, especially on an empty stomach, and that she always eats dinner at five o'clock, and that it's long past her bedtime.

Bella apologizes, relieved that the purported emergency involved nothing more dangerous than plummeting blood sugar.

This is ridiculous. She's running around playing amateur detective for no real reason while her guests starve.

Tomorrow, Luther will assure her there's nothing to worry about. He'll say she's just jittery because of what happened to Leona Gatto. He'll remind her, in his sensible Luther way, that violent crime can't possibly strike twice in a bucolic place like Lily Dale.

Bella carries the hot food out into the night, where laughter and the warm glow of twinkling lights are waiting.

So is Johneen, eyes blazing.

"Isabella, is this your idea of a joke?"

"What?" Waylaid at the foot of the back steps, clutching a heavy tray of chicken cordon bleu in oven mitts, Bella looks around, wondering what can possibly be amiss.

Everything appears in order, and the guests, though perhaps ravenous, seem content.

"Did you think I wouldn't notice?"

Johneen must be talking about the belated dinner. Bella bites her tongue to keep from pointing out that the meal would have been served on time if the bride had been here when she was supposed to be.

"You need to change it this instant!" Johneen rails on.

"Change *what*?"

"The song. The *song*, Isabella."

Caught off guard, she listens momentarily to the music wafting from the speakers.

"Poor little rich girl," Judy Garland is singing, *"you're a bewitched girl, better take care . . ."*

"I have no idea what this is, Johneen, but I didn't put it on the playlist. I only put the songs you wanted."

"Then how did it get there?"

That's a good question.

"Cocktails and laughter, but what comes after . . ."

At a loss for words, she can only listen to the ominous lyrics, heart pounding as she remembers what Odelia said about Spirit's electronic manipulation.

Chapter Seven

On Saturday, Bella awakens just past four AM from a strange nightmare.

In the beginning, she was setting the table with Odelia, and they were arguing about whether the white place settings were identical. Then it shifted; Bella became the bride, and she was looking into a mirror. Everything—and everyone—in its reflection was slightly *off.* Her own face, the objects she held up to it, even the room behind her . . .

"We're identical twins," her reflection told her.

"No, we're not. Your hair is a little darker than mine, and your eyes . . ."

Her reflection's eyes glinted with something dark and dangerous, as if she knew something or was up to something . . .

"Well, we're dressed like identical twins," Mirror Bella insisted.

"No, we're not. Your dress is off-white. Mine is white. See?"

"Our bouquets are exactly the same."

"They are not. The flowers are different. You have to pay close attention to the details!"

"So do you."

"I am!"

Mirror Bella lifted her bouquet. Only it wasn't a bouquet. It was a hand. Only it wasn't a hand. It was a claw. It came straight through the mirror . . .

Bella woke with a start to a pair of kittens busily making a cozy nest in her tousled hair and a third kitten kneading her forehead with tiny razor-sharp claws.

"Ouch! Come on, guys!"

Sitting up and turning on the bedside lamp, she sees the furry cul-
prits stretching luxuriously on her warm, vacated pillow like social-
ites claiming a poolside chaise. A fourth kitten valiantly attempts
to scale the vertical quilt folds to join them, and a pair wrestles on
the rug below. Another—the striped tabby whose official name is
Wednesday, though Bella prefers to call him Wallenda—performs
a harrowing, death-defying leap from the dresser to the bed. Only
Chance and Spidey remain snuggled in the nest, calmly watching
the action.

Bella gets out of bed and grabs a couple of clean metal pet bowls
and cans of cat food from the closet shelf. As soon as she pops the tab
on the first one, every member of the feline family, even Spidey, stops
in its tracks to look at her, whiskers and ears perked like antennae.

"That's right, everyone. Breakfast is early today." She dumps in
the food. "Come and get it."

The kittens race over, skidding across the hardwood floor and
jostling each other. Wallenda dive-bombs the bowl and emerges covered in pinkish-brown pâté.

Bella makes her way to the shower, where she lingers to let the
steamy water soothe away the weary ache along with last night's tension and sheer exhaustion. She fell into bed just a short couple of
hours ago, much too tired to dwell on the day's troubling events.

Now she's almost relieved that she hadn't connected with Luther
after all. As a detective, he's all about the concrete evidence, and she
has nothing.

Well, she does have the note. But what does it prove, other than
that someone would prefer the wedding not take place?

An anonymous note doesn't amount to a threat, and it certainly
doesn't indicate imminent danger.

Yes, that's what Luther will say when she shows it to him.

For now, she can't let it distract her from the many tasks at hand.
After last night, she wants everything to go smoothly.

Despite the blips, a great time was had by all . . .

All but Odelia.

And, of course, the bride.

Masking displeasure is hardly Johneen's specialty. She glowered until finally excusing herself to go upstairs shortly after dinner. Parker reluctantly but dutifully joined her, even though the party was in full swing.

The others stayed until midnight, talking, laughing, drinking. They'll undoubtedly snooze away the morning, unlike Bella, who was up even later on cleanup duty.

Odelia should have been right there with her but said she wasn't feeling well and left while the guests were eating dinner.

"I hate to do this to you, Bella, but I'm afraid I'll be useless tomorrow if I don't rest tonight."

Bella assured her that she could handle it on her own, though she wasn't convinced Odelia's ailment was purely physical. She suspected her friend just couldn't stomach the sight of Calla with Blue Slayton.

Ordinarily, Bella would have attempted to discuss it with her, but she had her hands full with the party, and she was still rattled by the Judy Garland song that shouldn't have been played.

By the time she ran inside to turn it off, it had ended. And when she checked her iPod, "Poor Little Rich Girl" wasn't even on the playlist.

How, then, had it made its way into the rotation?

She'd never heard the song in her life, but it was stuck in her head last night. Right before she headed up the stairs, she returned to the study to look up the lyrics.

Reading through them on the screen, she didn't find them particularly menacing. Earlier, though, with Odelia's comment fresh in her head, she was certain Spirit was sending Johneen a message.

That, too, seems ridiculous now.

While she was at the computer, against her own better judgment, she decided to revisit her earlier investigation into Johneen's background. She typed the first few letters, hit enter when the remembered search popped up, and glanced over the list of results. Nothing of note jumped out at her, and fatigue and the late hour swiftly got the better of her. She closed the screen and went to bed, not even sure exactly what she'd been looking for. A recent brush with danger, maybe? A restraining order against an old boyfriend? Some kind of—

Without warning, Bella's hot shower goes bone-chilling. She jumps out from under the spray, glad she's no longer covered in suds.

As she hurriedly wraps herself in a towel, shivering, she notes that this hasn't happened in weeks.

Is it, too, a message from Spirit?

If so, it's that she'd better get moving, because she has a million things to do.

Back in her room, she gazes at herself in the mirror, wondering how she's going to make herself presentable. Her eyes are bloodshot and deeply underscored with exhaustion, well beyond remedy by simple eye drops and drugstore concealer.

You just have to get through the next . . . not even twenty-four hours, she reminds herself. *And then . . .*

And then Johneen and Parker will be off on their honeymoon and life will be back to normal around here.

Normal, with Maleficent in their midst?

Her mother-in-law had stayed tucked away throughout the evening. As Odelia excused herself to head home, she wondered aloud if she should knock to make sure Millicent was all right.

"Please don't," Bella told her. "Trust me, she's the first to let someone—*everyone*—know when she isn't all right."

Judging by the look on Odelia's face, the words came out sounding more callous than she'd intended, or even than she was feeling. But it wasn't the right moment to explain that when it comes to protecting Max, she takes no chances.

Of course Millicent loves him, just as she loved her son. But Sam, as an adult, was able to grasp that his mother saw Bella as a third wheel. He was usually adept at deflecting Millicent's manipulation, but not always.

Max, as an impressionable little boy, could easily be blindsided by his strong-willed grandmother.

Bella might very well be overreacting to her visit, but she's pretty sure she didn't miss a hint of suspicious behavior yesterday, and she can't expect Millicent to stay hidden away all day today.

At some point this morning, she's going to have to squeeze in at least a brief conversation. Or confrontation, if it comes down to that. All the more reason to get busy on the day's tasks while she has the quiet house all to herself.

But when she heads downstairs, she sees light spilling from the back of the house and hears voices in the breakfast room.

Stepping across the threshold, she finds . . .

Even Valentino's ghost wouldn't be as shocking as the sight that greets her.

She must be hallucinating in the blinding glare of overhead light. She squeezes her eyes tightly shut.

But when she opens them again, there they are: Millicent and Johneen, companionably sipping tea at a round café table.

Johneen appears wan and plain, free of makeup and wearing glasses. Her long hair falls in straggly wisps over the appliquéd bodice of her white cotton nightgown.

Millicent is wearing eye pencil, rouge, and lipstick. She's fully clothed and accessorized: gold jewelry and a tweed blazer over a creamy silk blouse and brown slacks. *Maybe*, Bella thinks hopefully, *she's donned a traveling outfit to catch an early flight home.*

Catching sight of her, the two women curtail their conversation so abruptly that Bella's certain they were discussing her, or something they didn't want her to overhear.

"Good morning, Isabella," her mother-in-law says as Johneen pushes back her chair.

"Good morning. What are you doing . . . up?" Bella was about to say *here* instead, but Johneen, after all, is staying at the guesthouse.

"I've had terrible insomnia," Johneen announces, getting to her feet. "I finally decided to come down to make some chamomile tea. I'm hoping it'll put me back to sleep. I'd like to get at least eight hours. Be sure to keep the house quiet."

Bella murmurs that she'll certainly try, then watches the bride-to-be disappear in a billow of white cotton, leaving her chair pushed out and her used mug on the table.

As her footsteps retreat up the stairs, Bella looks over at Millicent. "Did you . . . um . . . are you leaving town?"

"Leaving? I just got here."

"No, I know, but . . . you're already up and dressed."

"I've always been an early riser. I don't believe in lying around the house in a slovenly way."

Is it Bella's imagination, or is that a personal dig? Unfair, considering she's up, showered, and dressed, even if she is just wearing an old flannel shirt and yesterday's tattered jeans with threadbare knees. She may not have on makeup, but her hair is clean and brushed, held back in a plastic banana clip.

"I was just wondering how you happened to be here at this hour, that's all," Bella tells her mother-in-law, trying to give her the benefit of the doubt.

"Your friend invited me in."

"My friend?"

"Miss Maynard."

Ah, Miss Maynard. Her friend. Okay.

"How did she happen to—"

"I was about to make myself a cup of tea in your neighbor's kitchen across the way when I glanced out the window and saw a light on here. Someone was in the kitchen, and I assumed it must be you, so I came across and knocked."

"And Johneen let you in." Bella nods, piecing it together—sort of. She still can't seem to wrap her head around the odd little Johneen/Maleficent wee-hour coffee klatch.

"The poor thing needed someone to talk to. She's getting married today," Millicent adds, as if that might be news to Bella.

"Yes, I know."

"It sounds like she's estranged from her own mother, so I gave her some advice."

"About the wedding?"

"Among other things. She's had a difficult time."

"With what?"

"With . . . relationships. Some people do."

"What do you mean by that?" Bella asks, wondering if Johneen confided something relevant.

But Millicent suddenly seems fascinated by the sodden tea bag's paper tag dangling over the edge of her mug. She peers at it, folds it, unfolds it, and tears it off the string.

"Millicent? Did Johneen—"

"I don't feel comfortable discussing this."

No, of course not. Nor is Bella comfortable kicking off a long day with this little tête-à-tête. They're here, so she might as well be direct.

"What exactly brought you here, Millicent?"

"Isabella, please do call me Mother."

She nods politely, though she has no intention of complying. Calling Maleficent *Mother* isn't exactly the same thing as calling Doctor Bailey *Drew*.

Her mother-in-law toys with the tea bag tag. "As I said, I saw someone in the kitchen and assumed it was you, so I knocked, and—"

"No, I mean what brought you to Lily Dale in the first place?"

"Why . . . you and Max did." Millicent gives a nervous laugh. "This isn't exactly the kind of place I'd visit otherwise."

"But . . ." Bella gathers her thoughts. "You didn't let us know you were coming, and I just spoke to you on the phone the other night."

"It was a last-minute decision."

"Based on . . . ?"

"Based on . . ." Millicent shakes her head. "Max is my only grandchild. I haven't seen him since . . ."

She can't bear to say it.

Nor can Bella.

As often as she thinks about last winter and losing Sam, she rarely speaks about it.

That, she realizes, is one of the advantages of living in Lily Dale, where no one knew Sam or anything of their life in Bedford. Her new friends aren't aware of exactly what she's lost, only that she *has* lost, like just about everyone else who finds their way to this village. And since the locals don't believe that the dead are truly gone, they tend not to view Bella's tragedy as . . . well, tragic. This is probably one of the few places in the world where her status as a widow doesn't seem pervasive.

Millicent sighs heavily, and Bella sees that her eyes are shiny.

"It doesn't get any easier, does it?" her mother-in-law asks.

Bella shakes her head, unable to push a word past the sudden lump in her throat, unable to decide which word it would be if she could.

Yes?

No?

She's cast off bits and pieces of the ache, but the weight of loss is no more likely to leave her than Maleficent's steamer trunk is to drift into the sunset like a helium balloon.

She finds herself picturing it, with Maleficent perched atop for the ride, and the lump subsides.

"I'm sure Max will be glad to see you," she hears herself telling her mother-in-law as she sits down in Johneen's vacated chair.

"Does he know that I'm here?"

"I haven't mentioned it yet. I wasn't sure . . ."

What you wanted, or if I should trust you.

"I had hoped to spend time with him last night," Millicent says when she trails off, "but I was so exhausted that I dozed off. I hadn't slept a wink since . . . what's today?"

"Saturday. Why haven't you been sleeping?"

She sidesteps the question. "By the time I woke up from my nap, it was long past Max's bedtime."

And I wouldn't have let you see him one-on-one anyway.

"Well, I'm glad to hear that you're comfortable over at Odelia's. I'm sure she made you feel right at home."

"She certainly tried, and she seems like a decent person . . ."

The emphasis on *seems like* strikes an ominous chord. It sounds as though Millicent doesn't believe Odelia really *is* a decent person.

How much, Bella wonders, *does she know about Odelia? And the Dale?*

She wants to come right out and ask. But if she's misreading her mother-in-law's wariness, the last thing she wants to do is put suspicion into her head.

"You said you haven't slept in a few days," she says, as an entirely different idea strikes her. "Are you all right? Have you been sick?"

What if Millicent is seriously ill? That would explain the impromptu visit. Maybe she wanted to tell Bella in person. Maybe she's hoping to mend the fences before it's too late.

"Of course not. I'm healthy as a horse."

"Then why aren't you sleeping?"

"I've been tossing and turning ever since I found out . . ."

Bella holds her breath as Millicent levels a stern look at her.

"Isabella."

"Yes?"

"I should have known something was amiss months ago when you suddenly told me you were staying here for the summer instead of coming to Chicago. But I convinced myself it was plausible that your car had broken down, and you'd found a temporary job—"

"It *was* plausible. The truth is always plausible!"

"Be that as it may . . . I'll admit that I might have been a little bit relieved you weren't coming right away."

"Relieved? Really?" Taken aback by the honesty, Bella recalls their previous conversation. She remembers only Millicent's blatant dismay and yes, anger at the change of plans.

"I wanted you and Max to feel welcome in my home, but it all happened so quickly that I didn't have time to prepare. I thought the summer would allow me to get the apartment ready and that I'd have additional time to . . . adapt. It's been a while since I've had anyone living under my roof," she adds wistfully.

"Why didn't you just tell me that? Why did you make me think you were disappointed?"

"It wouldn't have been polite under the circumstances. I didn't want you to think—well, you and I aren't exactly—we've never . . . but we aren't talking about our relationship, are we?"

Maybe we should.

"By the time September came," Millicent continues, "I was ready for your arrival. In fact, I was looking forward to it. So when you said you weren't coming—*ever*—I was terribly disappointed."

"This time, for real."

"I—yes. Yes, I was disappointed. So disappointed, in fact, that after a couple of weeks, a friend suggested that I visit you and Max."

A friend.

Bella is dumbstruck by the fact that Millicent actually *has* one. Somehow, the possibility had never entered her mind. Then she considers the slight hesitation before the word and the inflection, and she comprehends that Millicent is referring to a gentleman.

She stares at her mother-in-law, seeing her in a new light. *Wow. Just—wow.* The prospect of a pair of semipermanent overnight guests might have cramped Millicent's lifestyle in ways Bella had never imagined.

"Since you hadn't invited me to come stay with you . . ." Millicent pauses to let that sink in. "I decided that you couldn't turn away a paying guest, and I looked into Lily Dale online. That's when I found out . . ."

Oh.

So *that's* what this is about.

Unwilling to engage in a round of fill-in-the-blanks, Bella waits for her to go on.

Millicent just looks at her.

Unsure whether she found out about Leona Gatto's murder or the Spiritualism, Bella weighs her words carefully. "I know what you're thinking, because I thought the same thing when I got here. But it seemed like an ordinary little town, and you know what? I realized that's exactly what it is. It's just like any other town."

"Really? In what way?"

"Lily Dale is a true community, just like any other. There are houses and parks, schools and businesses, people . . ." True, some of those people aren't alive, if your philosophy aligns with that of the locals, but she's not about to spell that out to Millicent.

"I strongly disagree. You can't pretend that it's exactly like any other town, Isabella."

"Well, no, not *exactly*," Bella agrees. Bent on wiping the smugness from her mother-in-law's face, she goes on. "The people here are much warmer and more welcoming than I've ever encountered anywhere else. They open their arms to strangers. They embraced me and Max as if we were family."

If anything, Millicent is even more smug as she nods and says, "I'm sure they did. That should have been your first clue."

"My first clue . . . to what?"

"That's how these things operate."

"Which things?"

"These religious cults."

Bella's jaw drops.

"People just like you come along, people who are feeling lost and lonely, and they pounce! They reel you in by making you feel as if you belong, and they brainwash you so that—"

"Brainwash?" Bella manages to spit out. "Cult? What are you talking about?"

"I'm talking about Lily Dale. From the moment I realized what was going on here, I was heartsick. I'm here to rescue you and Max from their clutches and bring you home."

Speechless, Bella shakes her head at the absurdity of her mother-in-law's perception. Surely she doesn't believe . . .

But she does believe it, Bella realizes, remembering the strange question yesterday about mass weddings. *No wonder.*

"I know you mean well, Millicent, but—"

"Please, Isabella, call me—"

"I can't do that! I just can't. I'm sorry, but I've told you before, I really can't call you Mother. It's not you, it's me. I can't call anyone Mother."

"And yet these . . . these bizarre strangers . . . you call *them* your *family*?"

"I didn't mean . . . I mean . . ." She rakes her hands through her hair, knocking the banana clip to the floor, ignoring it. "Okay, first things first. I'm not brainwashed. Really, I'm not."

"People who are brainwashed are never *aware* that they're brainwashed, Isabella," Millicent points out reasonably, and dammit, she has a point.

But she's missing Bella's.

"I promise you, Max and I haven't been swallowed up by some bizarre cult. I know those things happen, but not here, and not to us. Look, you met Odelia. I'll admit she may not be the most conventional person in the world, but she's not a dangerous religious fanatic."

"All I know is that she was wearing a strange orange robe . . ."

Thinking back, Bella remembers: the wedding sari. She opens her mouth to enlighten Millicent, but Millicent is on a roll.

". . . and then when we got to her house, she was brewing up an exotic elixir that had a strange name—it was called medusa, I believe. She kept urging me to sample it."

Under any other circumstances, Bella might be smiling. "It's called menudo," she says, "and Odelia can be very persistent. But she's harmless. She was just being hospitable."

"I can see why you'd believe that, Isabella." Millicent reaches out to pat her hand. "I'm just glad I got here before it's too late."

Her expression is frightened but determined: a woman with a mission. However misguided, she's here because she cares—certainly about Max, but perhaps about Bella as well.

About to set her straight, Bella hesitates, hearing footsteps in the hall. Apparently, she was wrong about the guests sleeping in after last night's party. Someone is already stirring.

"We can't talk about this right now," she tells her mother-in-law in a low voice. "And I've got to take care of the wedding today. Promise me you won't do anything or say anything to anyone for the next twenty-four hours."

"But—"

"Please. Please do this for me."

"I *am* doing this for you. I only have your best interests at—"

"Then do it for Johneen," Bella says hurriedly, keeping her voice hushed as a shadow passes by the hall outside the breakfast room. "Doesn't she deserve to have her wedding day go off without a hitch? If you throw a wrench into the plans right now, it won't."

"What, exactly, are you asking me to do?"

"I'm asking you to keep your suspicions to yourself, because they are truly unfounded. Even if you don't believe that, we can discuss it tomorrow."

"Tomorrow might be too late."

"Too late for what?" Bella pauses, hearing the kitchen door open and close. Whoever came downstairs has left the guesthouse, at least for the time being. But they'll be back, most likely in search of coffee and breakfast, and the others may soon be stirring as well.

She looks at Millicent. Her fingers are tightly clasped beneath her chin, and her expression is troubled.

"I don't like this, Isabella. I'm not comfortable here."

"I know you aren't. Why don't you head back to Chicago?"

"Not without you and Max."

"Well, we aren't going anywhere today with a wedding at the guesthouse and a storm on the way and—" She breaks off, hearing a distinct meow from the kitchen.

"Is that a cat?" Millicent asks, wrinkling her nose.

It's Chance.

"Sit here and finish your tea. I've got a couple of things to do," Bella tells Millicent, hurrying out of the room.

In the kitchen, she sees that sure enough, someone left the door ajar and Chance has slipped out onto the step. She's staring out at the dark yard, ears twitching.

Bella had warned the guests about the broken latch last night, but maybe someone forgot.

Or maybe it wasn't a guest. Maybe someone else was prowling around the place.

Is it Nadine?

Like many cottages in the Dale, Valley View purportedly has a resident Spirit. The house next door has Miriam, and this one has Nadine. Odelia told Bella that she's entirely harmless and that Leona had learned to appreciate the companionship despite Nadine's feisty streak. She likes to move things around, flicker the lights, and change television channels without warning. These things have occasionally happened since Bella moved in, but she knows enough about electromagnetic energy to reason that there's nothing paranormal about them.

Odelia had also mentioned that the resident Spirit likes to play with the resident felines. "So if you ever see Chance looking as though she's interacting with someone who isn't there . . ."

"Then she's just being a cat," said Drew, who was a part of that particular conversation. "They all pounce on invisible objects and stare into space like something's there."

"Maybe something is," Odelia said with a shrug, and they dropped the subject.

Now, watching Chance stare out into the yard, Bella would much rather believe she's watching a ghostly visitor than a human one. She scoops up the cat. Predictably, Chance squirms and meows a protest.

"Sorry, but it's dangerous out there."

Maybe more dangerous than she's been allowing herself to consider.

She latches the screen, closes the door, and carries the cat back into the kitchen. Chance's eyes bore into hers as if she's trying to convey a message.

"What are you trying to tell me, hmm? That it's time for your second breakfast? That there really is a little blue kitten out there in Odelia's garden? Or . . . Nadine? Is that it?"

Or is it something even more ominous?

She sets the cat on the floor and goes over to the cupboard to find a can of food. But when she opens it, instead of rushing toward the sound of the popped top, Chance strides in the opposite direction, back over to the door. And when Bella pours the food into a bowl and sets it on the floor, the cat stays where she is, meowing.

"Sorry, Chance. You're stuck in here with me." Bella shakes her head, staring uneasily into the predawn darkness beyond the house.

Chapter Eight

Bella has no idea what time Millicent left the guesthouse this morning or even whether she went back to Odelia's when she did. She only knows that by the time the sun came up, her mother-in-law was gone. She must have left through the front door. Busy in the kitchen and laundry room, Bella kept a wary eye on the yard and the back door, though not for Millicent.

She isn't convinced that an outsider was walking around the house earlier. But if it had been one of the guests, that person has yet to return.

As for her mother-in-law, there was no sign of her when Bella finally returned to the breakfast room to brew the coffee.

Good. Bella doesn't care where she is, as long as she isn't out alerting the authorities or the press about the so-called religious cult she's infiltrated here in the Dale.

By seven forty-five, the sun is shining brightly, and Bella's cell phone is buzzing with a text from Drew Bailey.

Be there by nine.

So he *is* coming today to fix the broken door.

Thumbs poised on her phone, she fully intends to tell him not to worry about it today—or ever. But somehow, she finds herself texting back in cheerful agreement.

Great! Thanks so much!

She hurries upstairs and changes into newer jeans and a blue fleece pullover Sam always said matches her eyes. Then she brushes her hair and, after only a moment's consideration, applies makeup after all.

She tells herself it's only because she might not have another chance to make herself presentable, but somewhere in the back of her mind, she suspects that it has something to do with Doctor Bailey.

Unsettled by that awareness, she reaches for the necklace she'd taken off last night before bed. It's too dressy for what she's wearing, but she resolutely fastens it on anyway.

There. The tourmaline pendant falls alongside her heart as if to remind it to stay right where it belongs.

But she can't help feeling relieved that down-to-earth Drew is on his way. Maybe she can tell him what's been going on around here.

All of it?

Maybe just some of it.

Which parts?

Millicent and the cult, Johneen's mysterious past, the overheard conversation, Spirit manipulating the iPod playlist . . .

All right, maybe she'll tell Drew none of it.

But she'll still welcome the companionship. Odelia is nowhere to be found despite her promise to be here at seven. Max is still asleep, and the guests are . . . well, even if they're awake, they're just guests, not confidantes.

She wouldn't mind a private word with Calla, though. She and Blue were the last ones lingering at the party, sharing a quiet conversation on the Adirondack chairs facing the lake.

Before heading home, Odelia's parting words had been, "I hope Blue Slayton doesn't think he's coming to the wedding tomorrow."

Bella isn't looking forward to breaking the news that he is, indeed, coming to the wedding. Johneen herself invited him, saying pointedly so that Parker would overhear, "My fiancé has decided the more the merrier, so please do join us tomorrow, Blue."

She wasn't flirting. She didn't seem the least bit interested in Blue, and it's clear that Calla is. Johneen was making a point to Parker, who simply rolled his eyes.

Back downstairs, Bella sets out a platter of sliced strudel, then pulls out her cell phone. Odelia always runs late, but not this late. Bella had tried calling her several times earlier, but she hadn't picked up.

In her hurry, Bella bungles the password three times.

That does it. She opens the phone's settings and disables the password feature. She can enable it again when life is back to normal and she's not scrambling to jam countless tasks into every minute.

Odelia's line again goes to voice mail. Bella leaves a quick message. "Hey, it's Wedding Bella. Where are you? We have chairs and tables to arrange and flowers to pick, remember?"

As she hangs up, Parker pokes his head into the sun-splashed breakfast room. He responds to her cheery "Good morning" with a terse "I'm just letting you know that my shower was ice-cold."

"I'm so sorry. There's a sign in the bathroom warning that the hot water tank acts up once in a while. If you wait it out, it gets warm again pretty quickly."

"It didn't. I saw the sign, and I waited ten minutes."

"That's unusual." So is the fact that it's happened twice in one day. Does it mean the hot water tank is finally on its last legs?

"You need to get a plumber here before Daisy wakes up. The last thing she needs on our wedding day is a frigid shower."

Bella smiles, assuming the irony is intentional.

Parker doesn't return the smile, indicating that it was not.

Alrighty then.

"It's not an easy fix," she explains, running the kitchen tap to test the temperature. "The whole thing needs to be replaced, and the owner is planning to do that soon. But it doesn't happen very often."

"It obviously happens often enough for you to have posted signs in the bathrooms."

Ignoring that, she turns off the steamy tap. "This water is plenty hot. I'm sure the shower will be fine for the rest of the day."

"Let's hope so. Is everything else under control?"

"Yes. I was just waiting for Odelia to come over so that we can gather the wildflowers for the tables and bouquet, but she's late."

"I'll come with you."

"You don't have to—"

"No, it's fine." He musters a brief smile. "What better way to start the wedding day than picking daisies for my Daisy?"

With a warm shower, maybe? Or even a lukewarm wife-to-be?

Eying his white dress shirt, navy slacks, and polished wingtips, Bella asks, "Do you want to change into something more casual?"

"This *is* casual," he informs her, taking his designer sunglasses out of his pocket and putting them on.

Ten minutes later, they're stepping out the back door with a couple of pairs of garden shears and two large buckets Bella found on a cobwebby basement shelf. As she cleaned them out and watched a couple of scary-large daddy longlegs wash down the drain, she remembered Odelia's vision.

Was Spirit warning them to beware of spiders lurking in buckets on the wedding day?

Probably not, but considering Bella's profound distaste for arachnids, you never know.

"I hope Daisy gets some sleep. She was up half the night," Parker confides as Bella pulls the back door securely closed behind them.

"Why?"

"I suppose she was worried about the weather. But on a morning like this, it's hard to believe it's going to snow later."

"I know. And this is my first winter in Lily Dale, but according to the locals, October snow isn't unheard of. Don't worry, because I'm sure—"

"Oh, I'm not worried. Our guests are already here, so no one has to travel on treacherous roads. As far as I'm concerned, let it snow."

His attitude is surprisingly cavalier. Is he thinking that the treacherous roads might just keep interlopers away?

Is now a good time to bring up the note?

Before she can figure out how to make that segue, Parker moves on. "But before it snows, we have to find our flowers, so we'd better get busy, right?"

Now is not the time.

"Right. There are some daisies in Odelia's garden. We'll start there. I'm sure she'll come out and join us." With luck, Bella's mother-in-law won't do the same.

A warm breeze off the lake showers them with brilliant leaves as they cross the dewy lawn, weaving their way through the maze of bare round tables. Before Bella can set them, she needs to run one more load of linens through the dryer.

Yet here she is, picking daisies with Parker, who doesn't seem thrilled with Odelia's crop.

"The stems are a little short, don't you think? And Daisy wanted baby's breath. I don't see any."

"I don't even know if that blooms at this time of year or where we can find it."

"Well, we need something white and delicate, and we need more daisies. And—" He jumps back, startled, crushing more blooms with his polished black shoes. "There are rodents in here! Daisy would be horrified."

"Rodents? Where?"

"There." He points, and Bella peers at a small furry creature darting into a clump of asters.

"That's not a rodent!" she realizes, watching it peek out from beneath a dense, grounded trail of morning glories. "It's a kitten."

Max and Jiffy were right. Its plush fur isn't quite as deep a shade as the sheltering blooms, but it *is* a startling silvery blue.

"I'm allergic. Scat, cat." Parker stomps his foot, and the tiny creature dashes into distant shrubs.

Bella bites her tongue and looks at her watch. Drew—kind, animal-loving Drew—will be arriving within the hour. Not soon enough for her taste.

Time to move Parker along, she decides, *away from innocent kittens and inferior flowers.*

"Odelia said there's a meadow filled with wildflowers by the main gate," Bella tells him. "Let's head down there."

She leads the way out to the street. On a summer Saturday, Cottage Row would have been clogged with slow-moving car and pedestrian traffic even at this hour. Today, it's deserted.

They haven't walked more than a couple of feet before Bella hears someone calling her name. Turning, she sees Pandora Feeney beckoning from the porch of her pink cottage across Melrose Park. Her gangly frame is swaddled in a long, red, floral-print bathrobe.

Her gray-streaked hair, usually worn in braids down her back, hangs in loose waves.

Bella waves at her but keeps walking.

"Come on over, luv!" Pandora trills in her English accent.

"*Who*," Parker asks, "is *that*?"

"It's Pandora Feeney."

"Bella! *Do* come across!"

"She seems to want to speak to you."

"Do you mind if we stop for a second?" she asks him reluctantly. "Not at all."

No, Bella is the one who minds. She doesn't dislike the woman, as opposed to Odelia, who loathes her. But she isn't in the mood for a lengthy exchange of pleasantries followed by the usual barrage of pointed questions.

As they approach Pandora's cottage, Bella sees that not only has her neighbor replaced her summer window-box geraniums with burgundy chrysanthemums, but she's gone all out with autumnal decorations. There are additional potted mums on her porch steps, along with fat white pumpkins. The pillars are adorned with cornstalks. Wispy cotton cobwebs are strung between them. Bats, ravens, and large spiders dangle in the gingerbread eaves.

All that's missing are the ghosts, Bella notes without surprise. Pandora might enjoy Halloween, but she takes Spirit far too seriously to display campy, white-cloaked figures with round black eyes.

"How is our dear Chance the Cat?" Pandora asks Bella. "I heard she had surgery yesterday."

Bella doesn't bother to ask how Pandora heard. Somehow, she seems to know about everything that goes on around the Dale.

"She's doing really well, thanks. It was just a routine spay."

"None too soon. I hear she's been a bit of a slag."

"A slag?"

"Let's see, how would an American put it? She's rather been . . . *getting around*."

Bella can't help but grin. "Are you calling my cat a slut, Pandora?"

"If the shoe fits, luv . . ." Pandora returns the smile, then focuses on Parker. "You must be the bloke who's marrying Calla's university friend this afternoon."

"I am. Please don't tell me *she's* been . . . getting around."

"Wouldn't dream of it!" Pandora laughs delightedly and shakes his hand. "Brilliant to meet you. I'm Pandora Feeney, and you're . . . Parker Langley, is it?"

"Is there anything you don't know, Ms. Feeney?"

"Now that you mention it, I don't know why I'm not singing 'Oh, Promise Me' at your wedding."

Oh, no. Bella should have known that was where this little summons was headed.

"I beg your pardon?" Parker looks from Pandora to Bella, who shrugs.

"When I heard there was a wedding at Valley View and that Bella and Odelia were trying to rent a grand piano and hire a singing pianist, I offered to bring over my portable keyboard and play 'Oh, Promise Me.' I had vocal training in my younger days, and I've serenaded many a bride down the aisle."

She pauses to clear her throat, then sings a few bars in an operatic soprano.

"Very nice," Parker tells her, then turns to Bella. "I don't recall being asked about this delightful lady singing at the wedding. Did Daisy say no?"

"She was very specific. She requested a grand piano and the song 'Fields of Gold,'" she reminds him, "but she's agreed that we can use a recording of it instead."

"'Fields of Gold'?" Pandora echoes.

"It's our song," Parker tells her. "It reminds me of my Daisy."

"And that reminds me, we'd better get moving," Bella says. "We have lots of flowers to pick and not a lot of time to find them."

"If it's daisies you want, I've a garden full of smashing Shastas," Pandora tells them, then adds, eyeing the meager contents of their buckets, "The stems are much longer than those. My, but they're in a dreadful state. Where did you get them?"

"In Odelia Lauder's yard," Parker says, and Bella sees a glimmer of satisfaction in Pandora's expression. "You wouldn't mind if we cut some of yours?"

"Not at all, and help yourselves to any other flowers you'd like."

"Do you have any baby's breath?"

"My Gypsophilia is long past bloom and mulched over," the always botanically correct Pandora informs them. "But if you need delicate white blossoms, I've scads of Queen Anne's lace. Take all you need. There's a killing frost coming tonight; most everything will be withered by morning."

Parker thanks her profusely, and she invites them to deposit the "beastly" flowers they've already collected into the rubbish behind the house.

"Meanwhile, I'll dash inside and take a quick listen to 'Fields of Gold,'" Pandora decides. "I'm sure I can learn it by . . . what time did you say the wedding is?"

They didn't.

"Three o'clock," Parker tells her. "I'd love to surprise Daisy with a live musician if you think you can do it."

"I'm quite certain that I can! I'll come 'round before three with my keyboard!"

She might as well, Bella thinks as she trudges into the garden with Parker. Pandora and her keyboard are the least of her troubles, what with Johneen's moods, Odelia's visions, anonymous letters, wedding crashers alive and dead, and a storm brewing.

As they move through the flower beds, stooped over and filling their buckets, she steers the conversation awkwardly to Johneen.

"I hate to see her so stressed. Is everything okay?"

She expects Parker to brush off the question, but he straightens and looks at her in a way that lets her know she's struck a chord.

"Why do you ask?"

"Just . . . all brides are jittery, but she really seems on edge."

He hesitates and then looks over his shoulder to make sure there are no eavesdroppers. "Please don't mention this to anyone, all right?"

Her pulse quickening, she nods.

"Before I met Daisy, back when she was still living in Philadelphia, she ended a difficult relationship."

"With whom?"

"I don't know his name. She never wanted to tell me. Maybe she was afraid I'd . . . I don't know." He shakes his head. "He was just someone she met at a charity ball."

"In Philadelphia?"

"I think he lived in New York but traveled in the same circles." *Vastly wealthy society circles*, Bella figures.

"All I know for certain is that he was a possessive control freak. That didn't go over well with Daisy. She likes her space. When she broke up with him, he told her that if he couldn't have her, no one would. She moved to Pittsburgh to get away from him, made a fresh start. She thought she'd put it all behind her."

"But . . . ?" Bella says when he trails off, shaking his head.

"Breakups are always difficult. Lots of people say things in the heat of the moment that they don't mean."

"But you think he did mean it?"

"Lately, Daisy's been feeling as though he might be . . ." Again he trails off, as if searching for the right way to phrase it.

"Stalking her?"

"Stalking is a strong word."

"So she's seen him around?"

"No. But there were a few times when she's felt as though someone might be following her. One night last month, she came home from work and thought someone had been in her apartment."

"Did she call the police?"

"She didn't want to because nothing was missing, and she thought she might have imagined it. I insisted she file a report, but that was the end of it."

"Is he . . . does he know she's getting married?"

"We haven't made any official announcements in the press or on social media, if that's what you mean. We've tried to keep it as private as possible." Toying with the clippers in his hands, he shrugs and looks at her. "Now you know why my fiancée is on edge and why we wanted the wedding to be low-key and in a remote location but within reach of our friends. This place is perfect."

She nods. It absolutely makes sense. The Dale isn't all that far off the beaten path, but at this time of year, it might as well be a deserted island thousands of miles from civilization.

But even a deserted island is within reach if someone knows where to look.

Her mind made up, she says, "Parker, I wasn't going to mention this, but I got a strange letter about the wedding the other day."

His eyebrows shoot up above the rims of his sunglasses. She can't see his expression, but she can sense the immediate concern as she tells him about it, especially when she mentions the Lily Dale postmark.

"Can I see the letter? Do you have it?"

"It's back at the guesthouse. I'll show it to you. I'm sorry I didn't say anything right away, but I thought it was some kind of . . . I don't know, practical joke." She stops short of mentioning that she thought it might have come from Odelia, who's been having visions of danger at the wedding.

There's no reason to alarm or burden Parker with superfluous details. The information she just shared is based on something tangible.

"Have you told anyone about it?"

"Not a soul." *Yet.*

Relieved, he says, "I'd appreciate it if you didn't mention it to anyone. I just don't know whom to trust. Even among friends. I just . . . you never know."

She considers bringing up Luther, but that's complicated. Instead, she asks simply, "Do you think we should call the police?"

"I don't know. It isn't a threat. What would they do?"

"I guess . . . I guess they'd just file a report."

"And Daisy will have to know, and that will be it. She'll want to flee. Even if I can convince her to stay, she'll be a wreck."

Bella nods. He has a point.

"The wedding is just a few hours away," he continues, looking at his watch. "If we can just hold out until then, she'll have her wedding, and we'll be married, and we can escape together if need be."

"But what if he"—whoever *he* is—"shows up here?"

Parker's jaw is set. "Then I'll protect her."

Working quickly, they fill two buckets with daisies, along with delicate white Queen Anne's lace plus goldenrod and sedum. All pass the sniff test, lacking fragrance per the bride's request. As they lug their floral bounty back across Melrose Park, Bella spots Drew's car pulling up in front of Valley View.

"Who is that?" Parker asks sharply as Drew steps out of the car.

"Don't worry, he's a friend." Bella picks up her pace, relieved to see him.

Wearing jeans, work boots, and a blue flannel shirt, Drew hoists a large, metal toolbox from the trunk and starts toward the house.

"Drew!" Bella calls, and he turns.

She sees him look from her to Parker, then down at the buckets of flowers.

"This is Parker Langley," Bella says when they reach him. "Parker, this is Drew Bailey."

"I'd shake your hand, but mine are full and dirty." Parker sounds jovial, as if he hadn't just been wondering whether Drew might be a violent stalker.

"It's all right. Good to see you, Bella. I didn't even have to remind you not to call me Doctor Bailey this time."

"You're a doctor?" Parker asks.

"A veterinarian."

"Are you here to see the cat?"

"I'm here to see Bella." Again, Drew looks down at the buckets of flowers they're carrying, then shoots a questioning look at her.

"These are for the wedding."

"You . . . you're getting married?"

She frowns. "What? No! He is. Didn't I mention that I was hosting a wedding at the inn today?"

"You probably did. I must have forgotten."

She can't help but notice that he seems relieved and that his attitude toward Parker is slightly warmer as he congratulates him on the upcoming nuptials.

"Thank you. I'm a lucky man. How about you?"

"Me?"

"Are you married?"

"No."

"Divorced? Widowed?"

"No and no." Drew clears his throat. "Never married."

"Well, I highly recommend it."

"You're not married *yet*," Bella points out.

"Well, no, that's true. Who knows? Maybe Daisy and I will be absolutely miserable." Parker laughs heartily, as if it's the most absurd idea he's ever heard.

Bella wonders if he's trying to convince himself, or her and Drew.

"That looks heavy, Bella," Drew says, turning to her and reaching for the bucket. "Let me carry it for you."

"I've got it. You're already carrying your tools."

"It's not a problem. I like to be balanced." He takes it from her and they head toward the house, accompanied by a slightly sheepish-looking Parker.

"I should have offered to carry your bucket," he tells Bella. "I'm sorry. I'm distracted this morning."

"That's understandable. It's a big day."

"Well, there y'all are!" a voice calls from the porch.

Parker's cousin Virginia is sitting on the swing smoking a cigarette, casually dressed in a crisp white blouse with rolled-up sleeves, jeans, and movie-star tortoise-shell sunglasses.

She's accompanied by Frankie and Tanya, both of whom are also wearing jeans and clasping coffee mugs. Unlike Virginia, they're looking much worse for wear this morning.

Bella introduces Drew, who greets them politely, then quickly sets down the bucket of flowers to gently grab a small tabby kitten as it makes a fast break through the open door.

"Hang on there, little girl. It's not safe out here."

"How did she get out of my room?" Bella wonders. "I thought I left the door closed." Locked as well, as she tries to remember to do when there are guests in the house.

"Maybe she found the hidden passageway," Tanya suggests. Her eyes are slightly red and her voice sounds nasal, as if she has a cold or has been crying.

"How did you know about that?" Bella asks, not missing the fleeting eye contact between Parker and Virginia.

"Blue Slayton told me there are tunnels that lead downstairs and outside."

"Not outside, just to the basement," Bella amends.

"I didn't hear about any of it," Frankie says. "That's cool."

Tanya shakes her head. "I think it's creepy."

"Well, I'll bet this old house is *full* of creepy secrets." Virginia's one-syllable words stretch like warm taffy into two. "Most old houses are, especially down South where Parker and I grew up."

Parker responds with a loud sneeze into his shoulder. He plunks down his bucket and covers his mouth as he sneezes again.

"Sorry," he says, taking a white linen handkerchief from his pocket and blowing his nose. "Allergies."

"To cats or to smoke?" Frankie asks.

"Or goldenrod?" Tanya adds.

"Cats." He gestures at the kitten in Drew's arms. "They make me physically ill."

"Goldenrod does the same thing to me." Tanya casts an unhappy look at the buckets. "Are all those flowers coming inside?"

"They're for the bouquet and reception centerpieces," Bella tells her. "But we can leave out the goldenrod if you're allergic to it."

"Or we can just do an arrangement without it for her table," Parker says. "We need a splash of yellow with all that white. You know how particular Daisy is about her color scheme."

Yes, but at the expense of her guests' well-being?

Knowing her, probably.

For a short time there, in light of what Parker had shared, Bella had almost forgotten how much she dislikes the woman. The self-centered Johneen would be difficult regardless of her anxiety that a jealous, and perhaps violent, ex-boyfriend might ruin her wedding.

Remembering Odelia, she asks if her friend is here yet. No one has seen her.

Bella sighs. "She was supposed to come at seven. We have a lot to do."

"Do you need help with anything?" Frankie asks. "I'm not allergic to cats or flowers."

Stubbing out her cigarette in her empty coffee mug, Virginia chimes in that she isn't either, and she'll help, too.

"So will I, but not with the flowers," Tanya says. "Maybe it'll keep my mind off Dan and the baby. I've been up since four thirty missing them."

"Four thirty? After such a late night?" Bella asks.

"I'm used to it. That's when Emmie wakes up."

"Bless your heart." Virginia gives her shoulder a languid pat. "You'll see your little girl tomorrow. Try to enjoy the break. You deserve it. We'll be sure to keep you right busy in the meantime, won't we, Isabella?"

"If you really want to help, I can definitely find something for you all to do." Bella has to catch herself from saying y'all. Virginia's drawl is infectious. "But first, I need to go put this little girl back upstairs. You haven't seen any other kittens roaming around the house, have you? Because the back door doesn't close all the way and their mom escaped early this morning when someone went out and left it open."

"It wasn't me," Tanya tells her. "I was awake, but I stayed in bed. I was too sad about missing Emmie to get up."

Frankie rolls her eyes. "And it wasn't me. I just rolled out of bed now."

"So did I," Virginia says. "Slept like a baby. But if I had gone out, I would have been careful to close the door all the way like you told me to last night, Isabella. I'll bet even my sneezy old cousin doesn't want those poor little things running away from home, do you, Parker?"

"Of course not. And it wasn't me, either. I slept in, too. I just got up an hour ago."

"You call that sleeping in?" Ryan, the maid of honor's fiancé, materializes in the doorway. "It's not even nine o'clock yet."

"Then what are you doing up?" Frankie eyes him with an expression utterly lacking affection.

Bella isn't crazy about Ryan either, but she's noticed that Frankie seems to judge people a bit harshly. Last night, she overheard her mocking Virginia's accent and complaining under her breath to Tanya that the chicken was too salty.

It *was* too salty. And yes, Bella was undoubtedly overtired and overly sensitive.

Still, I can live without criticism from the guests this weekend, thank you very much. I'm sure I'll get more than my share from the bride and groom.

Ryan steps outside and joins the group, wearing pajama bottoms, shearling slippers, and a designer pullover. "Liz kicked me out of our room. She said my snoring was waking her up and that she needs her beauty sleep." He glances at Drew's toolbox. "Are you the handyman?"

Bella opens her mouth to correct him, but Drew, looking faintly amused, responds, "You could say that."

"Then you need to take a look at the third-floor bathroom we're sharing with the room across the hall."

"Is the shower running cold?" Bella asks. "Because it does that sometimes."

"No, it was plenty hot, but it's leaking. Unless whoever else is using it isn't bothering to turn it off all the way?"

"That would be me. I wouldn't dream of letting a faucet drip." Virginia's tone is sugary, though her expression is anything but.

Ryan shrugs and mumbles that he was merely speculating, not accusing.

"Of course you were. And my mama always said that old houses are like old men. They don't just have secrets—they have old plumbing."

Everyone, even Ryan, chuckles at that.

"I'll take a look at the bathroom," Drew offers. "But first, I need to fix the back door."

He excuses himself and heads in that direction. Bella escapes with the kitten after reminding the guests to help themselves to more coffee, fruit, and pastries in the breakfast room.

Upstairs, she finds that the door to her room is still securely closed, but the closet door is not. The panel at the back is askew, leaving a crack wide enough for a kitten to escape to the basement. To her relief, however, Chance and the rest of the litter are all accounted for.

Now she knows how little Monday got out of the bedroom and into the basement. Bella herself was down there earlier and had left the door to the kitchen open. That must have been when the kitten snuck up onto the first floor.

"That's two too many close calls for today," she tells the feline family as she moves the closet panel back into place. "You guys need to stay put for the rest of the day, okay? Just until we have the house to ourselves again. And then . . ."

And then she'll have to see about finding families interested in adopting kittens.

Bella sighs. If she thought welcoming eight kittens into her household was difficult, saying goodbye to seven of them is bound to be even harder. But there's no way they can keep them all, no matter what Max says.

She thinks of Calla, who said she might be interested in taking one. That in turn leads her to think of Blue Slayton.

Funny that he knew about Valley View's network of secret tunnels. Then again, there are no secrets in the Dale, and Pandora Feeney isn't the only busybody in their midst. With the tourists gone, even Odelia has too much time on her hands to speculate about other people's business.

As Bella told her mother-in-law, Lily Dale is just like any other small town. Yes, it's an unusual place. But there's no way—absolutely no way!—that Bella has been brainwashed into staying here.

Somehow, she'll have to convince Maleficent that there's nothing to worry about.

Wondering whether Max is awake yet, Bella heads down the hall to the train-themed room. Leona always kept it vacant in case Grant decided to show up for a visit. Now it officially belongs to Max, courtesy of Grant himself the last time he was here.

"You can have it when you come and visit if there aren't any other rooms open," Max told him.

"That's all right, buddy. I don't want to put you out of your bed."

Max shrugged. "My mom has a big bed, and she misses sleeping with someone."

The comment was pure innocence, and of course Max meant that *he*, not Grant, was the one who would share her bed, but Bella didn't dare meet Grant's gaze.

"I'll keep that in mind," he said, sounding amused.

Now Grant's "I don't want to put you out of your bed" is the phrase that rings in her ears. As much as she wants to believe it's true, she can't expect him to hang onto Valley View out of the goodness of his heart. She has to show him that it can be more than just a shabby little guesthouse. She can make it more, if he lets her give it a shot.

Chances are he will, if this wedding goes as planned. What does he have to lose?

But if anything goes drastically wrong, there's no question that he'll get rid of it as soon as possible. He might not even wait to sell it before kicking her out. *He doesn't even need to sell it*, she reminds herself. *It's not as if he needs the money. He could just decide the place is cursed, board it up, and walk away.*

Opening the door a crack, she sees that Max is sound asleep. His glasses are on the nightstand and he's sprawled on his back, legs tangled in the covers, one arm flung over the edge of the twin mattress.

Sam slept in exactly the same position.

Bella closes the door.

Yes, she does miss sleeping with someone. But she has no intention of doing it again any time in the near future.

She heads into the room across the hall where Frankie and Tanya are staying. She might as well make it up now, while they're downstairs. One less task to worry about later. Two if she cleans Virginia's temporarily vacated room as well.

It takes only a few minutes to make the beds, straighten the room, and empty the wastebasket. Ordinarily she'd run the vacuum, too, but she doesn't dare risk waking Johneen.

Upstairs, the small third-floor room is flooded with sunlight. At this time of morning, the golden beam through the dormers falls short of the water stain, so it's barely visible. She doesn't want to think about what might happen later, when the rain starts falling.

Virginia's overnight bag sits open and empty on the luggage rack. A couple of garments wrapped in dry cleaners' plastic hang from a hook on the back of the door. The rest of her clothes are presumably stashed in the bureau. Toiletries and cosmetics sit on top of it—nothing more elaborate than moisturizer, mascara, lipstick . . .

It must be nice, Bella thinks as she catches her own reflection in the mirror, *to be naturally drop-dead gorgeous.*

She herself looks windblown, and her face is ruddy. Not in a bad way, but she could probably stand to powder her nose and brush her hair before she goes back downstairs.

Why do you care? Drew Bailey isn't here to see you.

He's here to fix the door. And maybe the leaky pipe as well, though perhaps not for Bella's benefit.

Who could blame him if he'd taken one look at Virginia and been smitten?

If Drew wants to flirt with her, he's welcome to.

It's a ridiculous thought, really, because Bella can't quite fathom Drew flirting with anyone. He's much too buttoned up and serious for that . . . or is he?

She wouldn't mind finding out. Firsthand, though. Not by watching him in action with the likes of Parker Langley's cousin, no matter how much Bella likes her—and no matter how grateful she is that Virginia's around to make sure things go smoothly today.

Again foregoing the vacuum, Bella dumps a crumpled lipstick-kissed tissue from the wastebasket and makes the bed. As she tucks in the sheets, her fingers graze something wedged between the mattress and box spring.

Uh-oh. She never did get a chance to double-check the room for Lego bricks before Virginia came upstairs yesterday.

But when she lifts the mattress to peer underneath, she realizes that it isn't a stray child's toy.

Lying on the box spring is a very real-looking pistol.

Her thoughts careen. The last time she saw a gun, it was aimed at her.

This is different, though. Virginia isn't a killer . . . is she?

Chapter Nine

Bella crosses the carpet from her bed to the window and back to the bed. Round trip, round trip, round trip . . .

She's been pacing for fifteen minutes now, wondering what she should do about the gun and realizing there's nothing she *can* do.

For all she knows, Virginia carries it for her own protection and has a permit.

For all she knows, it isn't even Virginia's.

Maybe another guest left it, or maybe it's been there for months. Years. She's made the bed countless times but never lifted the mattress off the box spring before. Why would she? She probably would have found it before now, though.

But . . . well, it might be a toy—Jiffy's toy, most likely, hidden amid the Lego bricks because Max knew Bella wouldn't like it . . .

Except it didn't feel like a toy.

She can't stomach the thought of her son innocently playing with Lego bricks in a room with a loaded gun.

Unless it belongs to Virginia.

Why would she have it?

In Bella's world, women don't walk around carrying pistols, but maybe in Virginia's world, they do. To each her own.

It's not like there's an official Valley View antiweaponry policy. There aren't "No Guns" signs taped up alongside the "No Smoking" signs. For all Bella knows, plenty of armed guests have slept under this roof over the summer.

It's just . . .

With all that's gone on, she's concerned.

Concerned . . . and suspicious.

If there's an uncomplicated way to ask Virginia about it, Bella hasn't thought of it, and she shouldn't waste any more time wondering.

For now, she'll have to let it go. Let it go, file it away, watch her step, and Max's.

Descending the stairs, she hears Virginia's drawl in the breakfast room, telling Ryan to wipe up the coffee he sloshed over the rim of his cup.

"And pick up those crumbs you dropped on the floor while you're at it. This isn't a damn barn," she scolds him.

"Well, listen to you. Do you always talk to strangers in that bossy way?"

"I do when they deserve it."

"What are you going to do if I don't listen?"

"Trust me, sugar, you don't want to find out."

"Trust *me*, maybe I do."

She responds with a perfunctory laugh—sharp and not the least bit flirtatious.

Then Bella hears Ryan ask, "Whose ring is that?"

"You mean this?"

Unable to see them, Bella is curious.

"Yes," Ryan says. "Are you married?"

"Now if I were married, would I be wearing my wedding ring around my neck on a chain?"

"Nah. If you were married, you might as well be wearing a ball and chain."

"Your Liz is one lucky gal," Virginia says dryly. "I need a smoke."

"Smoking will kill you."

"A lot of things will kill you, sugar. Choose your poison. I've chosen mine." A chair scrapes, and a moment later, Bella is face-to-face with her in the doorway.

"You look like you've seen a—well, around here, I guess you might expect to see a ghost, right?" Virginia chuckles. "But you look like you've seen something."

Oh, I have.

"I'm just . . . I—I'm—"

Why, oh why, can't she ever be graceful under pressure?

"Is everything all right?"

"Yes, everything's fine. Just busy."

"I won't get in your way, then. Holler if you need a hand."

With that, Virginia heads out onto the porch, and Bella makes her way to the kitchen.

Drew!

She'd momentarily forgotten all about him, but there he is, kneeling in front of the closed screen door. It doesn't seem to matter whether he's wearing a lab coat or work boots, holding a stethoscope or screwdriver. He always manages to look capable and masculine. She is, in this particular moment, very happy he's here.

"How's it going?" she asks.

"Already fixed."

"Really?"

He nods and gets to his feet. "Try it."

Bella opens the door and lets it close. It slowly swings shut and fastens with a loud click. Giving it a slight push and then a harder one, she nods her approval when it stays closed.

"Thank you. Now as long as Chance and the kittens don't figure out another escape route, we should be . . ."

Gazing out into the yard, she spots a stumpy, fur-tufted gray tail just as it disappears behind a barrel planter filled with white and yellow mums.

"Oh, no! I think I spoke too soon." She quickly opens the door and steps outside. "I think I just spotted a kitten out there, and I'm hoping it's not one of ours." She hurries across the yard with Drew on her heels.

Chairs are scattered on the grass, waiting to be arranged into neat rows for today's wedding. In her haste, Bella trips over one.

"Whoa!" Drew, behind her, reaches out to catch her as she starts to fall.

"Sorry. I'm not the most graceful woman in the world."

"Or even in the yard." He smiles down at her, holding her steady.

That's the nice thing about Drew. You think he's always dead serious, but then he pops out with an unexpected quip and you remember that somewhere deep down inside, he's just . . .

A guy.

A nice, normal guy.

A guy like . . .

No, not like Sam. Sam was chatty and poetic and he wore his heart on his sleeve. Drew is the opposite.

But Sam would approve, Bella tells herself before wondering what, exactly, requires his approval. The local veterinarian catching her before she face-plants in the dirt? Yes, of course Sam would approve.

A handsome, rugged guy holding his wife so close she can identify the brand of his soap?

Max telling another guy—less rugged, but no less handsome— that he should share her bed?

Yeah, not so much.

She reluctantly pulls away and breaks eye contact.

Drew is big and strong, and for a moment there, she felt safer than she has in a long while. Funny, since somehow she's now even more aware of the danger of . . . *falling*.

How long has it been since someone hugged her?

Max doesn't count. He's smaller than she is, and she's the one who does the hugging.

"Is that the kitten you were chasing?" Drew asks. A few yards away, in a sunny patch of grass, curled into a drowsy, little blue ball, lies the little guy she saw in the garden earlier.

"That's him. Not one of ours, but he's been hanging around since yesterday. Hey, there, fella. Are you okay?"

The kitten, no bigger than Bella's fist, opens kiwi-colored eyes. They're big and round, gazing up in alarm, as if he's belatedly realized he might be in mortal danger. He rolls over, but Drew scoops him up before he can scamper away.

"Let's take a look at you, little Blue."

"He *is* blue, isn't he?" Bella says. "Max and Jiffy saw him yesterday, but I'd never heard of a blue cat. I thought they made it up."

"He's a Russian Blue, although I'm guessing he's not purebred." Drew strokes his fur with one gentle finger.

"Aw, he looks like he's wearing a bowtie," Bella notices, seeing the angular crest of white fur beneath his chin when he lifts it to nuzzle Drew's hand. "You're a dapper little chap, aren't you?"

Drew sets him gently on the ground again and he scampers away.

"Wait, what are you doing?"

"He might have a mama cat out here looking for him."

"What if he doesn't?"

"Then finders keepers."

"No way. I can't take in another kitten. I need homes for the ones we already have."

"Well, hopefully, the little chap's mother will come back for him. But in case she doesn't do that any time soon, you might want to put out a bowl of water and some kibble. Maybe set out some old towels in a crate or one of those big plastic tubs."

"Seriously?" She looks around, imagining a tub full of towels and a kitten in the middle of the Maynard-Langley wedding. That might be taking the shabby a little too far.

"If mama cat doesn't show up, he'll have a safe place to nest."

"Good morning," a voice calls, and she and Drew turn to see Luther Ragland striding into the yard.

He's balancing a long, bulky object—a chuppah?—on one broad shoulder.

Tall and handsome, with dark skin and just a touch of salt-and-pepper in his close-cropped hair, Luther always reminds Bella of the actor Morgan Freeman playing a cop in a movie. Only this is real life, and Luther really is a cop—a retired detective.

"You can put it right over here," she says, hurrying toward the designated patch of lawn.

He sets it down with a huff. "I got your message. I was up in Canada last night, and I had my phone turned off."

"That's what I figured."

"Sorry I got home too late to call you back. What's going on? Is everything okay?"

She hesitates, not wanting to say anything in front of Drew. "I just had a question, but I . . . figured it out."

"Are you sure?"

"I'm positive," she lies.

He shrugs and looks around. "Hey, where's your friend Odelia?"

"Good question." In the bustle of activity, Bella had again forgotten all about her.

"Isn't she supposed to be here?"

"Yes, she is." Looking toward the house next door, Bella spots Millicent sitting on the back step. She's still dressed in what Bella hoped was a traveling outfit early this morning. A book lies open on her lap, but she isn't reading it.

No, she's staring straight at Bella.

She must have seen everything.

Not that *everything* was *anything*, but still . . . Drew, holding her in his arms, even for a few seconds, couldn't have made Sam's mother very happy.

Bella fights the urge to call out something like, "Don't worry, it was nothing!"

Whatever it was—nothing, something, *whatever*—it's Bella's business. If she wants to hug a man in her own backyard, she can. And if she wants to . . .

If she wants to be brainwashed by a religious cult—which she doesn't and isn't—but if she wants to, she can.

Oblivious to Millicent's presence, Drew asks Luther about the object on the ground.

"It's part of a chuppah. The rest is in my car. How about helping me unload it?"

"Sure," Drew says agreeably.

As they head toward the street, Bella escapes to the house, leaving Millicent to brood on Odelia's steps and the kitten to snooze in her morning glories.

In the kitchen, she nearly crashes into Parker. Seeing the urgent look on his face, she has a sinking feeling.

"Is everything all right?"

"No, everything isn't all right. I can't find Daisy's wedding ring."

"She lost her ring?"

"Not *her* ring."

"I'm sorry, I thought you said—"

"I haven't given it to her yet," Parker cuts her off curtly, "because we aren't married yet. And we won't be able to *be* married unless I find the ring."

Bella's overcluttered brain digests this, and she asks him where he last saw it.

"It was in my suitcase. Zipped into an inside pocket."

"Just the loose ring? Could it have slipped into a hole in the lining or something?"

"No, of course it wasn't loose. It was in a box from the jeweler," he says as if she should have known. He goes on to impatiently describe the box—turquoise, from Tiffany—and the ring—eighteen-karat-gold band encircled with diamonds—as if to help her differentiate it from other stray jewelry she might have stumbled across.

Insisting she hasn't seen it, she tells him she's certain it hasn't been stolen.

"Did you unpack your bag when you got here?"

"My clothes, yes. But not the ring. I didn't want Daisy to see it."

"But you're sure it was there, in your bag, when you got here?"

"Of course I'm sure."

"You saw it when you unpacked?"

After the slightest hesitation, he shakes his head. "No, but it was there. Someone stole it from our suite."

Her thoughts fly to Virginia. Earlier, Ryan had mentioned that she was wearing a ring around her neck.

And, face it—the fact that she's toting a gun isn't making her seem quite so sweet and innocent.

"What about Virginia?"

"What about her?"

Bella shifts uncomfortably under his gaze, not wanting to sound accusatory. "She has a ring around her neck on a chain. Maybe—"

"Are you suggesting that my own *cousin* stole the ring?"

"No! I just thought maybe you'd given it to her for safekeeping or something."

"Don't you think I'd remember doing that?"

"I . . . it's a stressful time." Plus, the drinks were strong last night. He hadn't seemed inebriated, but you never know.

"The ring Virginia wears belonged to our grandparents," Parker tells her grudgingly, as if it's none of her business. "She was Granny's favorite. So no, she didn't steal Daisy's ring. But there are all sorts of people on the premises who might have. Your handyman and . . ." He gestures at the window. "Who is that man?"

She follows his gaze to Luther and Drew, assembling the chuppah on the lawn.

"*That man* is my friend Luther. He's a police officer, so if you really think someone stole your ring, I'll call him in here right now."

"He's a police officer? Then why is he here, putting up a tent?"

"Because Odelia asked him to help. And he's actually a retired detective. Do you want me to get him?"

He hesitates. "He might want to go into our room to look around and . . . I don't know, dust it for fingerprints or something. Daisy is finally sound asleep. Let's hold off on that."

She nods, understanding his reluctance to wake the sleeping tigress. "Have you kept the door to the suite locked, whether or not you're in the room?"

"What do *you* think?" he shoots back. "Wasn't I just telling you"—he lowers his voice—"that I'm concerned someone might have followed us here? Of course the door is locked."

"Who's been in the room besides you and Johneen?"

"Not a soul, unless you have? You're the one who does all the housekeeping around here, right? You must have a key."

"I do," Bella agrees stiffly, "and I can assure you that I'm no thief."

"I didn't mean to imply that you were. Look . . . I'm sorry. Maybe I'm letting my imagination get carried away. Maybe I . . . I suppose I could have left it at home. I packed quickly, and I was running late for my flight, trying to do a million things at once. You know how that goes."

"Like I said, it's a stressful time."

"I'm going to try to get ahold of the neighbor who has the key to my apartment," he decides, "and have him go see if it's there. In the meantime, let's just keep this between us, all right?"

For the second time today, Bella agrees to keep Parker's secret. It isn't until he's left the room that she allows a troubled frown to replace the agreeable expression on her face.

She can't help but recall that she'd heard someone slip out the door early this morning—much too early for any of the guests to be up. What if an intruder had snuck into the house and right back out again with the wedding ring?

He'd have needed a key to get past the locked doors. Bella has two sets of duplicates to the front door and the doors to the individual rooms. She usually carries one set with her. The other is kept in the top drawer of her nightstand. The same drawer where she stashed the note.

Heart racing, she heads upstairs. Opening the drawer, she sees that the note is still there, along with the set of keys. But that doesn't mean someone didn't borrow them and put them back. Unlike the original antique keys to the guesthouse rooms, these new modern keys could easily have been duplicated.

Unless . . .

What if the intruder came up through the basement tunnel, crawled through the panel in her closet, and—

It could even have happened while she was asleep.

Bella's skin prickles as she imagines a prowler stealthily creeping through her dark bedroom.

A prowler—who?

A stranger? One of the guests?

Tanya's words echo back to her, then Odelia's.

Blue Slayton told me there are tunnels that lead downstairs and outside . . .

Why does he have to hang around here now, of all times?

Why, indeed?

But if he's behind the theft, what's his motive? Odelia said he has plenty of money. Or is that merely the perception because his father is a wealthy celebrity? Maybe they're estranged, like Johneen and her family. Maybe . . .

Something else comes back to Bella.

Johneen had a fling with Blue back in college. For her, it seemed casual, but what if he never got over her? What if he's the one who's stalking her?

And Hellerman—he, too, could be trying to sabotage the wedding, motivated by unrequited lust or love, or plain old spite.

I have to tell Luther, she thinks, pocketing the keys and hurrying back downstairs. *I don't care what I promised Parker. Luther should know what's going on here.*

Outside, she finds Luther and Drew attempting to drape white fabric around the poles of the awning. It snaps and billows in the breeze.

Millicent is still sitting on Odelia's back steps, chaperoning the proceedings from afar.

Remembering that Odelia was supposed to be here hours ago, Bella asks the men if they've seen her.

"Not yet, but you know Odelia. The world is her shiny object," Luther says with a shrug, consulting the instruction manual.

"What do you mean?" Drew asks.

"You know . . . she's a little bit flighty," Luther tells him. "Easily distracted."

That's true, but when Bella needs her, she's always come through.

Odelia knows she's up to her eyeballs in in wedding preparations, and the clock is ticking away. If her mother-in-law wasn't posted like a sentry next door, Bella would have long since run over there after her friend failed to answer her phone. But Odelia is scarce, and so are the guests who earlier volunteered their services. Either they all went back to bed, or they found something better to do.

"Actually, it looks like she has company, or a client," Luther says, indicating Odelia's back steps with a jerk of his head.

"You mean the lady sitting on her steps, looking daggers at us?"

At Drew's comment, Bella darts a sidewise glance at Millicent. It's impossible to get a read on her mood.

"I wouldn't say *daggers*."

"Maybe not at *you*," Drew tells Luther, "but I'm definitely getting daggers."

"That figures," Bella mutters.

"Who is she?"

"My mother-in-law." She quickly explains about Millicent's surprise visit and how Odelia is playing hostess since the guesthouse was full. She neglects to mention the part about her motive to rescue Bella and Max from an evil cult.

"Is that why she's glaring at you, then?" Drew asks her. "Because there's no room at the inn?"

"I thought she was glaring at *you*," Luther says.

"She's glaring at both me and Bella."

Luther looks from Drew to Bella and back again, wearing a thoughtful expression.

He's wondering if something is going on between us.

As is her mother-in-law, apparently.

Let her wonder. We haven't done anything wrong.

Even if they *had* done . . . *something*, it wouldn't be wrong. Tragic as her circumstances might be, she's no longer a married woman. Drew is a single man. A romance between them couldn't possibly violate any reasonable person's ethics—not that there is, or would be, a romance, she reminds herself.

Realizing she's staring at Drew—and that he's staring right back—Bella hastily turns her attention back to the matter at hand, which is . . . which is . . .

What the heck is it again?

She can feel Drew's gaze still fixed on her. Her face is flushed.

"Are you guys done with this?" she asks, gesturing at the chuppah.

"Almost."

Good. The moment they finish, she's going to have a private little conference with Luther. She heads over to a shady corner of the yard, where the buckets of flowers are waiting to be arranged for the wedding. She'd been planning to delegate the task to Frankie, Tanya, and Virginia, but she might as well work on it until they reappear.

She grabs a couple of Queen Anne's lace blooms from the bucket and shoves them into a mason jar, clumsily bending one of the stems in her shaky hands.

Sneaking a glance at Drew, she's relieved to see that his back is to her now. He's listening to something Luther is telling him—about the lake, judging by the way he's gesturing at the rippling, blue water. And her mother-in-law is looking down at the book in her lap, presumably reading.

Nerves calming, Bella sets aside the ruined flower and inserts another Queen Anne's lace blossom, then a few more, admiring the airy effect. She sets the jar aside. Only one more to go, and a bridal bouquet, before she can move on to the next task. And there are many. *Too many.* Where the heck is Odelia?

And what the heck is going on around here? Where's the ring, and who wrote the letter, and why does Virginia have a gun?

She has to tell Luther—

"Mom?"

Looking up, she sees Max on the back porch. He's barefoot, wearing pajamas and glasses.

"Good morning, sweetie. There's cereal in the—"

"Doctor Drew! And Luther!" Max lights up, seeing them. He darts down the steps and across the yard toward them.

Turning, Bella sees that her mother-in-law has spotted Max and is on her feet. She looks elated, making a beeline for her grandson, wobbling in her pumps on the uneven ground.

"Max! Look at how you've grown!"

He turns toward Millicent and his eyes widen. *"Grandma?"*

She throws her arms around him as Bella hurries over to join them. She's been careful never to say a negative word about Sam's mother in front of her son. Even with Sam, she kept her opinions about his mother to herself for the most part.

"What are you doing here?" Max's face is muffled against Millicent's tweed.

"I missed you. I was so disappointed when you and Mommy didn't come to stay with me in Chicago."

"You *were*?"

Millicent rests both hands on Max's shoulders and looks into his earnest little face. "I would like nothing better than for you and your mom to come to Chicago, Max."

"And Chance and Spidey?"

"And . . ." For the first time, Millicent acknowledges Bella, asking, "What does that mean?"

"Chance and Spidey are his pets. Cats. And don't forget the rest of the kittens, Max. There are seven more," she informs Millicent.

"You have . . . *nine* . . . cats?"

Relishing the look of displeasure on her face, Bella nods. After all, it's true, for the moment.

"Ten, kind of," Max tells his grandmother. "There's a blue one who lives out here in the yard, and he wants to come in, only mom doesn't believe me and Jiffy that he's really there."

"I do now, Max. I saw him. He's a cute little chap in a blue tuxedo with a white bowtie. Doctor Bailey says he's a Russian—"

She breaks off, struck by something.

"He's Russian?"

"He's a Russian Blue," Bella says slowly. She doesn't believe in this stuff, but . . .

"I'm going to make that his name, by the way," Max is saying. "Okay, Mom?"

"Hmm?"

"I'm going to call him Li'l Chap, like you said."

"What did I say?" she asks absently.

"You said he's a li'l chap. Where is he?"

"He's . . . he's taking a nap in Odelia's garden," she tells him, her thoughts whirling.

The kitten—a *Blue*—is suddenly hanging around here just like Blue Slayton. Can it possibly be a sign from Spirit?

"Can he come inside?"

"Hmm?" she murmurs, thinking that of course the cat isn't a sign. But that doesn't mean Blue isn't guilty.

Or maybe the cat *is* a sign from the Spirit world—and it still doesn't mean Blue is guilty.

Blue . . .

Sam called her Bella Blue. It wouldn't be the first time Bella had thought he was greeting her from beyond the grave . . .

"Mom!"

She snaps back to reality. "Sorry, Max . . . No, he can't come in. Doctor Bailey thinks his mom is looking for him."

"Doctor Drew!" her son bellows across the yard. "If Li'l Chap's mom doesn't find him, can we keep him?"

Drew grins. "That's up to *your* mom, Max."

Bella notices that both he and Luther are keeping their distance from Maleficent. They're still over by the chuppah, now moving rented tables around with purpose, though she has no idea what that purpose is.

"Mom, can Li'l Chap stay if he doesn't have a mom?"

"We'll see."

"We will? We'll see?"

"I mean, no! No, he can't stay, Max."

"Where on earth do you keep all those cats?" Millicent asks, forcing a smile as though she finds all those felines charming instead of repugnant.

Max shrugs, gesturing at the house. "We have a lot of space. When people are staying here, all the kitties live in mom's room. So she doesn't really get lonely anymore."

Millicent flicks a glance in Drew's direction, then at Bella. "No, I don't suppose she does."

"Do you want to meet them, Grandma?"

"The . . . *cats*?" She seems to choke a little every time she says the word, as if she has a fur ball lodged in her throat.

"Only one is a cat. Chance. The rest are tiny kittens. They were tinier before, and they're still tiny now, but not as tiny."

"Yes, well . . . that seems to happen with boys, too. I would love to meet your pets, Max. Will you make the introductions?"

"Yes, only they don't speak English." Max is earnest.

To her credit, so is Millicent when she responds, "And I don't speak feline. But I'm sure we'll manage."

As Max grabs her hand to lead her into the house, she glances over her shoulder at Bella.

Fully expecting to see her looking smug, Bella is shocked to see that she isn't.

She just looks . . .

Happy.

Like any grandmother doting on a grandson.

They disappear into the house.

A lump of emotion seems to have lodged in Bella's throat and another has made her eyes so moist that if she blinks, tears might spill down her cheeks.

It's been a long time since she cried over anything. Even Sam.

If he were here, he'd be glad to see his mom bonding with Max and glad to see Bella tolerating her presence. He'd probably be amused by the cult assumption and . . . everything else. He'd advise his wife to lighten up, about everything.

For his sake, she vows to try.

She turns to Luther and Drew, who have given up their urgent table-arrangement pretense.

"Guys?" she calls, heading toward them. "I could really use a quick hand with this wedding stuff, if you're willing."

Drew meets her halfway on the lawn. "Whatever you need. I've got about fifteen minutes before I have to get back to the animal hospital."

"My tennis game isn't until this afternoon, and I'll do anything except hair," Luther tells her. "I don't do hair. I barely *have* hair."

"And here I was going to ask you to do a French braid twist for the bride." Bella manages a smile at him as if nothing is amiss, because maybe, hopefully, nothing is.

She busies Drew hosing out several large coolers that were used last night and asks Luther to help her with the flowers.

"What's going on?" he asks in a low voice as soon as Drew turns his back.

Beneath the rush of spray from the nearby garden hose, she tells him first about the note. He doesn't seem particularly concerned, even after she explains that the bride has a spurned lover lurking in her past. In fact, he nods knowingly at that news.

"Happens all the time. Whenever a couple gets married, chances are there's a jealous, jilted ex. Or a lovelorn friend with a crush," he goes on, ticking them off on his fingers, "or a relative who's convinced the bride or groom can do better—a father who thinks his baby girl is marrying a gold digger, a mother who has no desire for a daughter-in-law . . ."

Naturally, Bella thinks of Millicent. *Fair enough*. But even she didn't resort to trying to sabotage Bella's wedding to Sam.

"I wouldn't give this a second thought. For all you know, it's just some kid playing a prank," he says so mildly that she wonders if she's overreacting, even to the gun.

She wonders if he'd change his mind if she mentioned the missing wedding ring. But before she can break her promise to Parker and fill him in about that and everything else, Drew reappears to say that the ice chests are ready, and he'd better get back to the animal hospital.

"I'll come back after office hours, though, to see how things are going."

"Do you mean with the wedding?" she asks, surprised.

"The wedding and the upstairs plumbing. I never had a chance to look. And I'll check on little chap out back, too. I've been keeping an eye out for his mama, but there's no sign of her. If he's on his own, he'll need some help. There are foxes and bears around here. I know your hands are full, so I'll see what I can do."

She probably should protest, but she doesn't. She wants to see him again, and not purely for the kitten's sake.

"I'll head out with you," Luther says. "I've got some stuff to do."

"Isn't it a little late for golf?" Drew asks.

"Not for tennis. I've got an indoor court reserved this afternoon. Do you play?"

"Me?" Drew shakes his head. "No time for playing these days. I'm just going to go grab my toolbox and then I'll walk out front with you."

"No time for playing," Luther says in a low voice as they watch Drew disappear inside, "but time to help a pretty lady with kittens and broken screens. I like his style."

"Luther, it's not like that."

He gives her a sideways glance. "Not like what?"

"You know exactly what I mean."

"And you know exactly what I mean. It's all good. Now how can I help you with this wedding? Because I'd be glad to run a couple of errands for you while I run a few of my own."

Flustered, she comes up with a couple of things she needs for the wedding. Not only can she use the help, but she doesn't want to hear any more about her little flirtation—if that's what it is—with Drew. Only a minute later, when the two men have walked away, does she remember she wanted to tell Luther about the ring and the gun.

Should she chase him down?

No. He'll be back a little later, and she can pull him aside. Or maybe everything will have been resolved by then.

Stepping back into the house, she finds the first floor still deserted. But the guests are stirring overhead. From the foot of the stairs, she can hear water running, a hair dryer blowing. Footsteps creak the old floorboards, descending from the third floor. A moment later, Virginia appears in the hall at the top of the stairs. She starts down, catches sight of Bella, and pauses slightly before continuing down.

"Hello again, Bella." Everything about her is casual—her tone, her expression, her posture, even the way she's holding a fresh pack of cigarettes in one hand, slapping the end against her opposite palm, packing the tobacco.

But there might be a barely perceptible note of tension in the air. Or is it Bella's imagination?

"Going outside for a cigarette?" Bella asks, completely casual as well.

"I am. And then I'm at your service. Whatever you need."

"Thanks."

About to step outside, Virginia pauses with her hand on the doorknob. "Oh, and Bella? It was so sweet of you to make up my room with all you have going on. Thank you."

"You're welcome."

She knows, Bella thinks as Virginia steps outside, closing the door behind her. *She knows I found the gun under her mattress.*

Or is that just more paranoia?

Thoughts muddled, Bella is rooted to the spot, staring absently upstairs. There's a gun up there.

There's also Max, mingling with Millicent and the kittens.

Tempted to check on them, she puts her foot on the bottom step.

What if Millicent starts talking to her about cults in front of Max?

What if Max has already been brainwashed by Millicent and asks if they can move to Chicago after all?

What if Millicent asks Bella point-blank if she's involved with Drew Bailey or has any intention of dating him, or anyone else, ever?

Now isn't a good time to discuss any of that.

Max is fine. Of course he's fine. She shouldn't go up . . . should she?

Sunshine spills through the stained-glass window on the stairway, casting a rainbow across the landing.

Sam's voice pops into her head.

Radiant, isn't it, Bella Blue?

He's only in her imagination, of course, but it's what he would say.

Wait a minute.

I love snow and all the forms of the radiant frost . . .

Snow and frost are radiant, according to Sam, and Percy Bysshe Shelley.

But the prism on the stairs is also radiant, Bella thinks, toying with the tourmaline pendant around her neck. Again, she hears Sam's voice, but he isn't talking about rainbows.

Don't go up there, Bella. Max is fine. Let him be. Let them bond.

As much as she longs to believe Sam is here, talking to her, she knows better. It's just her own inner voice, sounding like Sam. But she should listen to it.

Her foot comes down off the step, and she starts to turn away, toward the kitchen.

Something catches her eye, and she turns back.

Was that . . . ?

For a second, she sees nothing and is certain she was mistaken.

Then she tilts her head, and the angle of the sunlight changes, catching gossamer strands of silk.

About halfway up the stairs, a large, delicate web is strung from the banister to the wall, with a small, black spider at its center.

Not unusual in an old house, by any means. But the design is so intricate that it must have taken a long time to spin.

Virginia descended that stairway a few minutes ago. How can it be intact?

Maybe . . . maybe she somehow didn't shatter the web?

No, that would be impossible. It's like a net stretched across the steps, waist-high and so close to the stair tread that you'd have to limbo beneath it to avoid breaking the lowest strands.

Well, then, maybe the spider is just . . . an exceptionally fast web-spinner?

Anything is possible.

Yet, staring at it, Bella can't help but remember Odelia's spider vision.

Spirit doesn't like this. Not one bit.

Chapter Ten

When the phone rings an hour later, Bella is in the kitchen slicing still-warm baguettes, thinking about spiders and rainbows and guns.

"Good morning, Valley View Guesthouse," she answers as always, though she's certain it's Odelia at last. She's pretty much the only one who calls the house phone postseason.

"Good morning, Isabella," says the one other person who regularly dials this number.

For a change, Grant Everard's deep, familiar voice doesn't sound as if it's coming from a remote part of the planet. He's called her from mountaintops and deserts and the sea. Today, however, he's calling from his apartment in New York City, having flown in last night from New Zealand.

"Business or pleasure?"

"Both, as always," he says. "How is everything going there?"

"Busy. The wedding is today."

"That's why I'm calling. I need you to snap as many photos as you can, and we'll use them for an advertising spread to showcase the guesthouse as a wedding venue."

Her heart leaps. He's taking this even more seriously than she expected.

"Maybe some video, too, for the new website," he adds, as if the site is a done deal. "Got it?"

"Got it!"

Efficient as always, he thanks her and tells her to have a good day. As she hangs up, she realizes she forgot to mention the hot water situation. Maybe he'll want her to hire a plumber.

Should she call him back?

But that would just remind him that this is an old house, and if he keeps it, the plumbing will need to be replaced, and the furnace, and the wiring . . .

The door opens, and Odelia bustles into the kitchen with several shopping bags. Tall, paper-shrouded bread loaves poke from the top of one.

"Sorry I'm late!" She stops short, looking in dismay at the baguettes on the cutting board. "You already got them? I thought I was supposed to pick them up."

"You were, but the bakery always sells out early, and I didn't know where you were."

"So you went? But you have so many other things to do. I could have done it."

You were supposed to, but you didn't.

Aloud, she says simply, "I sent Luther. He's also going to go buy more liquor for the wedding and drop it off later. We used a lot more than I expected last night."

"Well, that's because we had more guests than we expected."

"It worked out well in the end," Bella says with a shrug, not in the mood to talk about Calla's plus-one. "Everyone had a great time."

"Did Johnny notice the mismatched plate?"

"Nope."

"Really?" Odelia seems surprised—and disappointed. The one she'd brought over for Blue to use had been chipped, just as she'd promised, and made of inelegant brown pottery. Clearly, she hoped Johneen would put up a fuss and ask him to leave.

Maybe her attitude toward Blue Slayton has less to do with his breaking her granddaughter's heart and more to do with . . . something else. Does Odelia suspect him of something?

"Where is everyone else?" she asks Bella.

"They're helping me," Bella tells her, wanting to add, *"Like you were supposed to."*

Frankie and Tanya are outside arranging folding chairs into rows and tying white satin bows onto the backs. Liz and Amanda are in the breakfast room folding napkins and polishing silverware. Ryan, Charlie, and Hellerman are at the beach shoveling sand into white paper bags for the reception luminaria.

After her cigarette and a whispered conversation with Parker in the breakfast room—undoubtedly about the missing ring, unless she was telling him about Bella snooping through her room—Virginia asked Bella what she could do. Her cheerful smile didn't quite reach her eyes, and Parker seemed morose as he trudged back up the stairs. Bella sent Virginia to buy more white votive candles for the wedding. Those, too, ran short last night when the party ran long.

Calla is down the street picking up the wedding cake from Paula Drumm—prominent local medium during the season, skilled pastry chef the other ten months of the year. "I used to babysit for her sons when they were little. Now Dylan and Ethan are in high school," she told Bella on her way out the door, then added, "Hey, do you know where Gammy is?"

"No, but she was supposed to be here by now."

"Maybe she's still sulking," Calla said.

With too much on her mind to get involved in their private family business, Bella pretended not to know what she was talking about, and Calla didn't elaborate.

Now, as Odelia begins unpacking the shopping bags onto the already cluttered counter, she finds herself tempted to confide at least part of the story about Johneen's jealous ex, the missing ring, and the letter.

Luther had almost convinced her to let it all go, but there's a nagging doubt in the back of her mind.

What if there really is something to it? What if, by mentioning it to Odelia, she's able to jar a more concrete wedding premonition? What if Odelia can shed some additional light on Blue?

As much as Bella wants to disregard those visions, there's a part of her that might, just might, believe. Just a little. Just . . . right now.

She watches the ordinarily chatty Odelia plunk a jar of olives onto the counter, then a can of mixed nuts.

"So . . . where have you been?" she asks, setting aside the bread knife.

"I told you, I went to the store."

"Right, but it doesn't even open until nine." Realizing she sounds accusatory, Bella softens her tone. "It's just . . . you said you were coming over at seven."

"I wanted to, but I couldn't."

Odelia doesn't sound like her usual chipper self, and she certainly doesn't look it. Clad in a black sweater and charcoal pin-striped trousers, she lacks her usual splash of mismatched color. Even her hair, pulled back in a velvet headband, seems a shade less vibrant, with some gray mixed in.

"I didn't mean to sound critical, Odelia. It's okay if you were too tired to get up early. I've got it all under control, and the guests are pitching in to help."

"No, it wasn't that." Odelia tosses a couple of boxes of crackers onto the counter, then wads up the empty shopping bag and tosses it toward the waste can. It misses by a mile. "I didn't sleep last night."

"Because you were upset about Calla and Blue? Or about what Spirit's warning about the wedding? Or maybe you just drank too much caffeinated tea yesterday?"

"All of the above." Odelia stoops to pick up the shopping bag and throws it away. "Except the last one."

"What exactly is it about Blue that you don't like?"

"I don't trust him. Never have, never will."

"Based on . . . ?"

She shrugs. "He isn't trustworthy."

"People grow up. Or they change." Bella thinks of Millicent upstairs playing with Max and the kittens.

Or maybe she isn't. Maybe she left after the first few minutes and didn't say goodbye.

Or maybe she's still up there but is pumping Max for information about the cult, or searching for evidence.

Bella opens her mouth to ask Odelia if she's had any contact with Maleficent today, but Odelia is in the mood to wax on about her own nemesis.

"If I thought Blue Slayton could make my granddaughter happy, then believe me, I wouldn't be so disturbed to see her with him again, no matter how much I adore Jacy."

"But maybe Blue isn't so bad. Maybe you can't see his positive qualities because you're so fond of Jacy."

"I've watched them grow up. Jacy has character. Nobody ever handed *him* anything." Emphasis meant to imply that it's the opposite with Blue. "Everything Jacy has, everything he's achieved, has been hard-won. He's overcome some major challenges in this life. In others, too."

Bella nods, well aware that Odelia—according to Odelia herself—has been reincarnated many times over the centuries. Clearly, she believes the same about Jacy. And about Calla, whom she once mentioned previously lived on earth as an Egyptian princess and a Viking warrior.

"A man like Jacy will always be strong. A man like Blue . . ."

"Is weak?" Bella asks when she doesn't complete the thought.

"You said it, not me."

"But I didn't mean it that way. I barely know Blue Slayton."

I have no idea what he's capable of. He might be a cheat, a prowler, a thief, maybe even dangerous.

He'd been involved with Johneen in college, but it was a casual fling, and it wasn't behind Calla's back—according to Johneen, anyway. Had she played it down for Parker's sake? Or had it meant more to Blue than it had to her?

"I love my granddaughter," Odelia says, "but she doesn't always have solid judgment."

Bella chooses her words carefully. "At Calla's age, who does have solid judgment? She's only—how old? Twenty-six? Twenty-seven?"

"Twenty-eight."

Hmm. At that age, Bella was married to Sam, head over heels in love and certain of their future together. But not everyone is so lucky . . .

Or unlucky.

But this isn't about Bella and Sam.

"Calla reminds me too much of myself when I was young, and of my daughter Stephanie—her mom," Odelia is saying. "Sometimes, our emotions can overpower our Spirit guides, and we miss important messages. I just don't want Calla to make the same mistakes Stephanie and I did."

"Everyone makes mistakes."

"They shouldn't make the same one twice. She should know better about Blue."

"Do you think Spirit is telling her something and she's not listening?"

"Could be," Odelia says. "But Spirit is certainly telling me, and I'm telling her, and no, she's not listening."

Is Spirit also trying to tell Bella herself something? Or is she letting Odelia's prejudice, and the power of suggestion, taint her own judgment?

Most days, she resists buying into the Lily Dale mentality. Most days, she tolerates her friend's strong opinions without a problem and is sometimes even charmed by them. But today . . .

She's concerned about the wedding, and her patience is wearing thin. Yet she manages to stay—or at least *sound*—reasonable.

"Sometimes, even when you care about someone, you have to let them figure things out for themselves. I didn't have a mom or even a grandmother to give me advice, but even if I had, I probably still would have made my own choices, good or bad."

"You made good ones, Bella."

"Not always. We live and learn, especially from our mistakes."

"Some mistakes are more serious than others. Ending a relationship with the right person, going back to the wrong person . . ."

"It happens. I don't think any of us can escape heartache, Odelia. One way or another, it does have to happen."

"Oh, Bella, I'm sorry. I didn't mean to make you think of Sam."

"No, I know. I just—look, you're used to constantly seeking guidance, and finding it, and sharing it with others. I'm used to . . . the opposite."

"But you know I'm always here to advise you, and so is Spirit."

"I know you are." Spirit, she's not so sure about, but that's not the point.

Odelia rests a hand on her arm. "Just remember to keep an open mind and heart to the infinite intelligence you've found here."

Millicent's words echo in Bella's head: *People just like you come along, people who are feeling lost and lonely, and they pounce!*

That isn't what's going on here, though. She can't let her mother-in-law's misguided assumptions start making her question the motives of her Spiritualist friend.

Nor can she let her Spiritualist friend make her start questioning her own common sense and reality.

"Odelia, this isn't about me. It's about Calla. You don't approve, and you won't accept—"

"No, I don't. I can't. Not when Spirit is telling me that she's on the wrong path."

Bella bites back a knee-jerk response and picks up the lukewarm cup of black coffee she set aside earlier. Suddenly weary, she takes a long, disgusting sip, willing the caffeine to revive her. How on earth is she going to muster the stamina to get through the rest of the day?

No longer tempted to confide in Odelia what's been going on behind the scenes, she puts the empty mug into a sink already cluttered with breakfast dishes. "You've told me that Spirit gives us what we need, Odelia. And that what we need isn't always what we *want*, right?"

"Absolutely."

"Well, I'm doing the same thing with you. I'm telling you what you need to hear, not what you want to hear."

"But you can't see what I can see."

"It works both ways. Sometimes, *I* can see what *you* can't see. Not just *you*. All of you. Everyone here in Lily Dale."

"What do you mean?"

"It wouldn't hurt to take a step back from a situation and look at it with pure logic," Bella says, reaching back to massage the tired ache between her shoulder blades. "You're always caught up in trying to find meaning in everything, everywhere."

"There *is* meaning in everything, everywhere."

"What if there isn't? What if things *do* just happen for no reason? What if there *are* plain old coincidences? And what if," she goes on—in for a penny—"when people die, they're just gone?"

"Oh, Bella. After all that's happened here?"

"Most of the time, I'm not even sure *what's* happened here. Sometimes a stray cat is just a stray cat and . . . and a spider web really is just a spider web!"

"What are you talking about?"

"Never mind. I'm overtired. I'm not even making sense."

"Did you see a spider web, Bella?"

Seeing the curiosity-tinged concern in Odelia's eyes, she wishes she hadn't brought it up. "I see plenty. This is an old house."

"Yes, but you know that Spirit has been showing me a spider in a web, and it does feel like a warning."

"Maybe the warning isn't even about the wedding," she says reluctantly. "Maybe it's about . . . something else."

"I don't think so. I always see the dress and Johneen's shoes in a puddle."

"Why don't you think that's just Spirit warning you a storm is coming on her wedding day?"

"It might be. But it feels more serious."

"She's a perfectionist. A rainy wedding day might be disastrous as far as she's concerned."

Who are you trying to convince? Odelia or yourself?

"The good news," Odelia adds, "is that I don't feel as though my vision involves Johneen slipping or tripping and falling, so I'm not worried about the stairs."

"That's terrific. Truly, the best news I've heard in ages."

"Are you being sarcastic?"

"Listen, you can't keep them from getting married today no matter what Spirit is telling you. And I don't think you should try."

Odelia tilts her head, digesting that comment, almost as if she's . . . considering a confession that she wrote the letter? Did she?

Bella closes her eyes and presses her fingertips against her temples. Every part of her aches with tension and exhaustion.

She feels a warm hand on her shoulder. "Are you okay?"

"I'm fine." She opens her eyes and sees the concern on her friend's face. "I didn't sleep very well either, and when I woke up, Millicent was here."

"Did she give you a hard time?"

"You could say that. But I don't want to talk about it right now. There's so much to do and not enough time."

"Let's get busy. You just need some fresh coffee to perk you up."

I need a lot more than that, she thinks as Odelia finds a filter and the can of grounds.

"I really am sorry I wasn't here earlier," she says, quickly rinsing the glass carafe at the sink. "I just needed to take care of something."

"What was it? Did something happen?" she asks with a belated twinge of guilt. Maybe Odelia was ill and had to go to the doctor or had some kind of emergency.

"I was at Inspiration Stump for hours, meditating, asking Spirit for clarity on all of this."

When you were supposed to be helping me pick daisies with Parker and fending off Pandora Feeney and her portable keyboard and "Oh, Promise Me"? Or at least keeping Millicent at bay, for Pete's sake?

Bella isn't being fair. But in this particular moment, she can't help resenting Odelia and yes, Spirit, and Lily Dale itself. Sometimes, the daily disconnect with grim reality is a welcome distraction, even charming.

Today, it's wearing as thin as her patience.

Why was she so certain this place was home? It's not as if she's reaping the spiritual benefits of living here. She isn't being shepherded through difficult times by mystical voices or immortal guides or . . .

Sam.

That's what this is about, isn't it?

And no, she isn't resentful just because Millicent put a flicker of doubt into her head.

She's spent months trying to grasp the "rules" of Spiritualism, all the while looking with a scientist's eye—all right, a skeptic's eye—for undeniable proof. She never found it. Not really.

Looking back on the evidence she wanted to believe in the moment might be a message from Spirit, or Sam, she can think of a thousand other explanations.

All right, maybe not a thousand. But at least a couple. Sensory phenomenology. Coincidence.

Sometimes a spider web is just a spider web. You just said it yourself.

If Spirit is real, and Sam is in Spirit, and Spirit is here, and Spirit gives you what you need, then Sam should be here. Period.

"So what happened at the Stump?" she asks as Odelia scoops dry grounds into the filter, dusting the counter and floor with little black specks. "Were you enlightened?"

"Not in the way that I'd hoped. I still don't have any answers."

"Welcome to the club. Most of us never expect them."

There's an uncomfortable pause, during which Odelia presses the start button on the coffeemaker and puts the can back in to the cabinet. "I'm sensing that you're angry at me, Bella."

I'm not. I'm angry at me. *I'm more mature, and much stronger, than I'm feeling and acting right now.*

Odelia rakes a hand through her hair, apparently forgetting she's wearing a headband. It gets caught in her fingers and flies across the room, landing with a splash in the red, paw-print-imprinted water bowl by the door.

"Oops." She goes over to fish it out, dripping, then tosses it directly into the garbage can.

"Wait, that was clean water. I just filled it. You don't have to throw away your headband."

"It was too tight. I think it was squeezing my brain," she adds with a faint smile. "I haven't been thinking straight all day. Guess I'll have to figure out some other way to deal with my hair until I can get it cut and colored. Got any ideas?"

"Maybe a nice veil?" Bella suggests, smiling back, feeling the tension ease just a little. "But not a white one, and not a puffy one either, because . . ."

Grinning, Odelia completes the sentence with her: "*I don't do puffy!*"

Equilibrium restored, at least for now, they get busy with the to-do list.

Bella might not see eye to eye with Odelia on some things—*most* things—but she does love her. Probably more than anyone in the world—other than Max, of course.

She didn't always get along with her own stubborn father, either, or with Aunt Sophie, her godmother, or even with Sam. Conflict is a part of every relationship.

After this conversation, she's inclined to believe that Odelia was responsible for the letter. That gives her some measure of reassurance that Luther was right.

If you look at the series of events with logic, there's no ominous threat. Lots of brides have angry ex-boyfriends. Lots of grooms feel protective. And, of course, wedding rings get lost or left behind.

Feeling slightly foolish for allowing herself to believe danger is afoot, Bella realizes her concern was due in part to the seemingly ominous lyrics of "Poor Little Rich Girl" and Odelia's troubling visions. Even if Bella chooses to believe in Spirit, and Spirit is sending a message to the bride and groom, then it's probably something along the lines of "Grow up and stop being so selfish, or you'll become a divorce statistic."

It's nothing to sneeze at. But at least, Bella thinks, relieved, *it's not a matter of life and death.*

Chapter Eleven

The rest of the morning passes swiftly and almost pleasantly in a flurry of preparations. Tasks that seemed insurmountable before are a breeze with Odelia and an army of wedding guests at her disposal. Bella snaps photos of the hustle and bustle on her phone, not just to document the "before and after" transition for Grant, but also so that Johneen can see how wholeheartedly her friends have pitched in.

If that doesn't warm her brittle heart, Bella thinks as she snaps a candid of Charlie and Hellerman clownishly balancing mason-jar centerpieces on their heads, *then nothing will.*

She makes countless round trips from house to yard, preparing table settings, flowers, food, and beverages and leaving kibble and water near the spot where she last saw the stray kitten.

"Here, kitty kitty . . . are you around here someplace?"

The only response is Parker's voice, calling her name in the kitchen.

"I'm right here." She hurries back inside. "Is everything all right?"

"Not exactly." He reports that the ring hasn't turned up and he hasn't yet reached the neighbor who has his key.

She can't help but feel sorry for him. "Are you going to tell Johneen you don't have the ring?"

"Not unless I have to. She's never seen it, so . . ." He shrugs. "Virginia offered to give me our grandparents' gold ring if it doesn't turn up. Daisy would never even know the difference."

But you'd be starting your marriage hiding a major secret from your wife.

It isn't up to Bella to point out that trust is an important ingredient in marital success, though she again wonders if Spirit has been trying to do just that.

"I want to bring Daisy breakfast in bed," Parker says, "if you have a tray I can use? And a vase for some flowers?"

She finds both and helps him assemble food on delicate china, along with some of the wildflowers they'd picked this morning. She shows him the bridal bouquet she'd assembled and tied with a white satin ribbon. He decides to bring that upstairs, too.

Fifteen minutes later, he returns with most of the food untouched. This time, he's wearing sunglasses and a jacket.

"She wasn't hungry?" Bella asks, sensing his romantic gesture hadn't gone over very well.

"No. She just wants to rest until it's time."

"Does she like the bouquet?"

"She thinks it's a little too large. She was expecting it to be more of a . . ."

"But . . . she didn't say nosegay. She said shabby-chic wildflower bouquet." Which is exactly what Bella created, following a website illustration the bride herself had preapproved.

"I guess she changed her mind. She says she'll fix it, and she can use the extra flowers for her hair."

Parker plunks the tray on the counter, sneezes twice, and takes off his sunglasses to wipe his eyes with a handkerchief. "I'm going outside to get away from all this cat dander."

He walks away, leaving the tray on the counter for Bella to clean up. As the door slams shut behind him, she notices that he left his sunglasses on the tray, but she doesn't bother to go after him. He can figure it out and come back. She's just about had her fill of him and Johneen, whom she's barely even seen today.

She puts the glasses, which are heavy and *feel* expensive, on the windowsill. Then she scrapes the untouched food into the garbage can, puts the dishes into the sink, and turns on the water.

Beyond the window, the sun doesn't seem to be shining quite as brightly as it was a few minutes ago. She'd better take a few more photos of the setting now. A wet, overcast backdrop won't exactly showcase the guesthouse for Grant's photo spread.

Thank goodness her benefactor has finally realized the off-season wedding business might be lucrative. He may not have sentimental reasons to hang onto the guesthouse, but it sounds like he'd be willing to keep it for financial ones.

Then again, does Bella really want to be in the wedding business ten months a year?

Not all couples will be as difficult as Parker and Johneen are. And while the two of them might not be destined for everlasting joy, at least their wedding will start off picture perfect—Bella's golden ticket to Lily Dale ever after.

She finishes cleaning the kitchen and folds the last of the laundry, then heads outside with her cell phone. The battery is nearly depleted, but she can get a few quick shots.

Parker and Johneen are sitting in the Adirondack chairs out by the lake. Bella captures the moment with her camera: a pair of blond heads so intent on conversation that they don't even turn to notice her.

Then, seeing a puff of smoke drifting into the air, she realizes that it's not Johneen. It's Virginia.

The two tall, slim, blue-eyed blondes really do look alike from a distance. But while Johneen's perpetual pout ruins her beauty, Virginia's dazzling smile completes hers. No surprise that Johneen seems to envy her. Bella does, too.

In this moment, with some distance and perception, the thought of a gun under Virginia's mattress doesn't seem as ominous as it did earlier. Bella is no longer convinced Virginia knew she was snooping. Perhaps her own guilty conscience read dark undertones into a perfectly innocent comment.

As for the gun, Virginia is a tough cookie, and she's worried that her cousin and his fiancée might be in danger. She might be armed, but it doesn't mean she's dangerous to anyone other than the person who might harm someone she loves.

Spotting Bella, Virginia waves her closer. Parker, also with a cigarette in his hand, quickly stubs it out.

"What are you doing?" he asks Bella.

"I'm taking a few photos of the setting for the owner."

"Not of us, I hope."

"Mr. Henpeck here is afraid his wife-to-be will catch him smoking!" Virginia says with a laid-back laugh. "Here, we'll pose for you, Isabella. It's been years since we've had a photo taken together, hasn't it, Parker?"

"Years," he agrees tersely, undoubtedly thinking that Johneen won't take kindly to a framed shot of him with Virginia, with or without a cigarette in his hand.

"You don't have to look so thrilled about it," his cousin teases him as Bella takes aim. "Stop scowling."

"I'm not scowling. I'm squinting. I've misplaced my sunglasses."

"They're in the kitchen." Bella steps toward the lake to get the whole guesthouse in the background. "You look great. Put your heads a little closer together and say cheese."

Virginia cheerfully obliges. Parker doesn't say cheese, but he does smile for the photo.

"I'd better get back to the house," Bella says. "I've got a million things to do, but everything is coming together."

Virginia clears her throat. "Wait, Isabella."

Uh-oh.

The lighthearted tone has evaporated. This is where Virginia accuses her of snooping in her room.

"Yes?"

"I know Parker told you the ring is missing, and he mentioned a letter you'd received about the wedding. Do you mind if I ask you a few questions?"

"Sure," she says, feeling vaguely uncomfortable, despite her relief that it's not about the gun. It sounds almost as if they suspect Bella herself of taking the ring, and . . . what? Making up the letter to deflect suspicion?

Virginia's questions are in the same vein as Parker's were earlier, though more pointed and efficient. She wants to know who might have had access to the keys.

"I have both sets right here now," Bella tells her, and takes them out of her pocket.

"But you don't usually, do you?"

"No. I keep them in a drawer in my bedroom, and my bedroom is locked," she says, pushing aside the thought that someone could have borrowed the entire set and duplicated them.

Virginia asks whether Bella trusts the friends who have been in and out of the house. At least Virginia, unlike her cousin, doesn't assume that they're hired help or insinuate that they're potential thieves, even if that's what she's thinking. Bella considers telling her about Nadine and her reported penchant for mischief when Leona Gatto was living here. But that might make Virginia think she's just trying to deflect suspicion from herself with a crazy story about a resident ghost.

"If you're sure that no one you know could have taken the ring," Virginia says, "and Parker is reasonably sure the other guests are innocent, then it had to be an outsider. Those tunnels everyone was talking about earlier . . . do any of them lead into the honeymoon suite?"

"No. I mean, not that I know of," she adds, reasonably sure of it, though in an old house like this, there can always be surprises. "Couldn't Parker just have misplaced the ring or forgotten it back home? Why assume it was a thief?"

Virginia and Parker exchange a glance. He gives a slight nod, as if to tell her it's okay—that Bella already knows about Johneen's jealous ex.

"We have reason to believe someone doesn't want the wedding to take place. We're worried that he's here in Lily Dale, and . . ." Again, she looks at Parker, as if for permission.

"He might be dangerous," Parker tells Bella.

"And you think he wrote the letter? And broke in here and stole the ring?"

"Who else would it be?"

"Well, you did mention that it was gold with diamonds, from Tiffany. It was obviously valuable, and anyone would know that just by stumbling across the box itself."

"So you're saying it's likely that a random burglar off the street managed to get into our suite and—"

"No!" Bella cuts him off hastily. "Of course not. This is a safe town, and the guesthouse is always secure. I'm just trying to say . . ."

She trails off, not even sure *what* she's trying to say.

"Mom!" Max shouts from the house. "Hey, Mom! Where are you?"

"Outside," she calls back, then looks at Parker and Virginia. "It's my son."

"Go ahead and take care of him," Virginia tells her. "I'm sorry to ask all these questions. We're just concerned."

Perhaps rightfully so.

Hearing the back door open, Bella sees Max in the doorway with Millicent behind him.

She'd forgotten all about her mother-in-law.

"Go ahead," Virginia urges her again, gesturing at Max, who's waving his arms wildly. "It looks urgent."

Yes, it does. Bella hurries toward the house, promising herself she'll get the letter and bring it back outside to show them.

"I'm hungry for breakfast," Max announces.

"Oh, sweetie . . . it's almost lunchtime."

"But I didn't have any breakfast yet."

Feeling a familiar twinge of bad-mom guilt, she expects reproach from her mother-in-law, but it doesn't come.

"Come on back inside," Bella says, "and we'll see what we can find for you."

In the kitchen, Odelia is rinsing salad greens at the sink. Though Millicent shoots her a wary look, she's not as stiff as she was earlier. Her makeup has faded a bit, softening her features, and her brown slacks are covered in short, silvery strands of fur.

Did her mother-in-law actually have kittens on her lap?

"How about some cereal?" Bella asks Max.

"I can't find any."

Probably because the cabinets are cluttered with wedding reception ingredients. Bella sighs, opening one to look. A box of crackers topples onto the equally cluttered counter and sends a paring knife over the edge. It skitters across the floor, landing a few inches from Millicent's pumps.

She looks down, then up at Bella, her expression slightly alarmed.

"Oops, I'm so sorry. That was an accident." Bella scoops it up.

Not looking entirely convinced, Millicent says, "I know you're busy here. I can take Max out to eat."

Rarely treated to a restaurant meal, Max promptly shouts, "Yes!"

"Splendid," Millicent says, as if it's all settled. "Isabella, if you can you point me toward a nice restaurant for brunch, we'll be on our way. I'll need to borrow a car."

Given the circumstances, Bella isn't comfortable with the idea of her mother-in-law driving away with her son. Nor, though, does she want him here at the guesthouse if Johneen's stalker is lurking.

"Why don't you just walk over to Solstice Bistro right here in the Dale?"

The suggestion comes from Odelia, and Bella is grateful. The recently opened café probably doesn't meet Millicent's definition of *nice*, or most people's definition of *bistro*. Nor does it serve a traditional brunch.

"Perfect! Max loves their hash browns," Bella says, "and there's a playground right across the way, so maybe you can walk over there afterward."

"Can we, Grandma?"

She hesitates, then nods. "Of course we can."

Off they go, hand in hand.

"They seem to have hit it off," Odelia tells Bella. "Maybe she'll decide to move here, too."

"I doubt that."

If you only knew what she thinks of Lily Dale.

But now isn't the time for talking. She hurries upstairs. In the Rose Room, she plugs in her phone on the night table and feeds Chance and the kittens. Then, picking up the phone again, she composes a quick e-mail to Grant Everard.

His messages to her are always short and businesslike, signed with just his initials. She follows suit, typing at an awkward angle because the phone is attached to the cord.

Attached, please find a few photos of the setting for the wedding today. More to come! I.J.

She adds the files, hits Send, and sets the phone aside. Then she opens the night-table drawer to retrieve the folded sheet of paper so that she can show it to Parker and Virginia.

It isn't there.

It must have gotten wedged against the top. She feels around. *Where is it?*

Heart pounding, she fumbles through the significant clutter in the drawer. Most of the contents, like a pair of reading glasses, a bottle of prescription pills, and a small, crystal stone, belonged to the room's previous occupant. Grant had instructed Bella to bag and donate Leona's clothing to charity over the summer, but he wants to go through everything else himself.

Bella is certain she left the letter stashed in the drawer, but it appears to have vanished. There's no way she herself moved it and then forgot, is there?

No. Absolutely not. She wouldn't forget something that important, although . . .

Didn't she just tell Parker he might have done exactly that with the wedding ring?

It's a stressful time . . .

Yes, it's been a long and hectic day. Is it any wonder she's losing track of her possessions?

She did take the spare set of keys out of the drawer a little while ago. She'd been in a hurry. She must have taken the letter, too, by accident.

Farfetched, but . . .

She checks her pocket. It isn't there.

All right, well, maybe she dropped it downstairs or outside when she took out her phone or the keys.

Yes, or it was Nadine.

Except you don't believe in ghosts.

Someone crept in here and stole it from the drawer while she was outside.

Spooked, she darts a glance around. The room appears in order—as much as it can with kittens romping around.

Walking over to the closet, she checks the panel at the back wall and finds it slightly askew. Didn't she straighten it earlier?

The cats could have knocked it out of place again . . .

Or an intruder did, she thinks, and fear prickles the skin at the back of her neck.

Chapter Twelve

Dashing downstairs, Bella finds Odelia rearranging the contents of the refrigerator to make room for the salad.

I have to tell her. I have to tell someone.

But before she can blurt it, the back door opens and Parker steps into the house. Spotting Bella, he asks, "Did you say my sunglasses were here somewhere?"

"Yes, they're . . ." She looks over at the windowsill, half-expecting to see that they, too, have gone missing. But there they are, right where she left them.

She hands them over, wondering if he can see her hand trembling, and he tucks them into his shirt pocket.

"Where's Virginia?" she asks, wondering if she can get the two of them alone again for a moment.

"She went off to buy more cigarettes. She's running low. Stress makes her smoke more. I'm going to go upstairs and see how Daisy is feeling." He turns on his heel.

About to trail him out of the room, Bella hears a cry and a crash behind her.

She turns to see a shattered jar of blueberry jam at Odelia's feet in front of the open fridge. Purplish goo oozes from shattered glass and is spattered across the floor, the lower cabinets, and—uh-oh—the bottom of Parker's trousers.

With a curse, he bolts from the room.

"I'm so sorry!" Odelia calls after him as his footsteps hurry up the stairs. She looks at Bella. "It was an accident. I don't

175

know if I knocked it off the shelf, or if Nadine did, or one of the others."

That gives Bella pause. *Others*, meaning last night's ghostly party crashers?

"Are they . . . here?"

"Of course." Odelia nods as if Bella asked her if today is Saturday. "There's a lot of nervous energy in the house today. But I warned them to behave themselves."

Bella grabs a roll of paper towels and unspools a length. "Oh, no, Odelia. You've got jelly all over you, too."

"It's okay. I'm going to change for the ceremony."

"But it stains. You need to go change and get those slacks into the washing machine," she says as a loud knock sounds on the front door.

"Go get it." Odelia takes the paper towels.

"But your clothes are—"

"They're fine. Go."

Bella goes, feeling as though she's being propelled through this day at breakneck pace, unable to resolve one thing before another pops up.

As she makes her way to the front of the house, she keeps an eye out for the folded paper she might have dropped from her pocket, though common sense tells her it probably happened outside . . .

Or perhaps one of Odelia's "others" took it?

That's not common sense at all, she reminds herself sternly.

After she deals with whoever is at the door, she'll run outside and search. It must be there. It *has* to be there.

As she reaches for the doorknob, it occurs to her that she shouldn't just blindly open it. What if the stalker is there, crazed and dangerous? Do stalkers knock?

"Who is it?"

"It's me, luv."

Bella sighs inwardly. A crazed and dangerous stalker might be quicker and easier.

She opens the door to Pandora Feeney, still wearing her bathrobe from this morning.

"I know you're not expecting me until later, luv, but I've been troubled since you left. I had to come 'round and see if I could make sense of it."

"Make sense of what?"

"Spirit isn't pleased at all."

"Spirit isn't pleased with what?"

"With this. Today. The wedding." Still standing on the other side of the screen, Pandora reaches for the doorknob with a bony hand.

Bella grabs the knob from the inside, poised to engage in screen-door tug-of-war. It's one thing for Parker or Johneen to have second thoughts or concerns, but Pandora is an outsider and a notorious busybody.

"Isabella, I need to speak with the bride at once."

"You can't come in here and disrupt the wedding, Pandora. Tell me what's going on. What are you seeing?"

"I just want to have a word with Ms. Maynard."

Bella shakes her head vigorously. "I'm sorry, but you've never even met her. You can't barge in with unsolicited advice."

"It isn't *my* advice. I'm just the messenger."

Ah, but if anyone could kill a messenger, it's Johneen Maynard. And if any messenger could incite a violent reaction from a complete stranger courtesy of sheer gall, it's Pandora Feeney.

"I only want to deliver truth. I'm . . . sensing danger."

Bella's blood turns to liquid nitrogen. "What kind of danger?"

"If I could just meet the bride, I might be able to tell."

Unnerved, Bella turns, looking up at the stairway, wishing Parker or Virginia would appear to handle this. There's no sign of them, nor of the web that earlier stretched from banister to wall.

She can't even see the rainbow that often falls across the landing via the stained-glass window on sunny days, as if to mark the very spot where she found the tourmaline necklace in July.

She wanted so badly to believe that Sam had sent it from wherever he is. In that moment, she believed—she *saw*—what she wanted, needed, to see and believe.

Right now, the angle of the light is all wrong. There's no rainbow. There's no intricate web strung across the stairway.

She turns back to Pandora. "Johneen is resting until the ceremony begins. She gave strict instructions not to be disturbed."

Pandora stares at her for a long moment, then nods. "All right. I understand. And you know that barging in here like this just isn't my style . . ."

Really? *Really?* Barging in and confronting a stranger is precisely Pandora's style.

"Anyway, I might be mistaken about what Spirit is showing me," she goes on, turning to leave.

"Wait—what is it? What is Spirit showing you?"

"It's a woodland pond." Pandora bows her head, closing her eyes. "Beside it, a lovely blonde woman in a white dress, falling. . . ."

A blonde woman? Lucky guess. A white dress—most brides wear white. Lovely is subjective.

As psychics go, she isn't very convincing. "She lands face down."

"In the water?"

"In wildflowers growing not far from the water's edge."

"Are they daisies?"

"Daisies, goldenrod, sedum, Queen Anne's lace. . . ."

Well, of course. Pandora must have seen Bella and Parker picking those very same flowers from her own garden just hours ago.

"I appreciate your concern, Pandora. I hope you understand why I can't bother Johneen right now. Thank you for stopping over. Have a good day."

"Oh, I'll be back 'round in an hour to sing at the ceremony," she reminds Bella. "I've already learned 'Fields of Gold.'" To prove it, she sings a few bars.

Bella forces a smile. "Very nice."

"Yes, well, cheerio!"

Watching her toddle off across Melrose Park, Bella spots the little blue kitten peeking out from beneath a shrub. When Pandora is out of sight, she descends the steps and crouches down, hoping he won't scamper away again.

This time, he doesn't.

"Hey there, Li'l Chap!"

They make eye contact. He offers her a slow blink—a sign of feline affection, according to Drew.

She offers a blink in return. "I left you some food out back. Come on, I'll show you."

She slowly reaches for him, and he allows her to pick him up. As she carries him around to the backyard, she can feel his bony little body rumbling with a sweet, steady purring.

The last thing she wants to do is leave him outside. But Drew said she should, so she gently sets him down next to the bowls she left earlier. He dives greedily into the kibble.

"Listen, if your mama doesn't turn up, I've got someone who's going to help you, okay? He's a good guy. He'll take care of you."

Still crunching, the kitten looks at her solemnly.

Yes, Drew will make sure he's safe and has everything he needs.

If only things were that simple in Bella's world.

Not that she wants or needs to be taken care of. She's proud of having gotten this far entirely on her own. But sometimes, it would be nice to let her guard down for a while and let someone else pay the bills and kill the spiders and . . . deflect the mediums' Spirit warnings.

She walks over to the Adirondack chairs, searching the ground for a folded note as a light breeze ripples the lake. If she dropped the note here, it could very well have blown away.

If it was ever even here in the first place.

She finds herself wondering if the note might be a figment of her imagination. Stress can do crazy things to a person.

No. It was real. You saw it.

Then where did it go? Did Spirit vaporize it? Or did someone steal it from her drawer? Either of those scenarios is more believable than the possibility that she made it up.

How can you even think that?

Because she's had two too many confrontations with the mediums today, that's how. Parker's paranoia, combined with the coffee and lack of food and sleep, had her jittery enough before Odelia and Pandora spouted their dire warnings.

Yes, they mean well. They always do. Bella is accustomed by now to mediums popping up to share a message from Spirit. Some are more provocative than others, though she tries to take them all with a grain of salt.

If only Pandora's warning weren't too close for comfort to Odelia's.

But what is Bella supposed to do about it?

The clock is ticking. Everything is ready. If they can just get through the wedding without incident . . .

Fully staged for the ceremony and reception, the yard is still bathed in splashy sunlight glinting off the blue lake.

A bar is set up on a rectangular table with mason jar glasses, pitchers of lemonade and Brandy Daisies, and decanters filled with white wine, tawny port, and amber bourbon. A long white tablecloth conceals ice chests and backup bottles beneath.

Rows of white folding chairs face the white canopy decorated with garlands of English ivy from Odelia's yard. The round tables are covered in golden linens and topped with wildflower centerpieces, white votive candles, and Odelia's pretty little jars of lemon-habanero marmalade.

Fan-shaped school-bus yellow leaves float lazily from the gingko boughs to carpet the grass as if Mother Nature herself had a hand in styling the wedding.

Bella reaches for her phone to take a few more photos, but it isn't in her pocket.

Darn. She left it upstairs, plugged into the charger.

Hurrying inside, she finds Odelia tossing the last of the purple-smeared paper towels into the garbage can.

"There," she says. "You'd never know there was a violent, sticky explosion here, would you?"

"Thanks, Odelia."

"Who was at the door?"

"Oh, it was . . ." She can't lie. "It was Pandora Feeney."

"What did *she* want?"

"She just wanted to ask me something about the wedding." Changing the subject quickly, she asks Odelia about the food preparation.

"Just a few more things to take care of and we'll be all set."

"Thank you. Why don't you run home and change, and I'll finish up here?"

Odelia shakes her orange head. "I'm not leaving you until everything is ready. I still feel terrible about this morning."

"It's okay. Really."

"No, I've got it. You go on upstairs and get yourself ready while Max isn't underfoot," Odelia says firmly. "They'll be back soon."

She's right. Bella wonders how it's going. Her mother-in-law almost seems human today, courtesy of kids and kittens working their magic.

Or maybe, courtesy of Lily Dale's magic?

Millicent can't be entirely immune to the convivial warmth of this little village, can she? Surely she must realize by now that Bella and Max haven't fallen into the clutches of a dangerous cult.

She thanks Odelia and backtracks to the stairs, stopping to correct minor imperfections along the way: a misaligned area rug, a crooked picture frame, a bunched-up curtain. In the parlor, she adjusts the old photo albums stacked on the coffee table. They're filled with a remarkably steady stream of vintage images of Valley View and its residents over a century, leaving off before the turn of the new millennium.

Maybe I'll reinstate the tradition. I can start with an album of wedding weekend pictures . . . as long as everything goes all right.

It will. It has to.

Wishing Parker would come back downstairs, or that Virginia would return, she steps into the front hall.

The room is aglow with autumn sunlight and vintage amber sconces and infused with floral fragrance. Oh dear. One of the female guests must have used too heavy a hand on the perfume atomizer.

Bella opens the front door for some fresh air. She props it against the wall with the unsightly boulder of a brass andiron she'd lugged outside before Johneen's arrival and tucked behind a pot of lavender mums sitting beside the purple welcome mat.

As the mild, leaf-scented breeze diffuses the cloying scent, she decides to lock both sets of keys into a drawer on the registration desk for safekeeping. They're too bulky to carry around, but she can keep the only two keys to the drawer in the pockets of the dress she's planning to wear.

She pauses to replenish the crystal bowl of M&Ms on the desk. Yesterday's check-ins depleted the supply, and Leona Gatto would have wanted it to be ready for new arrivals, even though none are scheduled until . . . November?

Watching the colorful candies fall from the bag like the leaves piling ever higher outside, Bella reminds herself that the Dale's ancient trees will soon be bare. According to the locals, the ground will be white for nearly six months.

Sam—who loved *"snow and all forms of radiant frost"*—died on the first day of winter.

Subsequent holidays held no joy. Christmas, New Year's, Valentine's Day . . . All were so bleak, she can't fathom ever looking forward to them again. Spring took an exceptionally long time coming. When calendar and climate marked its official arrival, her grief might as well have withered the tulips and lilacs. Its pervasive chill numbed her by day and kept her awake at night, huddled and alone in the dark.

Only when she arrived in Lily Dale on the heels of the summer solstice did she finally experience a flicker of warmth again. Ironic, because around here, all anyone seems to talk about lately is the harsh weather that lies ahead.

You can't scare me, western New York winter. I've dealt with far more frightening monsters than the likes of you.

She shoves the nearly empty candy bag into a drawer and replaces the bowl's crystal lid, then heads upstairs. Warily opening the Rose Room door, she wonders what she'll do if someone is there.

But she sees only Chance and her kittens. They're scattered around the room, snoozing peacefully wherever patches of sunlight fall across the carpet, the bed, and a slipcover chair.

Bella closes the door behind her and returns to the nightstand. If she was willing to believe she herself had removed the letter and forgotten about it, then maybe she should also consider that she'd imagined its disappearance.

But no, it isn't here.

She crosses the room, sidestepping a snoozing fur ball consisting of Spidey and Chance, and opens the closet door. Moving the hanging clothing aside, she sees that the panel at the back is precisely as she left it earlier. That's a good sign.

She turns her attention to finding the dress she's planning to wear to the wedding. A relic of the old days, when finances were different and she had a busy, newlywed social life, the simple hunter-green silk sheath is still shrouded in clear plastic from a suburban New York dry cleaner. She hasn't worn it in years, but it's a classic designer cut and the nicest thing she owns.

Quickly pulling it on, she realizes that the dress fits a bit differently now. She might weigh the same as she did before Max's birth, but she has curves where there were none before. The bustline especially seems a little snug and the V neck is cut lower than she remembers. A bit of décolletage strikes her as perfectly appropriate for a married woman, and Sam undoubtedly would have approved. But now that she's the hardly merry Widow Jordan . . .

Oh, well. Too late now. She has nothing else to wear.

She refreshes her lipstick and brushes her hair. She rarely wears jewelry anymore, other than her wedding ring and the tourmaline pendant. But the simple dress seems to need a little something more, so she adds a silver bracelet-watch and some delicate jade earrings that once belonged to her mother.

There. Surveying herself in the mirror, she decides she's good to go. Better than good to go, really, considering that she's not even a guest. She probably could have gotten away with the dark slacks and sweater she'd been planning to wear . . .

Until you realized Drew Bailey was going to show up again later?

She tells herself that this sudden urge to dress up has nothing to do with him. It's just been ages since she went to a wedding, and when was the last time she threw a party with festive food and cocktails and decorations?

For her, it almost feels like a welcome back to the land of the living . . .

Ironic, since some might consider Lily Dale anything but.

All right. She's ready. She slips the keys to the downstairs desk into the left-seam pocket of her dress, planning to put her cell phone into the other.

But when she turns toward the nightstand to grab it . . .

It isn't there.

Did one of the cats knock it off the table?

Stepping closer, certain she'll find it on the floor, she sees the charger cord dangling from the outlet, no phone attached.

But . . . it was here. She definitely plugged it in. She remembers using it to send that e-mail to Grant.

She gets down on her hands and knees to look for it. The cats might have knocked the phone off the table and . . . and yes, pulled it from the cord and pushed it across the floor . . .

Under the bed?

Behind the chair?

Into a corner?

No, no, no, and no.

Heart pounding, she struggles to maintain logic.

I must have taken it with me when I left, and . . . and I just forgot, that's all.

She whirls to grab the jeans she'd been wearing, positive the phone will be in one of the pockets.

It isn't.

It's downstairs. It has to be downstairs.

Turning back toward the door, she spots something on the floor beside the bed.

Virginia's evening bag. The one she had at the party last night.

"How on earth . . . ?"

Bella gazes at the small, black-satin pouch with sequined straps—*straps*! Of course!

She turns an accusing eye toward the dozing Chance. "You naughty girl!"

As Bella picks up the bag, it gapes open. Inside, she sees a pack of cigarettes, a fancy, gold lighter, and a flat, black, rectangular object. A small wallet or a billfold?

She shouldn't snoop—she *knows* she shouldn't snoop—but the gun weighs heavy on her mind.

She takes out the billfold. Flipping it open, she instantly realizes what it is: a badge holder.

It's from a local police department in a North Carolina town Bella never heard of. Virginia's face stares solemnly out at her from a laminated identification card.

So Virginia isn't a killer. She's a cop. That's why she has a gun.

The answers bring more questions, but Bella is momentarily relieved, despite her missing phone.

She slips the badge back into the bag. She has to give it right back to Virginia, who may not even realize that it's gone astray.

Yes, and you'll say . . . what? That your purse-snatching cat brought it to you, so you snooped inside?

She doesn't have to admit that part.

Still, Virginia is incredibly intuitive.

Of course she is! She's a cop!

Even if Bella doesn't confess to taking a peek, Virginia might suspect that she did. Violating someone's privacy may not be a crime, but it's a lousy thing to do. Virginia might tell Parker, and the last thing Bella needs is to further alienate the groom before the wedding.

All right. So Virginia doesn't even need to know Bella found the bag. She can just slip it back into her room while she's out. Let her wonder how it got there. She already knows about the kleptomaniac cat, having caught Bella red-handed with the bra yesterday. Let her think Chance was carrying it around the house, or—whatever. Let her think a ghost was playing tricks on her. It doesn't really matter, as long as Bella can get through this day and marry off the bride and groom as planned.

She hurries downstairs for the master keys, then back up two flights of stairs, arriving on the third floor panting as much from exertion as from nerves. She hesitates in front of the closed door to Virginia's room. What if she came back and is in there?

You can't just barge in. You have to knock.

She turns, looking wildly around for inspiration, and spots the cabinet where she stashes extra linens. Tucking the little bag inside for the moment, she grabs a small stack of clean towels. If Virginia is here, she'll hand them to her, pretending she thought she forgot to leave them earlier when she made up the room.

Yes, and she'll see right through you.

It's a flimsy ruse, but Bella is fairly certain she isn't here. She'd been waiting for her.

Sure enough, no one answers her knock. She unlocks the door, retrieves the purse, and drops it in the middle of the neatly made bed. Then, thinking better of it, she moves it to the floor, not quite hidden by the bed skirt. That's exactly how she found it in her own room, courtesy of Chance.

Mission accomplished, she locks the door again, puts back the towels, and hurries back down to the second floor, where she immediately spots . . .

Nadine? *A ghost?*

Seeing the pale, voluminous figure at the end of the hall, Bella stops and stares.

But this is *not* her first spooky specter in a town that's supposedly crawling with them. This lady-in-white is a flesh-and-blood bride named Johneen Maynard.

Gazing at herself in the full-length antique mirror at the end of the hall, she doesn't turn around. But her reflection meets Bella's gaze in the glass, and even from here, Bella can see that her eyes are troubled.

"You look radiant, Johneen."

There's that word again, handily spilling from the tip of her tongue.

Johneen's unembellished white silk-organza gown falls in a narrow column to an inch above her satin pumps. Her golden hair is pulled back in a chignon wreathed in sprigs of fresh white wildflowers. The bouquet in her hand is considerably smaller now, and Bella's floppy satin bow has blossomed into an elegant and precise pair of loops.

Walking down the hall toward her, Bella catches a floral whiff in the air. It can't be the bouquet, and it doesn't smell like perfume, either.

"Calla forgot the bracelet," Johneen informs her.

"Pardon? Which bracelet?"

"I'd asked her weeks ago if I could borrow her emerald bracelet. You know, as my 'something borrowed.' It was your idea."

"My idea?"

"Maybe it was Odelia's idea. But I was counting on it, and now Calla's claiming she accidentally left it home."

"Claiming?"

"It used to belong to her mother, so I don't think she wants to lend it to me. Back in college, she told some crazy story about how she lost it at her mother's funeral in Florida, and then it mysteriously turned up here in Lily Dale months later, covered in dirt from the grave."

Bella's heart skips, and her hand goes to the tourmaline pendant dangling above her cleavage. "Where . . . where is Calla now?"

"She went back upstairs to see if she has any other jewelry that would be suitable, but I doubt it. Plus, I still need 'something blue.' Parker says it's my eyes, but . . ." Johneen trails off, her gaze landing on Bella's hand clutching the necklace. She turns around and leans in to examine it. "This would work. It would be borrowed *and* blue."

"I'm sorry, I can't."

Johneen's eyes widen. "Excuse me?"

Before Bella can elaborate, footsteps descend from the third floor, and Calla appears in the hallway. Her face is fully made up but appears entirely natural, and her hair is swept into an updo that looks gloriously careless, as if plucking one bobby pin would send it tumbling past her shoulders. Coming to a halt beside the bride, Calla is a few inches shorter even in heeled black pumps. Her velvet dress is maroon, not white. Yet she somehow manages to upstage the bride.

"Here," she says, offering Johneen a small jewelry box. "You can wear this. It's a sapphire-and-diamond necklace—borrowed *and* blue. Just don't lose it. Jacy gave it to me for my birthday last year."

Johneen opens the box and examines the necklace, then shakes her head. "It's too small. I'd rather wear that."

She points again at Bella's pendant, and Bella fights the urge to back away.

"I'm sorry," she says simply, "but this is one thing I just can't lend you. It's . . . from my husband."

"You're married?"

"Widowed." Even now, she puckers her mouth around the word's bitterness.

"Oh. Sorry." Johneen looks as though it's news to her, though Bella is pretty sure she's mentioned it before. "I wouldn't lose it, Isabella. It's not as if I'm a reckless child playing dress up."

"No, I know. But I just can't let it go even for a little while," she says firmly, if uncharitably. She's tempted to add an apology but decides Johneen doesn't deserve one. For someone who seems to pride herself on being ladylike, she doesn't exactly have impeccable manners.

"I don't see why—"

"Johnny, stop!"

Taken aback at Calla's sharp command, she scowls. "I keep telling you that I don't go by that nickname anymore."

"And I keep forgetting. Sorry. But listen, Bella said no. You need to respect that."

"I'm just saying, it's not like it's the crown jewels."

"That necklace has sentimental value, which means it's priceless to her. Take mine."

"It isn't as striking. The stones are dinky. No offense," she adds airily.

"None taken," Calla says, just as airily. She reaches out to take back the jewelry box, but Johneen holds onto it.

"I didn't say I wasn't going to wear it."

"Are you?"

"I guess so, since it's borrowed and blue." She fastens it around her neck, examines the effect in the mirror, and gives a shrug that says it'll have to do.

As she starts back down the hall toward her room, Calla stops her. "John—*neen*?"

"Yes?" She turns back expectantly, still perturbed, although perhaps slightly less so since Calla caught herself this time before using the dreaded nickname.

"Are you feeling all right?"

"About the bracelet? Or the necklace?"

"Just in general."

Johneen frowns. "Why do you ask? Don't I look all right?"

She's bone-thin and pale. But isn't she always?

At Calla's hesitation, she narrows her eyes. "Did someone tell you that I wasn't feeling well today?"

"No. I just . . . sensed it."

She smirks. "That's right, I keep forgetting you're one of *them*."

"What?"

"You know . . . the ghostbusters."

"Are you talking about the *Spiritualists*?" Bella asks pointedly.

"Isn't it the same thing?"

Calla rolls her eyes, shakes her head, and repeats her original question.

"Yes, I feel fine." Without another word, Johneen retreats into her room with a rustling swoosh of silk and closes the door behind her.

Bella looks at Calla. "*Is* she fine?"

"I'm not sure."

"You didn't have a premonition about her, did you?"

When the answer isn't an immediate no, Bella's heart sinks.

"It wasn't a premonition exactly. More just a sense of malaise."

"Was it about her? Or were you channeling what she's feeling?"

"Sometimes, it's hard to tell."

"So you don't think she's going to . . . fall down the stairs or get bitten by a spider or anything?"

"What? No. Why?"

Though Bella can't betray Parker and Virginia's confidences, she quickly tells Calla about Odelia and Pandora's visions and about the letter.

Calla digests it all thoughtfully, then asks if Johneen knows any of this.

"No." Bella hesitates, not wanting to mention that she was about to tell Parker in light of his own suspicions. "I didn't think it was up to me to tell her."

"Can I see the letter?"

"That's the thing. I can't find it. I'm pretty sure I left it in a drawer, and now it isn't there. And now my phone is missing, too. So either someone took them, or I'm losing my mind, or . . . well, those are the only two explanations I can think of."

"You forgot—"

"Nadine."

"You know about Nadine?"

"Your grandmother told me about her. I know she supposedly lives here and that she likes to move things around and play little tricks, but that hasn't happened to me."

"I guess it might have been Nadine, but I was going to say telekinesis," Calla says with a shrug.

Bella is well-versed enough in paranormal terminology to know she's referring to inanimate objects that move around courtesy of psychic energy.

Telekinesis isn't exactly logical, though. Nor is a resident ghost, or "the others." Bella steers the conversation back to Johneen, leading Calla to the subject of her angry ex. As a friend, she must know about him.

"Is there anyone you can think of in Johneen's past who wouldn't want this wedding to happen?"

"Sure. There are plenty of people."

"*Plenty?*"

"Well, for one thing, her parents wouldn't be thrilled if they found out. This isn't exactly their idea of a proper wedding."

"But would they write an anonymous note?"

"It's definitely not dignified, but like I told you, they're pretty dysfunctional. And . . . let's see, Johnny was dating a guy back when she lived in Philly. I guess he went a little bonkers when she dumped him."

"Bonkers how?"

"I don't know the details. All I know is that he wasn't happy when she ended it."

"Do you think he could have written the note?"

"I never met him, so it's hard to say."

"What was his name?"

"I knew you were going to ask me that."

"Because you're psychic?"

"Because I feel like you're a cop interrogating me." Calla closes her eyes as if probing her memory. "I think his first name was Griffin? Graham? Something like that."

"What was—"

"I don't even think I ever knew his last name. But you said the letter was mailed here in the Dale, right? And this guy lived down in New York City. That, I remember, because Johnny used to complain about taking the train up there to see him. She's not big on public transportation, and she was afraid to drive in city traffic. That's pretty much why she ended it."

And not because he was too possessive? Did Johneen keep that, and perhaps other details, from her friends?

Jarred by the image of the ice queen as a vulnerable victim, Bella hears a car outside, slowing in front of the house.

There are a thousand other questions she wants to ask Calla, but she settles on the most important one. "Do you think your grandmother could possibly have written that anonymous note?"

Calla nods. "Look, I'm not saying that it's likely, or that it's not a lousy thing to do, but Gammy can be a little single-minded when it comes to getting Spirit's message across. So, yes, I guess she could have. But if she did, I'm sure it was impulsive, and she's probably wishing she hadn't. Gammy would never want to upset you, of all people."

Then maybe she's the one who crept upstairs while Bella was outside and took back the letter.

It could also have been Pandora. Maybe she'd mailed the letter earlier this week, regretted it after meeting Parker, and decided to reclaim it. If so, this wouldn't be the first time she'd snuck in and out of her former home via the secret passageways.

Outside, a car door slams, and Bella hears distant voices through the open front door below.

Hurriedly, she asks Calla, "Do you think Spirit is really trying to warn Johneen not to marry Parker?"

"I'm not sure."

"But if something really terrible was going to happen to her, you'd probably be getting a more specific feeling too, wouldn't you?"

"Not necessarily. It doesn't work that way."

Hoping that it doesn't work at all, Bella asks, "Do you think you should tell Johneen?"

"If a psychic had come to *you* on your wedding day with a cryptic warning that something terrible might happen if you married your husband, what would you have done?"

"I'd have been upset."

"Upset enough to call off the wedding?"

Of course not. But Sam and I were different from Johneen and Parker. We were soul mates.

Then again, petty disagreements aside, Johneen and Parker certainly seem to believe they're destined to live happily ever after.

"Bella?"

"No," she admits. "I would have gone through with it no matter what."

Nothing could have stopped her from marrying Sam. Even if she had known, beyond a shadow of doubt, that her marriage would end as tragically as it had, she'd have marched down that aisle and taken her vows with conviction.

But what if she had a potentially violent ex who might be planning to show up at the wedding to harm her or her groom?

As far as Calla knows, there's no concrete evidence of that, only psychic intuition. Bella had sworn she wouldn't tell anyone about the missing ring or that Parker believes Johneen's ex has been stalking her, but it's only Calla. She might be able to help.

Bella takes a deep breath, again noticing a strange floral scent in the air. This time, it's even stronger, but as before, there's no discernible source.

The door bursts open below and Max bellows, "Mom! Mom!"

"Wow, he sounds frantic. I hope everything's okay," Calla says.

He always sounds that way, and whatever it is can most likely wait, but Bella isn't taking any chances today.

"I'm coming," she calls, excusing herself to Calla and hurrying down the stairs.

She finds Max and Millicent in the entry hall with Luther, Jiffy, and Odelia.

"Hey, Mom, guess what? We're going to the movies!"

"Who's going to the movies?"

"I'm taking them," Luther tells her, "if that's okay with you?"

"You came over to take them to the movies?"

"No, I came over to drop off the liquor you needed. I ran into everyone outside."

"I ran into everyone, too," Jiffy says, "after I saw them through the window of my house."

Grinning, Luther goes on, "We got to talking about that new movie *Candy Corn* that just came out and how all the kids at school are going to the Saturday matinee."

"All of them?" Odelia asks with a wink.

"Every single one," Bella assures her, remembering to lock the keys back in the desk drawer. "I heard all about it yesterday."

"But you said you're too busy to take us," Max tells her.

"So is my mom, by the way," Jiffy puts in. "And Luther's been wanting to see it too, right, Luther?"

He nods solemnly. "But I haven't been able to find anyone willing to go with me."

"And you're lucky 'cause Max and me are willing." Eager to launch a new adventure, Jiffy bounces a little on his sneakers, one of which is untied, as usual.

Well aware that Luther is trying to get Max out of her hair so that she can execute the wedding in peace, Bella is grateful. Now, if there's any kind of trouble at the wedding, at least she won't have to worry about her son.

"What about your tennis game?" she asks Luther.

"It's not until later this afternoon. But we have to get moving if we're going to make it, so are you ready, boys?"

They're ready.

"Tie your shoe, Jiffy." Luther turns to Millicent, who's drifted across the threshold into the parlor. "Would you like to come along, Ms. Jordan?"

Looking slightly worse for wear, her hair wispy from the breeze, she says, "Pardon? To the movie? Oh, um, no, no thank you. I'm just going to sit here and rest for a minute."

She sinks onto the sofa as Luther and the boys blow out of the house like a tornado. For a moment, the only sounds are the ticking clock, a leaf blower buzzing somewhere outside, and the old floorboards creaking overhead as the guests get ready for the wedding.

Bella reluctantly breaks the tranquility, asking Millicent how she enjoyed her lunch at the café.

"It was . . . all right."

"What did you order?" Odelia asks.

"Minestrone soup. There were bean sprouts in it. And French fries."

Though the recipe sounds right up her alley, Odelia shakes her head and explains, "On Saturdays, they just dump all the week's leftovers into a pot, boil it up, and call it minestrone. If you want decent soup, I have plenty of menudo."

"I'll keep that in mind, but . . . not right now."

"Did you go to the playground after lunch?" Bella asks her.

"Yes. We swung on the swings."

"*Both* of you?"

Millicent nods and leans her head back, allowing her eyes to close lightly. "He's quite a persuasive child. I may need a nap."

"I was just getting ready to go back next door," Odelia tells her. "Come on with me. You can lie down."

Bella is surprised when Millicent agrees.

Walking the two women to the front door, Bella is just in time to see a kitten scoot behind the reception desk. Startled, she hurries after it as Millicent shrieks as if it were a rat.

"It's just a kitten," Odelia tells her. "Got him, Bella?"

"Not yet." On her hands and knees, she crawls after the tiny, black fur ball. After a brief scuffle, she manages to grab hold of him.

"Is that Spidey?" Odelia asks in surprise when she emerges. "I didn't think he was that mobile."

"Neither did I."

"You'd better be more careful about closing your bedroom door."

Bella nods, unnerved, positive she *did* close the door this time and that Spidey was safely inside.

"It's dangerous for him to be running around with people coming and going," Odelia goes on, looking thoughtful, and Bella realizes she's wondering whether her vision might have something to do with this.

A spider, a key sticking out of a lock in the door . . .

Maybe Spirit was warning them that they need to be more careful about securing the kittens in the Rose Room. Especially vulnerable little Spidey.

It makes as much sense as anything else, Bella thinks as she cups the wee kitten in one hand, using the other to unlock the desk drawer and take out the keys again. She locks the drawer and carries the kitten up the stairs, cradling him against her collarbone and feeling his wispy whiskers tickling her chin.

If anything were to happen to this little guy, Max would be devastated, and so would she. Especially if her own scatterbrained recklessness was to blame.

Her bedroom door is still closed and locked.

Did Spidey somehow sneak out when she stepped out into the hall? Maybe she just hadn't noticed. She'd been startled by the sight of Johneen, thinking she was a ghost.

That's the only logical explanation, because even if he managed to crawl into the closet and through the panel, a tiny, fragile little guy like him never could have made it down the shadowy tunnel to the basement and found his way back up to the hall again in such a short time.

There is another logical explanation: someone snuck into the room with a duplicated key after she left, and Spidey slipped out.

The moment Bella crosses the threshold, she knows that that's exactly what happened, because there, sitting squarely on the nightstand, is her cell phone.

Chapter Thirteen

"What time is it?" Odelia whispers to Bella. Neither of them is wearing a watch, but Bella is clutching her cell phone tightly in her hand.

Checking it, she whispers back that it's only one minute later than the last time Odelia asked.

The bride is late, and Pandora's serenade is getting on everyone's nerves. Parked with her keyboard beneath a tree long before the guests were seated, she'd announced that she was saving "Fields of Gold" for the ceremony. Then she launched into what she referred to as a "repertoire of romantic classics."

Her rendition of "Just the Way You Are" was accompanied by the keyboard's percussion setting with an offbeat samba rhythm. She ended "Can't Help Falling in Love" with an Elvis-like "Thank you. Thank you very much." Now she's belting "Feelings," wearing a soulful expression with her calico dress and sensible shoes.

Pandora, whom Odelia likened to "a bad Vegas lounge lizard disguised as someone's frumpy spinster aunt," might be frightful for her captive audience, but Bella is privately grappling with a far scarier situation.

How could her phone have disappeared and reappeared behind a locked door?

Just like Calla's bracelet. The one she dropped into her mother's grave.

Bella doesn't believe in mischievous, ghostly behavior. So she *must* have somehow overlooked the phone the first time she checked.

Except, she didn't.

Anyway, the battery is still low. It wouldn't be if it had been charging all that time.

Why would Johneen's stalker want to borrow her cell phone?

Unfortunately, Bella had removed the password-lock function, so anyone could have accessed her online accounts via the saved information in her phone. She hurriedly checked them all to make sure there was no unusual activity—there wasn't—and changed the log-in data for each one. She also reenabled the phone password and quickly created a new one.

She enters it now and flips through the applications, searching for something amiss. Her rarely visited social media accounts are all intact, no one has been shopping online courtesy of her credit cards, and her e-mail is free of spam.

Grant has yet to reply to the one she sent earlier with the photos attached, which reminds her that she's supposed to be taking pictures of the wedding.

The lovely blue sky has faded to what Bella prefers to think of as white-gold in honor of the wedding and not evidence of an approaching storm. At least she got some good photos earlier, when the sun was still shining brightly . . . or did she? She'd been so rushed and distracted that she'd barely glanced at them before sending them to Grant.

As she clicks on the image file to look them over, Odelia whispers, "How much longer are we supposed suffer through this?"

"The singing?"

"Everything!" Odelia shifts a meaningful glare from Pandora to Blue Slayton, sitting beside Calla with his arm casually slung across the back of her chair.

Every time she looks at him, Bella wishes she'd had a chance to continue her earlier conversation with Calla or to talk to Parker and Virginia again. But Parker remained behind closed doors with his bride, and Bella was reluctant to knock.

Engulfed in a wedding whirlwind from that moment to this, she kept an eye out for Virginia but didn't see her again until she came outside for the wedding with Frankie and Tanya. They aren't necessarily unattractive, but they might as well have been cast as ugly stepsisters beside the striking Virginia. She isn't wearing white, but that might not matter when Johneen spots her.

Nor is she in the bride's coveted spotlight. But she's close enough, in the front row. An unlikely bodyguard, she can't possibly be toting a weapon in her off-the-shoulder blue sheath, but Bella doesn't doubt that it's concealed in the sequined evening bag she's clutching as securely as Bella is her phone.

Beneath the chuppah, Parker is handsome as ever in his dark suit with a daisy boutonniere pinned to his lapel. She can't see his eyes, as he's wearing his sunglasses again. Behind the dark lenses, Bella knows, he's probably scanning the area, keeping an eye out not just for his bride but for a stealthy gate-crasher.

Maid of honor Liz is stationed at the foot of the back steps in her yellow bridesmaid's dress, poised to precede the bride down the grassy aisle.

Odelia, standing beside Bella, is ready to officiate. She's sedately dressed in a navy pillbox hat with a swoop of veil across her eyes and a conservative pantsuit Bella couldn't imagine had come out of her closet.

Turned out it hadn't. She confessed that she'd bought it for a dollar at a tag sale this week.

"Ordinarily, I'd wear a white robe, but this is a nondenominational ceremony."

"Plus the bride said no white."

"Exactly. No chance of upstaging her in this." Odelia glanced down in distaste at her conventional attire. "I can't wait to change back into my normal clothes."

Normal being a relative term.

"*Feelings . . . whoa, oh, oh, feelings,*" Pandora sings, her soprano just slightly off-key, her fingers pounding the keyboard with an oddly staccato jauntiness that doesn't complement the song.

Bella looks down at her phone again.

Wait a minute. Why is the photo folder empty?

What happened to all the shots she took earlier?

She scrolls through the camera files and then through others.

There's no evidence of them on her phone.

Could she have accidentally hit Delete instead of Attach when she sent that e-mail to Grant?

No. A quick check shows her that he did get the e-mail and responded a short time ago.

Nice shots! Keep them coming! G.E.

Okay. If she didn't do it, then did the person who stole her phone erase the files, perhaps by accident?

Or . . . on purpose? But why?

Pandora transitions from "Feelings" to Barry Manilow's "We've Made It Through the Rain."

Not yet, they haven't. The breeze off the water is still gentle for October, but the temperature has dropped enough to raise goose bumps on Bella's bare arms—if they weren't already there. A knot of fear tightens in her gut as she thinks of Johneen, alone in the house, unaware that she might be in danger.

"I'll be right back," Bella whispers abruptly to Odelia.

"Where are you going?"

"To check on Johneen."

As she hurries toward the house, the wind seems to shift direction. It isn't just cooler, it suddenly smells different, heavily scented with flowers.

Again, something grazes her consciousness—last night, the mirror, her dream self as a bride—but it slips from her grasp like a keep-away ball.

Stepping into the kitchen, she nearly crashes into Johneen.

"I was just coming to find you. Are you ready?"

"I've been ready." The bride stands her ground. "I just need another minute."

"Are you all right?"

"Of course I am." She sounds prickly as always, her upper-crust accent firmly in place. But her eyes have a wide, incandescent quality.

It's just makeup and anticipation, Bella assures herself. *This is her wedding day*

Still . . .

199

Oddly, the floral perfume is even stronger in the house. She looks around for the source but sees only the bridal bouquet and the sprigs of Shasta daisies and Queen Anne's lace in Johneen's hair.

"Are you sure you're feeling all right?"

"I'm . . . not," Johneen admits. "No. I'm not."

If she were anyone else, Bella might press a palm to her forehead or even put a reassuring arm around her. But she doesn't dare touch the bride, fearful she might leave a smudge.

"You haven't eaten much today. Unless you snuck away for a cheeseburger when I wasn't looking."

Her feeble attempt at a joke doesn't merit a smile. Johneen merely looks down at her form-fitting silk gown. "Even if I was starving—which I wasn't—this dress isn't very forgiving."

Taken aback by the glimpse of vulnerability, Bella almost feels sorry for her. Perfection can't be easy.

Imperfection is tough enough.

"Do you need some crackers or something?"

"You want me to eat in this dress? *Now?*"

"I just thought—"

"Are you crazy?" she barks. Same old Johneen.

"I just wanted to make sure you're okay."

"Why does everyone keep asking me that?"

"Who's asking you?"

"First Calla's grandmother, and now you."

"I didn't know you'd even talked to Odelia. When was this?"

"She texted me a little while ago. She wanted to come upstairs, but I told her I needed some time alone. Then she reminded me there was still time to postpone the wedding if I wanted to."

Funny. Odelia hadn't mentioned that to Bella. Then again, they'd been busy putting finishing touches on the food and trying to herd the guests outside.

"I asked her why she thought I'd want to do that," Johneen goes on, "and she said maybe we should just wait a little longer."

"What did you say?"

"What do you think? If I wanted to wait, would I be standing here in a wedding gown?"

"It sounds like you know exactly what you want to do."

"Yes, and if I didn't feel so dizzy, I'd be doing it right this second. Can you get me some cold water?"

No *please*, Bella notes, going over to the sink, and no *thank you* when she hands over a glass. But this time, she forgives the lapse in manners. Johneen might look beautiful, but she really doesn't seem well.

As for Odelia, if she's desperate enough to try to convince Johneen to postpone the wedding when it was her own idea to have it here in the first place, then she could very well have been desperate enough to write that note *and* steal it back. Bella supposes she could also have stolen the wedding ring, hoping that would be enough to stall the wedding. But why would she take Bella's cell phone, too?

How infuriating to imagine that her wedding-planning partner— her friend, the person who concocted the perfect plan to guarantee Bella and Max's future in Lily Dale—is now trying to sabotage the wedding.

Yet it's almost a relief. Better Odelia than some sinister stranger. For all her faults, Bella is certain she isn't capable of harming another human being. Not physically, and certainly not intention- ally. Whatever she's been up to, it's because she truly believes she's working toward the greater good.

Bella watches Johneen take a few sips of water, eyes closed.

"You said flowers bother you. Are you allergic, like Tanya?"

"I'm not allergic. I just don't like fragrance. That's why I didn't want a scented bouquet."

"So you can't smell it? Because it seems strong to me now."

Johneen frowns, lifting the bouquet to her nose and inhaling deeply. "I can't smell a thing."

"Are you sure?"

"Positive. Why? Can you?" She holds out the bouquet.

Bella shakes her head, somehow certain that even if she buries her nose in it, she won't locate the source of the perfume in the air. Either she's imagining it, or it's . . . what? Nadine?

No. No way. The phantom floral scent is simply another Lily Dale peculiarity that seems to defy science. It too has a perfectly logi- cal explanation—perhaps sensory phenomenology.

Just like when you heard those clanging wind chimes deep in the woods, Bella reminds herself, shuddering even now to remember that awful July day. At the time, cornered by a murderer, she truly believed the sound was a ghostly warning.

Now that logic prevails, she knows it was either a panic-triggered delusion or an acoustic aberration.

She's stressed, but she isn't panicking. This isn't a delusion. The scent is real.

Why can't Johneen smell it?

Because . . . because . . .

Because maybe she has anosmia.

It's a legitimate medical condition: the temporary or permanent impairment of one's sense of smell.

See? All you have to do is use your background in science and take a moment to consider the possibilities.

Pleased with her latest hypothesis, Bella takes the empty glass from Johneen. "Do you want a refill? Or do you want to sit down for a minute?"

"No." She takes a deep breath. "I'm ready to go."

This time, Bella doesn't ask if she's sure, and not just because she desperately wants to be back outside in the fresh air.

Johneen is anxious and tired and possibly coming down with something, but Bella is certain it isn't a case of cold feet. She isn't going to let anything or anyone—not Odelia, or Spirit, or even a stalker, real or imaginary—keep this wedding from happening.

Not just because my own future depends on it.

Because Johneen really does love Parker, and she wants to marry him.

Chapter Fourteen

Twenty minutes, two gold bands—one a secretly borrowed family heirloom—and an off-key rendition of "Fields of Gold" later, Parker and Johneen are finally married.

Odelia makes the pronouncement, wearing a smile that's simultaneously relieved and strained. She's obviously still concerned that something might go wrong.

But that's life, Bella thinks as she allows herself to exhale at last. *Married or not.*

Nobody knows that better than I do.

Growing up motherless, raised by a grieving single father, you can't help but be well aware that calamity might strike at any given moment of any given day. And when it does . . .

You muster every shred of inner strength to move on, because what else is there to do?

"Can I kiss the bride?" Parker asks, and laughter ripples through the crowd.

Smiling, Odelia assures him that he can.

Watching him gently cup his new wife's face in his hands as his lips tenderly brush hers, Bella remembers what it was like to be kissed that way. It was thrilling, and comforting, and—

"Guess I'm just in time."

Startled by the low voice close to her ear, she spins around and finds Drew Bailey standing behind her. To her surprise, he's changed from jeans into a pair of dark trousers, a white shirt, and a sport coat.

He's so close she can smell his aftershave mingling with the still-pervasive scent of flowers.

"Hey, you came back," she whispers.

"Told you I would."

Right. For the plumbing and the kitten.

But you don't get all dressed up to fix a leak or rescue an animal.

She doesn't dare keep looking at him, afraid he'll be able to tell what she's thinking.

She turns and watches Parker release Johneen. He's smiling; she looks a little shaky. Maybe because she's been swept off her feet.

Yeah, I get that, Bella thinks, longing to sneak another peek at Drew. She's never seen him this clean-shaven or dressed up. Nor has she ever seen him looking at her the way he did just now, as if . . . as if he wanted to . . .

The guests applaud politely, and Pandora belts "We've Only Just Begun" as the bride and groom recess down the grassy aisle. The guests are on their feet following them, and Odelia makes a beeline for Bella.

"We did it!"

Swept into her friend's fervent embrace, Bella can hardly start flinging accusations. As Odelia releases her and turns to greet Drew, she notices that the floral scent is still drifting heavily in the air.

Nearby, Johneen and Parker, arm in arm, accept congratulations from their guests.

Bella has witnessed plenty of weddings and has been a bride herself. This is how it always goes after marriage vows are exchanged. Loved ones flock to congratulate the bride and groom, who are giddy with joy and excitement.

But as a smiling Johneen accepts a hug from her maid of honor, she seems to be merely going through the motions.

Bella turns to Odelia, wondering if she, too, has noticed. But she's busy unbuttoning her navy jacket.

"If you ever get remarried, Bella, I promise I'll be your officiant. But I'm never wearing this clown suit again."

Remarried? Why would she even say that? And especially right now, with Drew here.

Bella feels her face grow hot.

"I think you look very regal," he tells Odelia.

"No, I look very ridiculous, and—" She breaks off to address the empty space beside her. "Yes, Mae, he is. But it's a good thing he can't see you, you naughty girl."

Drew raises an eyebrow at her.

"An old friend," Odelia explains. "She says you're handsome."

"Um . . . thank you?"

"What's that, Mae?" Odelia seems to listen, then relays, "She thinks Bella looks nice, too."

"Bella looks beautiful," Drew says, and Bella's face grows hotter still.

Drew Bailey thinks she looks beautiful?

"Thank you," she murmurs, and he replies, "You're welcome." At that moment, even the ghostly conversation has stalled.

Fumbling for something to say, Bella comes up with "Food."

Drew and Odelia just look at her, then at each other.

"We have to eat the food!" she tells them. "No, I mean, we have to *serve* the food. For the reception."

"First, we need to pop the champagne for a toast," Odelia reminds her.

"You're right! We need to serve the toast!"

"You're serving toast?"

"No!" she tells Drew. "I meant we have to serve the pop for the toast and pour the food!"

Drew grins. "Have you been drinking already?"

Giving up, Bella hurries toward the house.

Heading in the opposite direction, Odelia calls, "I'll be back!"

"But what about the champagne? And the food?"

"I have to change! I'll be quick!"

Suspicion dogs Bella as she strides into the house, nearly hitting Drew with the door as she pulls it closed behind her.

"Sorry! I didn't know you were coming with me."

"I figured someone had better help you, and your co-captain seems to have jumped ship."

You have no idea, she thinks, saying only, "It's okay. You don't have to help."

"I want to, and it seems like you need me."

"I don't want you!"

He tilts his head at her, brows furrowed.

She hastily corrects herself. "I mean, I don't need you."

Realizing she doesn't sound particularly convincing, even to her own ears, she turns away, face flaming, and opens the refrigerator. She grabs several bottles of Dom Pérignon, kicks the door closed, and clumsily sets the armload on the counter, where plastic-wrapped platters cover nearly every inch of space. One of the green bottles teeters too close to the edge and topples off.

Bella reaches for it and misses.

Drew, however, makes a diving catch. He looks up at her from the floor. "Still think you don't need me?"

Despite herself, despite everything, she can't help but grin as she takes it from him. "You just saved me two hundred bucks."

"My pleasure. But I don't think you should open that one just yet, unless you want to douse yourself and everyone around you in eau-de-champagne."

"Speaking of eau-de . . . Do you smell perfume, by any chance?"

Back on his feet, he leans closer to her, sniffing her neck, and she's reminded that her dress is, indeed, far too low-cut.

"It smells good."

"No, I didn't mean—I'm not wearing any perfume. But I smell flowers. Do you?"

"Is it my cologne?"

"No, that's not floral." The words seem to lodge in her throat. He's standing unnervingly close to her.

She dares to look up at him, hoping to find reassurance that she's merely imagining the connection between them, along with everything else that isn't really happening.

But when their eyes meet, she knows that this, at least, is real.

He reaches out and pushes a strand of hair back from her face. "Bella, I—"

"Mom!" The front door slams shut. "Mom!"

Bella and Drew leap apart guiltily. He grabs a dish towel from the counter as Max and Jiffy burst into the kitchen chattering about the awesome movie. Bella jerks open a drawer and rummages through it with trembly hands.

"Hey, guys, how's it going?" Drew asks.

"I didn't know you were here!" Max gives him a high five.

"Are you guys going on a date night?" Jiffy asks with interest.

"Date night?" Drew echoes, looking amused.

Dismayed, Bella asks, her voice a little too shrill, "Why would you think that?"

"Last time my dad came back to visit us, that's what he wore when he went on date night with my mom." He indicates Drew's jacket and dress pants, then waves a hand at Bella. "And my mom wears some kind of smelly perfume, just like you."

Bella looks sharply at him. "I'm not wearing perfume."

"You're not?" He shrugs.

"Why? Do you smell it?"

"Yep." He gestures at the three-tiered wedding cake on the table. "Hey, by the way, can I have a piece of that?"

"I already asked, and she said no," Max tells him. "It's for the wedding."

"What wedding?" Jiffy sidles closer to the cake.

"Some wedding."

"Can we please have cake, Bella?"

"Maybe later. Do you smell flowers, Jiffy?"

"I *see* flowers!" He leans over the cake. "They're made of frosting. Look, Max!"

"Can we have frosting flowers, Mom?"

"Not now. Maybe later. Jiffy, do you smell flowers?" she persists.

"Yeah. They stink. They should go outside and blow the stink off."

Both boys snicker. Then Max asks, sniffing so that his nose nearly touches the icing, "Do the frosting flowers have a smell?"

"Why? Can you smell them?"

"Nope."

"Well, I can," Jiffy says. "I smelled them outside, too, when Luther dropped us off."

"Is he here?" Drew asks.

"No, he had to go play tennis. But he said he'll be back later and save him some food," Max says.

Jiffy nods vigorously. "He probably wants cake, too, by the way. We should probably cut some for him now. And for us."

"Later." Bella takes a deep breath of the floral-scented air and levels a look at him. "So you smell the flowers right now?"

"Yep. Did you put perfume into the frosting? Because I don't know if that would be so good, but I can taste it to make sure."

"My mom didn't make the cake. Mrs. Drumm did."

"Did she put perfume in the frosting?" Jiffy wonders, and Drew rests a hand on both boys' shoulders.

"Hey, guys, how about if we go over to Melrose Park and throw a football around?"

"Yes!" they shout in unison.

"Great." He looks at Bella. "Okay with you?"

"It's more than okay. But Jiffy has to get his mom's permission."

"She'll permiss me. She always does."

"Well, you need to ask her to make sure."

"She's not here."

"Then we'll stop by the house," Drew says. "Come on, grab the football, Max, and let's go."

"I don't have a football."

"How about you, Jiffy?"

"Nope."

"Do you have a Wiffle ball and bat?"

"Nope. My dad said he'd give me that stuff sometime, but I think he forgot."

"My dad didn't forget! I'll go get them!" Max scampers from the room as Bella remembers, with a pang, how Sam used to play ball with him.

Jiffy gives Drew a pointed once-over. "Your mom prolly doesn't permiss you to play outside in your good clothes."

Drew grins. "I'm pretty certain she'd be okay with it."

"Well, you need to call her to make sure."

"I wish I could," he says so wistfully that Bella can't help but wonder about Drew's mom, and his dad, for that matter.

Really, she knows nothing about his past. So how can she possibly be thinking about kissing him?

Again, her face feels hot. She forces herself to think of something else, like . . .

Like flowers. How she can possibly smell them inside the house, where there are none?

And it isn't just her. It's Jiffy, too.

Jiffy, whose mother is a medium.

Jiffy, who occasionally says things that no ordinary kid would say and who often seems to know things that no one in the world could possibly know.

"Hey, sorry about that," Drew says in a low voice, and she looks up, startled, to see him watching her. "I shouldn't have done that in front of the boys."

"No, they didn't see."

"What?"

"What?" she echoes, realizing he might not have been talking about what she thinks he's talking about.

"I probably should have asked you before I suggested taking them to the park."

Oh! The park! Right, the park!

Not the near-kiss or whatever was going on when Max and Jiffy showed up.

"No, it's—it's fine! It's great! I was actually hoping the movie would last longer," she babbles, "because after he got home I was going to make him stay upstairs with the Chances. I mean the cats. I mean the cat and the kisses. *Kittens.*"

She hurriedly turns away from the faintly amused expression in Drew's eyes.

"He's not going to the wedding, then?"

"Max? No." She jerks open the fridge and begins plucking containers from the shelves. "Kids aren't welcome."

"In that case, I can take him out for dinner after the park."

"That would be great." Arms full, Bella kicks the refrigerator door shut and looks helplessly at the counter for a spot to unload.

"Here, let me get that for you."

209

As Drew reaches to relieve her burden, the back door opens and Odelia steps into the kitchen.

"We're here to help," she says.

Bella sees that "we" includes Millicent, who is holding a small stack of books. She's changed into her version of casual clothing: dark, wool pants and a cashmere cardigan.

Odelia now sports a one-piece purple jumpsuit with a zipper up the front. She gestures at her Nikes. "Bella, do you think Johnny will mind that these are white?"

"She probably won't even notice." Bella is conscious of Drew's proximity as he continues to take refrigerated items from her arms beneath Millicent's narrowed gaze.

"Who's Johnny?" Jiffy asks Odelia. "And why would he mind if your shoes are white? And why did you call him *she*?"

"Johnny is the bride, and he *is* a she. I mean, *she* is a she."

"Can I see him?" Jiffy hurries over to the door to peek outside, nearly sideswiping the two women. "Oops, sorry, Odelia and . . . Lady."

"Jiffy, that's Max's grandma, Millicent," Bella says. "Millicent, meet Jiffy, a good friend of Max's. And this is Doctor Bailey. He's . . ."

He's also a good friend of Max's, and of Bella's. But she's not about to admit that, given the way her mother-in-law looked at him this morning—and is looking at him again now.

". . . our veterinarian," she says instead. "He's here to rescue a stray kitten."

Yes, a *kitten*. Not a *kiss*. There are no kisses here. No, sir.

Millicent looks harder at Drew holding containers of strawberries and salad greens, not a kitten in sight.

"What are those?" Jiffy has zeroed in on the books she's holding.

"They're for Max. They . . ." She pauses to clear her throat. "They used to belong to his father."

"What are their names?"

"The books? *A Wrinkle in Time*, *The Phantom Tollbooth*, *Charlotte's Web*—that was Sam's favorite."

"Max already has that book."

Yes. When Sam became too sick to play catch with Max, he bought *Charlotte's Web* and started reading it aloud, chapter by chapter. They never did get to finish the story.

Once in a while, at bedtime, Max asks Bella to continue it. "Please, Mom? I want to know what happens to Wilbur the runt."

"We'll get to it," she promises, but she hasn't had the heart to do it just yet.

Remembering father and son snuggled together in bed with the book, Bella turns to face the sink and runs the tap for no reason.

"Maybe you can give me some books," Jiffy suggests to Millicent. "I like to read. I'm good at all the two-letter words and three-letter words. Now I'm learning some four-letter words."

No comment from Millicent, but that gives Odelia and Drew a chuckle, and even Bella has to smile. She turns off the water and dries her dry hands on a dish towel.

"I found it, Doctor Drew!" Max bursts into the room. "Let's go!"

"Where are you going, Max?" Millicent asks.

"To the park to play ball."

She says nothing to that, but her face is taut.

"We don't have time to stop at my house," Jiffy announces, "'cause it's going to rain pretty soon."

"Soon?" Bella follows his gaze to the window. "Oh, no."

"Oh, yes," Odelia tells her. "We'd better start pouring that bubbly. If they drink enough, maybe they won't notice that the weather's turning."

"Hey, how come Johnny's wearing a Halloween costume?"

"That's not a Halloween costume, Jiffy," Odelia says. "She's a bride."

"A dead zombie bride?"

"No, just a regular beautiful bride."

"Well, she looks like a dead zombie," Jiffy insists.

Glancing out into the yard, Bella confirms that Johneen is still upright. She does, however, look even more peaked as she chats with Calla and Blue.

"What do you mean, Jiffy?" Bella asks, uneasy once more. "Why do you think she looks like a dead zombie?"

"She just does." He shrugs. "Can we go now, Doctor Drew?"

"Do you need me, Bella?"

She assures him once again—perhaps a tad too firmly—that she does not.

He ushers the boys out the front door, and Odelia hurries over to join Bella at the back, murmuring, "I don't like this."

"You don't like what?" Bella asks in a voice too low for Millicent to hear.

"What Jiffy said when he looked at Johnny."

Bella doesn't like it either, but the last thing she wants is for Odelia to start getting crazy again.

"We need to talk," she says. "I know what you—"

"Pardon?" Millicent asks pointedly from across the room.

"Sorry, we were just trying to figure something out."

Millicent doesn't ask what it is. Nor does she ask if she can help them, but Bella puts her to work anyway, hulling strawberries to dip in chocolate fondue. Then she rounds up Pandora, still mingling in the yard, to help serve.

A short time later, the guests are seated at the tables, toasting and sipping Dom Pérignon as Pandora and Millicent prepare main-course platters in the kitchen and Bella and Odelia serve the salads.

According to the hourly forecast, they'll make it through dinner before the rain begins. According to the heavens, that seems less likely by the minute.

The lake has gone from cobalt and placid to a dense, rippled fog-gray. Overhead, drying foliage whispers ominously. The air is thick with the scent of storm and wood smoke. Chimney tendrils snake from Dale rooftops into a murky sky that's darker than it should be at this hour, casting the tables in shadow.

Odelia was right, though. Now that the champagne is flowing, the guests don't seem particularly concerned about the weather. The men are still wearing their suit coats, and a few women have donned wraps, but everyone seems blissfully oblivious.

Everyone . . . except Johneen.

The bride alone appears troubled, though perhaps not by the prospect of rain. She begins to pick at her salad as the others dig in.

Is it any wonder? Odelia's warning is probably still ringing in her head. Perhaps she's wondering whether she just made a colossal mistake.

Or she might be pouting because Virginia is seated beside her. As Parker pointed out earlier, it wouldn't be right to put his cousin at a table filled with strangers.

Leaving the guests to eat their salads, Bella follows Odelia back toward the house but stops her on the back steps.

"What's wrong, Bella?"

"I need to talk to you for a second." Hearing a distant growl of thunder, she cuts right to the chase. "I know what you've been up to."

"What I've been *up to*?"

"Trying to get Johneen to call off the wedding."

Odelia shrugs. "I know you didn't want me to talk to her, Bella, but—"

"But you did it anyway." She sounds like a mother scolding a naughty child, but she can't help herself.

"We all do what we have to do, Bella. I deliver messages to those who need to hear them."

"Well, your delivery method isn't terrific. And it didn't change anything. She still married him."

"Yes, but I—"

"So maybe you caused this big stir for no reason," Bella goes on, frustrated by Odelia's mild expression. Doesn't she realize that you don't go around . . . stealing wedding rings and erasing people's private files? "Did you ever think that maybe you misinterpreted the warning?"

"That's always a possibility, but—"

"Daisy!"

The shout comes from the yard behind them.

Turning, Bella sees that Parker has jumped to his feet and is waving his arms wildly.

Johneen seems to have disappeared altogether.

Did she throw a tantrum and run off? Or flee the approaching storm?

No, there she is—lying on the ground beside the table. Her dress is askew, and her bouquet, which had been on the table beside her plate, lies scattered around her. She must have tripped and fallen, just like Odelia predicted, although . . .

I don't feel as though my vision involves Johneen slipping or tripping and falling.

The other guests, looking alarmed, are hurrying toward her as Parker flails and shouts.

"Please, someone . . . help her!"

But as Bella rushes to the stricken bride, she realizes it might already be too late.

Johneen's eyes are fixed on the stormy sky, and her lovely face is no longer pale.

It's blue.

Chapter Fifteen

Borne away on a stretcher within a few frantic minutes of Bella's 9-1-1 call, Johneen Maynard is barely clinging to life.

"What's wrong with her?" Parker asked repeatedly in the rush to save her. "Is she choking?"

It seemed the logical assumption. Frankie, well-trained in first aid as a coach, reached her stricken friend before Bella could get across the yard. She repeatedly tried the Heimlich maneuver to no avail, so switched over to CPR.

The medics took over the chest compressions as they rushed her to the ambulance, and the panic-stricken groom rode off with them.

As whirling red lights and sirens fade into the distance, Bella struggles to catch her breath. Her chest is tight with panic, her lungs filled with inexplicably floral-scented air.

The guests, still clustered by the tables, appear shell-shocked by the catapult from joy to sorrow. Several of the women are weeping.

Calla is not, though she's clearly distressed. Her hair has fallen from its updo, and she's leaning heavily on Blue Slayton's shoulder.

His expression is more thoughtful than disturbed. He's absently stroking Calla's hair, staring at the storm clouds mounting over the water.

Odelia and Pandora aren't teary-eyed either. The two women appear to have called a temporary truce and are whispering to each other. Like Calla and Blue, they seem to radiate a unique calm in the eye of this terrible storm.

Is it because they're Spiritualists? Do they react to matters of life and death differently because to them, there simply *is* no death? Certainly there's a level of comfort in the idea that the soul survives.

Plus, at least three of the four had premonitions that something might happen to Johneen, so unlike the rest of the group, they weren't entirely caught off guard.

As for the fourth . . .

She looks at Blue, then drags her gaze—and her thoughts—away from him and from her earlier suspicions.

Focusing on Virginia, Bella sees that she stands apart from the others. She, too, had been on high alert, expecting trouble. What is she thinking now that it's come in an unexpected way?

Her back is turned and she appears to be furtively fumbling with something in her hands . . .

The gun? Or just her badge? Is she going to whip it out and announce that she suspects someone here of foul play?

But it's not as if someone took a shot at Johneen or leapt from the shadows and tackled her to the ground. That much is clear. Whatever happened to her appeared to be natural and health-related.

Some kind of seizure, as far as Bella could tell.

She sidles toward Virginia and realizes that she's not holding a gun or a badge. She's simply trying to light a cigarette in trembling hands, positioned to block the wind, not the gazes of potential suspects.

"Does Johneen have some kind of medical condition?" Ryan is asking Liz. They'd both been seated at the newlyweds' table. His arm is wrapped tightly around her as she shivers in her yellow dress, dabbing at her mascara-streaked face with a cocktail napkin.

"Not that I know of." Her voice is high pitched and wavering. "But she told me she was feeling dizzy right before it happened. I thought it was just nerves. I didn't think anything was going to happen to her!"

"So what *did* happen, exactly?" Frankie asks, still panting from her heroic CPR efforts. "Was she just sitting there one minute, and the next, she fainted?"

"She didn't just faint. She couldn't breathe!" Liz snaps. "Didn't you hear that horrible sound?"

"I did. She was gasping for air," Andrea agrees.

Bella heard the wheezing, too. She shudders, hugging herself against the chill and the horror.

Hellerman, who topped off his glass of bourbon somewhere along the way, suggests that it might have been a heart attack.

"How could someone like Johneen have a heart attack?" Charlie asks.

"Stress."

"She's young and in shape."

"It's a freak thing, but it happens. Especially with someone like her. Trust me, I'm the one who works with her. She can be one uptight—"

"Shut up, Hellerman!"

At Andrea's admonishment, he throws up his hands in defense. "*Woman*. I was going to say *woman*."

"Yeah, sure you were," Andrea says. "I've heard you call her a—"

"Come on, babe, don't bring that up again!" Charlie tells her.

"Bring up what?" Tanya asks.

"When Hellerman first met Johneen," Andrea explains, "he was into her, but she wasn't interested, so he—"

"Babe," Charlie says again. "*Stop*."

"So he what?"

The sharp question comes from Virginia, who's stepped closer, eyes probing Hellerman.

"Nothing!" he protests. "I didn't do anything!"

Andrea looks from him to Virginia and shakes her head. "It's no big deal."

"What," Virginia asks in a low, steady voice, "did he do?"

"I didn't do anything!" Hellerman repeats.

Ignoring him, Andrea says, "It's just, as far as Johneen knows, they're friends and he's moved on. That's why she invited him to the wedding. But whenever he has too much to drink, he . . . says things."

"What does he say?"

"You know. He just . . . talks about her. Behind her back." She shrugs. "He says she isn't that nice."

That's such a glaring understatement that Bella has to hold back a hysterical laugh that surges from her gut. It isn't funny—none of this is amusing—but her emotions are volatile.

Virginia shrugs and fixes her gaze on Hellerman. "True?"

"Did I ask her out? Yeah. Did she say no? Hell, yeah. I already told you about that."

"Not all of it."

"So? Come on. Look at her. Look at me. Yeah, maybe I don't think she's all that *nice*."

"Sometimes she isn't," Charlie speaks up, and even Andrea nods.

"But I sure as hell didn't want her to have a heart attack," Hellerman says.

Virginia seems to consider this, then nods. "Y'all shouldn't speculate about what happened. We'll have to wait and see."

She walks over to the bar and pours herself a bourbon, straight up. She takes a long sip and then a long drag on her cigarette, heaving its acrid vapor into the night air.

Bella herself has never smoked, and she isn't tempted. Nor is she much of a drinker, though maybe she could use a stiff one now. But as she moves toward the bar, she spots her mother-in-law.

Hovering alone at the edge of the group, she's darting fearful glances from face to face. Her gaze settles on Bella's, and she raises a hand to beckon her over.

Bella quickly looks away, pretending not to have noticed.

I can't. I just can't be fair to her and her suspicions right now.

So much for a nerve-calming cocktail. There's no way she's going to pour one under Millicent's watchful eye, much less risk loosening her tongue and saying something she might regret later.

A cold gust sends leaves whirling around them, and thunder grumbles in the western hills.

"We need to get everything inside," she calls as lightning slashes the churning lake. "It's going to pour."

"What should we do with everyone now?" Odelia asks, sidling over as the others begin clearing tables and heading toward the house.

"What *can* we do? Tell them the party's over and send them on their way?"

"The ones who aren't staying here, yes."

Bella levels a look at her. "You mean Blue."

"And Pandora." She nods at the woman, who's recruited Ryan and Charlie to manhandle her portable keyboard into the house. "I have a feeling she's about to cause a problem."

"More singing?"

"Not that kind of problem. She doesn't think that whatever just happened to Johnny was an accident."

Bella's mouth drops open, and the reverberating thunderclap she hears in that instant might as well have fallen out of it.

"Shh, don't say anything." Odelia shakes her head at Bella as Millicent comes striding over.

"Isabella, I need to have a word with you. In private." She shoots a meaningful glance at Odelia, who holds out a hand, palm up.

"It's starting to sprinkle," she announces, then begins clearing the bar table. "We need to get the rest of this inside."

Finding her voice, Bella tells her mother-in-law that they can talk in the house.

"No, I don't want *them* to hear." Millicent emphasizes the word as if . . .

As if they're an evil cult?

The sprinkles are turning to rain. Hard rain.

"Come on, we're going to get soaked." Bella snatches the pitcher of lemonade and a few remaining mason-jar glasses from the bar. Then she spots something on the grass, poking from beneath the long, white tablecloth.

"Maleficent, can you please take this for me?"

"I beg your pardon?"

"Please just carry this into the house."

"*What* did you call me?"

Bella is incredulous. There's never a good time to have the "Please call me Mother" conversation, but could there be a worse one?

"I called you Millicent," she snaps.

"You called me *Maleficent*."

Uh-oh. "I did?"

"You did."

Remorse oozes in. "It was . . . it was a slip of the tongue. I'm sorry."

Wordlessly, Millicent takes the pitcher and marches it toward the house, sloshing lemonade and juggling delicate glasses.

She'll get over it. The only thing that matters right now is Johneen. Bella stands for a moment, eyes closed, face tilted to the sky. She lets the rain wash over her as if it might scrub away the ordeal, but it only succeeds in soaking and chilling her to the bone. She needs to get inside.

Kneeling on the grass beside the twitching tuft of blue fur poking from beneath the tablecloth, she lifts the fabric hem. There, crouched beside an ice chest, is Li'l Chap.

His pale-green eyes are trusting and frightened. Bella gently scoops him up and carries him toward the house.

Drew will understand that I couldn't leave him out here alone.

Chaos reigns inside the cluttered kitchen. There isn't enough room for all these people, let alone everything they're carrying.

Bella pushes past Pandora's portable keyboard and through the crowd with the kitten. She hurries up the stairs, unlocks the door to the Rose Room, and finds everything just as she left it. Chance is contentedly lying on a chair, keeping an eye on her energetic family. Several kittens wrestle on the rug, a few are playing paw hockey with Bella's lip balm as a puck, and one is engaged in tug-of-war with a strand of carpet fringe.

Not sure what to do with the little blue stray, Bella tentatively sets him on the cushion beside Chance.

"This is Li'l Chap. He was lost, just like you were."

Listening to the rain hammering on the porch roof beyond the open window, Bella stands poised to grab the kitten at the slightest sign of aggression. Chance might be sweet-natured, but felines are notoriously territorial, and this is her family's safe haven.

Cat and kitten eye each other warily. Then the baby opens his mouth and lets out a surprisingly loud, high-pitched mew. Chance arches a fat tabby paw toward him, and Bella's heart sinks. Before she can grab the kitten, the paw settles on his fragile little back.

But it's not a hostile gesture. It's a protective one. Chance snuggles the baby against her and begins licking his fur, tenderly grooming him as she does her own offspring.

Bella longs to cocoon herself in this hushed little haven for the rest of the night. But she forces herself to leave, sidestepping kittens as usual before locking the door and trudging back downstairs to harsh reality.

In the kitchen, Virginia is barking orders as she scrapes the remains of the salads into the garbage and stacks the plates in the sink. "All of y'all need to find a spot to put stuff down and then clear out of here!"

"I'm not putting this down, but I'm happy to clear out of here." Hellerman wields the bourbon decanter. "I'm heading out to the porch. Who's with me?"

Charlie is with him. Ryan, too. They gladly escape, leaving Pandora's keyboard propped against the refrigerator.

Hellerman turns to the lone male left in the kitchen. "Coming, Slayton?"

"Go ahead," Calla tells Blue, and he follows the other guys, though not with much enthusiasm.

Catching her grandmother's critical look, Calla asks, "What?"

"Did I say anything?"

"You didn't have to. But you usually do." Calla gestures at the table centerpieces she's retrieved from outdoors. "I'm going to go put these in the parlor."

"Me too." Tanya follows her from the room with the rest of the flowers. "And then I'm going to go upstairs to call my husband. I really need to talk to him. I'm so upset."

"We're *all* upset." Andrea shakes her dark head.

"Why is it that the women are always left in the kitchen with the mess?" Liz asks peckishly.

"It isn't fair," Frankie agrees.

"You should go with them," Bella tells them. "All of you. Really. I can do the cleanup."

Not waiting to be asked twice, Andrea, Liz, and Frankie make a beeline from the room.

Virginia is filling the sink with water and suds. "I'll wash the dishes. I'd rather be in here." She sounds as though she means it, and she probably does, being odd man out among the wedding guests now that Parker is gone.

What's going through her head now? Is she relieved that what-ever happened to Johneen, as disturbing as it was, hadn't been born of the violence Virginia was determined to prevent? Or is she still wary? Does she, like Bella, wonder if someone under this roof might have stolen the wedding ring out of vengeance? Blue, perhaps, or Hellerman?

"Where do you want these, luv?" Pandora asks, her gangly limbs juggling several napkin-lined bread baskets. "Everything got wet."

Bella takes them from her and dumps the soggy bread into the garbage on top of the salad scraps, wondering again if Pandora could possibly have been behind the missing ring and the anonymous note.

Hearing a clatter, she turns to see her mother-in-law wedging the pitcher of lemonade into a few square inches of counter space. It teeters, and she moves it to a different, equally crowded area. She picks up several used glasses, awkwardly looks around for a place to put them, and sets them back in the same spot.

Clearly, she's trying to make an effort to at least appear to be helping. Bella almost feels sorry for her. Though not enough to want to talk to her.

"Let's get your keyboard out of here," she tells Pandora, "so that we can open the refrigerator. I'll take one end, you take the other. We can put it in the study."

Together, they carry the unwieldly instrument through the house. Thunder and rain and voices from the porch float through open parlor windows.

She opens the French door, and she and Pandora prop the key-board against the wall of the small study.

"Careful not to nick the hardwoods," Pandora says with the pro-prietary air of one who painstakingly sanded them on her hands and knees when she lived in this house.

Does she feel a sense of obligation toward everything—and everyone—in it? Was it enough to make her trespass and meddle again, despite the havoc she wreaked earlier in the summer?

"Can you shut the door, please, Pandora? I want to ask you about something."

"Of course, luv."

Bella flips on the desk lamp. It casts a yellowish haze over the small, drafty room. Beyond the screen, rain patters into the shrub border. She closes the window to shut out the damp chill. As soon as it's down, she feels claustrophobic.

"Odelia told me that you don't think that whatever happened to Johneen was an accident?"

"She did, did she?" Pandora's eyes, behind her glasses, blink rapidly. "That woman can't keep a bloody thing to herself, can she?"

Funny—Odelia often says precisely the same thing about Pandora.

"Did someone try to hurt her? Is that why she collapsed? Or did someone say something that upset her?"

"Perhaps."

Bella digests that, along with the guilt that comes with it. "Earlier, you were here with a message for her. Only I wouldn't let you deliver it."

"It wouldn't have changed a thing. I'd only have told her that my guides were concerned about her safety, and I'd have warned her to be careful. But we all have free will, Isabella. I couldn't have stopped her from doing anything, and neither could you."

"What makes you think that this wasn't an accident?"

Stupid question. What are the odds that the answer will involve concrete evidence or logic?

Around here, absolutely zero.

"Spirit is showing me a hand at her throat."

"So someone strangled her?"

"Of course not!"

"But you said . . ."

"I didn't mean *that*."

No, of course not. Lily Dale logic prevails.

"She was right there in plain sight, luv," Pandora points out. "She wasn't actually strangled. That's just the symbol I see when someone leaves this world at the hands of another."

"Spirit shorthand," Bella murmurs, thinking she has to tell Virginia about this immediately. It isn't concrete evidence, by any means, but she should know that there's a chance . . .

And then it sinks in.

"Wait a minute . . . did you say 'leaves this world'?" she asks Pandora, who nods. "So then you think Johneen is . . . ?"

"In Spirit?"

Phrased that way, it sounds almost pleasant. Just another day in the Dale: Odelia is in the kitchen, Max is at dinner, Johneen is in Spirit.

"I can't be certain," Pandora tells her.

Bella thinks sadly of the beautiful woman who should have had every reason to live a long life with the man she loved. She may not be the warmest, fuzziest person in the world. Most of the time, she isn't even likeable. But she's human, and she doesn't deserve this. Whatever . . . whatever *this* is.

"I don't suppose . . . did Spirit show you whose hand was around her throat?" she asks, allowing fear to creep over her once again.

"The guides don't have all the answers, Isabella. Neither do I."

"But what good is knowing what's going to happen if you can't . . . make it *not* happen?"

"It doesn't work that way. Surely you know that by now."

Bella closes her eyes, inhaling through her nose. This room, too, is enveloped in the smothering scent of flowers.

"Pandora . . . do you smell anything?"

She sniffs the air. "Yes. The house always gives off this aroma when it rains, or on humid days. I remember it well."

"It smells like flowers?"

"No, it smells a bit musty, of old wood and damp paper. Do *you* smell flowers, Bella?"

"I've been smelling them all day."

"There are wedding flowers around."

"No, it isn't those."

"Of course it isn't." Pandora nods as if Bella had argued. "The ones you chose aren't particularly aromatic."

"And there are no flowers in here now."

"Yet you smell them?"

"I . . . yes. I smell them."

"How peculiar." Pandora looks thoughtful. "And what does this particular scent mean to you?"

"Absolutely nothing. Why?"

"Spirit often uses fragrance to send a message."

"But I'm not . . . I don't . . ."

"Everyone *is*. Everyone *does*. They just don't realize it."

Here we go again.

But this time, Bella was asking for it. And she's giving herself permission to momentarily suspend disbelief and accept the possibility that there might be a paranormal explanation to what she's experiencing, because . . .

Because it makes as much sense as anything else.

And because it might have something to do with Johneen's . . . illness. For now, until she hears otherwise, she'll think of it as an illness or an episode. She'll think that the medics and the doctors are working on her, that they can help her, that she'll pull through this.

Because she can't bear to consider the alternative.

"Just open your mind and accept what you're given," Pandora quietly instructs her. "All will become clear in time. Are you smelling *Hyacinthoides non-scripta*?"

The botanical name for bluebells.

Back in July, Bella wanted so badly to believe Pandora was channeling messages from Sam that she convinced herself a few off-season blooms might mean something.

Bluebells.

Bella Blue.

Funny, in that case, all did *not* become clear in time. On the contrary, time blurred her conviction that Sam was here, reaching out to her.

"I'm not smelling bluebells," she assures Pandora. "I know what they smell like, and it isn't them."

It isn't Sam. It never was.

So much for an open mind.

"Think back on your past. Are there occasions when you've smelled flowers?"

"Yes. Whenever there are flowers around," she says logically, ready to end this game.

"Be more specific."

"In a garden . . . in the summer . . ."

Pandora tries a different approach. "Close your eyes and try to focus. Do certain fragrances remind you of someone? Or something that happened? For example, when I smell carnations, I think of church on Easter Sunday. And you?"

Lilacs remind her of spring mornings back in Bedford.

Roses remind her of her wedding day.

Stargazer lilies remind her of funerals—of Sam's funeral.

And yet . . .

"This isn't any specific scent, Pandora. It's just . . . flowers."

"Spirit is using the scent to convey a message in language you'll understand. Does that make sense to you?"

Not entirely.

A scientific explanation like sensory phenomenology would make more sense.

So would a medical one.

What are the odds that Pandora, and everyone else in the house—everyone except Bella and Jiffy—is experiencing sudden onset anosmia?

Greater than the odds that dead people can communicate with the living?

There's a sharp knock on the French door.

Bella opens it.

"I'm sorry to interrupt. I've been looking for y'all." Virginia is standing there, holding her cell phone, tears in her eyes. "Parker called. She's in critical condition. It doesn't look good."

"Oh, Virginia . . ." Bella reaches out to hug her.

For a moment, they just stand there, arms wrapped around each other. Then she steps back, remembering Pandora, who holds out a bony hand.

"I don't believe we've been properly introduced. I'm Pandora Feeney."

"Virginia Langley."

"I know how upset you must be about your cousin."

"Thank you, but . . . I'm Parker's cousin. I don't really know Johneen well, although I'm sure she's a lovely person."

Trying to process it all in her brain's breakneck spin cycle, Bella asks Virginia, "Did Parker say what happened to her?"

"Medical emergency—sudden cardiac arrest."

Medical? So someone didn't try to murder her?

Bella looks at Pandora. Her face is a mask of concern, but her expression betrays a glimmer of doubt.

Uncomfortable, Bella shifts her gaze back to Virginia and rests a comforting hand on her shoulder. "We should update the others."

"I already have."

"How are they handling it all?"

"Not well."

Leaving Pandora to ponder whatever she's pondering, Bella follows Virginia out of the room.

The grim guests have moved from porch to parlor. Odelia is there, but there's no sign of Millicent. Frankie and Tanya are also missing—upstairs packing, according to Calla.

"Tanya wants to go home to Dan and the baby," she reports, "and Frankie is driving her."

Blue's arm is wrapped around her—a protective gesture, or a possessive one? Is he the jealous type? Is he secretly in love with Johneen?

"Liz and I would love to get the hell out of here too, but it's not a good idea in this weather," Ryan says. His fiancée is quietly sobbing into his designer suit coat, but he's craning his neck to see past her bowed head to the phone in his hand. "The roads are bad and there are trees down all over the place."

Bella's thoughts fly to Max. She pulls her own phone from her pocket and excuses herself, stepping into the kitchen.

The home screen bears a warning message that her battery is dangerously low. Ignoring it, she hurriedly dials Drew's number.

He answers on the first ring with a succinct, "We're fine. Don't worry."

"Where are you?"

"We ate dinner in Dunkirk and were on our way back to the Dale, but we just had to turn around. The road is blocked by branches and wires. Do you have power there?"

"Yes."

"You may not have it for long. Listen, I'm going to take the boys to my place. I've got a generator. Is that all right with you?"

"I probably would have asked you to do that anyway." She explains quickly about Johneen.

Drew listens, not saying much. Of course not, because he won't want to upset the boys, who are in the car with him. And because he's Drew. He doesn't ever say much.

"I'm sorry this happened," he tells Bella. "Is there anything I can do for you from here?"

"Just keep my boy safe, and make sure Jiffy calls his mom to tell her where he is. She's probably worried."

"One would hope so."

They hang up, and Bella finds herself wishing he were here with her. He may be a man of few words, but he radiates a strength that she could really use right about now.

Hearing footsteps and thumping on the stairs, she returns to the parlor. Through the archway into the front hall, she sees Frankie and Tanya lugging their rolling bags downstairs. Strong-armed Frankie, who's changed into jeans and sneakers, is carrying hers. Tanya is still in her black taffeta cocktail dress and heels, thumping her bag down the flight step by bumpity-bumpity step.

Pandora emerges from the study to scold her. "You're going to destroy the treads!"

"I'm sorry, but it's heavy!"

"Who cares about the stupid treads at a time like this?" Bella hears Andrea murmur to Charlie.

"I'll help you." Swaying and slurring slightly, Hellerman sets his bourbon glass on the coffee table. He takes the bag from Tanya and nearly swings it through the stained-glass window.

"Bloody hell!" Pandora glares and moves his glass to a coaster as Bella hurries over.

"You can't leave. I just spoke to a friend who said the road is blocked by limbs and wires."

"No! I have to get home to Dan and Emily!" Tanya is frantic. "I don't want to stay here!"

Odelia hugs her. "You can go home in the morning, sweetie. You don't want to take any chances. It's dangerous out there."

Her troubled gaze meets Bella's, and Bella can't help wonder whether it's dangerous in here, too.

Odelia propels Tanya into the parlor. The young woman sinks on the sofa to lament her plight to Calla, who sits beside her. Blue perches on the arm. He, like Virginia, is set apart from the rest of the group by virtue of not being a close friend of the bride.

"I'm going to make some tea," Bella says, because she has to say something, has to do *something*.

Pandora brightens. "Proper tea?"

"Oh, good grief," Odelia mutters. "Tea is tea."

As Bella follows her from the room, Hellerman announces, "Bourbon is bourbon, and I'll be happy to pour you a proper one of those, Ms. Feeney."

She takes him up on it, albeit with a sly, "*You've* had so many of those, it's bordering on *improper*."

Some semblance of order has been restored to the kitchen. Odelia fills the teakettle at the sink. Millicent is seated at the table in a lonely, inelegant posture, shoulders hunched and head bent. Bella realizes that she's leafing through one of the books she brought over for Max.

She looks up, and her expression transforms in a flash from bereft to disturbed. "I hope your friend pulls through, Isabella."

Bella's instinct is to deflect, as Virginia had in the study. She, like Parker's cousin, barely knows Johneen.

Parker—poor Parker, married a matter of hours—is alone at the hospital. She pictures him there—ashen, in shock, hoping against hope that his bride will survive.

How well Bella remembers her own awful nights keeping a hospital vigil, and then . . .

Afterward.

Afterward you face the unpleasant necessities that arise in the wake of a spouse's death. People materialize almost immediately. Suitably somber strangers come out of the woodwork with paperwork, offering sympathy yet quietly doing their jobs, going about the business of death.

Some parts of that horrible time in Bella's life are a blessed blur. But she remembers the nurses who wept with her and the kindly priest who prayed with her in the chapel. She remembers the less kindly but well-meaning attorney who advised her to cancel Sam's credit cards immediately.

"Why?" she asked, bewildered.

"Because identity thieves are opportunists, and they act very quickly after someone passes away."

Numb and grief-stricken, she was grateful for the people who guided her through the terrible aftermath, grateful for the countless questions they asked and the tasks they assigned, like signing her name over and over again on paper dampened with her own tears. It delayed the inevitable task of returning home, where Millicent and Max were waiting, to tell them that Sam was gone forever.

In those terrible moments, aware as she was that Millicent had lost her son, Bella was consumed by comforting her own. Her mother-in-law later channeled her own grief into efficiency. She made sure that Max was fed and clothed, and she dealt with the people who dropped by with food when Bella was too exhausted for coherent conversation, much less common courtesy.

Did I ever thank her for all of that?

Of course she did. She must have.

As she gazes at the woman holding a dog-eared children's book in hands that are veined with age, she sees not Maleficent, but a mother who lost her only child.

She pulls out a chair and sits beside her. "I'm sorry I didn't have time to talk when you wanted to earlier. So much was going on."

"I know that."

"What did you want to say?"

"That I've booked a return flight home for tomorrow afternoon."

"You're leaving?"

"I bought three tickets, Isabella."

Grasping the news, she shakes her head wearily. "Max and I can't just walk out of here. Even if we wanted to, we . . . can't. We just can't."

"I think that you *do* want to. I saw the look on your face earlier."

Startled, Bella thinks back, wondering if there was a moment when her expression might have betrayed her, a moment when she wanted to escape this place for a little while. Maybe even forever.

It's been a difficult day spent surrounded by difficult people and situations. But it doesn't mean she should flee.

"You and Max don't belong here any more than I do, Isabella."

Over Millicent's shoulder, Odelia is busily arranging tea bags in a bowl—*improper tea*, according to Pandora, who prefers the loose-leaf variety. Her back is turned to the table, but Bella knows she's listening intently to the conversation.

"Maybe you're right," she tells her mother-in-law. "Maybe we don't belong here."

"Oh, thank goodness. I was worried you'd been brainwashed to think you're like *them*."

"No, we aren't like them."

"Of course not. Max told me about them over lunch."

"What did he say?"

"That these people pretend to talk to ghosts."

"He said they *pretend*?"

"Not in those words, exactly."

No. Those are Millicent's words.

"And they claim they can predict the future," she goes on, "and convince people that they can heal them without medicine. I tried to talk some sense into Max, but I'm not sure I got through to him. I'm glad I'm getting through to you."

"Loud and clear."

"Then we're going."

"No. *We're* staying. You're going. Although I wish you'd at least stay long enough to give those books to Max. Or maybe even read them to him."

Millicent stares at her in stunned silence.

For a moment, the only sound is the rain.

Pitter-patter . . . pitter-patter . . .

Bella thinks of last night, in the garden. The music over the speakers . . .

"When Sunny Gets Blue."

Blue.

Nothing is an accident . . .

Millicent asks her where Max is, and she drags herself back to the conversation.

"He's with Doctor Bailey. They're at his house because they couldn't get back here."

"You trust a strange man to drive your son away from here, but you didn't trust me?"

"Drew is a friend."

"I'm Max's grandmother."

"Who seems to think we've been kidnaped by a cult."

At that, Odelia turns around, wide-eyed. She opens her mouth to speak, but Bella shakes her head at her.

Nothing Odelia can say will help the situation. In fact, anything she says is guaranteed to make it worse.

"I know religious fanatics when I see them."

"How?"

"By the way they act and the things they say. I've only been here a day, and it's obvious to me that these people are nuts. That poor Johneen felt the same way about them, and now look. Look what's happened to her."

"What are you talking about?"

"She told me this morning that she didn't feel comfortable here."

Bella remembers that she'd found Millicent and an insomniac Johneen together in the breakfast room.

"What did she say, exactly?"

"That she felt as though she and Parker were being followed and that someone might be rummaging through their belongings, because things weren't where they'd left them. And don't go telling me it was the ghosts."

"I wouldn't. Did she say who was following them?"

"She didn't have to. It was these people. That's what they do. They snoop around and they learn everything about a person, private information, so that they can use it to convince them they're mystical."

"That isn't what goes on here," Bella says decisively. True, there are times when she isn't sure exactly what does go on, but she won't believe for one moment that Odelia and the others are trying to dupe their clients or anyone else.

Millicent's lament continues. "That poor girl. She didn't believe in any of this Spiritualism mumbo jumbo. She thought it was ridiculous. And now look."

"But that has nothing to do with it! What happened to her was medical, not—"

"Is that what you believe?"

"Of course." Bella forces conviction into her tone.

"Do you?" Millicent turns to Odelia.

She doesn't believe it. Not entirely. Bella can tell by the look on her face. Either she thinks Pandora was right about someone wanting to hurt Johneen, or she's had a similar hunch of her own.

Odelia simply asks Millicent, "What do *you* think happened?"

"I think someone around here decided to bump her off because she wasn't a believer, and then they made it look like an accident."

"That's ridiculous." Bella pushes back her chair and stands. "No one here would ever . . . 'bump her off.' I think you've been watching too many cop shows on TV."

Millicent, too, is on her feet. "I'm leaving."

"Where are you going? You can't get out of the Dale."

"I heard. The roads are conveniently blocked—or so you say."

"Do you think I'm making it up?"

"No. I think *they* are."

They . . . as in Drew? Or Ryan?

Somewhere in the back of Bella's mind, Millicent's accusations stack into kindling for a lick of white-hot paranoia.

What if they *aren't* telling the truth?

Drew? Drew wouldn't lie. She knows him.

And Ryan . . .

You don't know him at all.

How well does she know any of these people, really, except for Millicent?

Even her closest ally, Odelia, let her down this morning and may have been going to desperate measures to stop the wedding.

If she had been behind it all, then her motives, skewed as they were, had probably been pure. But she must have known the anonymous note would make Bella uneasy, and the rest of it . . .

How could she have let me worry—especially with Max here—and not have said anything?

It just doesn't seem in her character.

Unless I never really knew her at all.

Bella tries not to allow mistrust to mingle with her lingering disappointment, but it's there. Odelia said she was meditating at the Stump, and Bella took her at her word. But she could have been anywhere, doing anything.

And Drew Bailey—right now, he, too, could be anywhere, doing anything . . . with her son.

She hurries from the room, pulling her phone from her pocket.

"Where are you going, Isabella?"

She ignores Millicent's question, rushing past the parlor where the guests are still talking. At the stairway, she stops short. Virginia is sitting on the steps, deep in conversation with Blue Slayton.

They look up, then stand so that Bella can by. She thanks them and climbs the stairs, glancing back over her shoulder to see that they're seated once more.

Maybe they're drawn together as the only two outsiders at the wedding.

Maybe there's an attraction brewing between them.

Or maybe Virginia, too, is suspicious of the man who came out of nowhere and has a questionable connection to the bride's past.

Right now, Bella doesn't know, or care, about any of that. Her thoughts are on Max.

Try as she might to reassure herself, Millicent has made her wonder.

She unlocks the door, steps into the Rose Room, and impulsively locks it after her. As she redials Drew's number, she sees that most of the kittens are now asleep, including Li'l Chap. He's snuggled, along with little Spidey, against a vigilant Chance, whose gaze meets Bella's. She offers a slow blink.

Just minutes ago, Bella was wishing Drew were here to lend a strong, comforting presence in the midst of tragedy and bedlam. Now . . .

He answers the phone on the first ring. "Bella? We're just walking in the door. It took us a while to get here."

"Where are you?"

"At my house, like I told you."

She can hear a dog barking wildly in the background.

"And Max is there?"

"Max and Jiffy. And my little animal kingdom," he adds, over the barking. "Hey, guys, careful not to knock over those stacks of papers. They're organized, believe it or not."

"It's kind of messy in here," Bella hears Max say in the background, and the tension cord constricting her heart loosens enough for her to start breathing again.

"It is messy," Drew agrees. "One of these days I'll clean it up."

"Do you got any snacks?" Jiffy's voice asks.

"You just ate dinner."

"Not for me! For her!"

"Hang on and I'll let you feed her. But don't let her put her paws on your shoulders. She's bigger than you are. She'll push you right down!"

Bella hears laughter, and more barking.

"Sorry," Drew says into the phone. "I rescued a greyhound puppy a few weeks ago. She's excited to see the boys."

He's a kind man who rescues animals, Bella reminds herself. Puppies . . . kittens . . . even ducklings.

"Can I please talk to Max for a minute?"

"Sure. Hang on. Hey, Max, your mom wants to say hi. And then you're going to call your mom and say hi, too, Jiffy."

"We already called her. She doesn't need me to say hi again."

"Yes, she does. I told her you'd call her when you got here so that she won't worry."

Listening to them discuss whether Jiffy's mom will worry—a genuinely debatable question, as far as Bella is concerned—she's relieved by the ordinary images in her mind's eye. A messy bachelor pad, an overgrown, overzealous puppy, a couple of curious kids.

"Hi, Mom! Guess what?"

"What?"

"Doctor Drew doesn't make his bed!"

She smiles and nudges her mind's eye to move past Doctor Drew's rumpled sheets. "What did you have for dinner?"

"Chicken wings. What did *you* have for dinner?"

Her smile fades as she remembers the dinner that was supposed to be served to the happy newlyweds and their guests.

"I haven't eaten dinner yet," she tells Max. "Are you okay with sleeping over at Doctor Drew's house tonight?"

I want you there, safe, with him. I trust him.

"Yes!" Max shouts. "We're going to sleep on the couch with Peewee! She's the best dog ever!"

"She's a puppy, by the way," Jiffy says in the background.

"She's a giant puppy, by the way," Max tells Bella. "That's why her name is so silly."

Certain Max is in competent hands, Bella tells him goodnight and asks him to put Drew back on the line.

"Thank you for taking good care of him," she tells Drew.

"Not a problem. I've never had kids over here before. It's nice . . . for the animals."

And maybe for their master as well, Bella thinks.

"One quick thing, Drew. You know that kitten from the yard?"

"The little chap?"

"Yes. I know you said not to, but I brought him inside when the storm hit."

He assures her it was the right thing to do, then adds, "I can't believe you finally remembered."

"Remembered what?"

"To call me Drew."

She did, didn't she? The word fell out of her mouth just as readily as Maleficent had earlier.

She hangs up the phone, relieved that at least her mother-in-law had been wrong about one of "them."

But then, Drew Bailey isn't part of Lily Dale.

Now that the perfect wedding has ended in tragedy, she and Max won't be, either. She needs to tell Grant what's going on.

So much for Wedding Bella.

She quickly changes out of the green silk dress. She returns it to its hanger, but not to the closet, certain she'll never want to wear it again. It's wrong for her figure, and it's . . .

Tainted.

She hangs it from a curtain rod for now and swiftly dials another familiar number, hoping her phone's battery will hold out a little longer.

Luther doesn't answer on the first ring, or even the third. Just when she expects the call to bounce into voice mail, he picks up, sounding a bit harried and out of breath.

"Are you in the middle of something?" she asks, suspecting that he has female company.

"My roof is leaking and I'm bailing the kitchen. This is some storm and the roads are bad. I hope you're safe at home."

"I'm home . . ."

But is she safe?

In a rush, she tells him what happened to Johneen. Predictably, he's dismayed and troubled by the news.

"It was a medical problem?" he echoes. "Are you sure?"

"Doesn't that seem strange? She was young and healthy."

"It happens. Maybe she had an undiagnosed heart condition. Or an aneurysm."

"Maybe." Those theories make so much sense that Bella almost doesn't want to mention the rest of it—the ring and the phone—and ask him the question weighing on her mind.

When he tells her he has to hurry back to his leaky roof, she blurts, "Can a person get away with murder by making it look like natural causes? Or does that only happen in fiction?"

There's a long pause.

"It happens. Not just in fiction. I've seen a few cases."

"How does it happen?"

"Bella, are you thinking someone tried to kill Johneen Maynard?"

"No." She clears her throat. "Maybe."

"Why? Is it because of that letter?"

"Not just that. It's—" It's so many things, she doesn't even know where to begin. "Pandora Feeney thinks—"

Luther cuts her off with a groan. "Pandora lives to stir up trouble."

Wrong place to begin. Bella doesn't want Luther to discount her suspicions just because Pandora can be less than credible.

"I know what you're thinking, but Pandora saw something that made her think—"

"Did she see something?" Luther asks. "Or did she . . . you know, *see* something?"

In other words, did she witness a crime, or is she relying purely on a psychic vision?

"She *saw* something. In her head," Bella admits. "She saw hands wrapped around Johneen's throat. She said that was Spirit shorthand, but . . . is it possible for strangulation to be mistaken for a medical condition?"

"No," he says flatly. "It isn't. Not like that. I don't suppose the divine Ms. Feeney happened to mention whose hands she saw? Or a potential motive?"

"No, she didn't. But it could have been Johneen's jealous ex."

"Do you have his name?"

"No. If you can hang on, I can let you talk to Parker's cousin, Virginia. She—"

"Wait a minute," he says. "Back up. Before we drag anyone else into this, I need more information from you, because this all sounds . . . well, you know."

Yes. She knows.

And she knows he isn't entirely skeptical, although he's no fan of Pandora Feeney. Like Odelia, he's convinced the woman is a busybody. In some ways, that's true.

But it doesn't mean she doesn't care, and it doesn't mean she isn't gifted—if you're the kind of person who believes there's something to Spiritualism.

Some detectives are open to working with psychics, and Luther is one of them.

Just—not *all* psychics.

"I wouldn't be surprised if Pandora wrote that letter you told me about," he tells Bella. "She's been seeing murder and mayhem at every turn ever since Leona died. I heard from a friend at the precinct that she keeps calling the crime hotline with tips."

Bella doesn't doubt it. Still . . .

She quickly explains about Pandora's visit this afternoon, then tells him about the letter's disappearance, and the ring's, and her cell phone's.

"You say your phone is back, but the photos are gone?"

"Yes, but I sent a copy to Grant Everard. I was thinking maybe I could see if I can access them from the e-mail and see if there's anything unusual in them, but I haven't had a chance."

"That's a good idea. You should—" He breaks off with a curse.

"Luther?"

"Sorry. I just skated across my kitchen floor. There's a flood in here. I need to take care of this. But listen, Bella, you shouldn't jump to conclusions."

"Can you ask your friends at the hospital what's going on?"

"What makes you think I have friends at the hospital?"

"You have friends everywhere. See what you can find out. Please? For me?"

"For you, I'll do it, but I probably won't hear right away."

"Thank you. Do you want to talk to Virginia?"

"You say she told you she's law enforcement?"

"She didn't exactly . . . tell me. I overheard." She stops short of mentioning that she was eavesdropping . . . or that she snooped around and found Virginia's weapon and badge.

"I do want to talk to her, but give me some time to take care of this flood or build an ark or something."

She forces a laugh.

"I may sound like I'm taking your situation lightly, but I'm not," he tells her. "You don't feel like you might be in danger, do you?"

She hesitates. "I'm not sure."

"Maybe you shouldn't stay there tonight. Why don't you and Max come here?"

"Because the roads are blocked," she reminds him. "Anyway, Max is at Drew's house, so I'm not worried about him. Should I be? You know, because of the storm and all?" she adds, not wanting to admit she'd had a moment of doubt over Drew earlier, and again now.

Darn you, Maleficent.

"Drew Bailey is a rock. He's one of the best men I know. You can rest assured that nothing is going to happen to Max with him around. Just watch your step at Valley View, okay? And see if you can get copies of those photos."

"I will. And I'll tell Virginia—"

"Don't tell her anything just yet, Bella. Okay? Don't tell anyone anything. Including Odelia."

"Odelia?" She frowns. "You don't think—"

"I don't know what I think. I guess I need to be *able* to think. But right now, it's raining harder in my kitchen than it is outside. I'll get back to you, I promise."

She hangs up and looks around at the peacefully sleeping felines. As much as she'd like to hide away in the Rose Room with them until morning, she has to go downstairs and see if she can access those missing photos. Her phone's battery needs to be charged, and it will be much easier to study them on a computer screen anyway.

Outside in the night, thunder is still booming ominously. Luther's words, echoing in her head, are just as persistent.

Don't tell anyone anything. Including Odelia.

She plugs in her phone and reluctantly leaves it on the nightstand, locking the Rose Room securely behind her.

What good will that do, though, if someone has the keys or wants to crawl in through the tunnel?

She slowly descends the stairs, taking her time. Blue and Virginia are no longer perched at the bottom. She can hear the teakettle whistling in the kitchen, muffled conversation in the living room, rain and thunder.

Is it possible that someone under this roof isn't who he—or she— appears to be?

What if—

Startled by an explosion, she stops short and grips the railing.

Her first thought is that it was a gunshot.

But the house is plunged into darkness, and she realizes that it was a tree snapping outside, bringing down wires and knocking out the power.

Chapter Sixteen

Bella has endured her share of difficult and endless nights—most of them within the past year.

This, however, has been one of the worst.

With her phone's battery dead and the Internet down along with the power and phone lines, she has no way of reaching out to Luther again or even attempting to access the missing photos.

She's helpless to do anything but brood in the dark chill, surrounded by fretful people who are drinking too much or saying too much, complaining about things that can't be helped.

Pandora wants proper tea.

Hellerman wants more bourbon, but the bottle is empty. He settles on Dom Pérignon but jostles it so much in his clumsy efforts to pop the cork that he sprays the kitchen and everyone in it with champagne.

Everyone is wet, cold, uncomfortable, unbearably sad . . .

Bella is all of those things, and afraid as well.

Thank goodness for Virginia. She appears unafraid but vigilant. Bella longs to pull her aside and talk to her, but Luther said not to.

Tanya weeps softly like a homesick little girl, missing her husband and daughter. "I just want to go home," she says every so often, and somehow, the others refrain from snapping at her.

Millicent, too, wants desperately to escape, though she hasn't said much. She huddles around the flickering candles in the parlor with the rest of them, sipping hot improper tea and wrapped in one of the blankets Bella handed out when the room grew too chilly.

Now she's dozing on the sofa, her head resting on the arm at an uncomfortable angle.

Nobody mentions Johneen, but her presence shrouds the room.

"Gammy . . . you're snoring." Calla reaches over to nudge Odelia, who has, indeed, dozed off in a chair.

She sits up straighter, yawning. "I'm sorry."

"Why don't you go home to bed?"

"Maybe I will. Come on with me."

"No, I want to stay here." Calla doesn't look at Blue, sitting beside her.

Odelia does. "How about you?"

"Me?"

"You. Are you heading home?"

"I don't think I can get there," he says as Calla rolls her eyes at her grandmother's question and shakes her head silently.

"Of course you can't get there, mate." Pandora is kneeling on the window seat, peering through the front windows. "You live outside the gate, and there are trees and wires down at the end of the lane. I can see them from here. But you can get next door, Odelia, and there's a clear path across the park to my place. Come along, let's be off."

Odelia taps the snoozing Millicent. "We're going."

"Hmm?"

"Next door. To bed. Come on."

Looking slightly dazed, Millicent gets to her feet without argument. Perhaps she's too weary to remember that Odelia is the enemy, bent on brainwashing her grandson.

"I'll be back 'round in the morning to get my keyboard," Pandora calls, headed for her pink cottage just across Melrose Park as Odelia and Millicent, stooped against the wind, hurry next door.

Bella stands on the purple welcome mat and watches the three shadowy female figures disappear into the night, pelted by an icy snow. It crystalizes along fallen tree branches and encrusts fallen leaves.

Radiant frost . . .

Virginia stands silently beside her, watching until they're safely home, blowing white smoke into the arctic air.

I know, Bella wants to say to her. *I know you're a cop. I know you think someone hurt Johneen. I know you think he might be out there . . . or in here.*

She's too exhausted to form the words in one moment, too exhausted to hold them back in the next. She opens her mouth but hears a voice behind her before she can speak.

"Think I should try it?" Blue asks, looking out into the storm.

If he goes, Bella might feel safer, and yet . . .

"No," she hears herself say. Of course he shouldn't try it. Beyond Odelia's house, downed branches rise from the lane like the straining claws of a felled beast, entwined with live wires sparking dragon fire. *The danger is there*, Bella tells herself. *Not here. Not with him.*

"You can sleep in Max's bed," she offers, and he thanks her.

She closes the front door, shutting out the storm, then locks it. Inside, the rest of the guests are climbing the stairs to their own rooms.

She might as well go to bed too, though she doubts she'll sleep. She starts up and then turns to look back at Virginia, still standing thoughtfully by the closed door.

"Are you coming?"

"Not yet. Parker said that if she stabilizes, he'll try to dash back here. He wants to change and get a few things he'll need at the hospital. I'll go back with him. I don't want him there alone. He's so upset."

Is he really coming back here while his wife is at death's door?

Or does Virginia just want to wait up to keep an eye on things?

"Do you want me to stay here with you?" Bella offers.

"No, that's all right. You should go to bed."

Climbing Everest couldn't be more daunting than this final trudge up the stairs. Every part of her aches with exhaustion. She hasn't had a decent night's sleep since . . . when? Wednesday? Even then, she tossed and turned, worried about the wedding.

She locks the Rose Room door securely behind her, pulls on a pair of flannel pajamas, and climbs into bed.

Suddenly, she's wide-awake. Calculating predators roam her mind's eye, lurking behind innocuous faces. No one here seems capable of murder, but she'd been fooled once before into trusting the wrong person. Any second now, her closet door might creak open and someone might creep into this room to . . .

What? To kill Bella?

No, of course not. If there really is a predator, and Johneen was the target, then the danger is past.

Except . . .

Her phone. If an intruder erased her photos, is it because they showed something he didn't want anyone to see?

Does he think she saw it, too?

On high alert, she's too cold, too rattled, too frightened to let down her guard enough to get the rest her body desperately craves.

Yet eventually, sleep does claim her, if only in fitful spurts.

The house is eerily quiet without the background hum of electrical appliances. Every time she dozes, she's soon jolted by the ear-splitting crash of another tree snapped by a windowpane-rattling gale.

At last, she opens her eyes to a tiny gray kitten purring and kneading her shoulder and a room bathed in golden light and the scent of summer gardens.

For a wonderful, mistaken moment, she assumes the whole thing was a nightmare. This is Saturday morning, the wedding day. The air is balmy, the sun is shining, and the bride and groom are safely asleep down the hall.

Then she sees that the kitten isn't gray at all. He's blue. The early dawn beyond the windows is gray, swirling with snowflakes. The floral scent is as pervasive as it had been last night, but it isn't wafting in the windows. They're closed. And the room isn't bathed in sunlight. It's the lamp she'd left on earlier.

That, at least, is a good sign. The electricity is back, though the house is still frigid. Extracting herself from the kitten, Bella creeps across the chilly room. She opens the door and peers into the hall. Lights are on there, too, but the house is quiet.

Squinting and yawning, she makes her way down the stairs to adjust the thermostat in the brightly lit front hall.

The furnace kicks on with a house-rattling shudder. She crosses the chilly threshold into the parlor, heading toward the study to look for her missing photos at last. Then depending on what she—

"Bella?"

She whirls to spot Virginia, still curled up on the easy chair. Somehow, despite a traumatic, sleepless night, she's just as lovely as she was yesterday morning. A crocheted white blanket is draped around her slender shoulders, and her phone is poised in her hand as if she's expecting a call.

"Are you still waiting for Parker?"

"Yes. He texted that he left the hospital twenty minutes ago. He should be here soon. The roads are icy but passable."

"Any news?"

"She's still hanging on. The nurses told him to go while he had a chance."

"How is he holding up?"

"Sad. In shock. He shouldn't be alone at a time like this. If she doesn't make it . . ." Virginia shakes her head. "I'm sorry. I know you've been there."

Yes, but it was worse for me. I'd been married for years, not hours. Sam and I had a child. I loved him more than Parker could possibly have loved Johneen.

She hates herself for thinking that, for qualifying and quantifying grief.

Maybe Parker and Johneen aren't the most down-to-earth couple in the world, but he loves her. Of course he docs.

Pain is pain. Loss is loss.

"I'll go make some coffee," she tells Virginia.

"That would be nice. Thank you."

In the kitchen, Bella measures grounds into a filter and sets the coffee to brew, jittery as if she'd already ingested a potful. She's eager to get to the computer, but the place is a disaster.

Every surface is sticky with champagne. Empty glasses fill the sink, along with plates and utensils from someone's midnight snack. The dish rack is filled with the salad plates Virginia had washed. They need to be put away before anything else can be done, yet productivity is elusive.

I just need to go take a quick look, Bella decides, heading into the study. *And if I can retrieve the shots and see something unusual in one of them, I can show Virginia before Parker gets here.*

Beyond the French door, Pandora's keyboard is leaning against the wall, just as they'd left it before Virginia interrupted the conversation about whether someone might have reason to harm Johneen.

Still unsure of the answer to that question, Bella moves the keyboard out of the way and sits down at the computer. It seems to take an excessive amount of time to boot up after having abruptly lost power. At last, she's clicking into her e-mail account's sent-messages folder.

There it is—the note to Grant with the photos attached.

She opens the file and begins clicking through them.

By all appearances, yesterday was a carefree celebration, she thinks, studying the guests' smiling faces. She remembers it differently, laced with dread and uncertainty. But, of course, she's not in any of the photos. Those who are look as though they're having a wonderful time: the former college roommates posing arm in arm, the guys clowning with flowers on their heads, even Virginia and Parker, squinting into the sunshine without a care in the world.

That wasn't exactly the case, she recalls. The ring was missing, and he already knew about the letter.

If he and Virginia managed to come across as unencumbered in a moment that was anything but carefree, then what about the others? Is one of the guests hiding a dark secret behind a happy grin?

She flicks slowly through the pictures again, finding nothing amiss in anyone's expression. Then she goes through them another time, zooming in to look at the backdrop of each one.

Now it's harder to tell whether there's something suspicious. Shadows that appear potentially human become too grainy when she enlarges the spots. What looks like a hand in a shrub border turns out to be, most likely, a dead leaf stuck amid the boughs . . . or is it? In the photo of Parker and Virginia, there might very well be a figure behind the lace curtains of the honeymoon suite.

Johneen?

Someone else?

"Bella?" Virginia calls from the next room. "Is the coffee ready?"

"Almost," she calls back, closing out of the photos for now, frustrated that there's nothing incriminating or conclusive.

Before she leaves the desk, she remembers to type a quick e-mail to Grant. He should know what happened here last night. Rather than delivering the news in writing, she simply asks him to call her as soon as possible.

After hitting Send, she notices a floral scent wafting in the air.

Was it there all along? Was she so used to it that she just didn't smell it anymore?

There's a scientific explanation for that, of course. There's a scientific explanation for everything.

In this case, it's sensory adaptation. When you become accustomed to a certain scent, odor receptors stop sending messages to the brain. The scent is still there, but you stop noticing and, in effect, stop smelling it.

Then why am I smelling it now? she wonders as she hurries into the kitchen. And why is it everywhere, mingling with the scent of stale champagne and fresh coffee?

The pot is missing a cup or so. Virginia must already have gotten hers. It smells so good that Bella pours some into a mug and sinks into a kitchen chair, clasping it in her icy hands as she sips.

Her gaze falls on the stack of novels Millicent left last night. Setting down her mug and reaching for *Charlotte's Web*, she imagines Sam's chubby, little-boy hands turning the dog-eared pages.

She opens the book. A word jumps out at her.

Radiant . . .

There it is again. It kept popping into her head yesterday. The first time was when she saw the light filtering across that spider web across the stairs.

Spider web . . . radiant . . . *Charlotte's Web.*

It all comes nicely full circle, but what the heck does it mean? Does it have something to do with Odelia's vision about the spider? Is Spirit trying to tell her something about . . . about what?

Spider . . . spider web . . . radiant . . . *Charlotte . . .*

She's had enough. She tosses the book aside and leaves the room, leaving her coffee to grow cold on the table.

"Is everything okay?" Virginia calls as she hurries toward the stairway.

"Yes. I'll be back down. I just want to . . . take a hot shower."

The bathroom, lacking a radiator, is frigid.

Radiator . . . radiant.

Spider web.

Charlotte's Web.

What about it?

She's delirious. A shower will rejuvenate her. She hurriedly turns on the tap and peels off her clothes.

Five minutes is all she needs, and she'll be good as new.

All right, maybe not, but somehow, she'll get through this day. She'll help Parker, and she'll tend to the guests until they leave, and Millicent will fly away, and Max will come home, and Johneen will pull through . . .

By tonight, everything will be back to normal and life will go on.

Yes, all she needs is a hot shower to warm her through and wash away the unpleasantness. But the water, gushing from the tap, refuses to heat.

Fidgety from the cold, she stands naked beside the old claw-foot tub, staring out the window. Wet snow swirls in the dim morning light, and a thickening silvery layer coats the grass. Trees, still heavy with foliage, bend and buckle beneath the slushy weight.

Bella checks the water. Cold.

She turns back to the window. The lake is purple, churning whitecaps and awash in debris. Splintered limbs litter the yard. Chairs are toppled around the tables, and the borrowed chuppah seems to have blown away.

Weary at the thought of the massive outdoor cleanup job ahead, Bella checks the water again. Still cold.

The heater is probably taking longer to kick on because the power was out, just like the computer downstairs. It'll start warming up any second now.

Outside, she hears a car, tires crunching slowly along the slick, narrow lane. Parker is back.

It's okay. Virginia is down there. They probably need some time to talk privately. He might not want to see Bella at all.

She continues waiting for hot water. Five minutes pass. Ten. Every time she sticks her hand beneath the faucet, it's doused with an icy deluge.

At last, she gives up and turns it off.

It's too early to call Grant about a plumber, but she can e-mail him again.

First, however, she'll have to greet Parker Langley. She isn't looking forward to that at all. His situation hits close to home, and her emotions are dangerously close to the surface. What if she bursts into inappropriate tears when she goes to talk to him?

She'll ask him if there's anything she can do. What else is there to say?

"Is there any chance that your wife's stalker tried to murder her? Or could it have been one of your guests?"

At the sink, Bella brushes her teeth and splashes cold water on her bleary face, then rubs it vigorously with a towel. In the mirror, she sees that her eyes are smudged with black. So is the towel.

Makeup. Unaccustomed to wearing it, she'd forgotten all about it. Yesterday was a lifetime ago—getting ready for the wedding, excited about the prospect of seeing Drew all dressed up, of letting Drew see her all dressed up. She remembers the rain, pouring down over her face last night when she thought it might wash away the tragedy.

She slathers cold cream on a tissue and wipes until her face is clean, then braves another bracing splash of water. Pulling on her flannel pajamas to walk back down the hall, she hears footsteps overhead and then the clanking gush of water running in the third-floor bathroom. It must be Virginia, about to get some sleep at last.

Maybe Parker is doing the same. Bella glances at the honeymoon suite's closed door as she hurries down the hall, wondering if he's behind it now. She can't bear to think of him alone there, sick with worry over his bride.

At the end of the hall, the door to the Rose Room is ajar.

Did she leave it that way?

She must have, because when she left the room, she only meant to run downstairs for a moment to turn on the heat. But it was careless of her, and not just because the kittens might have escaped.

She pushes open the door and gasps, spotting a shadowy figure looming beside the window.

Then she realizes it's just the green silk dress, hanging from the curtain rod where she left it last night.

Nerves on edge, she quickly counts ten feline heads. All present, including the little blue stray, still sleeping in the protective arc of Chance's furry limbs.

Standing near the warm, cast-iron radiator as she changes into jeans and a sweat shirt, Bella remembers her cell phone.

Today it's exactly where she remembers leaving it: charging on her nightstand, alongside the jewelry she'd taken off in the dark. She tucks it all back into the jewelry box, including the tourmaline necklace.

On second thought, she takes that out again and clasps it around her neck, tucking the blue pendant beneath the sweat shirt.

The necklace makes her feel close to Sam, regardless of whether it's truly a gift from him.

"I'm sorry I didn't let you borrow it," she whispers aloud to Johneen, then finds herself pausing to listen for a reply.

She hears nothing but the rustling of a couple of kittens rooting around beneath her dresser.

Johneen might die.

Sam is dead.

Dead is dead.

It's just hard to keep that in mind around Lily Dale.

Maybe she and Max should use those plane tickets Millicent purchased. Why wait around for Grant to tell her the inevitable? She should probably get a head start on making some semblance of a fresh start in Chicago, unless . . .

What if Johneen doesn't die? What if what happened to her really was some kind of illness or injury?

It's tragic for a bride to collapse on her wedding day, but Grant shouldn't sell the inn as a result. Even if someone had targeted her, and even if she doesn't make it . . .

It's a long shot that he'd keep Valley View under those circumstances, but maybe if he knew how desperately Bella wants to be here . . .

I should tell him. Just speak up and explain my situation.

Maybe she's delirious with exhaustion and maybe it doesn't make any sense to try, but there has to be a way to make this work.

If Grant would just give her some time here, at least a year, she could prove that Valley View is a worthwhile investment, and so is she. By then, she'll have worked her way out of debt and saved enough money to rent a cottage here. She might even find a teaching job.

Feeling slightly better about her situation, she checks her texts, hoping there might be one from Luther. There isn't. Nor has Grant texted or e-mailed back.

She hears a mew and looks down to see the little blue kitten at her feet. He cries out again, kiwi eyes wide with need.

"Aw, what's the matter, Li'l Chap?" She plugs her phone into the charger and picks him up. "Are you hungry?"

He informs her in no uncertain terms that he is, and she opens several cans of cat food. Predictably, the sound of popping metal tabs jars Chance and her family to consciousness.

For a few minutes, Bella sits watching them devour their break-fast, wishing that there was only this: an ordinary morning. Cats. Max. Normalcy.

With a sigh, she tears herself away. Stepping out into the hall, she hears someone whisper her name and looks up to see Calla wrapped in a thick white terry bathrobe. Her hair is damp.

"Good morning," she whispers. "Any word on Johneen?"

"She's stable."

"Is she going to pull through?"

"I don't know."

For a moment, they look at each other in somber silence. Then Calla says, "I just took a cold shower. The water won't heat up."

"I'm so sorry. I'm waiting to hear back from the owner so that I can call a plumber, but it might have something to do with the power outage."

"That makes sense. I bet the water heater just needs a jump start or a reboot or whatever you call it."

"I don't suppose you know how to do that, by any chance?"

"Sorry, I don't, but I bet you can find something online. Hey, look out—someone's making a run for it!" Calla bends over and picks up a ball of fur. "Hey! Either Spidey turned blue, or there's a new kid in town."

Bella smiles. "That's Li'l Chap. I brought him in last night right before the storm."

"Oh, he's precious! Where did he come from?"

"He just kind of showed up out of the blue. He's a stray."

"Out of the blue," Calla echoes thoughtfully, "and he *is* a Blue."

Bella nods and can't help but ask, "Do you think that . . . means something?"

She expects Calla to say that it doesn't or to spout some stock Spiritualist line about everything meaning something.

But she nods solemnly. "Yes. It means something. Gammy won't want to hear this, and you have to swear you won't tell her. She has to hear it from me. Today when I get back home, I'm going to tell Jacy I'm moving out."

"Why?" Bella asks, wondering what this has to do with Li'l Chap.

"Because I'm still in love with Blue," Calla says simply.

Okay. Now Bella gets it.

She wants to tell Calla that it's natural, in the midst of a traumatic situation, to feel bonded with the people who are going through it, too. But taking a stray kitten as a sign to go home and break up with her longtime love is extreme.

"I know what you're thinking," says Calla, who probably really does, "but Jacy and I have been talking about taking a break. And Blue and I have been . . . well, we've been talking. That's kind of why he's here."

"What do you mean?"

"He hates California, and he doesn't get along with his father. He's been thinking about coming back here for a while, only there was nothing here for him."

"And now . . ."

"And now I'm here." Calla shrugs. "I mean, he knew I was coming back this weekend for the wedding, and he knew Jacy and I were having problems, and he knew—*we* knew—that we might still have feelings for each other."

"I thought he broke your heart."

Calla shrugs, cuddling the kitten as he burrows into the crook of her neck. "It happens. Especially when you're young."

"What about Jacy?"

"Jacy," she says almost curtly, "will be fine. Trust me, he'll welcome this—whatever you want to call it. *Break*."

"You mean *breakup*?"

"People outgrow each other, Bella. It happens all the time. One minute, you think you're with the love of your life and the next . . ." She shrugs.

It's true, Bella knows. And it might happen all the time, but not to everyone. It didn't happen to her and Sam.

Would it have, eventually, if they'd had more time?

The thought is so distressing that she wraps her arms around her middle as if she's been seized by a horrible ache.

You and I never would have left each other, Sam. We were meant to be, and it isn't fair that we didn't have a chance or that people who have a chance can't make it work.

"Are you okay, Bella?"

"Yes, I'm just . . . cold."

"Do you want him back?" Calla holds out the kitten. "Nothing like snuggling with a little bundle of fur to warm you up."

"No, keep him."

"Can I really?"

"Sure. You can play with him for a bit—all of them," Bella adds, gesturing at her room. "I feel like I've been neglecting these guys, but I need to get downstairs."

"That's not exactly what I meant, but of course I'll play with them. Gladly."

"What *did* you mean?"

"He's the one I want to adopt." Calla runs a gentle finger along a fuzzy spot between the kitten's ears. "He's here for a reason. He's a Blue. Spirit is telling me to open my heart to Blue."

It's what Calla wants to believe.

"If you got to know him," she goes on, "you'd see that he's a good guy."

"I didn't say he's not."

"But you don't trust him. You think I'm making a mistake."

True, but Bella shakes her head.

"Come on, admit it. I'm sure Gammy told you all about him. She means well, but she doesn't always have the best judgment."

It's almost exactly what Odelia said about Calla.

Bella isn't in the mood to smile, but she finds one trying to sneak over her face as she hands Calla the key to her room. "Just make sure the door is closed and locked when you leave the room, okay?"

Heading down the stairs, she decides that Blue Slayton, for all his faults—real or imagined by Odelia—is no threat to anyone's safety, and wasn't to Johneen's.

Maybe it's Bella's turn to believe what she wants to believe.

Maybe, sometimes, that's enough.

As she heads down the stairs, Virginia calls her name from the parlor.

So she didn't go up to bed. Bella must have been hearing Calla's footsteps overhead earlier.

"Parker's back." Virginia pokes her head into the hall. "Come see him for a second while I pour him some coffee."

"Are you sure he wants me to?"

"Of course." Virginia heads into the kitchen.

Bella finds Parker sitting on the sofa in a desolate posture: elbows on his thighs, forehead propped on his hands. She calls his name softly, and he looks up, his handsome face etched in misery and exhaustion. His wedding suit is rumpled, his tie unknotted.

"Is there anything I can do?"

"There's nothing anyone can do."

"It's really hard to watch someone you love suffering so terribly."

"I just don't understand why."

"Did they tell you what happened?"

"They said she had some kind of—I don't know, a medical emergency. She just stopped breathing. It was a freak thing." His voice breaks, and he stares down at his hands clasped on his lap.

She swallows hard.

"Do you know what caused it?" he asks, and she looks up, startled.

"Do *I* know?"

"Aren't you . . . you know, psychic? In touch with Spirit? Not that I believe in any of that," he adds hastily. "Daisy doesn't either. We both thought it was a bunch of bull—I'm sorry."

She shrugs. "It's fine. And no, I'm not in touch with Spirit, and I'm not psychic. I don't . . . do that."

"Do you think someone here can tell me what the hell happened?"

"The doctors can tell you, can't they?"

"I don't know. Maybe. But that's not what I meant."

"Parker, if you want . . . spiritual guidance—then you should talk to Calla about it, or Odelia."

"Maybe I will." He exhales heavily and looks around. "Where's Virginia?"

"She was going to get you some coffee. I'll go check on it."

In the kitchen, Bella finds Virginia putting away the clean salad plates from the dish rack.

"You don't have to do that. I thought you were going to get Parker some coffee?"

"I am. In a minute. How is he?"

"He's . . ."

"I know. Not good. Stupid question. Did he ask you if you know exactly what happened to Johneen?"

"Yes, how did you know?"

"Because I told him to. I thought some kind of answer might be comforting for him, even though he doesn't believe."

"Do *you*?"

"Not really." Virginia puts the last plate into the cupboard and turns on the water. "But I might as well keep an open mind since we're here, right?"

"I guess so. But I'm not a medium."

"You're not? I thought y'all had to be one to live here."

Bella quickly explains the Dale's real estate regulations. Only members of the Spiritualist Assembly can own a house within the grounds. The houses, being built on land that belongs to the Spiritualist Assembly, are effectively leased to their residents.

"Well, that is just fascinating." Virginia reaches for the dish soap. "Is it hard for you to live here, though? Being a widow?"

She cringes.

Widow may be accurate, but it's always been such an ugly, uncomfortable word.

As Bella weighs her answer, Virginia thrusts her hand under the tap, then yanks it back again. "Oh, my goodness! That is just ice-cold!"

"I forgot—there's something wrong with the water heater. I need to go look it up online. Be right back."

She heads into the study and settles in front of the computer again. She quickly checks her e-mail to see if Grant has responded, but he hasn't.

She opens a search engine, positions her fingers over the keys, and begins typing.

W-A-T-E-R H-E—

A list of results appear, prompted by a recent search—which is strange because Bella has never before looked up information on water heaters.

But then, she isn't the only one who uses this computer. A guest must have conducted the same search, and the search engine remembered it.

She clicks the top link and sits back, hoping that whatever is wrong with the heater will be an easy fix. It can't be a simple matter to find an available plumber on a stormy Sunday morning. And the guests won't be pleased by the prospect of cold showers after a traumatic night in a chilly house—*although the touchiest guest of all is no longer a problem*, she realizes with a speck of guilt.

A website pops up, but it has nothing to do with water heaters.

Bella finds herself looking at a photo of . . . lacy, white flowers?

Oops. That must have been triggered by her many recent online investigations into wedding bouquets and centerpieces. She must have somehow clicked the wrong link.

She hits the back button and again scans the search results for *water heater*.

Wait a minute. That's not what it even says.

She typed in *water he*—and the search engine returned pages for a flower called *water hemlock*.

A guest must have conducted a recent search for water hemlock.

Again, she hits the remembered link and takes a closer look at the images.

Water hemlock is identical to Queen Anne's lace or . . .

No. Not identical.

The flowers are different!

Where has she heard that before?

She closes her eyes.

You have to pay close attention to the details!

That's right—the strange dream about the mirror. She was a bride, but her reflection was different. Her face was different, her dress was different, her bouquet was different . . .

She shudders at the eerie coincidence.

No coincidences!

Her eyes snap open. One thing at a time. This isn't about a dream, and it isn't about flowers. It's about a water heater.

Bella is about to hit the back button again when a word jumps out from the page just as *radiant* did from the book in the kitchen.

Seizures.

Chapter Seventeen

Heart pounding, Bella stares at the screen.

Water hemlock, an herbaceous perennial native to North America, is one of the most toxic plants in the world. Merely brushing against its stem or blossoms can make a person sick. Ingesting a tiny amount of the root, with its potent concentration of cicutoxin, violently stimulates the central nervous system, leading to seizures and, in sufficient doses, almost instantaneous death.

"Bella?"

She screams.

Virginia is standing in the doorway. "I'm so sorry! I just wanted to tell you the hot water is back on."

"It is?"

"Yes. So you don't have to bother with that. I'm filling the sink now, and it's nice and steamy." Virginia peers intently at her, and a familiar edge creeps into her voice again. She's back in cop mode. "Are you all right?"

"No. I need to show you something. I know . . ." She pauses, taking a deep breath. "Look, I know about you."

Virginia's blue eyes narrow. "What do you know?"

"That you're a cop."

She doesn't deny it. Nor does she ask how Bella knows. She just nods, looks over her shoulder, and then steps into the study and pulls the door closed behind her.

"What's going on?" she asks in a low, urgent voice. "What did you find?"

"I don't think Johneen's 'illness' was an accident."

Virginia's eyebrows rise, but she doesn't seem stunned. She, too, has been thinking someone tried to kill the bride.

In a rush, Bella tells her everything, right up to, and including, the water hemlock search on the computer.

Though Virginia says very little, Bella can see the growing alarm in her eyes.

"I knew it," she finally says, shaking her head. "I just knew it. I knew I saw him."

"Saw whom?"

"Johneen's ex."

"Here? In the house?"

"No, I thought I saw him yesterday, out on the lake in a boat, watching the guesthouse. I pretended I was going out for cigarettes, but I was really trying to track him down. Needless to say, I didn't find him. But it looks like he found Johneen."

"Does Parker know?"

"Not the whole story. And he's so distraught right now that I can't tell him until I have more information. I need to run upstairs for a minute, all right? Don't do anything, don't go anyplace, don't say anything about this. Not to anyone. Got it?"

"But . . . what should I do? I can't just . . . I need to do something."

"Wash the dishes," Virginia suggests. "Come on. Let's go into the kitchen."

Bella follows her, thoughts racing. Is she going upstairs to call for help? Or to get her gun? Was she, too, lulled into a false sense of security now that Johneen is gone?

Virginia turns on the tap at the sink.

"There. Nice and hot. I'll be right back," she says. "Go ahead. And I promise everything is going to be okay. I've got your back."

The words are perhaps the most comforting Bella has heard in ages.

I've got your back.

Sam always had her back.

Of course, Millicent thinks she has Bella's back, and Max's, but she's misguided. And Odelia—

Forget it.

I'm on my own, Bella thinks. *Thank goodness for Virginia.*

Left alone in the kitchen, she plunges her hands into the sudsy water, searching for a sponge among the dishes, barely noticing or caring that it's scalding her skin. The air is heavy with the scent of flowers.

There are no coincidences.

Terrible thoughts gyrate as she viciously scrubs a mason jar that doesn't need scrubbing.

She'd been looking for a would-be murderer. What if she herself might have been responsible for Johneen's collapse?

She's the one who picked the poisonous flowers . . .

Because Pandora told me to.

She can hear the woman's voice, trilling into the morning air, *"If you need delicate white blossoms, I've scads of Queen Anne's lace."*

The woman is obsessed with horticulture. Wouldn't she have known that it wasn't Queen Anne's lace?

Of course she would have. She'd lured Bella and Parker into her garden and steered them straight to the water hemlock. Poor Johneen wore it in her hair and carried it in her bouquet. No wonder she wasn't feeling well. She was being slowly poisoned.

But wouldn't Bella, too, have been poisoned? She had bare hands when she picked the flowers and arranged them.

Plus, the seizure came so quickly and violently. Would that happen to a person who didn't even eat the toxic root?

Unless she did . . . in the salad.

Bella herself had served that course, along with Odelia. The greens had been plated in the kitchen by Millicent—and Pandora.

How could a stalker—a stranger—have gotten past them to intercept the salads and deliver the poison only to Johneen?

He couldn't have. Not unless he, or *she*, was hiding in plain sight.

Any one of the three women could have looked up water hemlock on the inn's computer. That makes a lot more sense than Johneen's stalker breaking in to do research. And any one of the women could have smuggled a bit of the poisonous root onto the bride's dish.

But what possible motive could they have had? Johneen is unlikeable, but she isn't evil. It couldn't have been revenge . . . could it?

She does have a history with Odelia. Maybe she also has one with Pandora, who claimed she was a stranger. Or even with Millicent.

People hide things. People lie.

Had Millicent made up the ridiculous cover story about a religious cult to mask her true reason for coming to the Dale this weekend?

Okay, that's insane, Bella tells herself. Paranoia is taking hold, and her imagination is running away with this outlandish plot in which Sam's mother is a cold-blooded murderess.

But what about Odelia? She was acting strange.

Yes, because she was worried about her granddaughter and was trying to figure out what her visions meant.

Living in Lily Dale is like playing an endless game of telephone with a paranormal spin. Indirect communication should never be accepted at face value, and yet . . .

The bride's shoes standing in a puddle, the bottom of her white gown, a locked door . . .

Lock!

Hem*lock*.

The bottom of the gown—the *hem*.

A puddle—*water*.

The clues drop effortlessly into place like the last few pieces of a jigsaw. Only one remains.

The spider.

What could it have meant?

Bella has to talk to Virginia right away. The wedding flowers are here in the house. If Johneen was poisoned, they're the evidence.

Bella turns off the water and heads for the parlor, drying her hands on her sweat shirt. Prepared to act as though nothing is out of the ordinary, she finds Parker still sitting morosely on the sofa.

She sneaks a glance at the centerpieces lined up along the mantel, in front of the mirror.

"Are you all right?" she asks, and then cringes at the words.

Every time someone asked her that, as Sam lay dying, she'd had to hold back rage.

"I know you're not all right," she says quickly. "It was a stupid question. And I'm not going to say that I know how you feel, because

I know that's the other stupid thing people say to you at a time like this."

"Did people say it to you when your husband was . . . sick?"

"Yes. I wanted to strangle them every time."

As soon as the sentence leaves her mouth, she wishes she could take it back.

"What I mean is, no one can possibly know how you feel."

"You watched your husband die."

"Yes. It was different."

"How?"

"It wasn't . . . sudden." And he wasn't Johneen. He was a good man, a wonderful man, the perfect man . . .

Except, he wasn't.

Not in real life. He was good and wonderful, yes. But Sam had flaws, just like any other human being. It's so easy to sanctify the dead.

And just as easy to vilify the living. If Millicent—

"Did you get a chance to say goodbye?"

Startled by Parker's question, Bella nods. The last few months of Sam's life were one long, agonizing goodbye.

"See, I won't have that with Johneen, if she—if she doesn't make it. It would be easier to know it's coming and get to say goodbye."

"*Get to* say goodbye?" she echoes incredulously. "It's not easy either way."

"I didn't mean easy. *Easier.*"

She says nothing to that.

Again, she looks at the flowers.

They're reflected in the mirror, just like in her dream.

Was her subconscious mind already aware, somehow, of the poisonous blooms? Had she perhaps glimpsed that page on the computer when she was checking the weather and then forgotten about it?

Even the floral scent could have been psychosomatic . . .

Except Jiffy smelled it, too.

"What?"

She turns to see Parker watching her. "Excuse me?"

"Why are you staring at the flowers?"

"I'm not."

"Are you sure?"

"I'm positive."

Of course he had nothing to do with the poison.

The jarring thought seems to come out of nowhere. But it was there in front of her all along, fuzzy as a distant horizon trained in a binocular's crosshairs, suddenly brought into sharp focus.

She turns away, her heart pounding. "I'm going to go call a plumber."

"I thought the hot water heater was fixed."

"It is, but . . . I don't trust it."

Nor does she trust him. She doesn't trust anyone right now.

Bella goes into the study. Maybe she can check the browsing history to see when that water hemlock search was conducted and what other sites were visited. Somewhere in there, there might be a clue to the searcher's identity.

She closes the French door behind her, then, after a moment's hesitation, locks it.

She steps around Pandora's keyboard and sits at the desk.

Pandora Feeney is many things—busybody, know-it-all, snob, trespasser. But is she a cold-blooded killer?

Back in July, the idea didn't seem particularly preposterous, though in the end, it wasn't her. She hadn't murdered Leona Gatto.

That doesn't mean she's innocent this time. It doesn't mean she hasn't been creeping around the house again. But was it out of some misplaced sense of belonging or malicious intent?

Bella reaches for the mouse and finds that it's well beyond her grasp.

Frowning, she leans over and pulls it closer.

Clicking on the browser's history, she finds . . .

It's empty.

The entire search history has evaporated.

Did someone erase the history from the computer?

Did someone delete the photos from her phone?

Why? They seemed innocuous.

But the one of Parker and Virginia . . .

She opens her e-mail and finds her way back to that shot, looking again at the window in the background. This time, she isn't so sure she sees a figure there. It might just be the folds of the curtains.

She shifts her gaze to the foreground. The faces. Virginia is smiling, Parker merely squinting. He wasn't pleased at the prospect of her taking his photo, she recalls, especially without his sunglasses.

At last, giving in to suspicion, she types his name into a search engine.

Nothing relevant comes up. There are several Parker Langleys in this world, and at least one in the next. Sadly, a teenage boy by that name died in a car accident a few years ago.

The others bear no resemblance to the man she's looking for.

That doesn't mean anything . . . does it?

He lives in Canada. She adds that to the search.

Nope.

She adds *photographer*.

Still nothing.

How can he not be here?

What if Parker Langley isn't his real name?

If it isn't . . . then what else is he hiding? And how the heck is she supposed to find out who he really is with nothing more to go on than a picture?

A picture—

Remembering her image search for the perfect shade of yellow, she jerks the cursor back to the photo of Parker with Virginia.

She's about to crop it on his smiling face when a floorboard creaks somewhere on the first floor beyond the study.

Bella freezes.

It sounds as if someone is nearby, poised, spying . . .

Of course no one is *spying*. The glass panes looking into the parlor are covered in maroon drapes.

Bella whirls around, almost expecting to see a face pressed up against the window behind her. There's nothing but a snowy shrub border.

Radiant frost . . .

She jerks the blinds closed.

Having lost the patience to crop the photo, she hurriedly pastes the entire image into a facial-recognition search engine and hits Enter.

It doesn't take long to produce results.

Clicking on the first hit, an engagement announcement from a Florida newspaper, she sees that she was right about his name.

It isn't Parker Langley.

It's Thad Driscoll.

Or is it?

The hair is different. A little longer, parted on the side. And Thad Driscoll wears glasses.

You have to pay close attention to the details!

She zooms in on his face. It really does look like him.

Opening a new search engine tab, she quickly types "Thad Driscoll" and again hits Enter.

She's instantly rewarded by a series of hits. Some include photos. Most are of a centenarian named Thaddeus Driscoll, honored at a Founder's Day celebration in the Deep South. But one of the Thad Driscolls, pictured on a couple of social media sites, is familiar.

There's no mistaking that it's the same person she knows as Parker Langley.

Clicking back to the engagement announcement, she looks more closely at the photo. This time, she notices that the bride is a beautiful, sophisticated-looking blonde. She isn't identical to Johneen, but there's a strong resemblance.

According to the announcement, the bride graduated from a prestigious boarding school and an Ivy League college and lives in Palm Beach. There's no mention of her parents. Her name is Charlotte Ackerly-Toombs . . .

Charlotte.

She's an artist . . .

There was a whirlwind courtship . . .

A destination wedding is planned for August in Colorado . . .

There are indeed coincidences.

Destination wedding.

Whirlwind courtship.

Charlotte.

Charlotte's Web . . .

Bella opens a new screen and swiftly types "Charlotte Ackerly-Toombs."

There's the engagement announcement again, and . . .

There's an obituary.

"No way," she whispers, scanning it.

Mrs. Charlotte Ackerly-Toombs Driscoll collapsed and died of natural causes at her wedding reception in Denver. Her mother died when she was an infant, her father more recently. Her husband, Thad, is her only listed survivor.

Which possibly means he was her only heir—and, equally likely, the sole beneficiary to any life insurance policy.

Bella is well aware that a widowed spouse would collect in the case of accidental death and illness. She had expected to do just that until she discovered that Sam, feeling immortal, had let his own meager policy lapse prior to his illness.

Murder wouldn't be considered accidental death or illness. But according to Luther, it could certainly be disguised as natural causes.

Who stood to gain from Charlotte's death?

Who stands to gain from Johneen's, if she doesn't make it?

The grieving widower.

Drenched in a cold sweat, Bella reaches into her pocket for her phone. She has to text Luther right away. He might say it's circumstantial evidence, but—

Where is it? Where is her phone?

How could he have—

No, wait. He didn't steal it. Not this time. She left it up in the bedroom. She pushes back her chair, then freezes.

What if someone really is lurking on the other side of the glass door?

Parker, who isn't Parker.

Chances are, he isn't Thad either.

So who is he?

Bella grabs the mouse and clicks to the original image search results, hurriedly skimming the photo matches one by one. The pictures of Thad Driscoll don't go back further than about eighteen months. It's as if he didn't even exist before that.

Probably because he didn't.

Did he start using the identity when he met Charlotte?

Did he borrow it from one of the other Thad Driscolls—perhaps the elderly Thaddeus? The Founder's Day celebration was back in 2010. He may very well have since passed away.

And Parker Langley . . .

Remembering the teenage boy who died in a car wreck, she shakes her head.

It's sick, but it happens all the time, just as that lawyer warned her after Sam died. Identity thieves are opportunists.

Hands trembling now with more outrage than fear, she makes several attempts before she's able to enter both "Parker Langley" and "Johneen Maynard" without typos.

This time, she gets results.

The bridal couple may not be active on social media accounts of their own, but they do appear in photographs on pages belonging to a couple of their wedding guests: Hellerman, Frankie, Amanda . . .

Again, there's no online record of this Parker Langley's existence until about six months ago—right around the time he started dating Johneen.

All right. Then who was he before he borrowed Parker Langley's and Thad Driscoll's identities?

Bella returns to the facial-recognition search results, back to the photo of him with Virginia. As she glances down the page, she spots something that chills her in a cold sweat.

It's a wedding photo from a Houston newspaper published a few years ago.

The groom's name is Levi Joe Hicks, but he's unmistakably familiar.

So, this time, is the bride.

Blonde, sophisticated, beautiful . . .

Virginia.

The shocking truth slams into Bella.

She isn't his cousin. She isn't a cop. She's his wife. His *first* wife, his *real* wife . . .

His accomplice.

For a moment, she's too stunned to read on. She just sits with her eyes closed, her mind racing through the horrible implications.

That front porch conversation she overheard between Parker and Virginia was staged for her benefit. They were manipulating her all along, feeding her information. *Lies.*

But—the gun she'd found under the mattress, and the badge . . .

How on earth do you do it all? Virginia had asked on that first day. *You must have housekeeping help . . .*

They knew I'd be the one cleaning the guest room. They left the evidence where I could find it. She isn't a cop, and he . . .

Bella forces herself to look again at the photo, just to be sure.

That's definitely him. He's unshaven, his hair is longer, and he's wearing a cheap-looking suit without a tie. But it's him.

And it's her. Her name, according to the wedding announcement, is Brooke Marshall. She's wearing a smile so smug that she might as well have given the camera the finger.

After quickly searching the name "Brooke Marshall," Bella grasps that she was indeed gloating. She was flaunting her Mr. Wrong husband to the world—or at least to the billionaire father who'd shunned her.

A quick search reveals that she's the illegitimate daughter of a stripper and a wealthy Texas oil baron. Her father embraced her when she found her way to him as an adolescent following her mother's fatal overdose, then disinherited her a few years later in a public scandal after she was arrested for violent assault on household staff. It wasn't the first time she was in trouble with the law, but most of her prior offenses were relatively minor. Traffic violations, shoplifting, trespassing. Apparently, assault was the last straw for her rich daddy.

Reading between the lines, Bella discerns that Brooke Marshall appears to have a long history of mental illness. She hasn't exactly kept a low profile—social media or otherwise. She freely shared the details of a pampered existence in the lap of luxury and a romance with Levi Joe, all accompanied by the hashtag #lovemylife.

Cut off from her father's money, she and Levi had apparently come up with a scheme. It's unclear how they crossed Charlotte's path. He married and murdered her, inherited her fortune, spent it recklessly—then sought another conquest.

Johneen Maynard fit the bill. She was wealthy, lonely, estranged from her family, and—added bonus?—Levi's physical type.

So with Brooke's blessing, he seduced her, got her to marry him, and then tried to murder her? Only she's still alive.

Brooke's earlier comments echo in Bella's head.

He wants to change and get a few things he'll need at the hospital . . .

I don't want him there alone . . .

What were the "things" he needed to retrieve? More deadly blooms? Is he heading back to the hospital to keep a vigil at Johneen's bedside or to finish her off, with Virginia's help?

Bella needs to call Luther right now.

She grabs the desk phone.

No dial tone.

Did the storm take down the telephone wires, or did someone cut them?

Does she dare leave the room to get her cell phone upstairs?

She pushes back her chair and starts to rise.

Hearing, or perhaps just sensing, almost imperceptible movement on the other side of the door, she plops back down in the seat.

She's trapped.

He's out there. Maybe they both are. Parker and Virginia.

Levi and Brooke.

She opens a blank e-mail. In the subject line, she writes, "Urgent."

But people always write urgent. Grant does.

This isn't about business.

She changes it to "SOS."

In the address box, she types the first few letters: L-U-T . . .

The computer autofills the rest.

She'll have to hope Luther sees this message right away.

What if he doesn't?

She adds another name to the Send list.

D-R-E . . .

drewbailey@lakeviewanimalhospitalandrescue.com

Luther's words echo in her head. *Drew Bailey is a rock. He's one of the best men I know.*

"He is," Bella whispers. "And I need him."

Then, hating herself for her earlier misgivings, she adds a third name: O-D-E . . .

Her most trusted friend in the Dale is right next door. If Bella is in trouble, Odelia will come running.

But I don't want her to do that. It could be dangerous. I just want her to call the police.

Bella quickly types the e-mail, fingers fumbling at the keys.

Parker and Virginia poisoned Johneen. Guests unaware and asleep. I'm locked into first-floor study. Send police immediately.

About to hit Send, she hears a knock on the door.

"Bella?" someone calls.

It isn't Parker.

Nor is it Virginia.

It's Calla—the one person under this roof she's willing to trust.

"Yes?"

"Max is on the phone."

"What?" Her eyes dart to the phone on the desk.

Is this some kind of trick? Is Calla in on it, too?

"Your cell phone . . . Max."

Oh—Calla was in her room playing with the kittens. Her phone must have rung, and Calla answered it.

Bella opens the door.

Calla is standing there . . . with a gun pressed to her temple.

Chapter Eighteen

"I'm so sorry," Calla says in a miserable rush. "He was going to—"

"Shut up!" Parker, holding the gun, nods at Bella. "Let's go. Both of you."

A hard lump of fear rises in her throat. For a brief, frantic moment, she considers slamming the door closed in his face.

But if she does, she has no doubt that he'll press the trigger. He'll shoot Calla, then he'll shoot through the glass, reach in to open the door, and shoot her.

"Come on! I said let's go!"

"Where are we going?" Bella asks with a dangerous burst of defiance. He can't just . . . do this. He can't—

He nudges her with the gun.

Yes. He can.

"Walk. Not a sound."

Bella walks. Out of the study, into the parlor. She can hear kittens scampering in the upstairs hall and on the stairs. *The Rose Room door must be open*, she realizes dully. *They've escaped.*

Escape—I need to escape.

Parker—Levi—propels her and Calla into the foyer. Through the window in the front door, Bella sees his car parked at the curb. The engine is running.

Virginia—Brooke—is in the driver's seat.

"All right. Here we go." He opens the interior door. A blast of wet, frigid air blows through the screen door.

The Dale is shrouded in early-morning light and blanketed in white. A single set of black tire tracks mark the road. Sugary white crystals dust the porch floor that only yesterday was dappled in warm sunlight.

Bella's gaze falls on the pot of lavender mums beside the purple welcome mat.

"Y'all are gonna walk straight to that car and get into the back seat. Take one step in the wrong direction, and I shoot you both. Say one word, and I shoot you both."

Gone is the refined accent that had rivaled his bride's. His *third* bride's. His drawl has emerged loud and clear. He pronounces *shoot you* as *shootcha* and adds that if anyone happens to be out there and anyone tries anything, he'll *shootch'all.*

"Got it?" he asks.

Bella nods. Got it. If she or Calla hint that something is amiss, he'll kill them along with any innocent person who crosses their path.

If this were a sunny summer day, someone might actually be out there, even at this hour. Someone might witness the scene from afar and realize that this is an abduction. A bystander might at least get the plate number and call for help.

But at this time of year, especially at this hour and in this weather, the Dale is deserted. The only person out there is Brooke Marshall at the wheel of what is essentially a getaway car.

If she drives us out of here, we're never coming back.

Bella sneaks a glance at Calla. Her eyes are wide with fear and uncertainty, but she's calm.

Just a few days ago, Bella was convinced of her mind-reading capabilities. Now she tries desperately to send her a message: *As soon as we step over that threshold, you run!*

Calla steadily meets her gaze. It's impossible to tell whether she got the message.

Only one way to find out.

Bella swallows hard, conscious of Levi behind them, holding the gun. He pushes the screen door open.

"Ready? Let's go."

She steps out onto the purple welcome mat. The mums are beside her, just inches from the fingertips of her right hand. All she has to do is reach, and . . .

Hearing Levi's startled outcry behind her, she doesn't bother to turn and see what's happened. She swiftly grabs for the andiron.

"Duck!" she screams to Calla as her fingers close around it. She lifts, whirls, and swings the heavy object toward its target.

Calla ducks. The andiron makes contact with human flesh, slamming Levi in the gut. He doubles over and crumples to the ground. Beside him, Bella spots a wriggly pile of blue fur.

"He tripped him!" Calla says breathlessly, bending to pick it up, and Bella realizes she's talking about the kitten.

The kitten tripped Levi. Rather, Levi tripped over the kitten.

It isn't unusual. It's happened to Bella countless times. Kittens are dangerous underfoot. But this one might have saved her life. The momentary blip provided the opportunity to take him down.

"Get my phone!" she tells Calla. "And call the police! Hurry!"

Clutching Li'l Chap, Calla rushes for the stairs. Bella drops the andiron with a thud onto the snowy porch. She bolts back into the house, leaping over Levi, out cold on the floor.

His pistol flew out of his hands when he fell and landed a few feet away. She needs to get it.

No, first, she needs to close the door and lock it.

She starts to pull it closed, but he's in the way. She bends to push him aside.

He's dead weight. With a grunt, she pushes harder and manages to move him only a few inches.

Just a few more, and she can close the door and grab the gun in case Brooke tries to get in. But why would she? She'd have to be insane not to make a fast getaway. There's no way she—

"Isabella? Is that you?"

The familiar voice stops her in her tracks. She looks up to see Millicent out on the lawn, dressed in her traveling clothes. And the car—

The car is still parked at the curb. Only now the door is open, and Brooke is climbing out.

"I just wanted to say goodbye. My driver will be here in fifteen minutes."

Bella just stares at her.

"Good morning," Brooke calls to Millicent, her voice colder than the wintry air.

Millicent glances over her shoulder. "Good morning," she says politely, then looks back at Bella.

For one wildly illogical moment, Bella tells herself that Brooke is going to pretend nothing happened. She'll greet Millicent and then she'll get back in the car and drive away.

Yeah, sure she will. Because she's not insane?

The moment passes.

Bella sees that Brooke is holding something, and it isn't her keys. The badge Bella found might have been fake, but she's certain the gun was real, and now it's trained on Millicent's back.

Brooke calmly addresses Bella through a curtain of falling snow. "Can you please come over here?"

Not daring to move her head, Bella lowers her eyes desperately at the pistol on the hardwood floor. All she'd have to do is bend slightly and reach. Just like she did with the andiron. Just reach down, and in a split second's time, the gun would be in her hand.

But the moment she allows a hand to even twitch in that direction, Brooke is going to pull that trigger.

"You know I will," she calls.

So she, too, is a mind reader.

So close and yet so far. Bella rolls her gaze away from Levi's pistol just as Millicent, perhaps hearing the strain in Brooke's voice or bewildered by the cryptic conversation, turns around to look at her. Spotting the weapon in Brooke's hand aimed squarely at her chest, she cries out.

"Please be quiet and get into the back seat."

Millicent is frozen in place.

Her back is to Bella, but it's not hard to imagine an appalled and frightened expression on her face.

Brooke motions with the gun. "I *said*, get into the back seat!"

Millicent walks toward the car in silence. Her black pumps wobble a bit on the snowy, uneven ground, but her posture is straight, head held high.

Bella watches her open the door and get into the car.

Oh, Sam. I'm so sorry.

"Good. Thank you." Brooke's tone oozes saccharine. She keeps the gun leveled at Millicent, but her gaze flicks back and forth between the car and Bella.

"Come on out here."

Bella stays rooted to the threshold.

"*Now.* Or I kill her."

Bella steps out onto the porch.

Surely Calla has called 9-1-1 by now. Surely help is on the way.

But even in the best road conditions, it would take at least a couple of minutes to get here. It did last night, as Johneen lay convulsing on the grass. Today, the roads are treacherous.

Millicent said she has a driver on the way. But fifteen minutes—fifteen minutes is forever when there's a loaded gun involved.

"Come on over here, Isabella."

Bella slowly crosses the porch and descends the steps. She has a clear view of Millicent, huddled in the back seat in her tweed suit.

"Come on, hurry up," Brooke tells her. "It's freezin' out here!"

Bella continues walking, but she doesn't hurry up. Her pace is steady, her mind flying through the possibilities, though there are few. All right, there are only two. One, if you consider that they have the same outcome.

If I don't do something, she's going to kill us both.

If I do something, she's going to kill us both.

Either way, Max won't just be an orphan. He'll be left all alone, without any family in the world.

Maybe that isn't entirely true. He'll still have Odelia, and Drew, and Luther, and Jiffy . . .

They're *like* family, and they adore Max.

But they only know *now*. This life. Lily Dale.

They don't know the past. They don't know about Bedford, or New York, or Chicago. They don't know about Bella Blue, or Christmas-cookie wreaths, or breakfast for dinner. They don't know about reading *Charlotte's Web* in bed.

They don't know Sam.

A few months ago, when she was fighting Leona's killer for her own life, Bella was desperate to keep her son out of his grandmother's clutches. Max having to go live with Millicent was the worst thing she could imagine.

Now . . .

If only Millicent weren't here. Here in Lily Dale, here in the back seat of that damned car.

If only she were safely at home in Chicago. Then if something happened to Bella, Max would be certain to grow up in the care of a woman who knows how to raise a good man.

But that's not going to happen, unless . . .

Bella abruptly stops walking.

"What are you doing?"

She just looks at Brooke.

Slowly, she swivels the gun toward Bella.

"What are you *doing*?" she repeats, and there's a warble, ever so slight, in her voice.

Behind Brooke, out of the corner of her eye, Bella notes movement in the car. She doesn't dare allow her gaze to shift even a fraction.

Keeping it focused on Brooke, she clears her throat. "I'm thinking."

"You're thinking?"

"That's right."

"Well, if you were thinking, you wouldn't be thinking," Brooke drawls. "You'd be moving."

Bella stands her ground.

Brooke's blue eyes flash with warning.

"Don't you want to know what I'm thinking?" Bella asks her.

"No."

"Are you sure?"

Brooke says nothing, but Bella doesn't miss the bolt of curiosity on her face.

She does want to know what Bella is thinking.

That makes two of us.

But I'd better come up with something, because right now, I've got her.

"You made it up, didn't you?" she asks. "There was never a jealous jilted ex who was stalking Johneen. He didn't exist."

Even as she says it, she knows that can't be right. Calla, too, had mentioned him.

"Wrong!" Brooke shakes her head. "For someone who seems so smart, you're pretty stupid."

Fine, Bella thinks. *Let her think I'm stupid. Let her tell me exactly what they did, and why. We can stand here talking all day, as far as I'm concerned.*

"So there really was a guy?"

"Of course there was a guy. Some big shot she dated a while back, from New York." She waves a hand as if to indicate that she knows very little about the relationship, and it doesn't matter.

"And Johneen broke up with him, and maybe he didn't take it well—the breakup," Bella goes on, not daring to look toward the car again. "Is that right?"

"Who takes a breakup well?" She shakes her head at Bella's ignorance.

"But you two made Johneen think it was more than that, didn't you? To throw suspicion away from yourselves. You figured that she'd start to get paranoid and tell people she was being stalked by an old lover after she got engaged. You thought that when something happened to her, even if anyone suspected that it was murder, no one would look at the two of you. Right? A jealous ex . . . it happens every day."

Brooke says nothing.

"The ring . . . if there ever was a ring—you stole it yourself, or he pretended it had been stolen. And my phone—you took that, too."

Brooke shrugs, and Bella sees the bored look in her eyes. She's losing interest, running out of patience. This is all old news to her.

"How did you get in and out of my room, though? Did you use the tunnels?"

"Is that what you thought?" Brooke looks pleased.

It's what she wanted me to think.

"Or did you get ahold of my keys and copy them?" Bella asks. "Was that you, sneaking out of the house early yesterday morning?"

"Does it really matter?"

"Yes. I want to know."

"No, you don't."

"I want to know that, and I want to know if you planted your purse in my room after I found your gun, so that I'd see your phony badge and not suspect you. You did, right? You knew I'd think the cat had done it."

"You're answering all your own questions. You don't need me."

"But am I right?"

"You're stalling. And I'm done playing games. Let's go."

Bella has to come up with something else. Right now. Or—

"You wanted to know what I'm thinking," she hears herself say.

"Yeah, well, I changed my mind, so—"

"I'm thinking about love."

Brooke blinks. "*Love?*"

Gotcha.

"Yes. I'm thinking about the things we're willing to do because we love someone."

"Good grief. Shut up and get in the car."

"See, that . . ." Bella shakes her head. "That's something I'm willing to do because I love someone. Not *you*. I don't love you."

To her surprise, and maybe to Brooke's own surprise, Brooke snickers at that.

Bella pries a smile from her own mouth. "I do love my family, though. My son, and . . . my mother-in-law. How about you?"

"I don't love your son or your mother-in-law." Brooke snickers again, this time at her own cleverness.

"Aha! Well-played," Bella says, wearing an admiring expression.

Millicent is moving, inch by painstaking inch.

"But you loved Levi, didn't you?"

Brooke's eyes narrow. "Who?" she asks, not very convincingly.

"Levi. Your husband. The guy you've been calling Parker."

"His name is Parker."

"Yeah. Sure it is." She hesitates, and adds a deliberate, "*Was.*"

"What?"

"Then again," Bella muses on, struggling to keep her voice level, "maybe you *don't* love him. If you loved him, you wouldn't have been willing to just take off and leave him there."

"I didn't leave him. That's why I didn't go. I was coming back for him."

"Really? It's too bad you were too late."

"What are you talking about?"

"It looks like you and I have one more thing in common. We're both widows." She pauses to let the ugly word sink in.

Brooke pales. "*What?*"

Bella chooses an even uglier one. "He's *dead.*"

"He is not!"

Bella is reasonably sure Brooke is right. Any second now, he could regain consciousness, grab his gun, and burst out of the house shooting.

Brooke glares. Then she steadies the gun, aiming at Bella.

Before she can pull the trigger, two things happen in such rapid succession that Bella isn't even sure which comes first. Maybe they're simultaneous; maybe they're cause and effect.

The barely audible sound of a siren reaches her ears. In that split second, or perhaps the next, Millicent leaps from the car and tackles Brooke to the ground.

She's tiny, but she's a force to be reckoned with. "Get the gun!" she shrieks as Bella leaps into action. "Get the gun!"

Brooke, pinned on her stomach beneath Millicent, is still clutching the weapon. Bella struggles to pry it from her hand. Two on one. It shouldn't be difficult.

But the angle is awkward, and Brooke is armed, and she's strong.

She manages to turn the gun so that it's aiming directly at Millicent's head. Seeing her finger bracing to shoot, Bella screeches, "Noooooo!"

She makes a frantic, wrenching move, hurtling herself forward.

The gun goes off with such violent, deafening force that for a terrible moment, Bella is certain she's been shot, or that Millicent has.

But Millicent is still breathing.

Brooke, too, is breathing, panting beneath their weight. But blood is pooling beneath her left forearm.

"Bella!" Millicent screeches, seeing the blood. "Bella, no!"

"It's okay! I'm okay! It's her. It's not me."

Bella extracts the gun from Brooke's limp right hand. Holding it gingerly, she gets to her feet, then extends her other arm to help Millicent up.

"Owwww." Brooke moans. "It hurts." After a moment, her eyes close.

"Is she . . . ?"

Bella bends over and presses her fingers against Brooke's neck. "No. She's alive."

She and Millicent stand listening to the approaching sirens, the sound of their own breathing, and the wet snow sifting through the foliage-laden trees.

Then Bella says, "Bella."

"No. *You're* Bella. I'm *Millicent*. It's all right. It's just the shock. You're in shock."

"No . . ." She manages a laugh. "I mean, you called me Bella."

"Excuse me?"

"Just now—when the gun went off. You called me Bella."

"It's your name."

"You've always called me Isabella."

"And you've always called me Maleficent."

Her jaw drops. "No. I—"

"Yes. Of course you have. And I don't blame you."

Bella digests that. The sirens are coming closer.

"I do. I blame me. It was wrong."

"I deserved it."

"No. You're Sam's mother."

"And you're his wife."

Why, Bella wonders, are they talking about him in present tense? As if dead isn't dead?

Police cars are wailing into the Dale, their rotating, red lights tinting the falling snow at the end of the lane.

"He loved us both, Millicent. And so does Max."

"Oh, I don't know about that. Max barely knows me."

"We can change that. But he does love you."

"Max loves a lot of people. He told me about all of them yesterday at lunch. And a lot of people love him. You were right."

"I can't believe you're standing here saying that now. After . . . this." Bella gestures at the unconscious woman on the ground at their feet. "I mean, this is crazy. It's dangerous."

"But I have to say it, in case—if anything happens to me, I need you to know. I was wrong about Odelia, and this place, and everyone who lives here. I was wrong about what they do and what they are. They're Max's family. Lily Dale is his home."

"You're his family, too. You share his name, and his blood, and . . . you're a part of Sam. You're the only one in the world who can tell Max what his daddy was like when he was Max's age."

Millicent smiles a faint, faraway smile. "I can do that—if you can do something for me."

Bella holds her breath, knowing it's going to be the one thing she can't do. Not even now. Not even after all that's happened.

I can't call you Mom. I just can't.

"Can you forgive me?" Millicent asks. "Please? I know I haven't been very kind to you. I suppose I've resented you, coming along and stealing my boy's heart."

Bella allows her eyes to close just for a moment.

She can't predict the future, but she's pretty certain that someday, a woman is going to come along and steal her boy's heart, too. When it happens, she's going to feel wistful, wishing it were just the two of them again. Wishing he were here with her, needing her . . .

Missing him.

She opens her eyes and looks at the woman standing in front of her, seeing not the monstrous, meddling Maleficent, but just a mom. A mom who wishes time had stood still, so that she could keep her little boy with her forever.

"I do," she tells Millicent. "I forgive you."

"Oh, and one more thing . . ."

Here we go. Here comes the impossible request.

"Can I read *Charlotte's Web* to Max?"

"Absolutely," Bella says, "as long as I get to listen."

Epilogue

It's been a little over two weeks since Brooke Marshall and Levi Joe Hicks were arrested. To Bella, it seems as if entire seasons have passed.

Maybe because here in the Dale, they have.

The wedding weekend snowstorm wasn't the first this month, though it was by far the worst. The ground was white for a solid week, after which there was a rainy spell complete with a tornado that tore through a neighboring town.

Now it's Indian summer again.

Holding the phone holding against her ear with her shoulder as she finishes washing two dinner plates, Bella tells Millicent, "The sun is shining and it's supposed to get close to eighty tomorrow."

"It was seventy-five here yesterday," her mother-in-law says. "We went for a stroll along the lake."

Bella doesn't have to ask who "we" is. The *friend* Millicent had mentioned to Bella is indeed a gentleman, a widower named George.

"I hope the weather will cooperate when you and Max come for Thanksgiving," her mother-in-law says. "He really wants to ride the Ferris wheel at Navy Pier."

Millicent has lots of other plans for next month's visit: a trip to Shedd Aquarium, baking Christmas cutout cookies, and, of course, finishing *Charlotte's Web*. They were only halfway through the book when she flew home two weeks ago.

"I wish you could stay longer," Max said sadly, and Bella was surprised to find that she felt the same way.

But Millicent had to get back to George. They've been seeing each other for a few months now, and she missed him.

"I never expected to date again," she confided over lunch with Bella and Odelia on her last afternoon in Lily Dale. They were at the Solstice Cafe, where—wisely—no one ordered the soup.

"Well, everyone deserves a second chance at happiness," Odelia told Millicent, though Bella felt as though the words were meant for her own ears as well.

Her—*friendship*—with Drew Bailey has yet to officially progress to anything more. But on that memorable Sunday when he safely delivered Max back home, Bella impulsively threw her arms around him in gratitude. He held her there for a little longer than was necessary for a proper *you're welcome.*

Who knows what the future will bring?

Well, Odelia claims to know.

She's certain that Johneen, who is out of intensive care at last, is going to make a full recovery.

"Maybe not emotionally," she said sadly, "because how do you heal after something like that? But physically, she'll be okay."

She also told Bella that she sees another wedding at the guesthouse.

Bella shook her head. "No, Grant wants to put that plan on hold, at least until we finish all the work on the place."

"I didn't say I saw a destination wedding or that your role was to plan it," Odelia said mysteriously. "Your Wedding Bella days aren't over just yet."

Bella stopped her right there. "No offense, Odelia, but I don't want to hear any more of your premonitions for a while. Yours either," she added to Calla, who was with them that day.

She's been spending a lot of time here in the Dale lately with her grandmother, and with Blue Slayton. Odelia still doesn't approve of their rekindled romance, but she's learning to live with it, and she's pleased that her granddaughter is planning to rent a cottage here for the next couple of months.

"Why don't you just move in with me?" she asked when Calla first broached the subject, after breaking the news that she and Jacy had broken up. "You can have your old room back."

"Thanks, Gammy, but we might get in each other's way. I'm working on a new book, so I need some solitude, and there are plenty of places available around here for the winter."

Tomorrow—November first—Calla and Li'l Chap are moving into a small place on East Street. Like everything in the Dale, it's within a few minutes' walk of Odelia's cottage but secluded enough to give Calla some privacy.

"I know Gammy only wants me to be happy," she told Bella when she came to pick up her new kitten. "But sometimes, she gets a little too . . . involved."

Yes, she does. Just not as involved as Bella had suspected. When all was said and done, she was relieved to know that Odelia hadn't been behind the letter or anything else that had happened surrounding the wedding. Brooke and Levi Joe had written that note, laying the groundwork to deflect suspicion away from Parker.

"Grifter sleight of hand," Luther called it.

The pair had confessed to the rest as well. They had deleted the photo evidence on Bella's phone. They'd planted the fake police badge—one of many in Virginia's possession—in the Rose Room after Virginia realized Bella had probably found the gun. And they'd accomplished it all by borrowing and copying Bella's keys so that they could sneak past locked doors. The police confiscated the duplicate set along with other evidence, but Luther advised her to change the locks again.

"Better safe than sorry," he said.

"That's true, but Grant has already arranged to install a high-tech alarm system and electronic entry on all the guest room doors."

"Sounds expensive."

"It is, but he said it was a good investment."

Luther nodded. "Potential buyers will like that."

"Oh, he's not selling it. Didn't I tell you? He's keeping it."

She'd been prepared to beg Grant to let her stay for a while, but it didn't come to that.

"Aunt Leona wouldn't want me to give up so easily," he'd told Bella. "This place was such a big part of her life. I can't just hand it over to strangers."

"You sort of handed it over to me, and I was a stranger."

"*You*? Nah. You're the kind of person I feel like I've known all my life," he'd said so casually that he almost seemed like a regular person.

Maybe the rich aren't so different after all.

Luther was happy to hear she'd be sticking around the Dale for good, and not just because he and Max are good pals. "You're shaping up to be quite the detective, Bella. Maybe you should think about becoming a private investigator in the off-season."

"No, thank you," she said firmly. "I have plenty to keep me busy."

She's been talking to Grant about all the renovations he wants to do on the guesthouse. Overseeing the work will keep her busy in the off-season. So will Max and his enterprising sidekick Jiffy, finding homes for the remaining kittens, and, of course, the Thanksgiving trip to Chicago.

"Max and I were thinking you might like to come back here for Christmas," she tells Millicent as she dries the plates she and Max used for dinner and puts them back in the cupboard. "You can bring George too, of course. We'd love to meet him."

"You will, at Thanksgiving," Millicent promises. "And we'll see about Christmas. George has grandchildren, too, and I'm not sure what our plans are. But thank you for the invitation."

Hanging up the phone, Bella glances out the window to see that dusk has given way to darkness. It's almost six o'clock, meaning that any second now—

"Mom!" Max hollers from the front hall. "Come on! Are you ready?"

"I'm ready!" Smiling, she tosses aside the dish towel and grabs a flashlight waiting on the counter.

In the hall, she finds—

Hmm. She isn't sure exactly what Max is supposed to be. Last week, she'd bought him the Halloween costume he'd requested. Today, he'd announced that he no longer wanted to dress as an animated yellow, orange, and brown triangle courtesy of *Candy Corn*. Apparently, that movie is already old news with the elementary school crowd.

"Then what do you want to be, Max?"

"Me and Jiffy have it all figured out. We're going to be something scary so that we can fight the bad guys."

"Which bad guys?" she asked, wondering if he knows more than she thought about what happened here.

"You know—the kidnappers. Jiffy says they're coming in the big snowstorm."

That gave her pause. But then, Jiffy says a lot of things. She can only hope that he, like Max, has an overactive imagination.

"Good thing it's not going to snow again any time soon," was all she said to Max.

Now he stands before her dressed all in black. The exaggerated smudges around his eyes tell her that he found her makeup.

"What are you, Max?"

"I'm a kidnapper-fighting zombie," he says as if she should have known.

"Of course. A kidnapper-fighting zombie," she says agreeably as the doorbell rings. "Do you want to get that? It must be a trick-or-treater."

As her son races to the door, Bella reaches for the crystal bowl on the registration desk. Today, it's filled not with M&Ms but with miniature chocolate bars.

"Trick or treat," someone says from the porch. It isn't a kid's voice.

"Doctor Drew!" Max's zombie eyes are gleeful. "What are you supposed to be?"

Drew Bailey, wearing jeans, a jacket, and glasses attached to a large nose and fake mustache, looks down at Max, deadpan. "What do you mean, what am I supposed to be? I'm a veterinarian—and your friend," he adds.

And yes, a little bit more, Bella acknowledges as Max giggles, pointing at his face.

"Is that your costume?"

"I would appreciate it if you didn't laugh at my new glasses, young man. Now are we ready to go?"

They are.

"Careful," Drew warns Bella as she locks the door behind them and Max dashes ahead. "There's another kidnapper-fighting zombie lurking out there."

"You can't scare me." She flicks on the flashlight and holds out a candy bar. "Here you go."

"What's that?"

"Your treat."

He looks at it, shrugs, and tears off the wrapper. "This wasn't exactly what I had in mind, but I guess it'll do—for now."

Down the walkway, Max shrieks in delight as Jiffy pounces on him from behind a shrub.

"See? I told you things were lurking out there," Drew tells Bella.

"You can't scare me," she repeats with a shrug, eyes twinkling.

"Yeah, something tells me nothing can scare you. And I'm guessing you don't need me around to protect you from zombies or anything else, do you?"

"To protect me? Nope." She adds, boldly sneaking her hand into Drew's, "I'm glad you're here anyway, though."

Together, they scuff through dead leaves into a Dale that's teeming with zombies and goblins, clowns and princesses, and—yes—maybe even a couple of ghosts.

Acknowledgments

With gratitude to Matt Martz, Dan Weiss, Sarah Poppe, and Heather Boak at Crooked Lane; to publicists Dana Kaye and Julia Borcherts; to my agents, Laura Blake Peterson and Holly Frederick at Curtis Brown; to Dr. Robert Seaver and Cristina Gastesi for their medical and pharmacological assistance; to Marnie Zoldessy; to Carol Fitzgerald and the Bookreporter staff; to the Writerspace gang; to Margery Flax and MWA; to RWA, ITW, and Sisters in Crime; to Anjellicle Cats rescue for helping me save, foster, and adopt an imperiled Russian Blue kitten; to Mandi Shepp at the Marion Skidmore Library; to my many friends in Lily Dale; and to my supportive readers, booksellers, and librarians everywhere.